FIRE IN THE NIGHT

"You're chilled," Tanner said. He slowly undid her camisole and removed the clinging wet fabric from her body. With a corner of the woolen blanket he dried her, rubbing her limbs to bring the blood to the surface. Her skin was warm now, burning.

Tanner let his clothes slide off into a heap on the ground. Unashamedly Sarah looked at his body. She'd never dreamed a man could be so magnificent. With every movement muscles rippled. A mass of curly hair swirled across his chest. He was a burnished, golden giant of a man.

Then Tanner lowered himself to her, and Sarah welcomed him with open arms and sweet sensuous kisses, as her young body yearned for his. . . .

TENDER BETRAYAL

Peggy Hanchar

AN ONYX BOOK

NEW AMERICAN LIBRARY

PUBLISHER'S NOTE

This book is a work of fiction. Names, characters, places, and incidents either are the product of the author's imagination or are used fictitiously, and any resemblance to actual persons, living or dead, events, or locales is entirely coincidental.

Copyright © 1988 by Peggy Hanchar

Onyx is a trademark of New American Library.

To Jenny, who walked the Lolo trail with me, and to Dorothy Texter, Florence, and the other ladies at the Delton library who with unfailing courtesy and cheerfulness help me find the material I need, and always to Steve, with love.

PROLOGUE
Wallowa Valley, 1866

The heavy, insistent beat of the drums was mournful in the cold morning air. A rim of silvery light outlined the eastern peaks of the Bitterroot Mountain range, but down in the river valley the village of the Nimpau was shrouded in darkness, the bark lodges silent. An Appaloosa tied nearby whickered, then all was quiet again, save for the drums. The children and dogs slept.

Silently the warriors and their wives huddled in the morning chill, their faces solemn with grief, their eyes intent as they studied the white drift of ash rising from the smoke flap of Chief Wellamotkin's lodge.

The old chief was dying. He was well loved, for he had led his people wisely for many moons. Now the villagers drew closer, seeking and giving comfort to one another just by their presence.

A stirring at one side caused them to move apart.

Two warriors shouldered their way toward the lodge. Heinmot Tooyalakekt looked neither to the left nor the right. His rugged features were grim, his deep-set eyes sad but resigned. Beside him walked Ollokot, his younger brother. The people exchanged knowing glances. The medicine man had sent for Wellamotkin's sons. The end must be near. One of the women began to wail, throwing her buffalo robe over her head.

Heinmot Tooyalakekt walked among the Nimpau with great dignity. His air of wisdom and patience reassured them, quieting their fears, so their wailing stopped and they whispered among themselves. The men entered the lodge and the people waited.

Inside, a row of fire pits had burned down to winking coals except one at the far end. A woman knelt beside the fire slowly feeding wood chips to the flames. Heinmot paused, his eyes troubled as he watched. It seemed as if the Nimpau, the Nez Percé as the white men called them, were on the verge of a cataclysm that would devour them in the same manner as the greedy blaze ate the wood chips. He shook away the fanciful thought and knelt beside the pallet of the old chief.

"You sent for us, my father?" Weakly Wellamotkin turned his head, his watery gaze taking in the strong, handsome features of his sons. Of the two of them, Ollokot was the hunter and warrior. Younger, quicker to anger, he was bright and intelligent, able to draw the trails and boundaries of the Nez Percé land with great accuracy. Yet he lacked the wisdom of his brother and was willing to follow another's lead. It was to Heinmot Tooyalakekt that the people turned. When he spoke in council, it was with such dignity and persuasiveness that even the oldest warriors and chiefs listened in respect. Quick-witted and even-tempered, Heinmot would lead the Nimpau people wisely. Even his name, which meant Thunder Rolling to Loftier Mountain Heights, was given to him by the Great Spirit in a vision and evoked much power. Pride flashed in the old man's eyes and, raising a gnarled hand, he motioned his sons nearer. It would take great power and wisdom to rule the

Nimpau in the years ahead. The white men, greedy for the land and gold of the Nez Percé, had invaded their valley.

"What is it, my father?" Heinmot Tooyalakekt asked, taking the old one's hand. He could feel the fragile bones beneath the wasted flesh.

With an effort Wellamotkin half-raised himself from the sleeping robes. "My son, now you will be the chief of these people. They look to you to guide them."

"I will not fail them, my father."

Wellamotkin's frail body trembled from the effort it took to speak, yet he hurried on. There was much of which to warn his son. "You must remember this," he gasped. "Your father never sold his country. You must stop your ears if the white men ask you to sign a treaty and sell your home." He paused. His chest rattled as he drew a breath. The cords of his neck trembled and his glazed eyes were fixed as he sought a last remnant of strength to speak. His voice was little more than a hoarse whisper. "A few more years and the white men will be all around you. They have their eyes on this land."

"Kautsas, you must rest. Save your strength." The young chief pressed his father back against the robes. Wellamotkin's hands clutched at the muscular shoulders. Yes, his son would be a strong leader, but still he feared for him and for the Nimpau people.

"Never forget my dying words," he hissed insistently. "This country holds your father's body. You must promise me that you will never sell the bones of your father and mother."

"I promise," Heinmot Tooyalakekt cried, his arms supporting his father's shoulders.

Wellamotkin's fingers bit deeply into his son's flesh.

"Give me your word as chief of the Nimpau," he cried with his old strength.

"I pledge it," Heinmot answered willingly. The old man stared into the young warrior's eyes. His son had promised, but would the white men let him keep that promise? Wellamotkin felt afraid and the fear bled away the last of his strength. He collapsed back against the robes.

"Promise," he whispered piteously, staring stoically into the unknown future that awaited him, no longer able to see the tears glinting in his son's eyes.

"I promise," Heinmot said, then repeated it in a loud voice. Wellamotkin smiled as if he'd just heard the words for the first time and nodded his head in satisfaction. It was done, all that he could do. Now he must go. He opened his mouth to bid his sons farewell, but the rattle came again, clogging his throat so he couldn't speak. The smoke of a hundred campfires filled his vision so he couldn't see and he fell back limply. Without a sound the old chief left behind the land of the Nimpau and began his long journey to A-kum-kinny-koo, the happy hunting ground.

1

"Sarah, you must promise me!"

"I promise, Kautsas," Sarah MacKenzie said softly. The lamplight lit red sparks in her dark hair and gilded her high cheekbones and straight nose as she leaned forward to tuck the blanket tighter around the shrunken figure of her grandmother. Unshed tears glittered in her dark eyes. She had never seen her sturdy, indefatigable grandmother idle in bed before. But the Missouri winter of 1875 had been long and hard, and the spring of 1876 slow in coming. Some mysterious ailment that baffled even the doctor had struck the old woman, steadily seeping away her vitality until she could no longer rise. Only her eyes, still lively and curious in her shriveled face, reminded Sarah of the delightful, funny childhood companion her grandmother had been.

"This is very important to me, little frog," Ruth MacKenzie said weakly. Born at the turn of the century, a mere child of five or so when Lewis and Clark first came to the village of the Nimpau, Ruth MacKenzie had once been known as Swan Necklace, but many years ago the white men began to call her Ruth because she'd left behind the Wallowa valley of the Nez Percé and followed a man into another land and lived among strangers. She'd loved James Mac-Kenzie and the two sons she bore him, but now he

11

was dead as was one of her sons and the other was a stranger to her. Except for the slim, dark-haired girl hovering over her, no one ever called her Swan Necklace. She sighed. She was seventy-six summers and she would never return to her home, never again be Swan Necklace digging camas bulbs with her mother, and never again feel the wind from the mountains on her face.

No, she must die as she had lived most of her life, here in a strange land where people only pretended to accept her while complimenting her for embracing the white man's ways. Here she was always closed in behind walls of stone and wood and other people's expectations. Instead of stepping upon the soft soil of the mother earth or the wild sweet grass of the riverbanks, now she walked on hard floors of polished wood and streets of cobblestone and brick. Windows were hung with heavy damask draperies, shutting away the healthy sunlight and the soothing sight of the sky and trees. Men hid themselves inside buildings away from the sight of God's creations and sought to find Him huddled on the hard, narrow pews of a church. She had lived among the white men for more than sixty years and still she did not understand their ways.

"This is important and you must humor an old woman," Swan Necklace repeated. "I know my bones cannot be buried among my own people. Take my spirit bag back so my soul will be free to wander through the mountains and prairies of my childhood once again. You must promise me this, Sarah." The wrinkled old hands clutched the girl's smooth, round arm.

"There is no need to talk of these things, Kautsas," Sarah hastened to reassure her grandmother. "You will grow strong again and take your spirit bag back to the mountains yourself."

The old woman shook her head. "Do not be sad or turn your face away from the truth, Sarah. I have taught you better than that. I will never rise from this bed again and so I must ask you to do this thing for me. Promise me, my child."

"I have promised you, Grandmother," Sarah replied stiffly, "and when a Nez Percé gives his word, he must keep it."

"Ah, yes," the old woman said, pleased with her answer. "If only I could go with you, Sarah, I would show you so much of my land. I would show you where the Coyote flung his fishnet into the hills and turned the greedy bear into stone, and where the ant and the yellowjacket are locked in combat throughout all time because they would not listen to the Coyote and settle the argument. He turned them to stone and where the—" The old woman's words were disrupted by the cough that racked her body. Sarah held a clean cloth to her lips and wiped away the spittle. Exhausted by the illness, the old woman lay back against the pillows, her face pallid and glistening with sweat. Sarah dampened a cloth in cool, scented water and knelt beside the bed to bathe her grandmother's cheeks.

"I think I would not like to be in this valley when the Coyote walked the earth," she teased lightly. "The Coyote would surely have turned us to stone for all our mischief." Humor flooded the face of the invalid and she chuckled, remembering the joy of trudging through fields and along streams, her tiny granddaughter in tow as they spent long afternoons discovering the bounties and mysteries of the mother earth although it was only here in Missouri and not the Oregon territory of her people.

"You taught me many things, Kautsas," Sarah said, taking up the hairbrush and smoothing the thin gray hair from the wrinkled forehead.

"It is the way of the Nez Percé for the grandmother to teach the young girls all these things. You were a good pupil, Sarah. You learned quickly. Our people live by the food we gather from the mother earth. Here it is different, but one day you may need to know these things, even about the Coyote."

"Did you teach Papa and Uncle Caleb these things?" Sarah asked idly and carefully began to braid the long hair into two braids, the way her grandmother liked.

"I tried," the old woman sighed, "but Zachariah would not sit still long enough to listen." Sarah smiled at the mention of her father's name. She had been a baby when her parents were killed, and it always pleased her to hear some little thing about him. "He was like you, a little frog always jumping around. Caleb," she sighed and the light left her eyes. "Caleb was like his father. James would not allow me to teach our sons the Indian ways. He claimed the customs of the Nez Percé were heathenish and since he was a minister of the church, I tried to honor the wishes of his god."

"But his god was not so different from yours," Sarah protested.

"I suspect James never discovered that," Swan Necklace sighed.

"What is this blasphemy?" a voice demanded sternly from the doorway. Sarah jumped and dropped the brush.

"Hello, Uncle Caleb," she said politely. "How are you this evening?"

"Mother, I've asked you not to discuss these things with Sarah," Caleb thundered. He crossed the room in long, angry strides and towered over the bed. Sarah crouched beside it. "You will only bring confusion to her young, untried mind."

"I'm sorry," Ruth MacKenzie said weakly. "We were just talking."

"Idle talk can only bring about mischief. I've told you this before. You should spend more time at your prayers rather than discussing these heathen savages." At his words Swan Necklace turned her face to the wall, and Sarah's heart was wrung with pity.

"Those savages are her family, your ancestors," she flared.

"I forbid you to say such things in this house," Caleb MacKenzie snapped. His face was mottled with barely repressed rage. A tall, handsome man, heavy-boned and spare of flesh, his face was grimly set toward the rigid path of his beliefs. A light of unwavering zeal glowed on his countenance, inspiring those of a like purpose, intimidating those who were not. Pride in his calling burned in every inch of his demeanor.

"I am a man of the cloth. I do not associate myself with these Godless heathens who live like animals in the mountains."

"Don't you suppose we all lived like that at one time? Surely we didn't spring from the womb of Abraham into such fine houses as this?" Sarah snapped back. "And why is it blasphemous to talk about your ancestors, no matter who they were? Didn't God make the Indians as well as us?"

"Do you see what you've done?" Caleb demanded furiously, turning on his mother. "You've confused her with your tales. She's a child and you've turned her head with your heathen talk."

"Stop it!" Sarah shouted, getting to her feet and

rounding on her uncle. "Leave her alone. She's ill. Besides I am not a child. I'm twenty years this winter and certainly of a mind of my own. I asked her to tell me about the Nez Percé. I want to know about my people."

Cold fury settled over Caleb MacKenzie's features. "You are not to speak of these things again, Sarah. I forbid it and as long as you live in my home, both of you—" he glanced at his mother—"will obey me in this."

Sarah sensed her grandmother was crying. Swan Necklace hated dissension and Uncle Caleb was her son. Sarah sometimes wondered how that could be. He seemed not to have inherited one whit of his mother's humor or humanity. Still, he had taken Sarah in when her parents died, and he'd never made her feel the weight of his charity, as had Aunt Margaret. "I'm sorry, Uncle Caleb," she said meekly. "I will obey."

"Humph, I will pray for you, Sarah, that God will remove these troubled thoughts from your mind and put your feet on the straight and narrow path of His teachings."

"Thank you, Uncle Caleb," Sarah said dutifully, eyes downcast while she gave a quick, fervent prayer of her own that she might never be forced to live the rigid, humorless existence of her aunt and uncle. She would seek the sunlight shining on an untouched field of prairie grass, for surely she would find God there.

"I came up here for a special reason," Uncle Caleb was saying, his good humor, such as it was, restored somewhat by Sarah's acquiescence. "We are having a special guest tonight. A young man who has just left the seminary and is about to embark upon a glorious mission to save souls among the

Indians in the West. He has paused long enough in his mission to seek a wife. I want you to prepare yourself for our guest. Dress demurely as becomes a young woman of faith and conduct yourself with restraint."

"But I'm not seeking a husband, Uncle Caleb," Sarah protested.

"As you so recently pointed out to me, Sarah, you are of twenty years and no longer a child. Besides, a man of Daniel Stone's character will be a good influence for you. He can help you turn your back on the confusion wrought by your grandmother and lead you toward the light."

"But if I have no wish to—"

"It is not for us to do only as we wish, Sarah," Uncle Caleb said sternly. "We must not succumb to the devil's ways of weakness and sloth and self-indulgence. We must be diligent in our efforts to eliminate such weaknesses from our souls."

Uncle Caleb went on for some time, his voice ringing with conviction as he warmed to his topic. Sarah suspected the things she was hearing tonight would be repeated again for his congregation on Sunday. "I have been praying for just such a man as this to come along. He is truly a godsend and you must show him you are worthy of his consideration."

Anger shot through Sarah. Why must she prove herself worthy to this Daniel Stone? Rather, she would ask if he were worthy of her. Wisely she kept such thoughts to herself. "I want you to read the first two chapters of Romans, Paul's thoughts on missionary work among the heathens. I heard Brother Stone preach on this a few Sundays ago and he was truly inspired. You can discuss it with him tonight after supper.

"If you wish, Uncle Caleb," Sarah replied.

He studied her face, secretly pleased that like him she showed little of her Indian blood. "Wear something plain and dark, and comb your hair flat. You're far too comely," Uncle Caleb said grudgingly. "A man of serious Godly pursuits might think you frivolous."

"Yes, Uncle Caleb."

Swan Necklace, peering over the edge of her blanket, caught the flare of rebellion in the stubborn little chin. Her glance caught Sarah's and she lowered one eyelid in sympathy. The soft, pink mouth quirked up at one corner, and quickly Swan Necklace covered her face to hide her own smile. What did the child have in mind? She should admonish her not to behave badly, she should urge her to follow Caleb's advice. Caleb was right. She'd been a bad influence on her granddaughter. Still, curiosity and a spark of the high spirit that had bound the two of them these many years made her lower the blanket and peer curiously at Sarah. Caleb was already leaving the room. Sarah stood swaying back and forth, her face thoughtful.

"Sarah, what are you going to do?" Swan Necklace asked with her conspiratorial fire. Sarah glanced at her grandmother and raised her eyebrows in the most pious of expressions.

"I'm going to do exactly as Uncle Caleb bade me," she answered primly.

Caleb MacKenzie should have been gratified by his niece's appearance when she came downstairs to greet his guest, but was not. Her dark hair had indeed been plainly parted in the middle and brushed into a severe knot at the back of her head, and her dark, high-necked dress was without ornament of any sort, its somberness unrelieved by even a touch of lace. But the material was cheap and showed many washings, and the fit was so poorly done, Caleb was certain it had belonged to one of the servants. His lips twitched with disapproval, but Sarah didn't notice. Her eyes were demurely cast down, her proud head bowed, her shoulders hunched in a parody of humbleness.

"Brother Stone, I'd like you meet my niece." Uncle Caleb made the introductions.

"My pleasure, Miss MacKenzie. I saw you from a distance last Sunday at church."

"How do you do, Reverend Stone?" Sarah mumbled without looking up. "The Lord has surely blessed us with your presence tonight."

Daniel cast a glance at Caleb. "It's an honor to be invited," he answered. And so it went for the whole evening. Whenever Daniel addressed Sarah, she answered with such simpering, pious words that even Caleb tired of them.

Daniel Stone was a lively young man, well educated by the day's standards and burning with the calling to go into the darkness and bring light to heathens who'd never heard of the white god. His first assignment was among the western Indians, and in his enthusiasm Daniel Stone was only sorry he couldn't have been the first missionary to reach them. He was well aware of Caleb MacKenzie's intentions. Upon receiving an invitation to the MacKenzie house, Daniel had taken care to catch a glimpse of Sarah before accepting. He'd been pleased by the spritely, beautiful young woman pointed out to him and was not averse to considering her as a wife to take with him in his missionary work. Now as he labored to talk with the drab, pious creature seated across from him, he wondered if someone had jested with him. This couldn't be the same girl.

He longed to have her raise her eyes so he might see if some spark of intelligence registered there. But she slumped in her chair, shoulders hunched. Her black hair, which had seemed lustrous and silky when he'd first glimpsed her, was dank and as limp as her personality.

For all his religious teachings Daniel was a practical, down-to-earth young man who would rather have a comely, loving wife at his side than a humorless self-righteous disciple with no mind of her own. His years of missionary work would be long and lonely without a proper mate.

Caleb sensed the young man's reserve and blamed his niece for it. Deliberately she'd set herself to thwart his plans for her. Silently he fumed, vowing to make her rue this day. She would do penance until her knees were callused and Christian charity be damned.

Politely, Daniel stayed for coffee to be served in the drawing room. Seldom used, furnished in the current popular trend of a seven-piece parlor suite of angular Renaissance lines, this room was Aunt Margaret's pride and joy. The dark wood of the furniture, carved with crests, roundels, and drops, was polished with lemon oil until it glowed. Despite Uncle Caleb's high-minded calling, Margaret MacKenzie had always had a love of pretty things. Smiling graciously, she poured from a gleaming silver coffeepot into delicate, hand-painted china cups. Settling herself into an unobtrusive corner chair, Sarah refrained from wrapping her feet around the cabriole legs as was her want and sat primly, her prayer book clasped in her hands.

"Tell us something about the Indians with whom you'll be working, Brother Stone," Aunt Margaret asked.

Daniel cleared his throat and warmed to the task.

He'd read every report ever written by other missionaries. "As you may know, ma'am," he began, "Dr. Marcus Whitman and Reverend Henry Spalding began this onerous task with the Northwest Indians back in the mid-thirties. At first they made incredible progress with the Cayuse, the Yakima, and the Nez Percé." Sarah's eyes flashed with interest and she forgot her humble, self-effacing pose. "Unfortunately, the savages turned on Dr. Whitman, murdering his innocent family and workers, and Reverend Spalding, fearing the Nez Percé would do the same to his party, fled to Willamette for a number of years."

"How dreadful," Margaret MacKenzie said, shaking her head in sympathy.

"Yes, yes. We've all heard about Dr. Whitman's untimely demise," Uncle Caleb said with an impatient wave of his hand. Sarah sensed he didn't want to talk about the Northwest Indians. It seemed with every year that passed, Uncle Caleb grew more uneasy about his Indian heritage. He seldom spoke of it unless someone asked him directly.

"It was a dreadful time for Reverend Spalding," Daniel continued, unaware of his host's discomfort at the turn of the conversation. "Fifteen years passed before he returned to the Wallowa Valley. During that time his wife had died, but he remarried and his new bride accompanied him to the Nez Percé lands. All his previous work with the Indians had been undone. He had to start over again."

"The poor man!" Margaret sipped at her tea and settled back comfortably in her chair, her feet propped on a footstool near the warmth of the fire. She was heartily glad Caleb had never felt the call to go into the missionary field.

"I understand Reverend Spalding was able to reclaim his converts and before his death had a great deal of influence in helping the government bring the Nez Percé to heel," Uncle Caleb said. He longed to change the subject, but could think of no polite way of doing so.

"A goodly portion, yes, he did," Daniel said. "But another portion have embraced the old faith. It got quite a toehold while Reverend Spalding was away from his mission. Although he was able to win back many of his converts, a stubborn lot of them refused to return to the Christian faith. Since his death, the fear is that these unbelievers, these dreamers, as they call themselves, might persuade the converts away from their peaceful, God-fearing ways."

"But surely the Indians wouldn't leave after all Reverend Spalding and his mission have done for them," Aunt Margaret exclaimed.

"Since Reverend Spalding's death two years ago, the mission has fallen somewhat into chaos," Daniel explained. "They're short of disciples to do the Lord's work. They need teachers and missionaries to carry on. There's always a danger the unbelievers will influence the believers away from God's teachings."

"Oh, dear, the task seems impossible," Margaret said.

"Not impossible, dear lady," Daniel said. "With the might and strength of the Lord behind us, we'll drive out the devil who has laid claim to these poor heathens' souls. It is our Christian duty."

Sarah had listened quietly, her irritation growing. "Perhaps the Nez Percé have simply decided they're better off without Reverend Spalding's brand of Christianity," she snapped. Daniel Stone was startled at the angry color in her cheeks and the disdainful flare of her nostrils. Sarah MacKenzie was not as humble and godly as she would have him believe. Furthermore, when she dropped that meek pose, she was a beauty.

"Sarah," Margaret admonished weakly.

"Why do you say that, Miss MacKenzie?" Daniel asked. He wanted to see that flash of fire in her dark eyes once more.

Defiantly she returned his gaze, her head thrown back proudly. "I've heard stories of the way Henry Spalding whipped the Indians for the slightest infraction."

"They had to be disciplined," Daniel answered mildly.

"Disciplined?" Sarah cried. "Is it discipline to whip a woman seventy lashes for running away from her abusive, supposedly Christian husband?"

"I don't know the incident," Daniel answered. "I couldn't say."

"If she had been a white woman she wouldn't have been whipped," Sarah challenged. "And what of children who are whipped for stealing corn?"

"Stealing is an intolerable crime against man and God," Daniel began.

"Taking food when you are hungry is a crime?" Sarah demanded. "And why must they steal food? Couldn't your Reverend Spalding have given food to his poor and hungry?"

"Perhaps they were not one of Reverend Spalding's flock," Daniel said tentatively.

"What difference would that have made if the children were hungry?" Sarah demanded. She was on her feet, glaring at him accusingly as if he himself had wielded the lash against the defenseless children. "Have you ever been hungry, Brother Stone?"

"I, ah, know of none of these incidences," Daniel stuttered. "Hearsay—"

"It is not hearsay, Brother Stone. My grandmother witnessed these things and she has told me."

Daniel swallowed and glanced at his host, whose expression was thunderous as he glared at his niece. Undeterred, Sarah waited for his answer. Daniel thought back over all the things he'd read. He'd been appalled, too, at Spalding's treatment of the Indians and had discussed it with his leaders. Now he offered Sarah the same answers given to him. "Sometimes the discipline must seem harsh to outsiders," he said tentatively. "These people are like children, untrained in the ways of civilized Christians. They simply don't behave as you and I do, Miss MacKenzie."

"Perhaps that's a credit to them, Mr. Stone," she said coldly.

"Sarah. I'll not have any more of that kind of talk." Caleb had regained his speech. "Mr. Stone is a guest in our house. Show him respect."

Sarah took a deep, steadying breath, her hands once again clasped demurely over her prayer book. But her eyes glowed with anger.

"All right, Uncle Caleb," she answered quietly. Her gaze was unwavering as it met Daniel's. "I wish you well in your mission, Brother Stone. May God give you more mercy and love for the Nez Percé than he gave Reverend Stone. Or Uncle Caleb, for that matter." Sarah's slender frame shook with repressed anger at her uncle's shame for his heritage and the blind hypocrisy of the young man who planned to force an alien culture upon her grandmother's people.

Caleb MacKenzie stepped forward and clasped her arm, his fingers digging cruelly into the soft flesh. "I will not hear another word from you," he bellowed. "Go to your room at once and stay there." His gaze was so fierce that despite her anger Sarah felt intimidated by it. Clamping her teeth against another scathing outburst, she left the parlor without a backward glance.

"I'm sorry," she heard Uncle Caleb say. "I'm not sure what's gotten into her lately."

Seething at his attitude, Sarah clasped her skirts high and ran up the stairs, her high-topped shoes making an angry staccato against the steps. She'd meant to go straight to her room as Uncle Caleb ordered, but in passing the door to Swan Necklace's room, she heard a sound and turned inside.

"Kautsas?" she said softly, drawing comfort from the use of the Nez Percé word for her grandmother. She felt guilty for the things she'd heard downstairs, as if she had spoken against the Nez Percé herself. Now she tiptoed closer to the bed, wanting to talk to her grandmother and be comforted by her gentle stories. "Kautsas?" she whispered.

The sound, strangled and desperate, came again. Alarm swept through Sarah and she rushed to the bed. Swan Necklace's face was shrunken, her eyes fixed as if on some distant mountain. Only her mouth worked to make a sound. Feebly she reached out a hand to Sarah.

"Kautsas," Sarah cried, clasping the frail brown hand. "Uncle Caleb!" Her scream echoed through the house, wild and startling. Fearfully Sarah searched her grandmother's face, praying the noise hadn't bothered her, but too afraid to leave her. She could hear heavy footsteps thudding up the stairs and down the hall. The door was flung back and Uncle Caleb was there. His fierce gaze took in his dying mother and Sarah kneeling beside the bed, tears washing down her cheeks.

"Send for the doctor, quickly," Caleb MacKenzie

ordered, clenching his fists in impotency. Margaret ran to find a maid.

Daniel Stone stepped closer to the bed and suddenly he understood Sarah's fierce defense of the Nez Percé. "Has this woman become a child of God?" he asked now.

Numbly Caleb MacKenzie shook his head. "She has," he answered in a broken voice. "She is my mother." Sarah glanced up sharply.

"Then we will pray for her that God will accept her into his kingdom," Daniel Stone said and knelt at the foot of the bed. After a moment's hesitation Caleb MacKenzie knelt as well. Their voices rose in supplication.

In her bed, Swan Necklace did not hear them. She was racing through the blue-flowered camas meadow, her hand tightly clasping that of Running Brook, her dearest friend. Their laughter was caught by the warm spring winds and flung far over the brown hump of mountains. Swan Necklace smiled as she held out her hand and took the digging tool from her friend, then bent her young back to gather the bounty of the camas root. She let her digging stick sink deep into the moist, brown earth. It was good to be home again.

"Kautsas!" The beaded spirit bag dropped from Swan Necklace's lifeless hand and fell to the floor beside Sarah. "Grandmother!" It was too late. The prayers and petition had done no good unless they had been meant only to ease Swan Necklace's soul into heaven. She died with a half smile, her wrinkled brown face peaceful in death, her spirit free of the burden of the white world she'd embraced so long ago.

Sarah buried her face in the side of the bed and wept for the tiny, indomitable woman. Caleb Mac-

Kenzie's mighty, ringing voice faltered only for a moment before he continued with entreaties to God. But Sarah could find no comfort in prayer. Her hand brushed against the small beaded bag her grandmother had held to the end of her life and slowly she picked it up. The promise she'd made Swan Necklace pressed in on her and her chin tightened in resolve. Somehow she would keep her promise. She would return her grandmother's spirit bag to the land of the Nez Percé. Rocking back and forth, Sarah keened as her grandmother had taught her was done when a loved one died. The high-pitched wailing sounded heathenish to Daniel Stone's ears, and he wished Caleb MacKenzie would ask her to stop, but for once the elegant, restrained preacher seemed lost in his own grief.

2

The men huddled in their saddles, hunching their backs against the biting wind and stinging snow. They'd left Fort Fetterman two weeks before, traveling along the old Phil Kearney road to the Powder River at Fort Reno and on to the headwaters of the Tongue River. A late winter blizzard had caught them as they followed the valley of Otter Creek toward their objective. Blinded by the driving snow, the men had pushed on until they'd reached the fork of the Tongue River, and now they waited patiently for their scouts to return and tell them what waited below the bluff.

Major Lucas Tanner wiped the snow from his hat brim and pulled it lower over his eyes, squinting to see through the swirling flakes.

"Do you think it's Crazy Horse and his band?" Gayle Nevins asked. He was a young soldier, without much experience fighting Indians, and he was nervous, torn between wanting to acquit himself in battle and fear for his scalp.

Tanner's gray eyes held a trace of amusement as he studied the young man. "If that were Crazy Horse's camp down there, we wouldn't be sitting up here," he said.

Gayle Nevins sat thinking about what he'd said. He'd quickly learned not to question Major Tanner.

Unlike some of the other commanding officers fresh out from the Point, the major knew what he was talking about. He'd seen combat with the Indians and earned a name for himself. He'd fought with Custer's regiment in the Black Hills the year before, going up against the fierce Sioux. Gayle considered it the best of luck that he was with Lieutenant Colonel George Armstrong Custer's 7th Cavalry. It was considered the crack Indian-fighting regiment in the United States Army. He turned his attention to the gray shadows across the river.

"Who's down there, then, if it's not Crazy Horse and his Sioux?" he asked, excited and apprehensive at the same time. Talking to Tanner made him feel better, more certain that everything would come out all right.

Tanner shrugged, sending a swirl of hard white flakes flying from his broad shoulders. "Some band trying to join forces with him would be my guess," he said quietly.

"You mean other Sioux? How many bands are there?"

"Haven't you been listening to the old-timers back at the fort?" Tanner asked flatly. He was irritated at the young man's lighthearted, fanciful approach to the Indians. Dazzled by the esprit de corps of Custer and his regiment, Nevins and many of the new recruits gave no thought to the dangers of fighting the Sioux. Like their leader, they sought the glory. Tanner's lips tightened. If some of them would just take a little time to find out about the enemy they fought, they might have a better chance at survival. "There are the Ogalala, the Brule, Sans arc, Minneconjou, Santee, Blackfoot, Hunkpapa." He ticked off the names on his fingers.

"They figure more than ten thousand redskins are

out here." Nevins rolled his head to indicate the wide, wild land of prairies and mountains. His blue eyes were eager.

"Not that many, son," Tanner said wearily.

"How many, then?"

"Enough!" Gayle waited for him to continue. Next to George Custer he held the major in the highest esteem. "Enough to scare the hell out of me," Tanner snapped.

Gayle was disappointed by his answer. He'd never imagined the big man could be afraid.

"Sir? Colonel Custer wants to see you." A young adjutant had brought his horse quietly alongside.

"All right, Corporal." Tanner saluted and turned back to the young Irishman. "Watch your back when we go down there," he said quietly and was gone. Nevins watched him disappear into the white mist and felt the first wave of fear tightening his chest muscles so he had trouble breathing. Jesus, what was he doing here?

Cautiously Tanner made his way along the line of men. Custer's 7th Cavalry consisted of the usual variety of emigrants, soldiers of fortune, and veterans of the Civil War. Forty Arikara also rode with the detachment as well as six Crow scouts, three of whom were scouting the Indian village below.

Tanner guided his horse toward a ridge where Custer sat astride his blaze-faced sorrel thoroughbred, Vic. He was surrounded by his usual entourage, a news reporter from the Bismark *Tribune* who'd joined him for his summer campaigns, and a man holding the four staghounds he always carried with him. Dressed in a fringed jacket and breeches of deer hide, a wide, sloppy brimmed hat pulled low over his long yellow hair, Custer stood out from his men dressed in their dull blue uniforms. Even the sporting rifle resting in its fringed hide case and the self-cocking English bulldog pistols strapped to his hip were not government-issue. Custer set his own rules and his men loved his flamboyance and daring.

Some of his men, Tanner amended. Like him, some saw through the flare and dash to the careless, glory-seeking man beneath, and they worried at his lack of understanding of the real Indian problem. Sure of his own destiny and the famous Custer luck, the golden-haired commander often led his men into danger without giving serious regard to their safety. Now Lucas Tanner made his way to the group surrounding the commander. Major Reno was already there, his expression disapproving and contemptuous as he listened to Custer's hushed commands. They were still a good distance from the Indian village below and the blizzard covered the sound of their horses, but even Custer knew enough not to underestimate the Indians.

"You wanted to see me, sir?" Tanner asked.

"Major Tanner," Custer said. "We're going down to attack the camp."

"Have the scouts returned?"

"We aren't waiting for them. The element of surprise will be better than any information our scouts can bring back to us. I want you to take your men and deploy them to the west of that ridge. Major Reno will take his unit to the east."

"Sir, I think we should wait for the scouts. We don't know what we're attacking down there. It could be a peaceful tribe of Indians."

"This is Sioux territory, Major," the Indian fighter said, his blue eyes commanding as they glared at Tanner, "and I'd bet my commission it's Crazy Horse's camp. That's how sure I am. Now, if you have some other information, let's hear it."

Tanner refused to be intimidated by the imposing leader. "There might be women and children down there, sir, and in this weather we'd be hard put to see the difference."

"Then don't worry about the difference, Major," Custer said. "We're going in hard and fast. I don't expect to take any prisoners. Understood?" He looked around the gathering. Several officers nodded their heads in agreement. Custer brought his hard, bright gaze back to Major Lucas Tanner. "Is that understood, Major Tanner?"

"Yes, sir," Tanner said and, giving a sharp salute, turned his horse away.

"Nice try," Major Reno said as Tanner rode by. "Our fearless leader has decreed and we must follow." Denial of the major's words rose hot and cloying in Tanner's throat, but he swallowed it. He'd often clashed with Custer and knew his commanding officer was only looking for an excuse to muster him out of the 7th Cavalry. He rode back to his men and gave the order to ready for attack.

Tanner took his men along the western edge of the ridge, while Major Reno went off to the east as Custer had instructed. Cautiously they crept closer until Tanner could make out the conical outline of the Indians' tipis across the river. The driving snow made it impossible to see the markings. High up on the ridge a shot sounded and with a howling almost as blood-curdling as any the Indians could make, the force rushed pell-mell down the embankment, across the ice-encrusted waters of the Tongue River, and into the Indian encampment. Now Tanner could see the markings on the tipis and his breath caught as he stared at the round sun emblem.

"Hold your fire. They're Cheyenne," he shouted but no one listened. Caught up in the excitement of the battle, the soldiers galloped through the camp, firing their guns into the hide tipis until the Indians cowering inside were forced to leave, running head on into a barrage of deadly gunfire. Lariats were thrown around the support poles and tipis pulled down. Flaming brands were tossed through hide openings, so the women and children were trapped inside. Women screamed, children cried, and everywhere was the smell and sounds of death and destruction.

The blinding curtain of snow parted for a moment, and Tanner saw Gayle Nevins astride his horse, his gun blazing death. Behind him a warrior crept forward, a tomahawk raised.

"Nevins, watch your back," Tanner shouted and rode his horse forward, knocking the warrior aside.

Whirling, Nevins fired, killing the Indian. He grinned jubilantly. "Thanks, Major," he called. "I owe you one." His horse danced away and the young soldier was swallowed up by the swirling snow. The white curtain closed around Tanner again until in the midst of pandemonium he felt isolation. The Indians had rallied and the warriors were beginning to return the soldiers' fire. Wounded men fell beneath their horses' hooves and in the melee were trampled. Blood lay bright red on the white snow, then was trodden into a pink slush.

Sickened by what he saw, Tanner had not yet fired his gun. Now as his horse reared and snorted in fear at the noise and blood smells, Tanner brought him under control and rode through the camp. Bodies lay everywhere, their limbs flung out in some grotesque dance of death. Why did it shock him now, he wondered vaguely. He'd witnessed this scene a dozen times before. What was different? But his numbed mind knew the difference. They'd rid-

den in here expecting to find a Sioux war chief and
his warriors. Instead they'd found a band of peaceful Cheyenne, fleeing with their women and children to the safety of the reservation.

The wailing of a child penetrated his numbness
and Tanner looked around. A small boy not more
than four or five years old stood beside the fallen
body of his mother. He wore only a hastily donned
leather shirt. His feet were bare in the snow. Helplessly he looked around, seeking a familiar face. Pity
swept through Tanner and he turned his horse toward the boy.

"I'm not going to hurt you, son," he said gently
and dismounted. Slowly he walked toward the boy,
his hand outstretched in friendship. The boy's dark
eyes watched him unblinkingly. "Come on," Tanner
said. The boy glanced down at his dead mother and
took a step forward. There was a flurry of hoofbeats
and a shot rang out. The small body dropped to the
snow beside the woman.

"No—o—o!" Tanner shouted, looking around. The
soldier who'd fired the shot wheeled his horse for a
second look. Gayle Nevins's gun was still smoking.
A look of satisfaction crossed his face. Black rage
rose in Tanner. Snatching his gun from its holster,
he took aim and fired. The first bullet ripped into
Nevins's shoulder, the second felled his horse.

Stunned surprise crossed Nevins's face before he
was thrown from his horse. "What the hell? What'd
you do that for, Major?" he cried out as Tanner took
aim again. "Jesus!" Nevins dove for the protection
of his dead horse. Tanner's vision cleared and he
stared at the white-faced soldier. Slowly he lowered
his gun and let it dangle uselessly at his side as he
walked to the Indian boy and knelt down. Major
Reno rode by and Gayle Nevins stood up.

"Jesus, Major, did you see that? He fired on one of his own men," Nevins said incredulously.

"I saw it, soldier," Major Reno said. "You're lucky you're not dead. That was a damned-fool thing to do."

"Damned-fool thing for me to do?" Nevins exclaimed. "It was him who fired at me."

"You just missed killing a commanding officer. You hit the Indian boy instead. Major Tanner had every right to fire before checking to see if it was one of his own men."

"He didn't—"

"I suggest you find yourself another horse, private, and be sure of where you're firing next time. This could have brought you a court-martial."

"Yes, sir," Gayle Nevins said sullenly.

"And have that wound looked to."

"Yes, sir." The soldier limped away. He might have known. Officers always stuck together.

"You all right, Tanner?" Major Reno asked. He'd gotten off his horse and stood nearby.

Tanner looked up at him, his cheeks wet with tears. "There was no need to shoot him. He was just a scared little boy."

"It was an accident, Tanner."

"Was it? Was this whole fiasco an accident? They were Cheyenne. They weren't at war with us. They just wanted to get to safety."

Major Reno watched the big man hunched beside the dead Indians, and some of the truths he'd tried hard to ignore pressed in on him. "Come on," he said. "The burial detail is coming around." He held out a hand much as Tanner had done to the Indian boy. Tanner stared at it for a long moment, then with a shout of anguish vaulted on his horse and dug in his heels. The roan leaped forward, carrying Tanner beyond the wall of falling snow.

Custer rode into middle of the destroyed village. "We'll camp here tonight," he said and the weary jubilant men began to set up makeshift tents.

"You say Tanner had a good look at you before he fired his gun?" Custer asked, his blue eyes gazing at the private intently.

"Yes, sir," Gayle Nevins said and swallowed hard. "He knew all right who he was firing at. He couldn't have mistaken me for an Indian."

"Thank you, Private. That will be all."

"Yes, sir." Private Nevins saluted smartly and left the room. Colonel Custer turned to the big, somber-faced man sitting across from him.

"What do you have to say about this, Major Tanner?" he asked almost pleasantly. He'd never liked his officer. There was a hard implacability to Lucas Tanner that Custer found threatening. The big man wasn't easily charmed as were his other officers. Rebellion showed itself in the slashing lines of his weathered face and the stubborn, tight-lipped mouth. Tanner always questioned his orders instead of blindly accepting them as was required of a good soldier. Even now, in the face of this inquiry, he showed no nervousness.

"I shot the soldier," he answered tersely. There was no explanation and no expression of remorse.

"Sir, I was there and saw the whole thing," Major Reno spoke up. "Private Nevins fired first, nearly hitting Major Tanner. Major Tanner fired in self-defense. It was snowing hard. Visibility was poor. Once Nevins called out, Major Tanner ceased firing."

"Thank you for your accounting, Major," Custer said. "You may return to your men."

"Thank you, sir." With a last anxious glance at his friend, Major Reno left the office.

Once again Custer turned to Tanner. For a long measuring moment he studied him. "I want your resignation," he said quietly.

Tanner's head came up. "Why?"

"I want you out of my regiment."

"You're going to need every man you can get to go up against the Sioux."

"Precisely," Custer snapped. "But I need soldiers I know are behind me."

"I can't be behind you when you lead us against peaceful Indian tribes. That attack on the Cheyenne camp drove them to join the Sioux."

"They would have done so anyway," Custer snapped.

"We'll never know that now," Tanner answered evenly. "You've made damned sure of that by killing their women and children in a needless bloodbath."

"I want you out of my regiment," Custer shouted. "I can't abide an Indian lover and a coward."

"Why don't you name the real reason you want me out of here?" Tanner flared. "You can't stand someone telling you you're wrong. Well, I'm not the only man in this outfit that sees you for what you really are."

Custer's face was red, his pale blue eyes glittering with rage. "But there will be one less man against me," he declared. "If you don't resign, I'll have you court-martialed."

"If there's a court-martial, some questions are going to be asked about the Cheyenne camp," Tanner answered evenly. "Are you prepared to answer those questions, Colonel?"

Custer's pale face swelled with fury. The cords in his neck bulged and contracted. Slamming his fist against the desk, he opened his mouth but no words came.

Tanner got to his feet and picked up his hat. "I won't be resigning," he said quietly and walked to the door.

"Tanner," Custer shouted, his arm outstretched, a finger pointing accusingly. "I will have you out of my regiment. Do you hear me? You'll be out—" Tanner closed the door on Custer's tirade.

The May sun burned on the back of his neck. Tanner wiped the sweat from his brow and clamped the hat back on his head. Squinting against the bright sunlight, he glanced up the track. The train was late. He crossed the platform to the thin line of shade afforded by the overhanging roof of the station house. His footsteps were loud against the wooden floor. Squatting with his back against the plank wall, Tanner rolled a cigarette and looked around. More than two months had passed since their attack on the Cheyenne camp, and although Custer and the 7th had gone out on skirmishes since, Tanner had not. Custer had deliberately assigned him to Fort Russell, while rumors of cowardice and Indian lover swirled around him. The men who'd once respected him now spat in the dust when he walked by. One night a group of enlisted men had jumped him and took turns beating him while his arms were held from behind. Although Custer claimed an investigation had been made, the men were never found.

Tanner had gone over Custer's head to General Crook, but to no avail. The general believed Custer's allegations of cowardice and madness. Now caught up in the coming campaigns, no one had been inclined to give him a fair hearing. He'd been accused and condemned with no chance to defend himself. Tanner would have preferred a court-martial. If not for the building tension with the Sioux, he wouldn't have minded this transfer to Washington Territory. Speculations abounded of a large Sioux village in the vicinity of Rosebud Creek. Even now a company of men were readying themselves for a long seige.

Striking a match against the rough siding, Tanner lit a cigarette and pulled deeply. Boots sounded on the platform. Gayle Nevins approached, two other enlisted men behind him. Tanner shifted his weight slightly so he could move swiftly. He wouldn't be caught off guard again.

"Hello, Nevins," he said easily and grinned. "Come down to see me off, did you?"

"What're you doing, Tanner? Running away? Did you hear we're going out to fight real Indians?"

The grin faded from Tanner's face and his eyes grew dark. "It's always nice to have a friend drop by," he said quietly.

"I'm not your friend," Nevins sneered. "I don't make friends with men who try to kill me. You ain't nothing but a chicken-hearted, white-livered, whey-faced—"

"Careful, son, before you bust something," Tanner growled without removing the cigarette from his mouth.

Nevins halted his tirade and took a breath. "What're you going to do, Major? Try to shoot me in the back again?"

Tanner sighed. They both knew Nevins's words were a lie. They'd been spoken for the benefit of the other two men. "Run on back to the fort, son, before I'm tempted," Tanner warned and pulled his hat brim over his eyes dismissively.

Nevins flushed with a shiver of apprehension. He wasn't fooled by Tanner's nonchalant pose. He knew too well the lightning speed and fighting skill of the big man slouching against the wall. Gayle wouldn't be here now except for his friends, who'd grown tired of his accounts of the shooting and had egged him on to seek a revenge he didn't need. Now, with a wary glance at the other two men, he stepped forward. "Get up and fight me, you craven coward," he challenged.

Tanner studied him for a long moment. "What're you trying to prove, Nevins?" he asked evenly and the young private fought against the thrill of admiration and envy he'd always felt for the older man.

"I'm here to prove what a coward you really are," he sneered. "I'm twice the man you are."

"Is that why you brought reinforcements?" Tanner asked, nodding toward the men.

"I don't need their help to take you," Nevins shouted. "Stand up and fight, coward."

With a flick of his thumb Tanner tossed away his cigarette butt and slowly pushed away from the wall. Before he was upright a fist slammed into his face. Another balled fist hit him in the chest, knocking him back against the station wall. Tanner ducked as Nevins threw another punch at his face. He could hear the crunch of knuckles against the wood siding. With a cry of pain Nevins reeled backward, his injured hand cradled against his chest.

"Let's get him," one of the other soldiers cried and both men advanced on Tanner. A foot lashed out, landing in the soft middle of one of the assailants. With a whoosh the air left his chest and he doubled over. The other man kept advancing, landing a blow on Tanner's unprotected head. Reeling, Tanner staggered against the station house and turned to meet his attacker. Nevins had recovered now and leaped forward. Both men grabbed his arms, but Tanner jerked them forward toward each other. They bumped together, losing their grip on him. Nevins fell away. Quickly Tanner gripped the shoulder of the soldier's uniform and swung him around into the wall. With a hand gripping the back of the man's head, he slammed his face against the wood until the blood flew from his nose and lips and, with a quiet sigh, the soldier slid to the ground.

Nevins was back on his feet and the man Tanner had kicked had regained his breath. Warily they circled Tanner. Tanner charged the man on his right, his long arms gripping and pulling forward as he flipped him over his shoulder. The man slammed to the platform and lay still. The train chugged down the track and came to a stop in the station. Tanner paid it no heed. Only Nevins remained and Tanner squared off with him. He could see the fear in the young soldier's eyes, but there was no pity left in Tanner. It was time Nevins learned a lesson. Doubling his big hands into hard fists Tanner hammered a series of quick blows to Nevins's chin. Nevins ineffectually threw a punch, but it was wild and never hit its mark. Tanner landed a poke in the young man's middle and a final blow to his chin. Nevins's eyes rolled backward and he fell across the body of his friend and lay still.

Faces pressed against the windows of the train as the passengers stared at the men. Without looking at them, Tanner gathered up his bags and his saddle and walked across the platform. Gayle Nevins groaned and raised his head. Pausing on the steps Tanner looked back at the young soldier. "Like I said, Nevins, watch your back," he said softly and boarded the train.

3

Like the other passengers of the Union Pacific, Sarah stared at the uniformed soldiers fighting on the station platform. One, taller and broader of shoulder, seemed to be holding off the other three. One soldier was knocked to the ground and lay with his eyes closed, his chest heaving. Another soldier was neatly dispatched over the shoulder of the big man and landed in a heap. A few lightning swings of his fists sent the third following. He sprawled across his friend, then struggled briefly to get up before admitting defeat. Without looking back, the victor gathered his belongings and walked toward the train.

Sarah's breath caught when she looked at the strong, angular face. Deep creases lined his tanned cheeks and radiated from the corner of his eyes: he'd spent a lot of time squinting into the sun. With a large bronze hand he smoothed back his sun-streaked brown hair and clamped on his wide-brimmed army-issue hat. It shadowed his eyes so she couldn't see their color.

The passengers settled back in their seats now that the show was over. Their number had diminished as the train moved farther west. Now many of the travelers were day passengers.

Audrey Keane, one of the few passengers who'd boarded the train with Sarah in Omaha, leaned over the back of the seat. A reporter for an eastern paper, Audrey fancied herself a freethinker. Her speech and manner were overly bold. "Hmmm. Looks like not all the savages are Sioux," she observed. "Maybe I'll take up Indian fighting myself."

Sarah had long since ceased to be shocked by the reporter's frank remarks. Audrey had come out West to report on the rising hostilities with the Indians. She was certain they'd been vastly overstated for the folks back home, and she intended to destroy the romantic myths surrounding the West and its settlement.

"If the rest of the army looks and fights like that one," she commented, "we don't have much to fear from the Sioux." Her observations were cut off by the bump and lurch of the Union Pacific starting up again.

"Unruly lot," another woman passenger exclaimed. "No wonder we have trouble with the Indians. The army's too busy fighting among themselves to fight the savages." Her contentious voice quieted abruptly as the door opened and the tall man stepped inside. Without glancing around the compartment, he stowed his gear in a corner near the door and made his way along the aisle toward a seat. All eyes were focused on his blue-clad figure.

"He's a major," Audrey murmured in a low voice from her seat. "Wonder why three enlisted men would dare to gang up on an officer?"

"Maybe they were deserters or something," Sarah suggested.

"Maybe," the reporter said doubtfully. "If so, why did he leave them back there? No, there's more to this man than meets the eye. Oh, he's coming this way." Sarah resisted the urge to look around.

The big man was nearly past Sarah when he turned

and with a sigh settled into the empty seat across from her. Wearily he took off his hat and gloves and studied his scraped knuckles.

At first Sarah tried to ignore the man's presence, keeping her eyes lowered and her shoulders hunched in the mousy pose she'd assumed ever since leaving Missouri. Although she'd ignored her uncle's orders not to leave his house or never return, she had not ignored the dire warnings he'd hurled after her of what happened to unchaperoned young women in the lawless and untamed West. Wearing the same shapeless, threadbare dress she'd donned the night Daniel Stone had come to call and a bonnet of unadorned wool, Sarah had liberally applied rice powder to her face. It dimmed her youthful high color. A little coal applied sparingly to the hollows of her cheeks, brow, and chin made her face ashen. Indeed, so diligent had been her efforts that her fellow travelers had speculated on a lingering illness.

From beneath lowered lashes she studied the big, rawboned man in the soldier's uniform. An officer's gold maple leaves decorated the shoulders. Gingerly he worked his jaw as if he feared it was broken. Blood trickled from the corner of his wide, firm mouth. Instinctively Sarah reached for her handkerchief.

"You're hurt," she murmured and sat forward to gently dab at the gashed lip. With a grunt of pain he jerked away, his knees bumping hers. "Sorry," she said and handed him the wisp of lace and cotton. His hand brushed against hers as he took the scrap of cloth and cautiously applied it to the cut. Sarah smiled at the grimace he made. There was something almost childlike in the way he nursed his wounds. It was oddly at variance with the invincible strength of him fighting the other three men back at the station.

Suddenly she was aware that his gray eyes were watching her intently and she quickly lowered her lashes. Curiosity was her downfall, though, and just as quickly she raised them again so she could study the big man. His face wasn't really handsome, she supposed, when compared with the smooth-faced men at home. He looked too hard-used, too weather-beaten to ever be admired in the genteel, restrained parlors of her uncle's congregation. Yet his expression possessed a strength such as she'd never found in any other face.

Shifting in his seat, the man winced and held out the blood-smeared handkerchief. "I'm afraid I've soiled it for you," he said. His voice was deep.

"No matter," she answered evenly. "I'll soak it tonight. It'll come clean." His gray eyes studied her until she glanced away, certain the rice powder couldn't hide her blush.

"I'm Major Lucas Tanner," he introduced himself.

"Sarah MacKenzie." She was unaware her smile undid all her attempts to hide her beauty. Tanner held out a broad hand and Sarah shook it, startled at how completely his hand covered hers.

"Where are you heading?" he asked, and she wasn't sure if he asked out of curiosity or politeness.

"I'm on my way to the Lapwai mission in Washington Territory," she said. "I'm to teach there."

"Out to bring enlightenment to the heathen savages?" he asked. Something in his tone caused Sarah to glance up.

"Certainly, if I can bring a message of God's love and a better way of life to the s—" she paused, unable to call her beloved grandmother's people savages—"to the Nez Percé, I will have done my Christian duty."

"That's an admirable attitude, ma'am," the big

man drawled sarcastically. "But wouldn't it have been more in keeping with your Christian duty to stay home and have babies?"

Angry color suffused Sarah's cheeks. "That might be the calling of some of my sisters, Major Tanner, but not for me. I wish to do something more meaningful for my fellow man."

"Did anyone warn you about what's happening out here?" he demanded abruptly. "Your fellow man is busy killing his red brothers so he can steal their land and the gold hidden there."

"You seem to hold the uniform you wear in some disdain, Major," Sarah said stiffly.

Tanner glanced down at the dusty blue suit and shook his head. "Not in the least," he said softly. "I've paid quite a price to keep this uniform, quite a price. The question is was the price too high." He raised his head and gazed out the window. He seemed not to be talking to her anymore at all. Sarah remained silent, watching him. There was a sadness around the eyes and mouth that touched her.

Instinctively she leaned forward and placed her hand on his. "You seem troubled," she said softly.

His attention snapped back to her and he shrugged, a slight smile curving the broad mouth. "Save your sympathy, Miss MacKenzie, for the Nez Percé," he said wryly. "After we've finished with the Sioux, like as not, they'll be next."

"I don't understand," Sarah answered.

He shrugged again. "No matter." This time when he turned his gaze to the window, she sensed he wanted no interruption. He'd drawn a wall around himself, and she was dismissed and forgotten as easily as that. She leaned back in her seat and tried to concentrate on her own plans, which had occupied her for most of the long trip. It was impossible to think of anything else but the big, lonely man with the bruised knuckles and sad eyes.

In the end, it had been Daniel Stone who'd befriended her. His letters had interceded for her to go to the Lapwai mission to teach. He'd been surprisingly understanding of her need to go there after hearing her grandmother was Nez Percé. Uncle Caleb had done everything to impede her plans. Sarah hadn't told either of them of her promise to Swan Necklace to return her spirit bag. They would have considered such a mission as heathenish. The beaded bag hung now around her neck and was safely tucked beneath the high bodice of her dowdy gown.

Lapwai, Wallowa Valley, Kamiah, home of the Nimpau, as the Nez Percé called themselves. She still couldn't believe she was going there. If only her grandmother were her traveling companion instead of the big man dozing uneasily.

The train chugged along in fits and starts as it had ever since she'd boarded in Omaha. Now it's clacking iron wheels had settled into a steady rhythm and just as steadily the miles rolled by, the landscape changing from the green of sagebrush in the prairie to the yellow and orange rock of buttes and mesas. Sarah watched the changing scenery, wondering about the mountains and valleys of her grandmother's tales. Would they be as she'd imagined them?

Across from her, Major Tanner shifted and mumbled in his sleep, his voice becoming louder and more agitated until other passengers turned to look at him. Finally Sarah leaned forward and shook him gently.

"No, no," he cried out. In one smooth motion he had his gun out of its holster and aimed directly at Sarah's chest. His eyes were dark and unfocused as he stared at her. Fear cut off her breathing so she sat silent, her face a paler hue than the rice powder had ever achieved. No one else made an outcry. Stunned, they stared, fearful to move lest they goad the major into firing.

Sarah took a deep breath. "Major Tanner," she said softly. "It's all right now. You can put your gun away."

Slowly the dark eyes focused, their gray color softening. An expression of shock rippled across his face. Quickly he dropped the gun to his lap and wiped the sweat from his brow and cheeks with a shaky hand. "I'm sorry," he said. Wiping his eyes, he opened them and looked at the startled faces of the other passengers. "I'm sorry," he repeated. "It was a bad dream."

A passenger, bewhiskered and nattily dressed in a fine woolen suit and checkered vest, rose and walked along the aisle until he was abreast the major. "We understand, son. We know you soldiers must see some fierce fighting out here," he said sympathetically, "but you can't whip out your gun here on the train. Someone might get hurt. Give it to me until you reach wherever it is you're going."

Major Tanner looked at the man for a long, measuring moment. Sarah was sure he'd never give up his gun. There was a strong pride about him that wouldn't allow him to submit to such restrictions. At first he made a move with his head as if to deny the request. Then he caught a glimpse of Sarah's expression. She'd made no sound, yet he could see the fear in her dark eyes and he felt ashamed he'd caused it. With a tight smile he nodded and handed over the gun. The whole car was silent except for the clacking of the train as it roared westward.

The bewhiskered man returned to his seat with an air of pompous satisfaction. He was more than a little surprised at his courage and at the results of his actions. He hadn't thought the big man would acquiesce as he had. The crisis was over. The rest of the passengers settled back into whatever pastimes they'd chosen to wile away the monotonous hours. Sarah sat stiff and straight in her seat, her eyes downcast. She was embarrassed, uneasy that Major Tanner might blame her for the turn of events. Whenever she found the temerity to raise her head, she encountered the unwavering gaze of those unfathomable gray eyes. Restlessly she fidgeted. Finally she took courage and spoke up.

"I'm sorry you had to give up your gun," she said faintly.

"I didn't have to give it up," he replied softly. "I didn't want to frighten you any more than I already had." His tone was so gentle and sincere that all anxiety left Sarah. Her smile was wide and infectious, and suddenly Tanner felt better just seeing it.

"I wasn't that frightened," she answered and grinned at her lie. Laughter danced in the brown depths of her eyes, and Tanner found himself caught up in the bright warmth he found there.

Why was she trying so hard to hide her beauty? he wondered. A woman could make herself plain, but she couldn't camouflage the natural grace and beauty of her movements and responses. Why had she chosen to go the Lapwai mission? It was located in harsh, lonely country, in the Bitterroot Mountain range. Despite her drab, prim appearance, she didn't seem the sort to bury herself among the Indians. Was she running from something or someone? Who was she? He studied the high cheekbones and ivory skin, the dark eyes with the fine black brows arching above, the small straight nose and well-formed chin. Her mouth captured his attention. It was wide and generous when she smiled, but in repose the pouty lips curved sweetly. Tanner glanced away.

"Would you like to tell me about it?" Sarah asked.

"What?" Tanner asked, jerking around to look at her again.

"Your bad dream. Grandmother always listened to my bad dreams. She said they were evil spirits and when you told someone about them, they had to flee and find another home."

Tanner grinned and nodded his head. "Telling won't make my bad dreams disappear," he said. Sarah didn't press, respecting another's private thoughts as Swan Necklace had taught her.

"Where are you headed, Major Tanner?" she asked instead.

"The same as you," he answered. "I've been transferred to Fort Lapwai in Washington Territory."

"That's splendid," Sarah said and couldn't understand the leap in her pulse. "However, I expect the territory is so large, we'll likely not see each other."

"Likely not," he answered flatly and pulled his hat over his eyes. Sarah was sorry she'd spoken, but she didn't like the responses the tall soldier awakened within her. Now she leaned back against the cushions and studied the passing scenery. Low hills and gullies dotted with sagebrush and scrubby trees had become monotonously familiar. The Rocky Mountains were a purplish smudge on the horizon.

Audrey Keane peered over the edge of her seat, her lips silently mouthing a message to Sarah. "Find out more about him," she signaled. Sarah glanced at the major, worried that he might have seen the reporter but his eyes were closed and he appeared to be sleeping again.

The Union Pacific halted for the evening at Rawlins at the foot of the Rockies. The depot was a raw, rough town with ragtag buildings sprawling away from the small whitewashed board station. The streets were already dark. The tinny notes of a piano mingled with the shouts and ribald laughter of the men frequenting the saloons. Sarah stood on the platform peering around. She was hesitant to walk to the hotel alone.

Audrey Keane had already started down the street with a group of other passengers. "Come on," she called back. Sarah started after her, then spied Major Tanner leaving the train car, his saddle and haversack over his shoulder. Instinctively she held back, waving Audrey to go on without her. Tanner glanced up and saw her waiting.

Taking a deep breath, Sarah approached the officer. "I wondered if you'd walk me to the hotel, Major Tanner?" she asked.

He gazed at her intently. "Aren't you afraid I'll shoot you, Miss MacKenzie?" he asked. She was surprised he'd remembered her name.

"No, I'm not afraid," she said, and by the very simplicity of her words conveyed the trust she was willing to place in him, in spite of the incident on the train. Tanner felt better and knew that was why she'd asked his help. Taking her elbow, he escorted her down the street. Walking beside him, Sarah was surprised at just how tall the major was. Her head barely reached his shoulders. Tanner was silent, exuding an aloofness that she found daunting. His mouth was tight and unyielding, his eyes, fixed straight ahead, were cold and unfriendly. He was an enigma. She never guessed how aware he was of her. He felt the rhythm and gracefulness of her movements as if they were his own. She was tall for a woman and easily matched his long strides in spite of her full skirts.

The moon was just showing itself beyond the line of buildings. Its light poured into the street, softening the bareness of the shabby little town. Except for the drunken laughter and the slap of cards from the open saloon doors, they might have been any young couple back in Mountain Grove, Missouri, going for a moonlight walk. Suddenly from one of the open saloons, a drunken figure staggered out onto the sidewalk, knocking Sarah to her knees. With a curse the man reached for his gun. Before his gear had hit the dust of the street, Tanner's hand was at his empty holster.

The drunk glanced at his empty hand and, grinning, whipped out his own pistol. "Looks like you're misshing shomething important there, Major," he drawled. Tanner's hand froze. His eyes were rock steady as he studied the other man, looking for a chance to jump him and wrest the gun from him.

Sarah saw the peril Lucas Tanner was in and somehow felt responsible. Instinctively she fell back on the only defense she had. "Could you help me?" she asked tearfully of the drunk. "I'm afraid when you knocked me down, I hurt my knee."

Startled, the drunk stared at her with bleary eyes. He hadn't been aware he'd knocked a woman down. Now all his chivalry came to the fore and, bowing gallantly, he held out a hand. "I'm most awfully shorry, ma'am," he slurred. "Welcome to our humble town. Yo—hic—your beauty does us an honor."

"You are so kind," Sarah said graciously and, taking the drunk's hand, got to her feet. "Thank you again, sir. My husband and I will be on our way." Desperately she clutched Major Tanner's sleeve.

"Shorry—shorry to run into you, Major," the drunk said and saluted with his gun.

"It's all right," Tanner said and returned his salute smartly. "Carry on."

"Yes, shir," the drunk said and reeled back into the saloon.

"Are you all right?" Tanner asked and at Sarah's nod gathered up his gear and hurried her along the sidewalk just in case the drunk decided to return with reinforcements.

His aloofness was gone now. "Which one of us was doing the protecting back there, Miss MacKenzie?" he teased when they were a safe distance away.

Sarah grinned. "Anytime you need a partner, Major, don't think we women are completely helpless."

"I'll keep that in mind. In the meantime, that was quick thinking."

"I don't think he meant us real harm. We just happened to get in his way at the wrong time."

"You may be right," Tanner said, "but don't take chances out here, Miss MacKenzie. There's too much land and not enough law to go around. Some men take advantage of that. Don't be a fool and walk into anything you can't handle."

"Thank you for the warning," Sarah said lightly.

Sheepishly Tanner glanced away. "You're never going to let me forget this afternoon on the train, are you?" She nodded her head from side to side, her dark gaze holding his. Tanner felt an urge to take her into his arms and kiss her smiling mouth. He backed away and curtly nodded at the building behind them. "Here's the hotel. I'll leave you now."

"Aren't you coming in?" she asked in dismay. She didn't want him to leave, not yet.

Tanner shook his head and took a step or two away. "I've got some things I want to do first," he answered. "I'll see you back on the train in the morning."

Disappointed, Sarah watched him walk away, then entered the hotel and took a room for the night. Her funds were fast dwindling. She hoped they would be nearing the end of their journey soon. She would need the salary she'd earn from teaching at the mission to return home. Yet what would she return home to? she wondered. Uncle Caleb had said she couldn't come back. Would he change his mind? She felt very alone and for the hundredth time wondered at the wisdom of her decision. Yet the promise she'd made to Swan Necklace and the tiny beaded bag hidden beneath her bodice kept her going.

Lucas Tanner walked into the nearest saloon and ordered a whiskey, which he threw down in short order. The saloon keeper poured him another and asked him a question. Tanner didn't hear or respond and with a shrug the man walked away. Tanner didn't notice. His thoughts were on the tall, slim young woman he'd left back at the hotel. He couldn't have gone inside with her then. His need for her had been too obvious. He would have made a fool of himself. For the first time in weeks he was able to think of something else besides that bloody morning in the Cheyenne camp. Now he sat wondering what it would have been like to kiss the prim Miss MacKenzie and to take her up the flight of stairs to the privacy of one of the rooms. Her sparkling dark eyes and sweet face haunted him. Tanner waved the saloon keeper back to pour another shot of whiskey and hunkered down for a long night of forgetfulness. Sarah MacKenzie never knew that when Major Tanner finally made his way to his room, he was in worse shape than the drunk who'd accosted them on the street.

4

Sarah was back at the train depot bright and early the next morning. The engineer already had the engines stoked and steam was building. There was no sign of Tanner. The conductor called out for all to board and reluctantly she followed the other passengers onto the train. Anxiously she peered back along the street, but no tall, broad-shouldered figure in a dusty blue uniform was hurrying to the depot.

Audrey Keane leaned over the seat. "Looks like your major isn't going to make the train," she said.

"He still has time," Sarah said tersely, "and he's not *my* major."

"Don't be cross, my oh-so-proper Miss Sarah Mac-Kenzie. If you aren't willing to claim him, maybe I will." Sarah felt a rush of irritation at the pretty reporter's words. Anxiously she strained to catch a glimpse of Tanner. With a lurch the train started to move, then picked up speed. Sarah put down her window and leaned out to peer along the platform. There was no sign of Major Tanner. Reluctantly she put up her window and leaned back. Likely she'd never see him again, she thought regretfully. Suddenly he was there making his way down the aisle much as he had the day before. His eyes were bloodshot, his expression grim. Without a word he slid into his seat across from her and leaned his head back against the cushions.

Silently she watched, trying to still the wild beating of her heart. Why should she feel this lightheartedness at his mere presence, she wondered in dismay. He was a stranger to her. She made no attempt at conversation, and Tanner wearily opened his eyes and gazed at her questioningly. There were fresh bruises around his chin as if he'd been in another fight. Sarah looked at his puffy eyes and shook her head disbelievingly. "At this rate, Major Tanner, you aren't going to last long," she said. She was rewarded with a crooked smile.

"You're right," he agreed and promptly fell asleep.

The train labored into the first canyons and steep slopes of the mountains. Sarah was caught up in the sheer majesty of the crags and peaks. Trestles of intricately wrought wood pilings spanned deep gorges. Sarah opened her window and leaned out, this time to stare down at the rushing waters of a creek more than a hundred and thirty feet below. The sheer walls of the gorge appeared tunnellike and suddenly she was dizzy, gripping the edge of the glass with white-knuckled hands while she slumped forward. Strong hands clasped her waist from behind and she was nearly thrown into her seat. Gasping, she closed her eyes against the whirling images of rock and water and bright sunlight.

"Don't look down," a deep voice advised and Sarah opened her eyes. Major Tanner was awake. He looked better for his brief rest. His gray eyes sparkled with teasing laughter and Sarah smiled in spite of herself.

"Thank you," she said. "You saved me again."

"Are you all right?"

"Umm." Sarah nodded. "It's incredible! I felt as if I were soaring." Tanner laughed outright, a deep, pleasant sound that delighted Sarah without her knowing why. "Can you imagine the men who built those trestles, the courage they must have possessed."

"Yes, courage," Tanner echoed and gazed out the window. The openness of the gorge had given way to a sheer canyon wall. She talked of courage so easily and certainly she had shown courage herself last night with the drunk. What would she say if she heard the accusations made against him back at the fort? What would she have done in that Indian camp? The image of the Indian boy came to him and once again he saw the small body jerk as Nevins's bullets tore through it.

Sarah watched his expression change from laughter to sadness and wondered what had caused the change. She thought to ask, but didn't want to pry. Audrey Keane had no such inhibitions. With a rustle of skirts she slid into the seat beside Sarah, opened a pad of paper, and with her pencil poised, fixed Major Tanner with a purposeful gleam in her eyes.

"Audrey Keane from the _Boston Herald_," she said. "Tell me, Major Tanner. What is your opinion of the Indian problem out here?"

Despite her rude, probing air, Tanner returned her gaze without retreating in any way. "Which Indian problem?" he asked calmly.

"Any Indian problem," Audrey insisted, "most particularly the Sioux. You've just left Fort Russell. What's going on back there? What's Custer up to?"

Tanner paused for a long moment, and Sarah thought he meant not to answer. "The Sioux are fighting to retain their homelands," he said finally. "We're trying to take them away. Yes, I've just left Fort Russell. The troops are doing what soldiers do everywhere, writing home and trying to stay clean. Who knows what Custer is up to? Now I've answered your questions, Miss Keane, and the interview is over." Hunching down in his seat, Tanner flipped his hat over his eyes.

"I have more questions to ask you, Major," Audrey said imperiously, but no answer came from beneath the hat. "What about those soldiers you fought with back at the station? Is this an indication of morale at the fort? Why didn't you have those men arrested? What if they'd chosen to assault a civilian that way?" She waited in vain for an answer. "I find your attitude most uncooperative, Major. Is this the way the army handles its public image?" Still no answer. With a sniff of anger Audrey Keane returned to her seat.

The train wove its way around and over the mountain slopes, its speed slow and labored at times and nearly runaway at others. Sunlit slopes gave way to narrow tunnels cut through the mountains. Sheer mountain walls rose on either side, casting the valleys in deep shadows. Tanner hadn't moved for some time and Sarah assumed he had dozed off. She was far too restless. As she gazed out the window, the train slowed further and came to a complete stop. Tanner removed his hat and sat up, his gray eyes alert. Perhaps he hadn't been sleeping after all, she thought. The other passengers had also sat up and were looking around in puzzlement.

"Don't worry, folks," the conductor said, coming along the aisle. "We've come to a bridge that looks unsteady. We'll have to ask you all to get off the train."

"Whatever for?" a woman asked. "This is quite impossible. I'll do no such thing."

"Suit yourself, ma'am," the conductor said, "but the engineer is going to take this train across that bridge. Maybe it'll hold and maybe it won't. You can stay on if you like."

Red-faced, the woman stood up and followed her husband down the aisle to the exit.

"What is your name, sir?" Audrey Keane asked the conductor as she went past.

"What do you want to know for?" he demanded suspiciously.

"Because I'm a reporter for the *Boston Herald*," Audrey replied. "Tell me, sir, hasn't the Union Pacific done anything to make these bridges safer for its passengers?"

"I don't know anything about that, ma'am," the conductor answered and began to sidle away. Audrey followed close behind, pummeling him with questions.

"We'd better go too," Tanner said and took Sarah's elbow to escort her from the train. There was little room on the narrow ledge for the travelers to stand. Long afternoon shadows slanted against the walls, so Sarah shielded her eyes with one hand and peered ahead. Tanner made his way forward to the bridge and the others followed. The rickety trestle was one of the original ones hastily built nearly ten years before when the Union and Central Pacific railroaders had raced to lay the most track. Looking at the aging timbers, Sarah was grateful to be off the train. Everyone was off now except the engineer and his grime-faced fireman who stoked the firebox. Smoke poured from the stack. Slowly the driving wheels began to turn, and with a hiss of steam the locomotive inched forward, trailing the freight cars and the empty passenger coaches behind. The bridge timbers creaked and groaned.

Breathlessly Sarah and the other passengers watched the brave engineer cross the bridge with a slow, steady speed. When he reached the other side everyone cheered.

"All right, folks, its our turn now. We're going to walk across in a single file, keeping close to the center of the track." There were cries of dismay and anger from the other passengers. Sarah gazed down the steep slope and felt her heart beat faster.

"Remember, don't look down," Tanner said.

"I—I don't think I can make it across," she said fearfully.

Tanner looked at her stricken face and his expression softened. "You'll be all right. Just stay to the center," he advised. "I'll be right behind you." He smiled reassuringly. Sarah followed him to the bridge and took a step forward. There were no solid planks as she'd anticipated. Supporting the gleaming rail was an open ladder work of boards, and between each board was a wide gap. Sarah could see the network of crisscrossing timbers below. Panic swept over her.

"I can't do it," she cried, clamping her hands over her eyes.

Instantly Tanner was there, pulling her back against the reassuring solidity of his big body. "You're all right," he whispered soothingly, his mouth against her ear. She could feel his hot breath against her temples and it sent worse chills through her than the high, rickety bridge ever could.

"I'm sorry," she said in a small, frightened voice. The other passengers had made their way along the bridge. "I've always been afraid of heights."

"You needn't be afraid now. I'm holding onto you." To demonstrate, he wrapped his arms around her waist, holding her from behind. Sarah's fingers curled around his arm, desperately gripping his sleeve. "We're going to take it one step at a time, all right?" Sarah shook her head. She felt his knee bump against the back of her leg as he took a step forward.

Quickly she moved with him, trying to match her stride to his. The canyon yawned below her. Sarah closed her eyes, leaning back against Tanner, letting his arms guide her. One by one they took each cross tie until they reached the other side.

"We made it," Tanner said against her ear.

Sarah opened her eyes and looked around. Indeed they were safely on the other side of the deep, narrow gorge. The other passengers were already climbing aboard the train.

"Thank you, Major Tanner," Sarah murmured sheepishly. "I'm sorry to make such a fuss."

"It was my pleasure," he said, and she was aware that he still held her against him intimately. She could feel every inch of his tall, lean body pressed against hers.

"I think we'd better get on the train before it leaves without us," she said lightly and pulled away from him.

Reluctantly he let her go. "I wonder if we have any more bad bridges along the way," he mused. With flaming cheeks Sarah hurried back on the train and settled herself into her seat.

"I see the cavalry is as fast on its feet as it is on a horse," Audrey Keane said leeringly, her knowing gaze sweeping over Sarah, "and our timid little missionary seems to have her own personal escort."

"I'm truly afraid of heights," Sarah exclaimed. "Major Tanner would have helped anyone who needed it to cross that bridge."

"Ummm," Audrey said disbelievingly. "I'll keep that in mind next time there's a bridge."

When Major Tanner returned to his seat, he found Sarah deeply absorbed in her prayer book, and he wondered at the high color in her cheeks. It made her very pretty. He spent the rest of the trip to

Ogden thinking of the way the prim Miss MacKenzie felt in his arms. Beneath the ill-fitting dress, her body had been slim and firm, yet flaring with the well-defined curves of a woman.

At dusk the train pulled into Ogden, where the westbound passengers boarded the Central Pacific cars for their journey onto San Francisco. From Ogden the Union Pacific would continue to Portland as far as the track was finished. Ogden was a thriving Mormon town where the passengers found clean accommodations for the night. Major Tanner had disappeared and rather than share supper with the abrasive reporter, Audrey Keane, Sarah had a tray in her room and retired early. The day had been long. Yet as she pulled the covers up to her chin and prepared to sleep, Sarah fell to thinking of Major Lucas Tanner and the feel of his long, hard body pressed to hers.

The passenger car of the Union Pacific was nearly empty for the journey beyond Ogden. Most of the previous travelers had been bound for California. To Sarah's relief, Audrey Keane was among them. Of the passengers continuing northwest, four were men and one was a matronly lady named Mrs. Soules. Her husband was the gentleman who'd taken Tanner's pistol for safekeeping. Now Tanner stretched out on a seat all by himself, his booted feet propped up on the opposite cushions. Despite herself Sarah missed his presence.

For a time the train traveled through a high, flat prairie, but by afternoon was once again laboring up mountain peaks and racing down deep gorges. This length of track had been built after the driving of the gold spike at Promontory and more care had been taken to lay down permanent tracks. Flat roadways had been blasted out of the granite mountains whose sheer walls towered over the locomotive. Time and again Sarah cast an anxious glance at the gouged walls of rock, fearful least a rock slide tumble down on them. Staring out hypnotically, she didn't at first notice the shadow racing along the ground beside the tracks.

"Indians!" someone cried, and the astonished passengers straightened and peered out their windows. Sarah blinked her eyes and looked at the long shadow of a rider astride a horse. The silhouette sported feathers and clutched a rifle high. Swiveling in her seat, she strained to see, while Major Tanner cursed and sat up.

"Sioux," someone shouted. The other woman passenger screamed. Men groped for guns.

"We're out of Sioux territory," Tanner growled and reached in vain for his gun. A shrill war cry was followed by gunfire. Sarah pressed her face to the window to get a better glimpse of the strangely painted and garbed men on horses.

"Get down, you little fool," Tanner ordered. His strong hands pushed her to the floor just as a bullet shattered the window, showering them with glass. Tanner threw himself over her, shielding her with his body, and then he was on his feet.

"Give me my gun," he shouted and stalked down the aisle toward the gentleman who'd taken it. Sarah peered around the corner of her seat and saw the man sprawled on his back as if he'd fallen asleep. His natty vest was stained with blood. Tanner spent only a moment examining the dead man, then reached across him to retrieve his Colt pistol. With the barrel he knocked out the window glass and began firing at the line of Indians.

The train picked up speed as the firemen added coal.

"He's going to try to outrun them," Tanner said. "There's a tunnel coming up. We'll lose them there." He fired out the window and an Indian dropped from his horse. One of the passengers gave a grunt and fell forward across the seat, his gun falling from his lifeless hand. Sarah screamed and watched with horror-filled eyes as the man's blood slowly seeped into a puddle on the floor.

Swallowing against the bile that pushed at the back of her throat, she picked up the dead man's gun and crouched on the floor between the seats once more. Should she try to fire at the Indians as Tanner and the other men were doing? she wondered fearfully. Before she could act, darkness closed in on them. They'd made the tunnel. The Indians would have to fall back and follow the train from behind. Surely the train could pick up speed again and they'd be safe.

"Miss MacKenzie? Sarah, are you hurt?" Major Tanner called.

"I'm all right," she answered and was touched at his concern. Light flooded the compartment as the train reached the open again. Sarah could feel it picking up speed now that it was clear of the tunnel. The Indians would never catch them now. She got to her feet and looked around. Two of the men were dead. Mrs. Soules was wailing in terror. Another passenger was trying to bind up a bleeding hand. Sarah moved to help him and was suddenly pitched forward. There was a loud clash of metal and rock, and the car lurched wildly. Rocks rained down the steep slope, crashing against the train. The floor slid precariously beneath Sarah's feet and she fell heavily, hitting her head against the seat. Once again blackness roared over her and dimly she perceived this was not another tunnel.

"Sarah." Tanner's voice brought her back. She groaned and opened her eyes, uncertain of how long she'd been unconscious. Still gripping his pistol, Tanner cast an anxious glance over his shoulder. Sarah could hear sporadic gunfire and the rattle of gravel and rocks on the slope.

"What's happening?" she asked.

"They've wrecked the train," he said in a low voice. "I think the locomotive is derailed."

"How did they do that?" Sarah asked in amazement. She couldn't imagine anything but the hand of God lifting the heavy engine off its track.

"They tore up the track."

For the first time Sarah noticed the gash on his forehead. He'd rolled his bandanna and tied it around his head to stop the bleeding. One arm hung limply; the shoulder of his uniform was dark with blood. "You're hurt," she cried and tried to sit up. Dizziness swept over her, so she gripped her head and lay back. When it passed she sat up slowly, pushing back the darkness that threatened to engulf her. Cautiously she looked around. The front of the car had been crushed. Mrs. Soules lay silent, her head tilted at an awkward angle as if her neck were broken.

"How did that happen?" she whispered in awe.

"A large boulder crashed down on us. The robbers started a rock slide."

"Don't you mean the Indians?"

Tanner looked at her intently, as if gauging her courage. He had no choice, he realized. He had to tell her the truth. He was growing weak from the loss of blood and he'd need her help before they were done. Glancing around, he began piling up loose baggage in the aisle.

"I don't think it's Indians," he said. "Whoever it is, they mean to kill all the passengers. I want you to get behind here and hide until I get back."

"Where are you going?" Sarah asked fearfully. He was going to leave her here.

"I'm going to check the rest of the train to see if there are any other survivors. If we hole up in here we may be able to hold them off, at least until help comes."

"I'll come with you," Sarah offered.

"No, it's best if you stay here. One person has less chance of being seen. I'll come back for you." He paused. "If I don't come back, stay hidden. They may not find you here. After they've gone, follow the tracks to the next depot."

"Major Tanner," Sarah cried as he started to rise. He looked at her expectantly. "I—good luck."

He nodded. "Stay down." Cautiously he eased open the door and looked along the side of the train, then he was gone. Sarah quelled the urge to call out or to run after him. He'd said he would return. She must trust he would. Breathing deeply to regain her composure, she waited, counting the gunshots, counting the seconds between each one and growing more afraid with each passing moment. The sound of voices came from outside.

"Have you looked in this car?" a man's voice called. The Indians must have been driven off, Sarah thought with elation. Men boarded the car, their heavy boots clomping loudly on the bare boards. Sarah pushed aside one of the carpetbags and prepared to show herself to her rescuers when a bright color caught her eye. One of the men had come into her line of vision, and now she saw he wore feathers and rawhide breeches. A rag was wound around his forehead, and bright paint was smeared on his face and bare chest.

Stunned, she ducked down, able to see only their leggings and leather boots. Reason returned to her and finally she discerned the reason for her nagging doubts. Indians didn't wear boots and spurs. At least not the Indians she'd been told about. Swan Necklace had often spoken of the beautiful moccasins the women made for their men in the Nez Percé villages. She'd never once mentioned boots. From the safety of her hiding place Sarah watched the boots move along the aisle. They paused in front of the seat where Mrs. Soules lay sprawled.

"She's still alive," one of the men said, and a gunshot rang out, reverberating in the quiet confines of the metal car. Mrs. Soule's arm slid off the seat and the chubby, beringed hand brushed the floor. Roughly her arm was snatched up, then callously dropped again. This time the rings were missing from her fingers.

Sarah clamped a hand to her mouth to keep from crying out. Taking a deep breath, she slowly let it out, counting to ten to calm herself. This was all a horrible nightmare, like the one Major Tanner had dreamed. Soon she would wake up and look at the sunshine gleaming on the mountain peaks. But she knew it wasn't a nightmare. She was trapped in here with men who wouldn't hesitate to kill her, and Major Tanner was out there somewhere, possibly dead.

Sobs of fear clogged her throat and she clenched her teeth to hold back any sound. Tears filled her eyes and poured down her cheeks, but she ignored them. She had to get out of here. It was only a matter of time before they discovered her and killed her as they had Mrs. Soules. Carefully she shifted so she could see the door. It was only a few feet away. Could she make it before they fired at her? It was her only hope.

Boot steps sounded on the metal platform outside and a man entered. Sarah caught a glimpse of a wide-brimmed hat and a fancy vest of embroidered satin. She couldn't see his face.

"How are you doing in here, boys?" the man asked, looking around.

Sarah ducked back. Her hand brushed against cold metal. Startled, she looked around. It was the gun she'd picked up earlier. Hope spiraling, she curled her fingers around the grip and glanced back at the man who'd just come in. He seemed to be the boss. The other men were following his orders to search the pockets of the other bodies. Taking care not to be seen herself, Sarah strained to see what the man was doing next.

"Take a few scalps to make it look authentic," he ordered and turned back toward the door. "Let's wind this up and get out of here. When the train doesn't reach Salmon Falls, they'll come looking for it." He ducked his head and left the car. Sarah gripped the pistol, hesitant about what to do next. If she stayed silent, they might not find her after all. She pulled back into her hiding place more tightly. Apprehensively she waited. The booted Indians were busy at something. Suddenly they stepped back, one of them clasped a bloody piece of hair. A body rolled to the floor and she could see the bloodied head, its hair cut away. A sound of revulsion escaped her. Clamping a hand to her mouth, she curled into a ball, fighting the waves of nausea that swept over her.

"Did you hear that?" one of the men asked. Sarah tried desperately to keep silent, but mewing whimpers escaped her lips. "Someone's still alive. The boss said no witnesses." The men moved back along the other bodies, checking each one for a pulse and firing a bullet into them just to be sure. Tears streaming down her face, Sarah gulped and fought back the sobs. At first she thought they wouldn't find her, then one of the men tore at the carpetbags Tanner had piled over her hiding place.

"Something's down here," he shouted to his companions.

"What'd you find, Luke?" they asked and helped clear away the baggage until Sarah's hiding place was revealed. "Well, lookee here," one exclaimed. "We found us a woman and a pretty one at that." He grinned at his companions. "Let's take her with us."

"Peppi won't like it. He don't like witnesses."

"So we'll take her with us for a little fun tonight, then we'll kill her in the morning."

Callously they discussed Sarah's fate as if she weren't there. She lay still and watchful, still gripping the gun hidden by the folds of her skirt. Finally all three agreed to take her with them. "Come on, girlie, come on out of there," one man said and reached down for her. Sarah brought up the barrel of the gun and fired point-blank. A round red hole appeared in the man's painted chest. His face registered surprise and he fell forward on top of her. At first the other two men weren't sure of what was happening.

"Jesus, he's killed her. We said we was going to wait." One of the men complained. "Jake, get up." He kicked the fallen man.

"He's dead," the other man cried. "She must have a gun." He reached for his pistol. Desperately Sarah tried to bring her gun up and fire again, but the dead man pinned it between them. She saw the blue metal of the gun barrel pointed at her head and closed her eyes. A shot rang out, but there was no pain, no impact of a bullet. Someone grunted and Sarah opened her eyes. Only one man remained and he had swung around, his gun in his hand as he looked out the window and door. Peering around the shoulder of the dead train robber, she saw a movement at one of the windows. Tanner hung there upside down and even as she watched he fired. The other train robber went down.

"Sarah," Tanner called urgently.

"I'm here," she yelled back and struggled to free herself from the crushing weight of the dead man. Her gown was smeared with blood when she finally wriggled free.

Tanner slipped through the door and glanced at her. "Were you hurt?" She was shaking uncontrollably, her face pale.

"I—I shot one of them," she stuttered. She was wavering on the edge of hysteria.

"Sarah," Tanner said roughly. His strong hands gripped her shoulders. He shook her lightly, then pulled her against him and kissed her. There was no passion between them. Passion wasn't intended. His kiss was meant as an affirmation that in the midst of death and terror could be found normalcy and human warmth. "You're going to be all right," he said harshly.

"Yes," she said, shaking her head numbly. He could feel her slender body still trembling, but the glaze of panic had left her eyes. "How did you know I needed help?" she asked, seeking anything to take her mind off the fact she'd killed a man.

"I was hiding on the roof," Tanner explained.

"The whole time?"

"Most of it. I searched the other cars, but—there are no survivors."

"None?" Sarah was stunned that of the whole train they were the only ones alive. "Are you sure?"

"I'm sure. We have to get out of here or we won't stand a chance."

"They'll kill us too," Sarah said almost too calmly. Tanner glanced at her. Was this the calm before a storm of hysteria or was she just giving in to shock and hopelessness? Neither, it seemed. Her eyes were alert and clear. "One of them said they can't leave witnesses," she explained.

Tanner nodded. "That's because they can't afford to have their cover blown. They want people to think Indians did this."

"Why?" Sarah asked.

"It makes a good cover for their own crime, but even more importantly the government will step in and do something about the Indian problem, so the white man can take their lands." The whole time he talked, Tanner was gazing out the windows on either side, gauging where the robbers were and looking for an escape route. "I saw a place where we can climb up into the mountains back there. It's pretty rugged. Do you think you can make it?"

"I know I can," Sarah answered stoutly.

"The farther up the mountainside we can get before they discover us, the better, so let's be careful."

"I understand."

"Have you still got your gun?" Silently she nodded, holding out the gun for him to see. She thought he almost smiled, then he led her to the door and cautiously looked out. A finger to his lips needlessly warned her to silence, then he motioned her forward through the next car, which was less damaged than theirs. Two men lay sprawled across the backs of their seats, their sightless eyes staring at the roof. An old Indian sat upright, gazing straight ahead. Sarah wasn't sure if he were alive or dead.

"Get down," Tanner ordered and shoved her to the floor. Two of the train robbers sauntered by the outside of the car. Tanner watched until they disappeared, then he motioned to Sarah. Crouched down, they made their way to the door and once again paused to see if all was clear.

"I'll go first. Wait two minutes. If you don't hear anything, follow. I'll be up in those rocks with my gun to give you protection." Sarah nodded. Tanner paused, his gray eyes searching her face. "If you hear gunshots, don't come out this way," he warned her. "Wait. My gunfire will draw their attention. Slip out the other way and try to get away."

"Without you?"

"Without me," Tanner said grimly, and she knew he wanted no argument. "Go in a southeasterly direction and I'll catch up with you."

She knew he only said it to make her feel better. "They won't find us. I'll follow as you said."

Tanner gripped her shoulders tightly. "Don't come out this way if there's gunfire," he repeated.

Reluctantly Sarah nodded her agreement. Her soft hand gripped his. "Thanks for coming back for me," she said.

A smile warmed his eyes. Then he was gone without a sound, and she was left with just the warm feel of his hand in hers.

5

Sarah watched as Tanner cautiously made his way along the edge of the track, then cut diagonally across the shale train bed to a sheer wall of rock. For a moment he disappeared behind an outcropping Sarah hadn't noticed before. Then he reappeared several feet up the incline, his long legs making quick work of the steep slope. When he reached a ledge, he took his gun from his holster and flattened himself on his belly so he could see the train and along the track.

Sarah was ready when he waved her forward. Skirts bunched around her thighs, knees churning, she followed Tanner's route along the tracks. For once she was grateful for the sturdy, plain boots she'd worn as part of her missionary attire. They served her well now as she crossed the loose shale to the outcropping.

Breathlessly she flung herself against the rock wall, gasping in air. She'd made it. Any moment she'd expected to feel the impact of a bullet ripping into her. From his perch above, Tanner signaled silence and with a thumb indicated someone was nearby. Sarah hugged the wall, trying to make herself smaller. Her heart was beating wildly. She could hear the crunch of shale as the man walked by.

"Cooper, the boss said go see what's keeping Luke

and the boys," someone called and the man disappeared. Frantically Sarah looked at Tanner. It seemed to her they waited for hours before he motioned her forward. Sarah scrambled up the incline, trying her best not to loosen stones and send them rattling down behind her. Tanner waited until she was on the ledge beside him.

"Luke was the name of one of the men in the passenger car," she whispered.

"Damn," Tanner swore. "That means they'll be looking for us. Let's try to get as far up that slope as we can before they discover us." He led the way. In spite of their hurry, he chose each toe hold, each grip carefully, making sure it would hold their weight before moving up to the next. Once Sarah slipped. A small cry escaped her lips, then Tanner was there, his hand steadying her. They were nearly at the top when a shout went up from below.

"There they are." Bullets bounced off the granite wall near Sarah. Involuntarily she screamed.

"Come on," Tanner cried and nearly pulled her the rest of the way up the slope. More shots were fired and bullets ricocheted off the rocks around them. Then they were at the top, rolling over the edge onto their stomachs. For a moment they lay gasping in air, then Tanner crawled forward on his belly and elbows and fired down on the heads of the robbers, who were already making their way up the slope. Sarah crawled forward to see, but Tanner pushed her back.

"Head off along that slope," he ordered. "I'll hold them off for a few minutes to give you a head start. Don't stop and don't look back."

"I can't leave you."

"Get going. I'll catch up. I can outrun you."

Without further argument Sarah started running

as hard as she could along the rocky spine and down along a little valley. She could hear Tanner firing at the robbers. She wasn't sure how far she'd run, but she feared Tanner wouldn't be able to find her. A stitch of pain in her side made her pause only for a moment, and then she ran on until her chest hurt from gasping in air and her steps lagged. Still she pressed on, until she lost her footing and went sprawling down a slope. Gravel and loose shale slid down with her. At the bottom, Sarah lay stunned, her chest heaving as she tried to sob and breathe at the same time. She couldn't go on. Suddenly Tanner appeared above her.

"Get up. Get going," he shouted, and somehow she found the strength to get to her feet and run again. They were going downhill now and ahead was a mountain forest of pine trees. "Come on," Tanner called and headed for the pines. Sarah followed. Once they were under cover of the trees, Tanner slowed only a little, breaking into a steady jog that Sarah found she could maintain after all. She'd given up trying to breathe normally and simply gasped in the air she needed. Her lungs burned and her legs ached. Back on the slopes she could hear the cry of angry men. Suddenly bullets whined around their heads, burying themselves into the tree trunks. But Sarah could see they were already out of range of the bullets, and the robbers seemed less inclined to pursue now. Still Tanner pressed on, putting plenty of space between them.

Finally, when Sarah thought she couldn't go another step, Tanner slowed to a walk and leaned against a tree to rest. His head lolled back as he drew in air.

"Are they gone?" Sarah gasped.

"I don't know," Tanner said. "We'd better keep

moving and vary our course until we know we've lost them. Can you make it?"

"Uh-huh," Sarah nodded.

Tanner looked at her, a half smile on his face. Her dark hair had come unbound and now it hung nearly to her waist. The lowering sun cast fiery, dancing lights in its sleek blackness. "You run very well for a missionary," he said lightly, and Sarah smiled in spite of her fatigue.

"Don't underestimate us, Major Tanner," she said.

"I won't ever do that, Sarah," he answered, pausing before using her first name. His deep voice made it a caress, and Sarah shivered in the afternoon heat.

Tanner saw the shiver and glanced around. The shadows were already growing long. "We'll have to keep moving," he said, "for two reasons. It will keep you from getting chilled, and we need to put some distance between us and them." He nodded back toward the train.

"I'm ready, Major," she said, pushing away from the tree.

"Call me—" He paused.

"Lucas?"

"Tanner."

She nodded. "What about your wound, Tanner? You've lost a lot of blood."

"They're superficial," he lied and shrugged dismissively.

They traveled north through the fragrant pine trees, then cut along a rocky shelf that led them around the mountain and back toward the tracks. It was their best chance to survive and find their way back to Salmon Falls. The afternoon shadows were giving way to dusk by the time Tanner found a place to pause for the night. The night air was already growing chilly and in spite of herself, Sarah shivered.

"Let's drag up some deadwood and build a fire here," Tanner said. "These rocky ledges will hide the glow of our fire."

"You don't think they're still looking for us, do you?" she asked fearfully.

"I don't know," he confessed, looking around. "They can't afford to let us live. We know too much about them. On the other hand, they may just clear out of the territory, move on someplace else."

Sarah scanned the ring of mountain peaks hemming them in. Could the robbers be out there somewhere, waiting to jump them?

Seeing her frightened eyes, Tanner gave her a gentle shove. "Come on, let's get some firewood."

They dragged a number of dead limbs and trunks back to their site. The light was fading fast now. The valleys and wooded slopes were in dark shadows. Only a rim of light at the peaks of the mountains still showed. Sarah glanced at Tanner, hunkered down over a flame. Smoke was drifting upward from the pile of dried needles and whittled shavings. Tanner's knife lay nearby.

"I'm going to the creek I saw down there," she said. "Mind if I use your knife?"

"Watch out for snakes," he warned.

Sarah stopped and stared back at him in consternation. There was a grin on his face. Still, she wasn't sure. "Snakes won't be moving around in this cold air," she said. "Didn't you know that?" The grin disappeared from his face.

Without another word she walked to the creek, where she washed her face and hands and scrubbed the dried blood that stained her skirt. She tried hard not to think of the man she'd shot. She'd had little choice. She wrung the skirt as dry as she could and stood up, shaking it away from her body. The petticoats beneath would keep the wet cloth away from her until it had dried. Making her way upstream, Sarah selected a stout branch and stripped it of its limbs and bark. Then she shaved a point on one end and settled down to wait. Her patience was rewarded, for soon a large trout moved lazily in the shallows and with a quick, smooth motion Sarah speared it. With a strong, swinging motion she threw the struggling trout onto the bank and, taking up the knife, dealt it a stunning blow before cleaning it into two generous fillets.

Carrying her bounty and Tanner's knife, she returned to their makeshift camp. Impaling the trout fillets on two sharp sticks, she set them to cook over the fire. Tanner was nowhere about, so Sarah settled beside the fire and spread her skirts to dry. Memories of the day's events crowded in on her and she pushed them away. She'd seen horrible things and had nearly been killed herself; all that was bad enough. The thing that bothered her the most was the killing of a man. Yet if she'd hesitated, she wouldn't be here now. She propped her elbows on her bent knees and rested her chin in her hands, gazing into the dancing flames. Its cheerful warmth soothed her.

A sound in the woods nearby made her swing around and slip into the cover of shadows. "Who's there?" she called shakily.

"Tanner," he answered and walked into the firelight. He'd been to the creek to wash and carried an armload of deadwood. "I was trying to snare a rabbit for our supper," he began and paused, catching a glimpse of the trout fillets slowly cooking. Perplexed, he looked back at her.

"Not bad for a teacher, huh?" she said, laughing.

Tanner's gleaming eyes studied her. "Not bad at all," he agreed, and Sarah colored under his gaze.

She'd washed away the rice powder and her long dark hair still tumbled in disarray around her shoulders. The planes of her face were cast in shadows, and Tanner thought he'd never seen a more beautiful woman. Sarah saw the admiration on his face and felt unaccountably timid.

Tanner dumped his armload of wood and turned around to gaze at her again. "What other surprises have you got up your sleeve, Sarah?" he asked softly.

"If I tell you they won't be surprises," she said laughingly, and to hide the blush of her cheeks bent to turn the fish. Glancing up, she caught his grimace of pain. "Your wound is bothering you," she exclaimed accusingly.

"It's all right," he answered. "The bullet went through and the bleeding's stopped."

"You'd better let me look at it," she insisted with such a no-nonsense air he complied, seating himself on a stump nearby. Sarah helped him strip away his shirt, unable to avert her gaze from the broad, muscular shoulders. His skin looked sleek and smooth to touch except his chest, which was covered by a soft mat of hair. His flat nipples shone darker against his tanned skin. Sarah had no more time for her perusal, for she caught sight of the blood-caked bullet wound and gasped. Fortunately the bullet had gone through the fleshy portion of his shoulder, but it had left an ugly, tearing wound. Without comment she tore away a piece of her petticoat and set about cleansing the wound, then went unerringly to gather a bit of pine moss. She packed the wound with the light green lichen and tied it in place with another strip from her petticoat.

"It feels better already," Tanner said.

Sarah colored under his frankly admiring gaze and moved back to the fire. "I believe our supper's ready," she said.

Tanner settled at the side of the fire and reached for one of the sticks. Silence reigned as they gobbled down the sweet white meat of the trout. Their hunger surfeited, they leaned back, enjoying for the moment the warmth of the fire and their safety.

"There was a man in charge of everything today. Did you happen to see which one he was?"

"He came into the car just before his men found me," Sarah said.

"Can you describe him?"

Slowly Sarah shook her head. "Not really. I never saw his face. He wore a wide-brimmed hat pulled down. I remember the sound of his voice. It was sort of a gravelly whisper. He also wore a fancy vest. That's all I remember about him. Did you see him?"

Tanner frowned. "I never got close enough to him. I wonder who he was."

"One of his men mentioned the name Peppi."

"Peppi?" He sat thinking over the name. "It sounds Spanish or Mexican."

"They weren't Indians at all, were they?"

Tanner shook his head. "Not like any Indians I know."

"Where are you from originally, Tanner?" Sarah asked. She was sitting with her arms wrapped around her bent knees. She seemed perfectly at home sitting on the ground around a campfire. He tried to think of one woman he'd known who could be so at ease in the wilderness.

"I'm from Ohio," he said, leaning forward to put more wood on the fire. "I joined the army when I was seventeen. My father sent me to West Point. I remember how badly I wanted to be finished with it so I could go fight in the war with the South."

"Did you?"

"I fought at Gettysburg," he answered and tossed away the twig he'd been chewing. His face was troubled, full of regret. "You should have seen those rebel soldiers coming at us in waves. Some of them were just boys. Our guns destroyed their lines and still they kept coming. The fields were littered with bodies. The streams—" He flung a rock at the fire and his voice was hard when he continued, "The streams ran red with blood. It was a slaughter, just like what we did at the Cheyenne camp." Abruptly he stopped talking and Sarah sensed he didn't want to talk about either battle anymore. Yet something else kept probing at her thoughts.

"Why have you been transferred to Fort Lapwai, Major Tanner?" she asked. "Are they having Indian problems? Will there be slaughters there?"

"I hope not," he answered wearily, and some of her alarm melted away. He meant no harm to her grandmother's people. "As for the Nez Percé, I know nothing about them."

"But you're being sent to govern them. Doesn't the government teach you the customs and traditions of the people among whom you will live?"

"I'm afraid not. Our government expects the Indians to conform to our traditions. That is our custom. Don't look too shocked, Sarah. You're part of the acclimation process. You and other missionaries and teachers like you. What do you know of these people you're going to teach? What will you offer them that's better than the customs you'll take away?"

Troubled by his words, Sarah shook her head. "I know a lot about the Nez Percé," she said sadly.

"Tell me about them," he urged, sensing her disquiet over the things he'd said. "Tell me about the Nez Percé."

Sarah looked at his tanned, smiling face. How had she ever thought it harsh? Hesitantly at first and then with increasing relish, she told him about the Nimpau, the real people who had somehow come to be called Nez Percé, "pierced nose." Few Nez Percé had ever worn ornamentation in their noses, yet the name had stuck with them from the days of Lewis and Clark.

Sarah told him the story of the Coyote and the heart of the monster that brought forth the Nimpau. She told him charming tales of the Nez Percé that explained creation and the movement of the sun and moon in the sky and how the animals came to be upon the earth. Tanner listened attentively to the gentle stories, moving only to place more wood upon the fire. He watched the dancing flames cast light and shadow on Sarah's beautiful upturned face, and something was renewed within him. For the first time since that bleak March day, he was able to think of the little Indian boy without pain. When at last her voice slowed and she stopped talking, he sat still, waiting for her to begin again.

"I'm very tired now," Sarah said in a small voice, and Tanner saw that she was shivering in the night air. Her arms were clasped about herself in an attempt to conserve body heat.

"Sarah, come here," he said softly. Without hesitation she got to her feet and moved around the fire to him. "Sit beside me. It will keep us warmer," he said, and without demur she sat beside him. Tanner wrapped his arms around her and drew her against his chest. Trustingly she rested against him. Tanner stared into the flames, remembering all the wonderful things she'd told him about the Nez Percé.

"How do you know so much about the Indians?"
he asked. When she made no answer, he gazed
down at her. She was sleeping, her face pale with
exhaustion. Her soft pink lips were parted. Her black
lashes lay along the creamy curve of her cheek. She
felt small and warm in his arms. Tanner eased himself back until he was leaning against the rock wall
and cuddled Sarah against his shoulder. She was the
most amazing woman he'd ever met. She'd shown
courage and common sense and unexpected skills all
day, and now she lay sleeping like a helpless, trust-
ing babe in his arms. He longed to kiss her and
knew he wouldn't. When he kissed Miss Sarah Mac-
Kenzie again, he wanted her to be awake and a full
participant. There would, he was sure, be unexpected surprises in store for him even there. He lay
his head back and tried to rest. Tomorrow he had to
find a way to get them safely to Salmon Falls and
from there on to Wallowa Valley, land of the Nimpau,
the real people.

The next morning Sarah was already up and gone
when Tanner awoke. Disoriented and still sleepy, he
sat looking around, certain she was not in danger,
yet wishing he knew where she was. As if summoned by his thoughts, Sarah returned to camp.
She carried a bundle of something in her hand and a
heavy, pointed stick in the other. "Don't tell me
you've brought more trout," Tanner said in dismay.

Sarah laughed and shook her head. "Something
almost as good," she said gaily and untied her bundle. "How's your shoulder this morning?"

Tanner moved his arm experimentally. "It's much
better," he said in surprise.

"Good!" Sarah smiled and portioned out the roots
and berries she'd gathered. Tentatively Tanner looked
at his makeshift meal.

"Eat. It's very good," Sarah urged and, taking up a piece of scraped and cleaned root, bit into it. Tanner did the same and was surprised at the nutlike flavor of the root.

"These are kouse," Sarah explained. "The camas bulb is better, but this is good and easier to find."

"How do you know all this?" Tanner asked wonderingly. Sarah's dark eyes gleamed with laughter.

"My grandmother told me," she answered.

"Your grandmother was a woman of rare knowledge."

Sarah's laughter faded. "Yes, she was," she said simply. "Her name was Swan Necklace and she was a Nez Percé Indian."

Somehow Tanner wasn't shocked at her news. It explained so many things about her, the glossy dark hair and eyes, the high cheekbones, the calm acceptance of a situation no matter what the danger. "How did Swan Necklace end up in the East?" he asked, and Sarah told him the story of her grandmother.

"I hope to find Swan Necklace's people and return her spirit bag," she finished softly. "I've promised."

Tanner was touched by the strong love Sarah bore her grandmother, and he felt closer to her for sharing this story. He longed to fold her in his arms, but sensed the time was not right. Each new thing he found out about this beautiful young woman only drew him more surely to her. He wasn't certain he wanted to be ensnared, yet he was inextricably captured by her beauty and courage.

"We'd better be on our way," he said gruffly. Springing to his feet, he kicked apart the cold ashes of their fire and gathered up his knife and gun. Without looking back, he started up the slope. Sarah would follow behind, he had little doubt. Later, when he paused for a breath and to get his bearings, he saw that Sarah was indeed not far behind, her digging stick in her hand. She'd plaited her long black hair into a single thick braid and tied it on the end with a strip from her petticoat. She smiled as she drew near to him.

"Is it safe to head back to the train?" she asked, and he didn't wonder that she was as aware of where they were and in which direction they were heading as he.

"Not the train," he answered. "They may be waiting there, hoping we'll return. We'll cut down to the tracks farther north and follow them into Salmon Falls. By now the town must be alerted to the fact there's trouble with the train and are already headed out to look."

"That makes sense," Sarah said approvingly. "Shall we go on, then?" Tanner smiled at her calm acceptance of their situation. His own good humor was restored.

They traveled along the mountainside, slowly working their way back toward the track. The morning sun burned down on their heads, its warmth welcomed at first and resented later. Sarah opened the collar of her high-necked gown and tore another piece from her petticoat to wear turban fashion over her head and thus gain some protection from the sun's rays. They were on the ledge right above the track now, and Tanner prepared to make the final descent. The railroad bed would at least be level and they could walk on the cross ties. As he turned toward a slope leading down to the track, he caught a glimpse of movement and signaled Sarah to wait. Instantly she froze, crouching down while she looked around. Her quick eyes picked out the movement below and when Tanner motioned to her, she nodded her head in understanding.

The robber had placed himself at a strategic spot. He could see the track for miles either way. Any movement to regain the track bed would be seen by him. They were fortunate they'd come down the mountain at this point. Now Tanner carefully crept closer. The man was seated on a small ledge, his feet dangling over the edge. His horse was tied about thirty feet behind him near a patch of scrubby mountain sage.

Cautiously Tanner worked his way toward the man until he was a few feet behind him. Then he stood. "Got a light?" he asked, walking forward. The robber swung around, a smile on his face, his hand already in his shirt pocket to retrieve a match. A look of astonishment erased the smile when he caught sight of Tanner. Tanner gave him no more time. He was close enough now to simply give the man a push. For a moment he teetered, his arms flapping, then with a yell he slid over the edge, bouncing against the stony slope on his way to the bottom. Tanner glanced over the edge.

Sarah ran to join him. "Is he dead?"

"If he isn't, he won't be able to give us any trouble," Tanner said and grabbed the reins of the train robber's horse. "This'll make the going a little easier." He swung into the saddle and motioned Sarah forward. Gripping her arm, he swung her onto the horse behind him. She wrapped her arms around his lean waist and held on tightly as Tanner headed down the slope. Swinging wide of the fallen man they gained the tracks. Traveling was easier now and they covered the miles quickly. They'd gone about five miles when Tanner pointed ahead to some riders.

"Let's get into those rocks just in case they're more of the train robbers," he said. Breathlessly they waited. The riders drew abreast, and Sarah could see they were all well armed. One of the men wore a badge pinned to his vest.

Tanner stepped out to hail him. "Sheriff," he called.

The man reined in his horse, his gun in his hand. "Who are you?" he demanded.

"Major Lucas Tanner of the U.S. Army, sir." Sarah showed herself and went to stand behind Tanner. "This is Miss Sarah MacKenzie. We were traveling on the Union Pacific out of Ogden."

"What happened to it?" the sheriff demanded. He was a large, fleshy man whose once powerful, lean body had long since grown more used to the comfortable pad of his office chair than to a saddle. Still, he was an honest man and determined to do his job. Now taking off his hat, he ran his thick fingers through his gray-streaked hair and waited for Tanner's answer.

"It's been derailed about ten miles back," Tanner informed him. "Men dressed as Indians started a rock slide down on it."

"Where are the rest of the passengers?"

"All dead," Tanner answered. The men in the posse swore grimly.

"We killed some of the train robbers. I just threw one of them off a ledge back there about five miles. He may still be alive."

The men conferred and the sheriff turned back to Tanner. "A couple of the men will take the little lady on in to Salmon Falls. I'd like you to go back with me to find the train and that man you threw off the ledge. He may be able to tell us who did this."

"All right," Tanner agreed.

"By the way, I'm Sheriff Hiram Knute." The fleshy man held out a hand.

Tanner shook it. "I'm pleased to meet you." He

turned back to Sarah. "Go on ahead. I'll catch up." She smiled at his words. How often had he repeated them during the harrowing hours just passed?

"What about your shoulder?" she asked anxiously.

"It'll be all right. I had a good doctor." Tanner grinned, the stark folds and lines of his face softening for a moment.

"Be careful," she said and on impulse kissed him swiftly on the cheek. "Good-bye, Major Tanner."

"Good-bye, Miss MacKenzie. If I don't see you sooner, we'll meet at Fort Lapwai." His voice dropped so only she could hear. "I think we could improve on that kiss."

"Perhaps we could," Sarah said and blushed at her boldness.

"All right, then," the sheriff called out. "Wilson, ride the pack mule and give Major Tanner your horse." Reluctantly the fellow named Wilson climbed off his horse. Tanner mounted and turned to give Sarah a parting salute. Smiling warmly, she stood watching until he'd disappeared with the rest of the posse. Two men were left behind along with a pack mule. Sarah had little doubt as to who would ride the mule. Raising her eyes heavenward, she approached the sad-eyed creature. The only good thing she could think about it was that it was better than walking. Before she reached Salmon Falls, she was to amend that thought as well.

6

Sarah delayed her departure from Salmon Falls on the pretense of waiting for her luggage. In reality, she hoped that Lucas Tanner would return and they could travel on to Fort Lapwai together. When her luggage arrived and Major Tanner did not, she was at first worried until she read the dispatch he'd sent. He was staying with Sheriff Knute's posse for a few days more in the hopes of tracking down the robbers. On her way to the agency, would she stop at Fort Lapwai and convey to Captain Perry the reason for his delay? Sarah had little choice but to leave. Transportation was arranged for her to Kings Hill, where she would take the stagecoach for the rest of her trip to Umatilla.

On the long, tiresome trip, Sarah thought of little else but Lucas Tanner, remembering the laughter in his eyes or the quick way he'd dealt with the train robbers or the way his strong arms had wrapped around her to warm her through the night. Was he safe? Would he take chances that might endanger his life? She prayed not.

From Umatilla she took the steamboat to Lewiston, sailing up first the Columbia and then the Snake River. It was a circuitous route, but the best she could effect over the mountains of Idaho and Washington.

Lewiston was a small, rugged frontier town. Once it had been a good-sized mining camp, but the mining reserve had been changed to another site and Lewiston had become a quiet village. A mill, newspaper, and several general stores supported those who'd remained.

As the boat docked, people gathered on the landing. The arrival of a boat was a primary event in their quiet lives now. Soldiers were prevalent in the crowd, their hats and uniforms setting them apart. Sarah looked around for a hired carriage to take her out to the Indian agency. Her attention was caught by a group of children crowded around a cage at one end of the dock.

A bear, its coat thin and shabby, gazed dully from behind the bars of its prison, which was too small to even move around in. The children pranced about the cage, shouting and thrusting sharp sticks through the bars to prod the helpless animal. In pain and frustration the bear raised its mighty head and growled in a hopeless parody of the fierceness it once had possessed. Screaming in mock terror, the children ran away, only to return and once again taunt the pitiful creature.

"Stop that," Sarah ordered, and the children paused to look at her. Sticking out their tongues, they ran away to join their parents elsewhere on the wharf.

A tall, fair-haired man with melancholy eyes approached her. "Miss Sarah MacKenzie?" he asked hesitantly. Sarah nodded. "I'm John Monteith, the Indian agent at Lapwai. We received word you were on this boat. Welcome to Lewiston."

"Thank you for coming for me," Sarah said with relief. She held out a hand to him. The earnest, thin face flushed, but he took her hand and shook it brusquely. Sarah guessed the agent was shy. "I'm afraid I'll have to prevail on your patience somewhat, Mr. Monteith. I must go to Fort Lapwai first and deliver a message to Captain Perry."

"It's on the way, ma'am," he said and gathered up her bags. Though somewhat diffident in the presence of a woman, he soon had her baggage loaded and Sarah settled on the hard plank seat.

"How far is the fort?" she asked, eager to make her report and go on to the agency, where she could begin her duties.

"It's about twelve miles from town. The agency is about three miles past that, near the Clearwater River," John explained.

"So close," Sarah said, pleased at the prospect of seeing Lucas Tanner often.

"I'll have to make a stop in town first," John said, picking up the reins. "Frances'll wear me out if I don't get her some flour."

"Is Frances your wife?" Sarah couldn't imagine the quiet, diffident man working up the courage to court a woman, much less marry.

"She's my sister-in-law," he replied. "My brother Charles is with the agency as well."

He pulled the team onto the dusty main street of Lewiston, and Sarah fell silent as she studied the meager, rough stores fronting it. A man came out of one of the buildings and leaned negligently against a post, a cigar clasped between his teeth. In contrast to the roughly clad cowboys and farmers on the street, he wore a dark worsted suit with a fancy satin vest and a string tie at the collar of his white shirt. His face was heavily jowled and the narrow eyes were set so close together his jutting nose seemed even more prominent. In spite of a sneering grin, his thin lipped mouth was stingy of humor. He stared at the Indian agent, and Monteith glared back until his wagon rolled passed.

"Who was that man?" Sarah asked.

"Owen Thatcher," Monteith replied in a grim tone. "He's a lawyer here in town, but I wouldn't recommend him." Sarah resisted the urge to turn around and stare at the man again.

John pulled the rig to a stop in front of the general store. "I won't be long."

"Take your time," she answered and sat looking around at the rugged little town. It seemed strange and different from the town of Mountain Grove, Missouri, yet she supposed it would become familiar enough in the months ahead.

Her musings were interrupted by shouting, and Sarah swiveled around to see the cause of the commotion. The lawyer called Owen Thatcher was shouting as he brought a leather strap down over the back of an Indian woman. The woman cringed, but made no outcry. Passersby stopped to watch the whipping, but no one made an attempt to stop the burly lawyer.

Fury washed through Sarah at the helplessness of the Indian and she leaped from the wagon impatiently brushing her full skirts free of the wheel. Thatcher didn't hear the angry staccato of her boots against the boardwalk or he chose to ignore her, never believing anyone would dare to interfere. His arm swung the strap back for still another blow on the hapless woman and Sarah stepped forward, shielding the Indian with her own body. Her dark eyes snapped angrily as they met Owen Thatcher's. Surprise washed over his face in that last moment before the lash descended across Sarah's shoulders and chest. She wasn't prepared for the pain and cried out, stumbling backward against the Indian woman. A murmur rose among the onlookers. It was one thing to whip an Indian, quite another to strike a white woman.

"Who the hell are you?" Thatcher demanded, his florid face growing even redder. "What do you think you're doing, woman?"

"My name is Sarah MacKenzie," she snapped, "and I'm trying to stop your inhumane treatment toward a fellow human being."

"Another do-gooder from the agency," Thatcher sneered. "Just get in from the East, did you, girl? You don't know how things are out here, Miss Mac-Kenzie." He grasped a handful of the Indian woman's hair and pulled her head up so her face was exposed. Sarah gasped at the ugly bruises that marred the smooth brown features.

"This is not a fellow human being," Thatcher went on. "This is an Indian and one who works for me, when I can get her to work."

Sarah was nearly speechless with rage at his words. "The two are one and the same," she declared.

"Not in my book," Thatcher answered. "Now take your do-gooding somewhere else and let me get on with disciplining my Indian."

"Living out here in the West, Mr. Thatcher, perhaps you haven't heard that we fought a war a dozen or more years ago freeing the oppressed from slavery and bondage. You have no right to treat this woman this way."

"Haven't I?" Thatcher challenged. "Ask her if she agrees with you. She's a lazy, stubborn Indian and she deserves to be punished. Ask her. Annie, tell this meddling woman whether you deserve the whipping."

Sarah turned back to the Indian and studied her closely. She was startled at how young and comely the woman was, hardly more than a girl. Though small in stature, the woman stood tall, her shoulders thrown back, her head held high. Only her eyes gave away her fear and resentment.

"Go on, Annie, tell her," Thatcher demanded and something flickered in the Indian's eyes.

"He is right," she said in a low voice, and now her head was bowed in humiliation. "I am lazy and deserve to be whipped."

"But he's hurt you," Sarah protested.

One small brown hand quickly covered the battered cheek. "I fell," Annie said. Her fearful gaze darted to Owen Thatcher, then lowered. "Thatcher is a kind man. He's most generous with me."

"Generous with the blows, no doubt," Sarah said, glaring at the smirking man. Frustrated, she turned back to Annie. "You don't have to work for him. You could leave."

"She's right, Annie," Thatcher said in a soft, menacing tone that struck shivers of apprehension along Sarah's spine.

"Oh, no!" Annie cried. "I don't want to leave. Thatcher is a kind, generous man, a—a good man." Her expression was pleading as she looked at the lawyer. "Please let me stay. I will do better."

Thatcher smiled triumphantly, his expression that of an indulgent benefactor. "All right, Annie. I'll give you another chance, but you'll have to work harder at pleasing me, girl," he warned.

"I will," she answered quickly and one of the men on the sidewalk guffawed crudely. Mortification swept over Sarah as she realized the true relationship of the lawyer and the Indian girl. Still, it didn't excuse the man's mistreatment of his mistress. Cheeks flaming, Sarah put a hand on Annie's arm. "You don't have to stay with him, if you don't want to," she insisted.

For the barest instant something flashed through the Indian girl's dark eyes and was gone, but not before Sarah had seen the despair and hopelessness Annie felt. "I want to stay," Annie said quietly.

"I think that's enough interference from you, Miss MacKenzie. Annie, go inside," Thatcher ordered. Without a backward glance the girl went back inside the building that housed the lawyer's offices and his apartment above. "Go on, folks, the excitement's over," Thatcher advised, and the people slowly broke apart and went about their business.

Thatcher's hard gaze came back to rest on Sarah. "Now, girlie," he said derisively. She could sense the rage in the man. "You may not know who I am."

"I know," Sarah replied with more calmness than she felt.

"Then you should know this. I'm not a man to cross. Don't ever meddle in my business again." With a final warning glance he turned back to his office and closed the door firmly behind him. Aware now that others were staring at her curiously, Sarah walked back to the wagon.

"What was the commotion?" Monteith asked when he'd loaded his supplies and climbed up beside her.

"Owen Thatcher was whipping his Indian," Sarah said dully.

"Poor Annie," the Indian agent said and slapped the reins against the horses' rumps. With a lurch the wagon started down the street, leaving behind the ugly scene Sarah had witnessed, but she couldn't put it out of her mind. If even John Monteith knew of Annie's plight, why hadn't they done something?

They traveled through brown humpbacked mountains and valleys of dark green pines, and reached the fort within an hour. Fort Lapwai wasn't a walled post, simply a cluster of stout buildings. John guided his team past the stables and rough log cabins of laundresses who were busy hanging their freshly washed clothes on rope lines strung between trees. The barracks, guardhouse, and officers' quarters all opened onto a dusty square.

"Welcome to Fort Lapwai," David Perry said graciously. He was a sandy haired man with a slim, sturdy body and a boyish air. He was younger than Sarah had expected and lacked the rugged countenance of Lucas Tanner.

"Thank you, Captain Perry," Sarah replied. "I've been asked to relay a message to you from Major Tanner. He was delayed on his way here." Sarah took the letter from her bag and handed it to the young officer.

"I trust it's no serious matter?"

"In fact, it was," Sarah replied and told him of the train holdup. "Major Tanner saved my life," she concluded.

"I look forward to having him under my command," Perry said. "In the meantime, Miss MacKenzie, won't you all join my wife and me for supper tonight? Faye will be delighted that another lady will be living nearby."

"I look forward to it, Captain," Sarah said, getting to her feet.

About three miles northeast of the fort, above the mouth of Lapwai Creek, the old mission had been located. Rough log cabins had been erected to house the agent's family and store the food the government doled out to the treaty Indians as supplement to the vegetables and beef they raised themselves.

"That's the schoolhouse." Monteith pointed to a

smaller building. "The sawmill, gristmill, and church are over there." Beyond the cabins Sarah could see vegetable crops neatly tended and fenced with split rails. In the distance were other structures, some newly whitewashed and some mere log cabins. Figures moved in and around them.

"Welcome to Lapwai, Sarah. We're so happy to have you here." A pleasant-faced woman stepped forward to grasp both of Sarah's hands. "I'm Frances, John's sister-in-law. This is my husband, Charles." A man who was a younger version of the Indian agent stepped forward to shake her hand.

"This is Callie Osgood, the miller's wife."

A slatternly woman nodded shyly. She held a baby in her arms and a young toddler gripped her skirts. "Pleased to meet you, ma'am," she said and ducked back, her face beneath its mop of unkempt hair growing pink. "These here are my girls, Lizbeth—" she pushed forward a ten-year-old who was the spitting image of her mother—"Nan, and Jane. The little one there is Kate and this here's Lucy." She jiggled the baby good-naturedly.

"I'm so pleased to meet you all," Sarah said. "I'm looking forward to seeing you girls in school."

"I ain't," Lizbeth said, but the youngest of the three, Jane, stepped forward.

"Theth ith for you, Mith MacKenthie," she lisped, holding out a wilting bouquet of wildflowers. Sarah could see her front teeth were missing with just the nubbins of new teeth beginning. She was enchanted by the little girl with the cornflower-blue eyes and pale hair.

"Thank you, Jane," she said, taking the bouquet.

"You young'uns run on now and let the new schoolteacher get her bearings," Callie ordered, and the three girls ran off toward the creek. Callie shifted the baby from one hip to the other. "I'll be on my way too," she said, bobbing her head. "My man don't like his supper late." Taking the arm of the toddler, Callie made her way toward the mill.

"Good-bye," Sarah called. Then caught up in the beauty of the mountains and wide sky and the green of the hills and sparkle of sun on the rushing creek, she swung around with eyes shining. "I tried hard to imagine what it would be like here. I never once thought it was this magnificent."

Frances put an arm around her shoulders and gave her a hug. "You're going to be good for us, Sarah," she said. "We've gotten to be rather stodgy and glum about things around us."

"Well, we should," John Monteith said. "I saw Thatcher in town."

"Oh no," Frances exclaimed anxiously. "Was there any trouble?"

John Monteith nodded. "He won't bother us. He knows this farce won't work."

"Still, he may try to cause trouble for you, John," Charles warned. "You're the one who stopped him."

John Monteith looked at his brother. "I'll walk around fearful of a rattlesnake's bite."

"He's not as trustworthy as a rattlesnake. At least the rattler gives you warning. Thatcher won't. See to your back, brother."

"Shush, now," Frances said. "You'll scare Sarah off before she's even settled. Come on, Sarah. We'll leave these doomsday sayers and get you settled in your room."

Sarah followed her hostess to the largest of the log cabins. "You'll be staying with Charles and me," Frances chatted in her gentle, breathless voice. "We don't have children, so we have the extra room. Our work with the Indians has been most rewarding."

"I'm sure I will find it so as well," Sarah said. She liked the motherly woman already.

"You'll have the room off the parlor," Frances said. "We thought you'd be most comfortable there."

"It's lovely," Sarah said, looking around the sparsely furnished room. The walls seemed freshly whitewashed and a vase of wildflowers sat on the washstand. Sarah picked them up to sniff their sweet fragrance, then turned to face her hostess.

"There was some trouble in town today," she said. "Owen Thatcher was whipping an Indian girl named Annie, and no one tried to help her."

"No one can," Frances said sadly.

"Why not?" Sarah asked, the wildflowers forgotten.

"Annie Red Moccasin is a reservation Indian. Her father, Whooper, owned land south of here near Wallowa Valley. White men can't own reservation land unless the Nez Percé sell it to them. Whooper sold his land to Thatcher; some say he was tricked out of it. When he protested he was murdered. His killer was never found. Whooper's wife and mother were told to get off the land, but old Half-Moon refused to go. Thatcher agreed they could continue to live there as long as Annie went to work for him. We all know what kind of work she does and we know how he mistreats her, but as long as she refuses to leave and makes no complaint against him, we can't step in."

"She'll never make a complaint as long as her grandmother wishes to stay on the land," Sarah said softly saddened by Annie's predicament.

"Exactly," Francis said disgustedly. Sarah thought of how much Annie must love Half-Moon. Would she have made such a sacrifice for Swan Necklace? she wondered. She knew she would have. Now she resolved to befriend Annie Red Moccasin whenever the opportunity presented itself.

"Owen Thatcher is a greedy, evil man," Frances was muttering angrily.

"Why would he hurt John?" Sarah asked curiously.

"He wouldn't," Frances declared without much conviction. "Charles is a bit of a worrier at times."

"Still, I saw the way Mr. Thatcher came out and stared at us as we drove past. He made me feel frightened."

"You mustn't," Frances said quickly. "Owen Thatcher tried to make what we call a mission claim against the Lapwai agency."

"What is that?"

Frances settled on the edge of the bed. "Back in 1848 our government passed an act which gave a square mile of land to each mission in operation at that time. Although Reverend Spalding abandoned the mission in 1847, he and another man sold the Lapwai claim to Thatcher about ten years ago. Thatcher never tried to claim the land until two years ago. He had the sheriff serve papers on John, but John refused to recognize the claim. He was ordered to stay here by the Secretary of Interior, but the sheriff returned and forcibly removed John and the rest of us from the property, claiming it was Thatcher's. Since then the agency has been renting back part of the buildings from Thatcher. You see there's really nothing for us to fret about," Frances said brightly, but Sarah saw her concern and asked no more questions.

When Frances left her alone, Sarah was too keyed up to rest. She unpacked, then stripped, and bathed in the cold water from the china pitcher. Since there was time before they must leave for dinner at the fort, Sarah stretched out across the hand-carved four poster bed and pulled the bright patchwork quilt over her. Every thought had been given to her comfort and she was grateful for Frances' warmth. Somehow the smiling, friendly woman made up a little for the desolate loss Sarah felt over Swan Necklace. Her thoughts drifted to Lucas Tanner. Where was he now? she wondered and wished he would be there at the fort tonight. Surprisingly she fell asleep and awoke feeling refreshed. Carefully she dressed for dinner, wanting to make a good impression on the people she would meet. In such a small outpost, friendships were bound to assume greater importance. She put aside the drab gowns she'd worn on the train and chose a modest one of pale green trimmed with darker green ribbons. Its bustle was modest yet fashionable and accented her slender, high-breasted figure. When she was ready she stepped back to assess the results in the mirror and wished again that Tanner would be there. He'd only seen her in the dark, unflattering missionary garb she'd affected for the trip out.

Faye Perry was an attractive and gracious hostess. The rough rooms in the officer's quarters had been thoughtfully decorated with touches of elegance that mingled with homey comfort. Obviously Faye adored her handsome young husband, and he, in turn, hovered over her solicitously. Yet beneath the gallantry Sarah discerned an anxiety of the captain for his wife, as if he feared she couldn't weather the harshness of life on a military post.

The Perrys shared a double set of quarters with the fort doctor and his wife, John and Emily Fitzgerald. Only a porch separated their two buildings, but more than that separated the wives. Emily was a straightforward, commonsensical woman with whom

Sarah felt an immediate kinship. She liked the obvious intelligence and sensitivity of the other woman.

"Welcome to Lapwai, Sarah," Emily said, shaking hands with the younger woman. "It seems you've had a most unpleasant beginning in our country."

"I wouldn't have been half so brave, if not for Major Tanner," Sarah answered, "and I'm quite happy it's behind me."

"I'm sure I would never have survived such an ordeal," Faye Perry said, shivering delicately.

"Nonsense, we suffer what we must," Emily said, "and we go on."

"Perhaps you would, dear Emily," the captain's wife said, "but we are not all so strong-spirited as you."

"You might surprise yourself, Faye," Emily answered generously. "We all find extra courage when the need arises."

"At any rate, we're grateful you've come, Miss MacKenzie," Faye said. "The more there are of us, the easier it is for one, especially when our husbands must go out and fight against the Indians."

"We've hardly been in danger of fighting the Indians, Faye," Perry said quietly. "The Nez Percé are peaceful."

"Why, everybody knows we're just sitting on a powder keg," Faye declared plaintively. "You should hear the tales of atrocities the Nez Percé have committed, Sarah. It fairly makes my blood run cold."

"I don't know as I'd put much stock in the stories being told in Lewiston," John Monteith said. "There's a passel of white folks up there in town just looking for a reason to take some of the reservation land."

"What's happened with Thatcher and his claim?" Captain Perry asked.

"Nothing so far. He doesn't stand much chance of making his claim good."

"I've been instructed to give you aid, should he try force again," Perry said.

"Oh, David, no," Faye wailed.

There was a knock at the door and David Perry hurried to answer, as if glad to end his wife's laments against the Indians. He turned back to the room with a broad smile, his gaze flashing to Sarah. "Miss MacKenzie, no doubt you'll remember Major Tanner?" he said, stepping aside so she could see the tall, broad-shouldered officer standing in the doorway.

Sarah gasped and jumped to her feet. Her face shone with surprise and happiness upon seeing Lucas Tanner again. She was never aware of the knowing looks the other women exchanged. Her gaze was only for the big man who stood smiling down at her with equal delight.

"How did you get here so quickly?" she asked softly and felt unaccountably subdued under his warm gaze.

His gray eyes sparkled with laughter. "I left Sheriff Knute's posse a few days ago. We tracked the men northwest until we got to the Payette River, where we lost their tracks. The country was so rugged, it didn't make sense to retrace my steps. I just followed the rivers north."

"I'm glad you're back safe," Sarah said softly so the others couldn't hear. "I worried about your wounds."

"My arm is nearly healed," he said dismissively. "I worried about you. No more Indian attacks or detours into the wilds with an unknown man?"

Sarah smiled. "I never thanked you properly. You saved my life, you know."

"Then I'll expect a reward," he answered. His words and the look in his eyes gave Sarah a warm glow that stayed with her the rest of the evening. She found it difficult to concentrate on the other guests. The meal was delicious, but Sarah hardly knew what she ate. After dinner, while the others gathered back in the sitting room, Tanner bent over Sarah.

"Would you care to step outside for a breath of fresh air, Miss MacKenzie?" he asked softly and quickly she got to her feet.

Faye arched an eyebrow in Emily's direction, but Sarah ignored it. Tanner's touch burned her skin as he took her elbow and guided her out the door. The moon cast a blue-silver glow over the square and the squat log buildings.

"You look very beautiful tonight, Miss MacKenzie," Tanner said.

Sarah felt a shiver run along her spine. "Thank you, Major," she said crisply and matched her stride to his as he turned her along the side of the building and into the deep shadows. Without a word he swung her around and into his arms. His mouth covered hers in a long, passionate kiss that left her breathless.

At last he released her. His breath came in warm gasps against her temple. "Much better than the last kiss we shared," he whispered huskily. Sarah sighed. "I couldn't think of anything else but you while I was in the mountains," he went on, "wondering if you'd arrived safely, cursing myself for a fool to have left you in the first place."

Sarah's heart thrilled to his words. "I worried about you every minute," she admitted. "You just dashed off. I was afraid your wound would become infected, or that you'd find the robbers and they'd shoot you from an ambush or something."

"Nothing could have hurt me. I had to be sure you were safe. I wanted to see your eyes again and kiss you like this." Once again his mouth settled over hers. His strong arms wrapped around her, pulling her against his tall, lanky body. Her breasts were flattened against his hard chest. One gold button dug into her rib, but she didn't care. She was too happy to be in Lucas Tanner's arms.

Reluctantly he drew away. "We'd better get back," he said. "If I ride out to the agency sometime, may I see you?"

Sarah felt like laughing at her happiness and the serious formal way he'd adopted after his passionate kiss. "I'd like that very much," she murmured.

Bright speculation burned in the eyes of Faye Perry and even Frances Monteith when Sarah and Tanner returned to the drawing room. Despite herself Sarah blushed, and Frances smiled sweetly.

"Major Tanner seems a fine man," Frances said on the wagon ride back to the agency.

"He is," Sarah answered and fell to dreaming of the rugged, handsome officer with whom she'd shared such harrowing adventures and such passionate kisses.

7

The next morning Sarah walked to the log school-house and went over the books and supplies she found there.

"We can order what we need from Lewiston and Portland," Frances said, helping her with her inventory.

"In the meantime we can begin school tomorrow," Sarah exclaimed. "I'm looking forward to working with the Nez Percé children."

"You'll find them bright and intelligent and quite diligent in their efforts," Frances assured her. "Their parents are hardworking and law-abiding. It's only the non-treaty Indians who create such a problem."

"Who are the non-treaty Indians?" Sarah asked. She couldn't remember Swan Necklace mentioning them.

"They're the Lower Nez Percé, who refuse to acknowledge the 1863 treaty. They won't come onto the reservation, and we have to constantly guard against their persuading our people to run away on one of their interminable buffalo hunts or root gathering expeditions."

"But isn't that the way of the Nez Percé?" Sarah asked. "What can be wrong with that?"

"Those are the old ways, Sarah. The Nez Percé must give up this traipsing around the countryside at a whim. They buy whiskey and race their horses and get into all sorts of trouble. There are killings and the Indians complain about the white men. John does his best to obtain justice for them, but the judges let the culprits go. They get up petitions signed by every whiskey seller and land grabber in the territory and try to have John removed. All this trouble would be over if the Indians would just move onto the reservation."

"But if the old ways hurt no one, why not let them continue? By what authority do we take away their rights?" Sarah insisted.

Frances looked at her in surprise. "Why, Sarah, you sound just like Chief Joseph."

"Chief Joseph?" Sarah's interest quickened at the name. Was this the Chief Joseph who was her grandmother's brother?

"Joseph is a young chief," Frances explained, "only thirty-seven years old, but his people look up to him. His father, Old Joseph, opposed the treaty. On his deathbed he instructed Young Joseph not to accept the treaty. He claimed the bones of his ancestor were buried there. Now Joseph won't listen to any proposals made by our government and the Nez Percé follow Joseph. John tries to do what he can for them."

"I'm sure the Nimpau are fortunate to have a man such as John Monteith to care for them," Sarah said.

Frances looked at her strangely. "Why do you call them the Nimpau?" she asked.

Sarah hesitated, torn between wanting to tell Frances about her grandmother and suddenly fearful it would drive a wedge between them and thus make impossible any hope she had of helping the Nez Percé. "It's what they call themselves," she said softly. "The real people."

"But how did you know that?"

Sarah hesitated again, loathe to lie to Frances. The sound of hoofbeats in the yard saved her from answering. Frances ran to the door and her plain face paled when she saw the mounted horsemen.

"Who are they?" Sarah asked, peering over her shoulder.

"Owen Thatcher and Sheriff Wilmot," Frances whispered, "and they've got a posse." Running to the opposite window, she threw up the sash and called out to a young Indian boy working nearby. "Little Fox, go to the fort at once. Tell Captain Perry that we need him immediately. Hurry." Spurred by her urgent tone, the young boy took off at a run, disappearing in the woods on the way to the fort.

Frances turned back to face Sarah. "My brother-in-law is in this position, Sarah, because of his work with the Indians. And my husband works with him. I fear for both their lives." Whirling, she ran to the door. Sarah followed her to the agency office and the angry, menacing group of men gathered there.

John Monteith walked out onto the porch. "What do you want, Thatcher?"

"I told you we'd be back," Thatcher called. "I've got the sheriff with me this time."

"Sheriff? More like your toady," the Indian agent replied derisively. With a curse the man with a badge pinned to his vest prodded his horse forward as if he meant to ride Monteith down.

"Wilmot," Thatcher said, and the sheriff reined in his horse.

"You're on my land, Monteith. Get your bunch and get off. I want all the buildings on this land turned over to me at once."

"And if I refuse?" Monteith asked stoutly.

Owen Thatcher smiled. "I had you evicted from

these lands once, Monteith. I can do it again. Throw him off, Sheriff."

"All right, men," the sheriff ordered.

"Burn down the buildings so they can't come back," Thatcher instructed. His glance fell on Sarah. "Start with the schoolhouse."

"No," Sarah cried and, whirling, ran toward the log building. One of Thatcher's men rode after her. She could hear his horse's heavy breathing and the staccato beat of its hooves. The rider galloped past her, then swerved his horse. Sarah dodged away, but another horseman was there blocking her path, hemming her in with their sweating mounts. Three of them made a game of it, circling her in an ever shrinking perimeter, taunting her, bumping their horses against her when she tried to break through. Beyond their menacing presence Sarah could see books and papers being flung from the window of the schoolhouse into a bonfire.

"No!" she screamed and forgot to dodge. A horse knocked her to the ground. The rider laughed, tightening the circle until she was fearful of being trampled underfoot. Quickly she rolled away, then scrambled to her feet.

Suddenly a shot rang out. Startled, the men jerked their reins and grabbed their guns. Their horses moved apart so now Sarah could see Lucas Tanner and a detachment of soldiers. They sat in an invincible line, rifle barrels aimed at Thatcher's men.

"What's the trouble here, Mr. Monteith?" Tanner asked, his hard gaze swinging to the lawyer and sheriff.

"Nothing for the army to concern itself with, Major," Thatcher spoke up. "This is a civilian matter."

"The agency is a government matter, sir," Tanner replied. "You're trespassing."

The lawyer drew himself up. "I'm Owen Thatcher and this land is mine, Major. Mr. Monteith and his people refuse to relinquish rights to this property."

"It appears, Mr. Thatcher, there's some dispute over the legality of your claim and until that's settled, I'll have to ask you to leave these people alone."

The lawyer's face grew red with fury. He wasn't used to being crossed. "If I may not have use of my property, Major Tanner," he snapped, "it is only fitting that these squatters not have access to it either. Therefore I am padlocking all buildings until this matter is settled. Sheriff, here are the keys. Will you see this is carried out?"

"You can't do that," John Monteith cried. "Can he, Major?"

"I'm sorry, sir," Tanner said. "I was instructed to keep Thatcher and his men from bodily removing you from the agency. I can't keep him from locking up some of those buildings."

"But the school," Sarah cried, seeing the sheriff lock the door of the little log building.

"I'm sorry," Tanner said.

With the school, sawmill, and even the storage sheds holding government supplies securely locked, the sheriff rode back triumphantly. "All done, Mr. Thatcher," he said with a grin.

"How can you do this?" Sarah demanded. "We can't continue our work with the Indians."

"That is not my affair, Miss MacKenzie," Thatcher said. "Until the government has paid me the one hundred and twenty thousand dollars it owes me for improvements on my land, you may not have access to it."

"This land belongs to the Nez Percé, Thatcher, and you know that. You bought this mission when it was abandoned by Spalding. He had no right to sell it to you. It should have reverted back to the Nez Percé. Now you're trying to bilk the government. They'll never pay you for this land."

"Then you and your Nez Percé will never have it," Thatcher said. His evil, triumphant gaze swung back to Sarah. "This should be a reminder, Miss MacKenzie, to never meddle in my business. To do so will cost you dearly." Turning his horse, he galloped out of the clearing. The sheriff and his posse followed close behind.

"Nasty characters," Tanner observed watching them leave, then he turned back to Sarah. "What did he mean?"

Sarah told them of her run-in with Thatcher the day before. "I'm sorry if I've brought this trouble to the agency."

"You haven't," Frances hastened to reassure her. "Thatcher was just looking for an excuse." But Sarah saw how John's shoulders slumped and she was unconvinced.

"What're we going to do now?" Charles asked and put his arms around his wife.

"I'll write the Commissioner of Indian Affairs," John said halfheartedly.

"Little good that will do," Charles replied bitterly.

"We've written before and how much support have we gotten?" Frances demanded.

"Don't give up," Tanner said. He'd dismounted and joined the others on the porch. "Thatcher and his lot will soon be found out and stopped. In the meantime, try to carry on the best you can."

"You're right, Major." John seemed to take heart from his words.

Tanner turned back to Sarah. "I'm sorry about your school."

"Don't be," she said with bright determination.

"He's only locked up the building, not the school."
Tanner smiled. Somehow he wasn't surprised at her
words. "I'll teach outdoors," Sarah hurried on. "I
brought a few books and paper with me. We'll make
do with those for now."

"Oh Sarah, can you?" Frances cried joyfully. She
looked at her husband. "You see, Charles, we can
go on. It will be all right. You'll see."

Callie Osgood came running up from the mill, her
baby clutched to her breast. "John, Thatcher's men
locked Dean out of the mill," she wailed.

"I know, Callie," John said calmly. "Tell Dean to
stay home until we get this straightened out." They
stood talking about Owen Thatcher and his latest
threats.

Tanner took Sarah aside. His gray eyes were som-
ber as he gazed down at her. "Be careful," he said.
"Don't go too far from the house without an escort.
Thatcher and his men may come back."

"There's no need to worry about me, Major," she
answered with more courage than she felt.

He grinned at her independence. "All the same,
don't take any chances."

"I won't," Sarah answered and grew breathless
under his steady gaze. His thick, sun-streaked hair
was too long, she noticed. It fell unruly and unyielding over his collar. Her gaze dropped to the wide,
muscular shoulders. One big tanned hand still gripped
hers. Everything about the man was disturbing and
reassuring at the same time.

"Tanner," she said quickly when he would have
turned away. "Can you help me with something?"

His expression softened as he looked at her. "What
is it?"

"I need help in locating Swan Necklace's people.
Frances Monteith says that Chief Joseph lives out-

side the reservation. I don't know where to begin to look for him."

"From what I've heard, feelings run pretty high against Joseph and the non-treaty Indians," Tanner said.

"Can you find out where his village is?"

Tanner studied her face. "Are you sure you want to do this? Things could heat up and you'd be caught in the middle."

"I haven't told Frances and the others about my connection with the Nez Percé yet. They seem so angry with the non-treaty Indians. I'm afraid they wouldn't understand, but I must find my grandmother's people. I promised her."

"This could be dangerous for you."

"I'm beginning to understand that, but I've come too far to run scared now."

Tanner grinned and shook his head. "No one could ever accuse you of that."

"Will you help me?" Sarah persisted.

"I'll see what I can find out." For a moment she thought he meant to kiss her in front of his troops and the agency people, but then he swung into his saddle and with a final salute led his men back to the fort.

With the help of some of the Indians and under John Monteith's directions, a makeshift shelter was erected of spindly tree posts and covered over with brush and leafy branches. Two sides of the shelter were open, but the interior shade was cool and comfortable for the children to gather and study. Happily Sarah set about teaching them the alphabet. They were quick to learn, their bright dark eyes eager.

Other problems were not so easily solved. Thatcher

rehired Carl Pepin, a man John Monteith had fired
for incompetence. Once more he was put in charge
of the mill and liquor was freely sold to Indian and
white men alike. Indian women were kept in the
mill and day and night men visited them.

"They've got a regular shebang down there in the
mill," Charlie muttered and Frances quietly explained
"shebang" was a local word for a house of prostitu-
tion. Diligently Sarah, Callie, and Frances tried to
keep the children away from the mill. Dean walked
around scowling darkly now that he had no job.
Bitterly John wrote to the Commissioner, but his
letters brought no results. He despaired of ever finding support. One day as Sarah and her students
labored under the leafy canopy of her schoolhouse,
she saw Dean Osgood run up from the creek.

"John," the miller shouted.

The Indian agent ran out. "What is it, Osgood?"
he asked.

"They've cut off the water the Indians need for
irrigation," Dean gasped, out of breath. "They
damned off the creek upstream."

"This must stop, by damned," the agent cried,
slamming a fist into the palm of his hand. "Dean,
prepare to ride into Lewiston with a letter." In short
order, John drafted a letter and Dean galloped off to
dispatch it on the next steamboat to Oregon. In the
days that followed, the people at the agency tried
their best to carry on as normal, but the hot June sun
burned away unwatered crops. One by one the children dropped out of Sarah's class. With the irrigation ditches dried up, they were needed to tote water
from the small springs to the withering crops.

One evening as Sarah stood watching Little Fox
and his mother struggle to carry water, anger washed

over her and in a fury she stalked down the hill toward the creek.

"Sarah, where are you going?" Frances called after her, but Sarah kept walking until she reached the mill, where a dam had been built. Grabbing up a stout stick she began to tear at the makeshift logs, trying to dislodge them. The noise she made aroused the men inside, and they came tumbling out.

"What the hell?" a man shouted, running out in his bare feet. His greasy hair was uncombed and his fancy vest was spotted and rumpled. "What're you doing, you fool woman?" he demanded and, doubling his fist, hit Sarah along the temple, knocking her to her knees.

"You can't keep water from the Indians," she cried, getting to her feet. Her head was spinning, but she squared her shoulders and stared back at the men defiantly.

"Who's she, Carl?" some of the men yelled. "You been holding out on us?" Sarah glanced back at her assailant. Carl Pepin! Something about him sparked a shiver of fear. She stared at him, striving to remember what seemed so familiar about him. Pepin seemed uncomfortable at her close scrutiny.

"She's the new schoolmarm at the agency," he snapped in answer to his men.

"You sure she ain't one of them Nez Percé all dressed up like white folks?" the man asked. "Look at them eyes and hair. She kind of looks Indian, don't she?"

Pepin studied her, then nodded, a nasty grin on his face. "Yeah, she does at that," he said thoughtfully.

"Reckon we could add her to our shebang?" one of the men asked and took a step closer. His rough, dirty hand brushed against Sarah's hair and along her cheek.

"You'd better leave me alone," she cried. "You'll have the agency and the army down on you."

"Will we?" He guffawed. He didn't notice the stick as Sarah swung it. She hit him low and he doubled over from the unexpected pain.

"Whoo-ee. We got a wildcat here," another man cried and ran to help his friend.

"Don't come another step closer or I'll give you the same," Sarah cried, brandishing her club. Warily the man circled her. Suddenly from behind, the club was snatched from her hands and her arms were pinned to her sides. She lashed out with her foot and felt it connect. A man grunted with pain and she was free. With a swiftness born of fear and desperation she scrambled up the creek bank.

"Get her," Pepin yelled and the other men were after her like a pack of hounds after a hare. Holding her skirts high away from her knees, Sarah tried to outrun them, angling across the open fields toward the agency. A hard hand clamped over her shoulder and she went down, crushing the tender new shoots of beans and potatoes. Blindly she struck out, but her hands and feet were caught.

"Take her back to the mill," Pepin ordered, and Sarah felt herself being lifted onto the shoulders of the men. What would they do with her? she wondered, but their rough hands settled too often at her breasts and hips for her to have any doubts about their intentions. Helplessly she tried to twist away from their careless, obscene touches.

Lucas Tanner pushed his stallion a little harder. He had a leave from the fort for only a few hours, and he wanted to spend as much of that time with

Sarah as he could. Try as he might, he couldn't get her out of his mind. The memory of her face when she smiled and the taste of her lips occupied every waking moment. He thought of their danger from the train robbers and her fearlessness. He remembered how her slim, strong young body had effortlessly kept up with him on their twisting, climbing flight and of the softness of that same body later when she'd slept in his arms. An ache rose in his loins and he urged his horse along.

Frances heard him coming and ran out on the porch. "Major Tanner," she cried.

He wheeled his horse to a stop and looked around. "What can I do for you, Mrs. Monteith?" he asked politely.

"It's Sarah," Frances said, twisting a corner of her apron in worry. "She headed down to the mill some time ago. She looked angry. Pepin and his men are down there with their whores. It's not any place for a decent woman to be."

"I'll go get her," Tanner said and nudged his horse to a gallop. He caught a glimpse of blue off in one of the fields, but when he looked again it was gone. Field hands were gathered around something. He prodded his horse on, then reined in, some intuition telling him to look again. This was Indian land. No white man would be working it this close to the agency. The men were gone now. He caught a glimpse of them near the creek: they appeared to be carrying something on their shoulders, something blue. The blood rushed to his head as he remembered that Sarah had a blue gown.

The men heard him coming and dropped their burden. Streamers of long dark hair tumbled over the blue cloth. The men drew their guns and fired. Fearful of hitting Sarah, Tanner fired over their heads.

"Let her go," he roared, but the men continued to shoot. A bullet creased a hole in the sleeve of his shirt, but missed the flesh beneath. Reluctantly he took aim and pulled the trigger. A man went down.

Sarah pressed tightly to the ground, covering her head with her arms. Guns roared above her and men cursed. She could hear hoofbeats. Someone was coming.

Tanner ignored the whiz of bullets past his shoulder and leaned low over his horse's neck. Taking care not to hit the blue-clad figure on the ground, he fired again and another man went down. Sarah raised her head and looked around. One of the wounded men had landed nearby, his gun flung from his limp hand. Cautiously she crawled toward him. Grabbing his gun, she fired into the air. Startled, the other men turned.

"Drop your guns," she commanded, and the men looked at each other in surprise. With the big officer bearing down on them and this determined hellcat holding them at bay, they had little choice. One by one they dropped their guns.

Tanner rode up in a cloud of dust. "Damn it, Sarah, can't you wait to be rescued?" he shouted, sliding off his horse. He waved his gun at one of the men. "Get over there with the others," he ordered and gathered up their guns. John and Charles were already drawing near. "Send someone to the fort," Tanner ordered.

"Already done," John Monteith said. The two brothers dismounted and, taking out ropes, began to tie up the men. "The judge won't get you off so easily for this, Pepin," John said. "You've attacked a white woman this time."

"Yeah? She looked like an Indian to me," Carl Pepin sneered. "Don't she, men?" he turned to his companions. They nodded in agreement. John looked startled.

"It won't work," Tanner said quietly. "Let's take them down to the agency until my men get here."

Before long Lieutenant Dillon and troops from the fort rode in, and Tanner gave Pepin and his men into their custody.

"I'll be along directly," he said. "I have some business here." He watched as the detachment rode away toward Lewiston, then turned to Sarah. She grinned impishly. She was perfectly aware Tanner was angry with her and hoped to tease him out of his bad mood.

"You had business with Mr. Monteith?" she asked lightly. "I'll get him for you."

"Come here," Tanner growled and, grabbing her arm, led her into the shade of a towering white pine. "Why did you take such a chance with those men?" he demanded. "What if they hadn't laid down their guns. What if they'd shot you?"

"They wouldn't have." Sarah shrugged.

"But you didn't know that for sure. It was a damned fool thing for you to do."

"Were you worried about me?" she asked lightly, her dark eyes studying him. For an answer he pulled her into his arms and kissed her. Sarah leaned against his strong body, marveling at how familiar and right it felt to her. The tip of his tongue touched her lips, and she sighed against his mouth.

"What do you think?" he asked gruffly. Sarah could smell the scent of mountain pines on his skin and clothes, and feel his wind-chafed cheek against her own. He awakened feelings of wonder within her.

"I think I'm grateful you came along when you did," she whispered.

"Just grateful?" His broad hands captured her small waist and held her close.

"And delighted," she answered teasingly. He wasn't sure if she were happy he'd rescued her or just that he was here with her. Either way he felt elated by her response. Once again he lowered his head and kissed her. His large hand molded her slender body to his. Fires raged inside him and he fought to keep his head. It wasn't easy. Sarah was like no woman he'd ever known and he'd known his share, women easy to forget, unremarkable, and predictable. Sarah was like one of the sturdy, slender white pines growing on the side of a mountain. No matter what the wind blew, she would sway and bend and always snap back as right and strong as ever. He was drawn by her strength and haunted by her beauty.

"Have you forgotten about your business, Major?" she inquired innocently.

"As a matter of fact, I do have business but it's with you." Her face grew serious. "I've made inquiries about Chief Joseph's village and I know how to get there."

"Will you take me there?" she asked eagerly.

"If that's what you want."

"It is. I can't get on with my own life until I've carried out that promise I made to Swan Necklace." She paused. "Will it be dangerous?"

"Would that stop you?" he asked with mock disbelief.

"Not if you come with me." Her simple response was serious and direct.

"We would have to go by horseback. A carriage or wagon would never make it through the mountains."

"I prefer horses," Sarah said, not mentioning that

Uncle Caleb had never allowed her to ride horseback. Now she smiled gamely at Lucas Tanner.

He grinned back. "We make a good team, lady, in case you haven't noticed."

"I have," she answered, and the lights in her eyes made him draw her near again.

On the way to the fort, Tanner berated himself. He was like a schoolboy in love, he told himself. He'd never taken time for a woman before. His career as a soldier had demanded all his thoughts and energy. He'd satisfied his physical needs with passion that was paid for and no commitment expected. Sarah would never be a woman to love and walk away from. She'd be with him for the rest of his life. Suddenly Tanner felt unaccountably happy. He'd be spending a few days alone with Sarah in the wild and beautiful mountains, and he intended to make their time together count. Did she love him? he wondered. No matter. When they returned from Chief Joseph's village, she'd love him. He had all the time in the world to win her. Yet he was impatient to claim Sarah and suddenly distrustful of his newfound happiness.

8

They followed the Snake River south. Tanner rode at the front, followed by two pack mules and then Sarah. He had surprised her when he'd arrived to begin their journey. Instead of his uniform, he wore a blue cotton shirt that made his gray eyes change color, a bandanna, leather vest, and britches of heavy denim shoved into scuffed leather boots.

Sarah had also made concessions for their trip through the mountains. Discarding bustles and extra petticoats, she'd once again donned a plain gown of dark muslin with buttonholes at the hem that allowed her to fasten the loose, full skirt at her waist out of her way as she rode. A straw bonnet tied beneath her chin with a satin ribbon protected her from the hot sun. She was as excited about this trip as a child at Christmas. She'd had to do a lot of reasoning before John Monteith had agreed to let her go. Reuben, one of the agency Indians, had taught her to ride horseback. When they'd started their journey, she'd felt confident she could ride to Chief Joseph's village without any trouble. By late afternoon she'd altered her opinion considerably.

They'd been traveling for hours. The shadows had lengthened. The valley through which they journeyed was deep in shade while the tops of the mountain were bright with sunlight. "How are you holding up?" Tanner called back.

Sarah's head bobbed up proudly. "Don't worry about me," she answered brightly, but Tanner could see the white line of fatigue around her lips. They'd been moving steadily since early morning, pausing only twice for brief respites. Sarah had never once complained at the pace he'd set. There was no need to push, he decided, and swung off the trail, looking for a suitable spot to spend the night.

"This'll do," he said at last. They were near enough to the river to bathe and draw water for cooking, yet away from the path of any wild animals wandering down to drink.

Sarah slid off her horse and stood flexing her legs to loosen stiffened muscles. Curiously she glanced around. "This is beautiful country, isn't it?" she asked, absently arching her back and shoulders.

"Let me," Tanner said and began kneading the muscles in her slim shoulders and back. Despite her height she was a slender girl, and the bones beneath his hands were delicate.

"That feels wonderful," she moaned, letting her shoulders go limp.

Laughing, Tanner caught her around the waist. "You're right, it does," he said, nuzzling her ear.

Shivers raced along Sarah's spine and she sighed contentedly. "I could stay here forever."

"If we're going to stay here at all, we'd better get camp set up," he said and let go of her. Sarah missed the feel of his strong arms around her and made a face at him. "Gather wood," he ordered. "Then we'll catch some fish for supper."

"Yes, sir, Major Tanner." Sarah gave him a mock salute and set about helping to drag deadwood back to camp. When they had enough, they took fishing lines and hooks and went down to the river.

"The water's too swift for fish here," Tanner said and directed them along a small stream that flowed into the river. He cut poles for them, and they sat in the grass, dropped their hooks into the water, and waited. The shadows in the trees were deepening now. Night came earlier to the valleys. Sarah remembered that first night they'd spent in the mountains. She'd been frightened and exhausted then, and Tanner had been wounded. Such was not the case now and she could feel the tension of unspoken questions building between them as the evening wore on.

When they'd each caught two fish, they took them back to camp. Tanner cleaned them while Sarah built a fire. She soon had coaxed a flame from twigs and dried leaves, and added the deadfall wood. Glancing up, she caught Tanner studying her, a strange expression on his face.

"What is it?" she asked. Her heart had begun to beat so quickly she could scarcely breathe.

"I was just thinking," Tanner said, putting the fish to cook over the coals. "I've never known a woman who could build a fire."

"I begin to wonder, Major, about the kind of women you've known," Sarah teased and felt annoyance at the thought of him with some other woman.

"I've begun to wonder too," he said softly, and his eyes glowed softly in the firelight. Sarah felt a warm flush color her cheeks.

"I'd better get water for coffee," she said, suddenly stammering like some of the silly girls she'd known back home. She'd never understood why they behaved as they had. Now she did. That fluttery, breathless feeling was overpowering. Shakily she got to her feet and picked up the metal pot.

"Let me get that for you," Tanner offered. His hand covered hers, his touch kindling a searing flame in her bloodstream.

"I can do it," she said and wondered why her voice came out all choked and whispery.

Tanner's eyes gleamed with some emotion she couldn't name. "Relax," he advised and trailed one finger tenderly along her cheek. "You must be tired after all that riding."

"No, not really," she lied, but she let go of the pot and watched as his tall figure disappeared in the direction of the river. Settling beside the fire, Sarah tried to calm her racing pulse. Unable to sit still, she went to look for berries in the gathering twilight, glad to be away from the intimacy of their camp for a while.

The knot in her stomach grew bigger as they ate supper. Sarah watched the flickering light play across Tanner's craggy features and wondered at the confusion he wrought in her. Unable to eat, she put aside her plate and sat staring into the flames.

"Sarah," Tanner said softly. She jumped at the sound of his voice. Quizzically Tanner looked at her, then rose and moved around the campfire until he towered above her.

"Yes?" she asked, trying to keep her voice crisp and sure, but it came out a shaky squeak.

Tanner squatted beside her until his eyes were level with hers. "Is anything bothering you?"

"Me? No, nothing." Sarah feigned nonchalance. "Why do you ask?"

"You seem worried."

"I'm not—not worried at all. What is there to

worry about?" She tried but couldn't quite meet his eyes.

"Me?"

"You?" Sarah squirmed on the hard ground. "No, no, not at all."

"Yourself, then."

"I—I don't understand what you mean."

"I mean," Tanner said, straightening his long legs out in front of him. His shoulder brushed hers and instinctively she moved away as if burned. Tanner glanced at her pale face. She was utterly beautiful in the firelight. She'd unbound her hair and it lay about her shoulders sleek and glossy, inviting a man's touch. He clenched his hands together to keep from touching her. "I mean," he continued, "you and me."

His voice was husky and intimate, igniting a fire that could melt the snow from the mountaintops. Sarah swallowed hard. "You and me?" she repeated shakily.

Tanner gave in to the urge and let his fingers glide through the silky dark strands of hair and caress the warm ivory curve of her cheek. "You're beautiful," he said softly. He felt the leap of pulse against the hand that stroked her slender neck. "I find you utterly desirable," he whispered. When her head came up and her wide dark eyes stared at him like a startled doe's, he leaned forward and touched his lips briefly to hers. She tasted sweet, like the berries they'd had for supper.

She sat still, neither answering nor resisting his kiss. Tanner drew back and forced himself to what he knew he must say. "What's happening between us is not bad, Sarah. You mustn't be afraid."

"Who's afraid and of what?"

"I think you are. Funny, you can face a man with a gun without a quiver of fear."

"I wouldn't say that." She shrugged, but he felt resistance in the small, delicate hand he held.

"Yet you're trembling sitting here beside me." Tanner paused and took a deep breath, cursing himself for playing the gallant when all he wanted to do was crush her sweet, slender body beneath his. "What I'm trying to tell you is you needn't worry on my account."

"Oh?"

Was it his imagination or did she sound disappointed?

"Although we're alone here in the wilderness, I intend to be the soul of propriety."

"Oh." She was disappointed.

"You can rely on me to protect you at all times. You have nothing to worry about from me."

"Thank you, Major Tanner," Sarah said flatly.

"Well, better turn in." He steeled himself to turn away from her. Springing to his feet, he undid the bedrolls, taking care to keep hers well on the other side of the fire from his. "There you are," he said. "That log will keep you from rolling away down the mountainside and into the river."

"Thank you for your concern," Sarah said.

Tanner thought he detected an edge of irritation, but could think of no reason for it. He'd done everything he could to reassure her she was safe with him. "Well, good-night," he said and with a final nod took off his boots and slid into his bedroll.

"Good night, Major," Sarah said crisply. Her tone was as icy as the river water tumbling down from the mountain peaks.

Sarah sat on staring into the dying fire and thinking of all Tanner had said. With a branch she raked the dying coals, trying to bring them to life again but to no avail. Irrationally she was miffed at Tanner. So what if she had been acting as skittish as a colt? Every woman had a right to feel that way when confronted with spending the night with a man such as Lucas Tanner. Now she sat pouting, angry with herself for her earlier fear and at Tanner for being astute enough to sense it and honorable enough to accede to it.

"Damnation," Sarah muttered under her breath, taking particular comfort in the spoken and forbidden curse. Flinging down the branch, she readied herself for sleep. It was long in coming. Perversely she wished the same sleeplessness on Tanner, but his deep breathing told her he suffered from no such problem.

In the morning Sarah awoke with an abominable headache. Tanner ignored her grumpy mood and whistled cheerfully while he made breakfast. He maintained the same impersonal, helpful attitude throughout the day as they climbed mountain trails and descended into cool, shadowy valleys.

"The Indians call this the up and down land," Tanner told her during one of their breaks.

"Aptly named," Sarah said, her good humor somewhat restored. "How much farther is Wallowa Valley?"

"A day's travel," Tanner said, looking at his map. "I figure we're here at this fork."

"We don't seem to be that far away," Sarah said, leaning closer to study the map.

Tanner was silent for a moment, taking in the scent of her hair. She was so close he would barely have to move to touch her. Taking a deep, shaky breath, he pointed to the area they'd already covered. "It's taken us almost two days to come this far," he said. "Remember this is up and down country. The distances are greater than they may look on a map."

"I see," Sarah said thoughtfully and sat back. They'd be on the trail together for at least another night before reaching the Indian village and there were all those nights together returning to Fort Lapwai.

Tanner was thinking the same thing. Groaning at the self-control he must exercise, he went for a walk just to be away from Sarah for a while.

She watched him leave. He seemed to be limping. Thoughtfully she leaned back against the rocks. She'd given little regard to these nights alone with Tanner, deliberately pushing them from her mind, but some part of her had acknowledged the desire she felt for him. Now he seemed set on an old-fashioned code of honor toward a lady. She could, she realized, choose to accept this chivalry and return to Fort Lapwai as much a lady as when she started, or she could end this awkwardness between them and persuade him to make love to her. Which did she want?

Tanner had returned from his walk and was now tightening the cinches on their horses. Sarah watched the proud set of his head and shoulders, the way his big body moved with effortless strength and purpose. She knew very little about Lucas Tanner, yet she knew enough to trust him, enough to feel desire for him. The time to be a coy maiden was long past. She and Tanner had been through too much together. In a short, intense space of time she'd come to love him, but how did he feel about her? Sighing, she remounted and followed him along the trail.

They covered several miles before Tanner called a halt. Sarah was more than willing to stop. After two days of riding horseback her unused muscles were protesting.

"We'll set up camp here," Tanner said. "There's a creek nearby for bathing if you want, although the water will likely be cold."

"Even a cold bath sounds heavenly," Sarah said and helped unload the packmules. When firewood had been collected and camp set up, she gathered up clean undergarments and went off to find the inlet. The water was icy cold, making her gasp when she first dove in. Vigorously she swam from one side to the other in an attempt to warm up. A splash near the river made her look around anxiously. Where was Tanner? she wondered frantically, and then she saw him, his long powerful arms cutting a clean silver line through the cold water. Smiling, Sarah swam toward him.

"It seems we had the same thought," she called when she'd drawn closer. Tanner stopped swimming and looked around, shaking the water from his hair and eyes. The silvery drops flew around him, catching the gleam of the rising moon before falling back into the river.

"Don't come any closer," he called and Sarah paused, puzzled and a little hurt. Did he want nothing at all to do with her now? She ignored his warning and swam closer.

"Sarah, stay where you are," he ordered, a desperate note in his voice. Chivalry was costing him dearly. "I left my clothes on shore." Sarah halted and looked at him, laughter bubbling up.

"So did I," she said and slowly swam closer, her dark eyes gleaming obsidian in the moonlight.

"Sarah, don't come closer," Tanner said tightly and retreated downriver.

"All right," she relented. "If that's what you want." She put her arms around her shoulders and shivered.

"You're cold. You should get out. I have a fire going."

"I can't get out," Sarah said. "I left my clothes down along the creek."

"I'll fetch them for you. Turn around so I can get out."

Sarah smiled but did as he bade, keeping low in the water, for the air had turned chilly as well. She heard a splash as Tanner climbed out. "Can I turn around now?" she called gaily.

"No, not yet," Tanner growled. A muffled curse came to her and she could see him hopping on one foot. He must have stepped on a sharp rock, she thought, and couldn't help smiling at the boyish side of this rugged man. Soon she heard him move along the creek bank to the place where she'd left her clothes. Dreamily she waved her arms in the water, watching its black, moon-gilded swirls wash against her skin. Delicious shivers raced through her.

"You can come out now," Tanner called from the bank. "I'll put your clothes right here." He placed them on a nearby stump.

"Oh, don't go," Sarah pleaded. "It's so dark. I'll be frightened."

She was certain she saw him flinch. Finally he sighed. "I'll be standing right over there with my back turned," he said. Sarah looked around and, true to his word, Tanner's broad back was to her.

Slowly she waded out of the inlet. Ignoring the stack of dry clothes she went to stand in front of him. "You can open your eyes now," she said softly.

Tanner did as she bade, tight-lipped control changing to consternation at seeing her attire. She had bathed in her camisole and pantalettes. Mischievous lights sparkled in her dark eyes at the trick she had played him. "I thought you—you said you—" His words stammered to a halt as he gazed at her. She wasn't even aware of how incredibly beautiful she looked standing in the moonlight.

Her long black hair hung in sleek, wet strands around her shoulders. Rivulets of water ran from her hair to the moon-burnished curves revealed by the low, lace-trimmed bodice of her camisole. Tanner's eyes dipped to the dark shadows of her breasts. The wisp of wet cloth and lace couldn't hide the darker shadows of her nipples or the way the cold water had made them pucker into hard buds. Below the lace the thin cotton clung to the young curves of her waist and hips and the long, slender legs. Tanner swallowed hard.

"I'm cold, Tanner," she said softly. "Put your arms around me?" He groaned and, reaching out for her blindly, pulled her against him. His mouth, hard and urgent, descended to hers and Sarah sighed, giving herself up to the swirl of desire his kiss awakened. He couldn't seem to hold her tightly enough or taste enough of the sweetness of her mouth. Again and again his mouth crushed her full lips. His rough chin scraped the soft skin of her neck and she shivered.

"You're chilled," Tanner said and, swinging her up in his arms, carried her to the fire. Gently he laid her on the bedroll. His luminous gaze captured hers as he slowly undid the laces of her camisole and removed the clinging wet fabric from her chilled body. With a corner of the woolen blanket he dried her, rubbing her limbs to bring the blood to the surface. She felt the heat of the fire and of her desire. Tanner's gray eyes held a passion of their own as his ministrations turned to sensuous caresses.

Her skin was warm now, burning at his touch, yearning for it.

Tanner let his shirt slide off his shoulders into a heap on the ground. His pants slithered down the hard columns of his thighs, and unashamedly Sarah looked at his body. She'd never dreamed a man could be so magnificent. With every movement muscles rippled across his powerful shoulders and sinewy legs. A mat of curly hair swirled across his chest. He was a burnished, golden giant of a man. Tossing aside the last of his clothes, Tanner lowered himself to her. Sarah welcomed him with open arms, sweet, sensuous kisses, and soft breasts. Her slender legs wrapped around his, her young body yearned toward his.

He had meant to take his time, to savor every moment of this first mating between them, to slowly awaken Sarah to the beauty of love, but as always she surprised him. Without false modesty she followed eagerly where he led. Captive to a passion he'd never known before, Tanner scaled the mountain ridges and fell into swirling space on the other side. His joyous cry mingled with hers until at last they lay still, locked in each other's arms beside the dying campfire.

9

The Nez Percé lands were located on a high plateau between mountain ranges. Centuries before, its flatness had been carved into deep valleys by tumultuous young rivers. Low mountains, rolling hills, and even prairies lay under the protection of the Bitterroot Range, mountains so formidable that until Lewis and Clark, white men from the East were held at bay. Only two trails allowed passage over the mountains and those were undertaken only by the most hardy.

As they rode along, suddenly Tanner put out a hand, motioning Sarah to caution. Warily she looked around. She could see nothing, but she felt someone was watching them. From a dark stand of pines rode a young brave on a beautiful Appaloosa. He wasn't dressed like the Indians at the agency. His face was lean and brown and very attractive beneath the long, loose flowing hair. A single braid was worn on one side while feathers were anchored in a topknot of sorts. His breechcloth and leggings were of fringed deer hide. A sash was belted about his loose-fitting shirt, and he wore pendants and ear ornaments of shells and bones. A bow and quiver of arrows were worn over his shoulder, and a dagger was strapped at his waist. A carbine rifle was seated in a decorated buffalo-hide gun case that hung from his saddle. He carried a spear in one hand and his dark eyes were hostile as he stared at Tanner and Sarah.

"Greetings to the Nez Percé," Tanner said quietly. Sarah could see that although he assumed a pose of ease and friendliness, his gun hand was free and rested casually on his knee. It would take only one quick smooth movement to draw his pistol.

The Indian warrior made no acknowledgment of Tanner's greeting. His dark eyes glittered dangerously, and Sarah felt a chill of fear sweep over her. "Go back," he said, motioning angrily back up the trail.

"We have come to see Chief Joseph," Tanner replied. How fool-hardy for them to have come like this, Sarah thought. How did she know these were her grandmother's tribe and, if so, whether they would be friendly. She quelled her fear and urged her horse forward.

"Go back!" the brave said sternly.

"Wait," Sarah cried in the Nez Percé language her grandmother had taught her. "I wish to see Chief Joseph. I am Sarah MacKenzie, granddaughter of Swan Necklace, who was sister to Old Joseph—she called him Wellamotkin. I am a niece to Chief Joseph."

"Joseph has no niece of white blood," the young brave spoke in English, his tone arrogant. "Is this another trick of the white man to claim our lands?"

"I do not desire the Nimpau lands," Sarah answered quickly. "I wish only to see Chief Joseph and tell him of Swan Necklace's death."

"He does not wish to know of this," the brave said.

"Are you sure about that?" Tanner spoke up. "I'd hate to face Chief Joseph if I had turned away one of his family." His gray eyes were cold as they met the warrior's. Sarah saw a flare of anger in the Indian's dark eyes, and she feared he meant to strike at Tanner with his spear.

"Look!" she cried, pulling at the neck of her gown. "I've brought back my grandmother's spirit bag as she requested." Sarah held the beaded bag high so that the Indian could see it. He stared at it, as if weighing Tanner's words, and at last nodded.

"Follow me," he commanded and turned his horse along the riverbank. Other Indian braves similarly dressed fell in behind them.

"Good work," Tanner said under his breath.

"I couldn't have done it without you," Sarah whispered back. "I think you frightened him a little."

"I hope so. He frightened me a lot."

Sarah glanced back at Tanner, wondering if he had been teasing, but his face was somber. He had fought against the Sioux, she reminded herself, and if he was worried, they well might be in danger.

"Don't tell anyone I'm with the army," Tanner said quietly. Perplexed by his request, Sarah nodded her agreement. Silently she followed the tall Indian brave. They traveled for some distance beside the deep-banked river before the Indian brave halted, motioning them to wait. He rode ahead and, putting two fingers to his lips, made a high-pitched trill. The answer was clear and sharp on the pure mountain air. He waved Tanner and Sarah on.

She could tell they were approaching the village long before it came into view. She could hear sounds of women calling to their children and the quick staccato start of ponys as warriors left the village. Evening was drawing near and the smoke of campfires wafted on the air along with the smell of roasting venison.

Finally they caught sight of the riverine village nestled against a steep, pine-covered hill. Lodges, some of them nearly a hundred feet long and covered with reed and grass mats, sat peacefully on the riverbank. Smoke curled from several openings along the ridgepoles of the sloping roofs. Smaller conical huts sat off away from the main part of the village. Canoes and nets were pulled up on dry land, and racks of drying fish gave off a pungent, welcoming smell that spoke of plentiful food supplies and filled cache pits.

The villagers were bent over their evening chores and didn't at first notice the newcomers. No alarm had been raised by their guards, so they gave little heed to the riders entering the village. The Indian brave took them to the center of the square and spoke to an old man sitting in the doorway of one of the lodges. Quickly he rose and disappeared inside. Now the villagers put aside their work and gathered around in curiosity, their bright eyes studying Sarah and Tanner closely.

"What's going to happen now?" Sarah asked Tanner in a low voice.

"Sit tight. Don't look worried," he admonished. "They aren't going to harm us and won't like it if we show fear." Sarah smiled at the curious onlookers, but they made no response. Still, she sensed they weren't hostile. Silently she studied the women.

Like the Indian brave who had brought them to camp, the women were dressed in fringed buckskin decorated with bits of fur and brightly dyed quillwork. Their faces were painted and their hair caught back in neat braids at the back of their heads. Some of the women wore conical beaded hats. All wore strung beads and shells around their neck and at their ears. Hanging on a tripod nearby was a chubby brown baby securely laced into his cradleboard, its headboard painted an intricate design of red and blue.

Everything about the Nez Percé reflected a love of beauty and individuality.

No two women wore dresses alike. Although they were all made of elk or deer skin, the ornamentation was personal and meant to show identity. Their skin and clothes seemed clean and attractive, and the Nez Percé, men and women alike, held themselves with great dignity. The younger children, Sarah saw, wore no clothes at all, whereas the older ones were dressed much like their parents.

The old man returned and spoke to the brave guarding them. Finally they turned to Tanner and Sarah.

"Chief Joseph is not in camp now. You wait until he returns."

"All right," Tanner said and dismounted. Sarah did the same and looked around the village. The older children had crept closer. Sitting in the doorway so she might catch the dying rays of the sun was an old woman. Her brown face was wrinkled and wizened, but her eyes were still alert. The woman reminded Sarah of Swan Necklace, and she walked toward her.

"Do I know you, little one?" the old woman asked, and Sarah couldn't help a smile. Even stretched to her full height, the wizened little woman would be much shorter. Still, her age gave her great authority among her people, and Sarah nodded her head in acknowledgment of the elder's prestige.

"I am the granddaughter of Swan Necklace, who lived in your village long ago as a girl."

A look of wonder touched the old woman's face, and she started forward. "Swan Necklace?" she cried eagerly. "She has come back?"

Sarah hastened to correct her. "Swan Necklace died in the winter."

The old woman sat back, horror crossing her face. "It is not good to speak the name of those who have crossed into the spirit world. It will bring them back to haunt our village."

"I do not wish to bring such trouble to you. My grandmother would not wish it, but I feared no one here would remember her."

"I remember her well," the old woman said. "I am Running Brook. We played together as children."

"Running Brook." Sarah knelt in the dust. "She spoke of you often." She longed to embrace the old woman as she had her grandmother, but Tanner's caution held her back. "I've brought back her spirit bag as she asked so her spirit may rest freely in its new home."

Running Brook nodded thoughtfully. "Tell me something of her, what she said and did," she requested. Sarah, never realizing the old woman was testing her claim, happily related the things her grandmother had told her about the village and her childhood friend.

"She spoke of you with love and called you her sister," Sarah said, ending her narration.

Tears puddled in the creases around Running Brook's eyes. "Was she happy in the white man's world?"

Sarah nodded. "Sometimes, sometimes she wasn't. She longed to be back here in the mountains with her people, but she couldn't bear to leave her son or me. Swan—, must we never speak her name again? Will she be forgotten here as well?"

"It is the way of the Nimpau," the old woman said softly. "We do not want to call her from the afterworld. Her spirit must dwell there untroubled."

"Sarah," Tanner called, and she got to her feet. A group of men were entering the village. At the head of them rode a tall, powerfully built man with a rugged, handsome face and eloquent eyes. Riding his white Appaloosa to the center of the village, the Indian alighted and looked in her direction. Sarah had little doubt this was the Chief Joseph about whom she'd heard so much.

Little wonder Indians and white men alike held him in awe. His presence was commanding. Yet his demeanor was amiable and he carried himself with solemn dignity. His gaze was direct and proud. He was dressed much as the other braves. The fringed hides of his clothes had been bleached almost white by the sun. Dyed quillwork decorated the yoke of his shirt, and he wore several strands of beads around his neck. His long dark hair was pulled to one side away from his broad brow. He raised a hand and motioned her forward. The gesture wasn't arrogant, as it might have seemed from some other man, but was simply a gentle beckoning that she trustingly obeyed.

"Welcome to our village," Chief Joseph said when she stood before him. His voice was deep and caring, his words slow and thoughtful. Sarah sensed Tanner standing protectively behind her and wished she could reassure him.

"Thank you," she said to the tall chief. "I am Sarah MacKenzie, and this is my friend, Lucas Tanner."

"You are here to find someone?" Joseph asked. "We wish to help you."

"I have come to the land of the Nimpau to return the spirit bag of my grandmother who was the sister of your father," Sarah said, taking care not to speak the names of those who had died. Clearly she told the story of Swan Necklace and when at last she fell silent, the chief shook his head.

"I understand," he said. "You are my kinswoman."

"So she claims," the brave who had brought them to the village exclaimed. His eyes flashed with anger. "It is a trick to try to gain Nez Percé land."

"Perhaps, Black Beaver, perhaps," Chief Joseph said placatingly, "but what if she speaks the truth? Would you have me turn away one who is of the blood of my father? This is not the Nez Percé way."

"She speaks the truth," a wavery old voice called. Chief Joseph turned to Running Brook, seated in the doorway of her lodge.

"Kautsas has spoken strongly and without hesitation," he said tolerantly. "Is her eye that sure?"

"My eye is as keen as when I was a girl," Running Brook said proudly. "The girl speaks of many things only known to me and one other. She is your cousin, Joseph." Sarah's heart warmed to the old woman.

Chief Joseph smiled. "I rely upon the wisdom of Running Brook," he said. "You are welcome to our lodges."

"Thank you," Sarah replied.

"Joseph," the old woman called again. "Heed me. You must call the shaman to perform the rituals of the dead. The spirit of one I knew long ago will not rest until this is done."

"I will see it is done, Running Brook," Chief Joseph said with a nod of deference to the old woman. Sarah was touched by his consideration and respect for her. Turning back to Sarah, Joseph spoke again. "You will rest in the lodge with my wife and family," he invited. "We are honored that you have traveled so far to be with us."

Sarah glanced at Tanner. His expression was still watchful, but he nodded his acceptance. "The honor is ours, Chief Joseph."

"I will begin the burial preparations," Running

Brook said. Taking the spirit bag from Sarah, she rose and disappeared inside her lodge.

Sarah was intrigued by the living arrangements in the longhouses. Several families occupied one lodge, but each had his own campfire placed with his neighbors in a neat row down the middle.

Along each side were spread sleeping mats woven of reeds and grasses. Joseph took his guests to the far end, where a slim, pretty woman bent over the fire tending the baking of flat bread against hot stones. Fish roasted on sticks nearby.

"This is my wife, Yellow Bird." Joseph made the introductions. Sarah could hear the love and pride in his voice as he spoke her name.

The Indian woman rose and smiled at Sarah. Her features were finely drawn, her coppery skin smooth. Her dark hair was neatly parted in the middle and pulled into two braids on either side. There was a serenity to her expression that made Sarah feel at ease immediately. "Welcome to our lodge," she said warmly.

"My grandmother often spoke of the hospitality of the Nez Percé," Sarah replied. "I see she spoke the truth."

Yellow Bird smiled, pleased by her words. "The spirits have been generous to us this season," she said. "Many salmon traveled upriver. Our pots are full. When such bounty is given, it must be shared or the spirits will not be as generous next year."

A warrior nearly as tall as Joseph entered the lodge. There was a striking resemblance to the chief. Joseph turned to Tanner and Sarah. "This is my brother, Spotted Frog," he said.

Spotted Frog put out a hand and clasped Tanner's arm at the elbow, Indian fashion. "Welcome," he said. As with all the other Nez Percé she'd met so far, Sarah was impressed by the warrior's handsome appearance and the attention paid to his clothes and hair.

"Chief Joseph says you leave in a few days for Camas Meadows," Tanner said.

The warrior nodded. "Our ancestors have done so since they came to this valley."

"Do you move your whole tribe there?"

Chief Joseph nodded. "Only a few of the old people who can no longer travel remain in the village. We will take tipis for ourselves and stay many weeks."

"The camas root is an important food for our people," Yellow Bird explained. "Once it has been cooked and dried, it can be stored for many moons. It helps us through the winter months when the spirits are tired and cold and not as generous."

"How will you move all your women and children?" Tanner asked, and Sarah looked at him quizzically. Why had he developed this sudden interest in the Nez Percé?

"We have many horses," Spotted Frog said proudly. His shoulders were squared and high, his expression, if not friendly to Tanner, was at least not hostile.

"I've heard of the Nez Percé horses," Tanner said. "They have the reputation of being highly prized here in the Northwest."

"That is true," Joseph answered serenely. "Unlike the other Indian tribes we take care to breed our horses for the qualities that please us most such as swiftness, intelligence, and beauty. Tomorrow we will take you to see our herds."

"I'd like that," Tanner replied, and Sarah was keenly aware she had not been invited to join them.

After the evening meal, the storyteller gathered the children around the campfire in Joseph's lodge. Even their parents crowded around. The women sat back, visiting one another in these few hours before they must return to their own lodges and sleep. Sarah and Tanner sat side by side on the ground listening to the murmur of voices around them. Tanner seemed to have relaxed his vigilance somewhat. Perhaps he had realized what she'd known from the first moment Chief Joseph greeted them: the Nez Percé would not harm them. Content to be here at last among the people about whom she'd heard so much, Sarah sighed and laid her head against Tanner's shoulder.

Smiling down at her, he wrapped his arm around her. "Tired?" he asked.

Sleepily she nodded. "It's been a long journey." She curled against him much as she had in the mountains when they were fleeing the train robbers. The storyteller's voice droned on, telling another of the myths of the Coyote. They were meant to instruct the children in the customs and values of the tribe, Sarah realized, and remembered how Swan Necklace had taught her young granddaughter to value the earth and its people. Swan Necklace had also taught her the importance of bravery, fairness, and generosity toward others. She had despaired of teaching Sarah stoicism. Sarah's face was alive with every emotion she felt. Suddenly Sarah could feel the warm presence of her grandmother and, closing her eyes, she slept as innocently as a baby.

Tanner held Sarah long after the storyteller had ended his tales and the children had been put to bed on their sleeping mats. He looked at her sweet face, soft and unguarded in sleep, and remembered her beauty and passion the night before. He would guard her for all time, he thought fiercely, his heart swelling with a love he'd never known before.

A shadow moved near him and Yellow Bird knelt beside him. "She sleeps as a child," she said softly.

"It's been a long trip for her," Tanner said.

"She must be a woman of great determination and character to come such a distance," Yellow Bird observed.

Tanner laughed, remembering Sarah holding a wavering gun on one of the train robbers. "Great character," he said.

Yellow Bird saw the love on his face and smiled. "I have your sleeping mats prepared," she said. "Do you need some help in putting her on one?"

Tanner nodded and, moving slowly so as not to wake her, gathered Sarah up and carried her to the mats. She never stirred when he settled himself on the mat next to her, but sometime during the night, he wakened to find her snuggled against his chest. Chuckling, Tanner pulled her closer, wrapping his long arms around her slender body. How would he ever be able to spend another night any other way? he wondered before dozing off again.

10

Tanner was already up and outdoors by the time Sarah awoke the next morning. Yellow Bird waited by the fire, a wide smile on her face as she held out a wooden bowl filled with gruel made from the kouse root. With a horn spoon Sarah dipped out a small bite. It tasted like parsnips, which wasn't her favorite food, but not wanting to offend her hostess, she ate it anyway.

"I've waited to take my bath with you," Yellow Bird explained. "We can go down to the river, when you're ready."

Other women had gathered for their morning bath, and they greeted Sarah at first with shyness, then with increasing friendliness. They splashed in the water and talked sometimes in English and sometimes in the Nez Percé language. Sarah's accent often brought giggles from the other women, but she felt their humor was not meant as an affront.

"I will braid your hair if you wish," Yellow Bird offered, and Sarah nodded. When she had neatly parted Sarah's hair in the middle and woven the strands into braids, Yellow Bird fastened a bead and fur hairpiece below each ear. Leaning back on her heels, she considered her handiwork. Shock registered on her face.

"What is it?" Sarah asked.

Yellow Bird reached out a hand to touch Sarah's cheek, her gaze going from her own dark skin to Sarah's lighter color. "Except for the lightness of your skin, you look like one of us," she said thoughtfully.

"I am part Nez Percé," Sarah answered, and the enormity of what she'd said washed over her. She glanced around. All her life she'd known she was different than the other people around her, but she'd never realized how isolated she'd felt until this moment. She was among the Nimpau, who were her grandmother's people, but even more, they were her people. Tears started in Sarah's eyes.

"Why do you cry?" Yellow Bird asked, distressed at her tears. "I have offended you with my careless words."

"Oh no," Sarah cried, putting a hand on the other woman's arm. "I'm not offended. You've reminded me that the Nimpau are my people as well. I'm pleased by this thought."

Delighted with the new kinship they felt, Sarah and Yellow Bird dressed. Sarah watched as the other women painted their faces and removed unwanted body and face hair with bone tweezers. "Why do they do this?" she asked.

"It helps to protect us against the sun and the little mosquitoes that bite us. It also makes us attractive."

Sarah was intrigued by the women. They might be readying themselves for a ball or the theater back in Missouri. Actually Uncle Caleb's conservative congregation would no doubt have found the Nez Percé women shocking. "Where do they get their paints?"

"We make them," Yellow Bird said in surprise. Where else would a woman attain such necessities? "We use ocher, tallow, fish oil, and mud."

"Sounds lovely," Sarah said brightly and thought she would never put such a combination on her skin. When Yellow Bird had completed her preparations, they returned to the village. Tanner and Spotted Frog were standing on the riverbank. Sarah couldn't tear her gaze away from the tall, familiar figure. His hat was tossed onto a bush nearby as was his shirt. His hair was dark and sleek against his head, and his broad chest gleamed with droplets of water. He must have taken a swim as well, she thought, and remembered the night they'd bathed together and made love afterward. Even now the memory of their mating brought the blood to her cheeks.

"Tanner is a good man?" Yellow Bird asked. "You are happy?" Sarah nodded, blushing at her bright, knowing gaze. "Tanner is also a man who cares for his woman."

"I'm not really his woman," Sarah replied hesitantly.

"You are not? How is it that he shows such tenderness for you?" Yellow Bird asked in surprise.

"He is a good and gentle man," Sarah answered, "but he has made no vows to me."

"Sometimes a man makes a vow without words," Yellow Bird said wisely. "I think this is the case with your Tanner." Sarah looked at the tall man at the river's edge. He turned and, catching a glimpse of her, waved. She waved back, then followed Yellow Bird to the longhouse. It would be unseemly of them to tarry where the men were bathing.

Before they left to find the herds, Tanner took Sarah to one side. "Are you sure you'll be all right?" he asked doubtfully.

"These are my grandmother's people. They won't harm me," she whispered and grinned to show she wasn't worried. Reluctantly he left her, looking back several times before riding away.

"Come with me," Yellow Bird said and led Sarah through the village, stopping at other lodges to introduce her to other women. Except for White Feather, Spotted Frog's wife, the names soon became a jumble to Sarah. The women paused only a moment to greet her, then returned to their chores of preparing food for the evening meal. They talked as they worked, their lilting voices floating on the morning air. Fascinated, Sarah watched their quick, capable hands at their tasks. With stone mortars and wooden pestles they ground seeds or a dried white-meated bulb.

"This is kouse," Yellow Bird explained. "It is the first root we dig in Ah-Pah-Ahl, what the white people call May. We make a bread with the ground root which we call ahpah."

"My grandmother told me of these roots and of the camas which you'll soon gather."

"You know much of our ways."

Sarah wandered from one group of women to another, stopping to chat with the few words of Nez Percé her grandmother had taught her and to kiss the fat brown cheek of a baby in his cradleboard. The Nez Percé she saw were loving but firm parents. She stopped to hear an old grandmother instructing a young girl in the skills of tanning a fresh deer hide, and was reminded of Swan Necklace patiently teaching her granddaughter. How much her grandmother had given her.

Yellow Bird was an excellent guide, explaining the functions of all the huts that sat out away from the village and in so doing revealing more of the Nez Percé customs. Children, Sarah learned, were seldom disciplined until they were older, and even then the punishments were meted out by a specially appointed community whipper. After the age of nine, young boys were expected to go off alone and seek a vision, a spirit who would guide and protect them the rest of their lives. Yellow Bird showed Sarah the shaman's lodge and the sweat hut where the men could renew themselves and the isolation hut used by women as they underwent their monthly cycle. Sarah saw the hot baths that the Indians used in the winter when the river water was too cold to be comfortable. A small, oblong pond had been cut into the riverbank, and heated stones were dropped into the water to warm it.

When they had completed their tour of the village, Sarah looked about, realizing she hadn't seen Running Brook yet.

"She grieves and prepares for the burial of the one she knew long ago," Yellow Bird replied. "Tonight the shaman will perform the rituals to send the spirit of the dead one to the afterworld, where she can dwell in peace."

"May I help?" Sarah asked.

"I think Running Brook would like that," Yellow Bird said and escorted Sarah to the old woman's lodge.

Running Brook accepted Sarah's offer of help as if it were the proper way. Side by side the two women made their preparations for the dead, and when all was as it should be, Sarah walked alone beside the river, remembering the happy years with Swan Necklace. There was a special joy in being here in the beautiful land of Swan Necklace's ancestors. The narrow green valley gave way to the implacable slopes of the mountains which rose to meet a sky that was high and cloudless. Swan Necklace must once have walked here, Sarah thought and held her arms wide as if to embrace the whole world.

She'd wandered farther than she realized. The tall, dark pines closed around her, and she might have feared becoming lost if not for the companionable gurgle of the swift-flowing water. She could always follow the river back to the village. She didn't see the men until she was almost upon them.

"I told you she was Indian," one of the men shouted gleefully. Sarah halted in her footsteps and studied them carefully. The three of them were shabbily dressed, bewhiskered, and dirty-looking. Behind them Appaloosa horses had been trapped in a makeshift corral made of ropes strung to trees. The man who'd spoken grinned with broken, yellowed teeth.

"We'll have to kill her," a long-haired man said. "She'll just go back to the village and tell them we're up here. We'll have the whole village down on our heads before we can get these horses out of the valley."

"Reckon you're right," the broken-toothed man said. His friend drew his gun, but before he could aim, Sarah spun and ran back along the riverbank.

"Don't let her git away," one of the men yelled. "She'll warn the others."

Sarah could hear their boots pounding after her. A rough hand clasped her shoulder, spinning her around. Where was Tanner? she thought in terror. She should scream. The village couldn't be that far. Surely they would hear her and come, but she was too winded from her flight and her struggles with her captor. With a mighty effort she wrenched herself free, but the path back to the village was cut off. The mountain was at her back. Sarah scrambled up the steep slope.

"Git her," the men shouted and came after her. Her breath caught in her throat. Her chest ached. Her legs trembled beneath her. Still she pushed on concentrating only on making the next step. Her boots dislodged stones and they rolled back on her pursuers. She heard them curse, but didn't look back. Suddenly an iron grip closed around her ankle and she was jerked backward. She went sliding down the mountain in a shower of rocks that cut her hands and arms. When the slide stopped, she lay stunned and bleeding. The three men stood over her, one of them with his gun drawn. Sarah's eyes rolled in fear as he pulled back the hammer and aimed.

"Wait a minute, here," the broken-toothed man said. "If we shoot her, they'll hear it back in the village."

The man with the gun relaxed. "What'll we do?" he asked. The long-haired man picked up a large rock and approached her. "We'll just bash her head in," he said.

"Good idea, Matt." His friends nodded their heads approvingly. Sarah whimpered and tried to roll away from him, but he knelt and caught hold of her shoulder, raising the rock high above her head.

"No!" Sarah screamed.

An Indian cry high and shrill echoed through the valley. Startled, the men looked around. The cry came again from a different direction. The man holding Sarah dropped the rock and leaped to his feet.

"Jesus, they got us surrounded," the broken-toothed man said. "Let's get out of here." All three men ran for their mounts. Horses thundered down the mountain slope, snorting and neighing shrilly. Above the sounds of stampede that high-pitched cry sparked fear in all who heard it. Without looking back, the men urged their horses to a reckless, headlong gallop toward the other end of the valley. The stampeding horses swept past Sarah, then slowed and stopped. A single Indian brave rode out of their midst, a smile lighting his handsome features.

"Black Beaver!" Sarah exclaimed, getting to her feet but wincing when she tried to walk.

"You are hurt," Black Beaver said and swung out of his saddle.

"My ankle," Sarah replied. "I don't think it's broken."

"Let me see." Tenderly Black Beaver examined the ankle, then the bleeding scrapes on her arms and legs. "I will take you to Yellow Bird," he said finally. "She will tend your wounds." Effortlessly he gathered her in his arms and carried her to his horse. Then he sprang up behind her and, cradling her between his powerful arms, gathered the reins and turned his horse back toward the village.

That was the way Tanner first saw them together, Sarah nestled against Black Beaver's chest, her head thrown back as she laughed with him. He had returned from seeing the herds with Spotted Frog only to learn that Sarah was with Running Brook. Out of respect for her privacy he'd refrained from going to the old woman's lodge. Now it was clear such consideration was unnecessary. Sarah had been out riding with Black Beaver! Jealousy, hot and unfamiliar, washed through him. Even as he watched, the Indian warrior slid off his horse and reached up to pull Sarah into his arms.

Fists balled, long legs churning, Tanner reached Black Beaver and swung him around. "Get your hands off her, you ba—" He halted as he caught sight of Sarah's battered, bleeding face. "What did you do to her? What's happened?"

"It's all right," Sarah said almost gaily. "Black Beaver's rescued me."

The warrior's dark eyes flashed with sudden knowledge. "White men tried to kill her," he said stiffly.

"They were trying to stop me from warning the village about their stealing Nez Percé horses." Sarah's bright eyes swung back to Black Beaver. "He scared them into thinking they were surrounded and they took off. Lucky for me, he was nearby."

"Thank you," Tanner said gratefully. Though jealousy still plagued him, it meant little in the face of Sarah's safety. Still he stepped forward and held out his arms. "I'll take her now." Black Beaver passed her over.

"Thank you again," Sarah said sincerely. Before she could add more, Tanner turned toward the lodge. Subdued by his grim face, Sarah was silent as he settled her on the pallet so Yellow Bird could tend her scrapes.

While Sarah rested from her ordeal, Tanner made his way to the riverbanks. He'd heard the whole story and felt somewhat mollified, but the memory of Sarah in another man's arms still rankled. Restlessly he watched young men balancing on platforms of rock and wood anchored out over the water so they could spear the blueback salmon. Weirs of wood and rope had been built to trap the fish. Large dip nets, harpoons, seines, gaffs, and hooks and lines all lay to one side. The men flung the large fish onshore. The women ran forward to strike them a blow and cut the red meat into fillets that they hung to dry over their racks.

"This is not very much salmon," Tanner said to Spotted Frog. "There's not enough to last your people through the winter."

"Later," Spotted Frog said, "after the camas gathering during Ta-yum, the time of midsummer heat, the Chinook will migrate to the headwaters of the rivers to bear their young. The spirits allow us much bounty then."

"We have many sources for food, but each comes to us in its own season," Joseph explained. "In the spring and summer our women gather the bulbs, and wild onions and carrots from the hills. There are also berries of all sorts. We gather the fish from the rivers and game from the mountains. We have managed enough to survive all these years."

"In the spring we cross over the Lolo Pass to hunt buffalo in Montana," Spotted Frog said. He seemed to be warming to the white man and Tanner, in turn, felt a growing respect for the warrior who was not only Chief Joseph's brother but one of the sub-chiefs of the band.

"That pass crosses the Bitterroot Mountain range, doesn't it?" Tanner asked and saw suspicion flash through Spotted Frog's eyes. "I've heard others speak of this pass. It was used by Lewis and Clark."

"That is true," Spotted Frog said, and the mistrust faded somewhat from his glance. He was a fearless man, Tanner guessed, less given to introspection than Joseph and slower to accept any white man as friend. Yet he was capable of great loyalty for his brother and his people. He was the kind of man Tanner would have been happy to fight beside, but he knew time and circumstances would more likely pit them against each other.

"But even with the bounty of the mother earth, sometimes hunger sits at the doors of our lodges," Joseph admitted. "When this happens we must forage for anything that will sustain life, the inner bark of the pine tree, even the moss on the dark side of the hills."

"Our people have survived here for many generations," Spotted Frog spoke up proudly. "We will continue to do so, despite what the white man wishes of us." These last words were issued almost as a challenge. Tanner's gaze was unwavering as he met the warrior's. Finally Spotted Frog rose and walked toward the lodges.

"Do not mind Spotted Frog," Joseph said in his gentle manner. "He does not trust the white man, and for good reason, but you are welcome to our lodges."

"Thank you," Tanner said. Thoughtfully he followed the stiff, proud figures of the Indian brothers. All day he had felt the resentment simmering beneath the surface with Spotted Frog and some of the other men. Only Joseph seemed to truly welcome them here in his village.

Sarah had awakened and was preparing for the funeral rites for Swan Necklace. If not for her gown, Tanner wouldn't have recognized her. Lines of paint had been daubed around her eyes and along her cheeks and chin. Only the flare of light in the dark eyes when she saw him dispelled the shudder of fear that coursed through him, fear that this was a Sarah he didn't know and couldn't hold after all. She seemed sad, unlike her normally ebullient self. Pushing aside his concern, he grinned lazily at her getup.

"Oh, Tanner, I am so happy to be here," she said, placing a hand on his sleeve. "Thank you for bringing me to the village of my people."

Her words startled him. "Whoa," he said, gripping her shoulders. "Don't lose your way here, Sarah. The Nez Percé are Swan Necklace's people, not yours."

"It's the same thing, isn't it?" she asked innocently. "I helped Running Brook prepare for the burial of my grandmother. Many of these things Swan Necklace told me, but at last I am here in her village and I'm part of the rituals. Do you know what a comfort that is to me?" Her face was earnest as she looked at him. Tanner wanted to crush her in his arms and carry her away from here, but she rushed on: "I never quite belonged to that world back in Missouri. People knew about Swan Necklace and although they professed Christianity, they condemned her for her Indian blood. My uncle felt that prejudice, too, and he spent his whole life trying to overcome it, pretending he was white. Swan Necklace taught me never to pretend."

"Sarah, don't condemn them too harshly," Tanner admonished. "Swan Necklace was someone they couldn't understand; she was from a world totally alien to anything they'd been taught."

"But what of the people here?" Sarah asked. "Will they be any different?"

"Give them a chance and find out. Do you think it matters to me? You're Sarah MacKenzie, the woman I love."

His words caught her unexpectedly, and she fell still under his grasp while waves of joy washed over her. "You love me?" she asked breathlessly.

"I love you, Sarah," Tanner repeated wonderingly.

Sarah stepped into his embrace, her own arms circling his hard, narrow waist, her head resting on his broad chest. "I love you, too, Tanner," she whispered and felt a prickle of tears behind her eyelids.

The Nez Percé women and children cast sheepish, smiling glances at them, then quickly looked away, respecting their privacy. Although loving people among themselves, they weren't used to this open display between a man and woman. Such demonstrations were reserved for the privacy of their sleeping mats in the darkness of their lodge.

Suddenly aware of the Indians moving around them, Sarah placed her cheek against Tanner's in a final, quick hug. Stepping away, she glanced up at him and burst into laughter.

"What is it?" he asked, feeling lighthearted as well. Sarah could always make him feel better.

"Now you're Nez Percé too," she answered sassily. She swiped across his cheek and held out a paint-smeared finger for him to see.

"Do the Nez Percé men beat their women for impudence?" Tanner inquired, grinning as he scrubbed his cheek.

"I don't think so," Sarah answered lightly. "They treat them with respect and love. They protect them and cherish them." Her laughter was gone and she spoke the words softly.

"Then I must be a Nez Percé," Tanner answered. "You can always count on those things from me." His expression was intent and loving. A large brown hand came up to touch one sleek braid.

"It is time for the burial ceremony to begin," Yellow Bird said, embarrassed to interrupt the two lovers.

"Thank you," Sarah said, glancing up at Tanner. Did he understand the importance of these rituals? she wondered. She'd sensed his resistance when he first saw her braided hair and painted face. Her small hand stole into his to placate his doubts.

The burial rituals had begun long before this final ceremony. Running Brook had made a doll of grass and clay. She and Sarah had spent the afternoon painting the clay face and dressing the doll in an old but still beautiful buckskin dress Running Brook had worn as a girl. Last, Swan Necklace's spirit bag had been placed around the clay figure and their preparations had been completed.

Now men came to carry the bundle up the steep hillside to a prepared grave in a secluded place. The villagers followed behind, their voices raised in a wailing death chant. Tears coursed down Sarah's cheek, and instinctively she raised her voice in the keening song she'd sung once before back in Missouri. Then it had been a song of sorrow; now it was one of hope and entreaty for the departing spirit. The shaman was there with his medicine stick with a swan's head on one end and his bundle of special herbs tied at the other. Solemnly he performed the elaborate ceremony that would free the soul of Swan Necklace. When the prayers were finished, everyone filed back to the village. Sarah was exhausted. The other villagers seemed subdued as well.

From the middle of the village went up a cry, and the men and women looked up with a quickening interest.

"People, lay everything aside," the village herald announced, "for we are going to have a feast. Get out your finest clothes and put them on and make ready for the celebration. People, we shall see the garments of our dead men of long ago, so everyone must come." Joyously the people called out in response.

"The spirit of your grandmother rests in the afterworld," Yellow Bird said with a gentle smile. "Now we must celebrate life. Our cache pits are full again. Joseph has called for a special celebration tonight. We call it *ka-oo-yit*. It is a special thanksgiving to the Creator and to the fish for returning and giving themselves to the people as food. It is our hope the fish will be pleased and will return again next year."

"What a lovely custom," Sarah exclaimed.

"It is also an important night for you, little sister. Come with me and we'll prepare for the feast."

Sarah followed her back to the lodge. "I have a gift for you," Yellow Bird said, laying out a handsome fringed and beaded garment of elk hide.

"It's beautiful," Sarah cried. The hide had been so carefully prepared that it felt velvety soft and supple beneath her fingers.

Yellow Bird also laid out a pair of knee-high moccasins. Their tops were completely covered with an intricately beaded pattern of flowers and vines.

"They must have taken hours to make," Sarah cried, gently fingering the bead work.

Yellow Bird nodded. "That is why I wish to give them to my new sister. I have drawn pleasure in making them, and you shall have pleasure in wearing them."

"I can't imagine wearing anything so beautiful," Sarah said, running her fingers over the moccasins and dress. Yet she knew she must or she would give offense.

Sunflower, one of the women Sarah had met earlier in the day, entered the lodge. She wore her special ceremonial clothes as well and carried a small bundle in her hands. "I have brought you a present," she said and held out the bundle.

Bewildered, Sarah glanced at Yellow Bird, then back at Sunflower. "Why do you bring me a gift?"

"It is a special day for you," Yellow Bird answered, "and it is the custom of the Nimpau to do this. You must take the gift."

Sarah took the bundle from the girl and unwrapped it, gasping with delight when she saw a beautiful beaded pouch with a zigzag design in red and blue. "I'm honored you've given me such a gift. I'll wear it with pride and remembrance of the friendship you've shown me," she said.

Other women came, bringing Sarah an additional piece of clothing, one of the conical hats, an intricately worked sash, a string of beads and shells, a brightly patterned apron. Yellow Bird helped Sarah into her new finery and stood back to look her over.

"You look like a Nez Percé," she said with a nod of approval. Sarah couldn't help wondering how Tanner would view her new attire.

Chief Joseph had called for the celebration, but the shaman presided over the thanksgiving rituals. Special dances were performed, led by a dancer with a wand made of eagle feathers, horsehair, beadwork, and buckskin. Woven-grass gathering baskets laden with food were placed at one end of the village square. Everyone would eat and drink their fill and dance until they fell to the ground in exhaustion.

Sarah made her way around the throng of people to Tanner's side. He stood, smiling and relaxed, watching the dances, succumbing to the festive mood of the village. He glanced at Sarah, then looked away. There had been no light of recognition in his eyes.

Sarah stepped forward, laughter bubbling through her as she touched his arm. "Don't you know me?" she asked.

Tanner jumped and turned around, his disbelieving gaze going over her from head to foot and back again. She saw the disbelief turn to anger. His lips tightened and then the anger was gone, replaced by a smile that was stiff and forced.

Sarah stared at him. "Tanner?" she said tentatively.

"You look beautiful," he said, but his eyes couldn't meet hers, and she couldn't forget that moment of anger he'd so quickly masked.

"Tanner, what's wrong?" she whispered.

He shook his head and shrugged. "Nothing, Sarah," he said tersely. "You just caught me by surprise."

Troubled, she studied his face. Was it just surprise she'd seen? she wondered. Tanner turned back to watch the dancers, and she sensed the disapproval in his stiff figure. Anger and disappointment swept through her. Was he unwilling to accept the Indian blood in her? He'd claimed he did, but now she felt his rejection. The light from the torches was blocked and a tall, bronzed-skin man stepped forward.

"Come. You will dance?" Black Beaver stood before them.

Sarah shook her head and backed away. "No, thank you. I can't," she said, but the Indian warrior stood with his hand outstretched.

"You do not celebrate with us?" he asked, and Sarah remembered how he'd rescued her in the afternoon and the new friendship that had begun at that time.

"Yes, of course," she said, sending Tanner a quick glance. Perversely he ignored her appeal. Resentment stiffened Sarah's resolve. Taking the warrior's hand, she smiled and moved forward to join the line of dancers around the campfire, her feet automatically following the rhythm of the drums in a dance her grandmother had taught her once long ago. She saw Tanner draw back, saw the thin line of anger around his mouth. It serves him right, she thought rebelliously. He must come to terms with her Indian background and if he could not— She left the thought unfinished, not wanting to think of a life without Tanner. Was it only a few hours ago that he had declared his love for her?

It seemed to Sarah the drums went on interminably. Her head was pounding. Black Beaver seemed

to be always at her side. Tanner had disappeared.
Just when she'd decided she would go back to the
lodge, a crier stepped forward and called the people
to attention. An expectant hush fell over the crowd
as Chief Joseph stepped into the torch light. He also
wore his finest clothes for the celebration. Around
his neck was a necklace of grizzly bear claws, and
over his right shoulder was thrown a sash made of
otter skin. Strips of ermine and six round mirrors
were sewn around it. The villagers fell silent, pleased
by their leader's appearance. Joseph held up his
hand and spoke.

"Tonight the Great Spirit has accepted the spirit of
one who lived with us long ago, and in her place he
has sent our little sister from the east. She has come
among us with love and friendship, and she is worthy of a Nimpau name." He paused, waiting for the
interest to build. Yellow Bird gently pushed Sarah
forward, and Joseph motioned her to him. Slowly
she walked the distance to the end of the dancing
ground and came to a halt a few feet from Joseph.
He smiled at her kindly and again spoke.

"We will call you Swan Necklace," he said gently,
"in honor of the old one we once knew."

Sarah gasped, immeasurably touched by his words.
It seemed as if her grandmother were not dead after
all. "Thank you, Chief Joseph," she said softly.

"You are Nez Percé," Joseph said, "and as such
you have a home among us for all time." He raised
his arms to embrace all his people. His strong, mel-
low voice rang out in the night air. In the flickering,
smoky light of the campfires, his people stirred and
were still again, soothed and reassured by their char-
ismatic leader and the power of his words. "Perhaps
the white man will see this blending of two bloods
and know that he and the Indian can live in peace.

All men were made by the Great Spirit Chief. We are all brothers and sisters. Let us live in harmony with one another and with our mother earth." Listening to Joseph speak, she understood why he'd gained such stature with John Monteith and Captain Perry. He paused and looked back at Sarah. "Welcome home, Swan Necklace," he said warmly. Unexpected tears ran down her cheeks.

Joseph stepped forward and gripped her hand, and Yellow Bird wrapped her arms around Sarah in a quick hug. Now other Indians surged forward to greet her and welcome her to the tribe. Then a dancer held up his wand and the drums started again. Everyone shuffled back onto the dancing ground, their bodies moving in rhythmic cadence with the chanted song.

Black Beaver was there, leading her out onto the square with the other dancers. Sarah looked around for Tanner, but could not catch a glimpse of him among the weaving figures. She danced for a long time until her legs ached with fatigue. Other couples had broken away from the dance and disappeared into the privacy of their lodges or along the moon-washed shores of the river. Sarah thought of Tanner and pushed her way through the villagers until she caught a glimpse of him standing off to one side. He looked lonely and isolated, and her conscience pricked at her. She'd been so caught up in the events of the evening she hadn't stayed by his side or made him feel a part of the ceremony. Now she walked forward and put an arm on his sleeve. Tanner turned to look at her and she smiled appealingly. There was no answering smile in his eyes. Her heart sank. After Joseph's words she'd hoped he would understand better.

Suddenly Tanner swept her into his arms. "Sarah,"

he whispered harshly. His hungry mouth descended to hers in demanding kisses that left her breathless with desire.

"Oh, Tanner, I was so afraid," she murmured.

"Afraid of what?" he asked between kisses. His strong arms lifted her, molding her soft flesh and delicate bones against his body.

"Nothing," she sighed helplessly. "I'm never afraid when you are here."

Tanner slipped his arm under her knees and effortlessly carried her along the bank to a secluded spot he'd found that afternoon. The throb of the drum matched the heavy, passionate beat of his pulse, and he concentrated on it, trying to erase the words she'd spoken. He knew her fear, for he was afraid too. Afraid that he'd already lost her.

11

"I'll come back again," Sarah said two days later as she stood in front of Joseph's lodge. Tanner waited nearby with their horses. The beautiful gifts the villagers had given Sarah were carefully wrapped in a leather parfleche and tied behind her saddle. Her time among the Nez Percé had come to an end for now. She sensed that Tanner was anxious to be gone and knew his uneasiness was not born out of fear of the Indians themselves, but out of concern for her. She felt no such disquiet. She'd been happy here in Chief Joseph's village, feeling as if she finally belonged somewhere for the first time in her life.

"I will miss my new sister," Yellow Bird said, a sad smile lighting her face.

"I'll miss all of you as well," Sarah cried, giving her a fierce hug. "You've made me feel at home here."

"That was our intention," Joseph said. "This is your home now, Swan Necklace." Sarah smiled at his use of her Indian name.

Tanner stepped forward and held out his hand. "My thanks also to Chief Joseph and Spotted Frog for their hospitality."

"Tanner is a good man," Joseph said. "He watches and he listens to what the Indian says. I do not think you mean us harm."

"No, I come and go in peace," Tanner said. "I've learned much in your village these few days."

"Perhaps you will carry this knowledge to the white man so he might come to understand my brothers and sisters and we can have peace here in the valley," Joseph said, his keen eyes watching Tanner closely. "We have no wish to be at war with our white brothers, yet we cannot live on the reservation as he wishes us to."

"I will tell my white chief," Tanner promised.

Joseph nodded and held out a hand to clasp Tanner's elbow. "This is good." He turned as a noise broke out at the other end of the village. A shrill, wailing death chant sounded as three horsemen rode forward. One of them was Black Beaver. They led a horse that at first appeared riderless until Sarah discerned the body of a man draped belly down over the saddle, his hands hanging limp and lifeless. The death wail increased in volume as more of the women caught sight of the dead Indian.

"Little Wolf, Black Beaver, what is it? Where is Eagle Robe?" Joseph asked, his expression heavy and fearful. The Indian braves paused and Little Wolf held out the reins to the dead Indian's horse.

"My father is dead," he shouted. "Shot by a white man under a guise of friendship."

Tanner dropped his reins and hurried forward to check the pulse of the dead warrior. His mouth was grim as he noted the bullet holes in the man's back. Shaking his head, he walked away, concerned now for Sarah and her safety should the hotheaded young braves wish to retaliate.

"Who has done this thing?" Joseph demanded.

"A man named McNall," Little Wolf declared angrily.

"How did it happen, son?" Tanner asked quietly.

Little Wolf glared at him, then looked at Joseph questioningly. At a nod from the chief the young brave reluctantly answered, "We were hunting, Red Fox, Black Beaver, and us. We had made camp for the night, and the next morning two men rode into camp and accused us of stealing their horses. We told them we had not taken them, but they wouldn't believe us. We were unarmed. Our rifles were on the ground nearby, but the white men were between us. McNall fought with my father and called to his man to shoot and he did." Little Wolf paused, his fists clenched, his teeth clamped together in grief over his dead father.

"Even dying," he said bitterly, "my father ordered me not to avenge his death."

"It is best you heed his wishes," Joseph said.

"My father's death cannot go unavenged," Little Wolf shouted.

"We will go to the white man and ask that he punish these men who have killed the Nez Percé," Joseph assured him.

"They will do nothing," Little Wolf said dully. "There is no justice for the Indian under the white man's law."

"I will see these men are brought to trial," Tanner said. "I give you my word."

"The word of the white man is as nothing," Black Beaver said. His expression was filled with hatred as he glared at Tanner. "You come to sell us whiskey, and take our gold and our women." His dark eyes swung back to Sarah. The friendly young man she'd come to know was gone. Suddenly she felt afraid of this hostile warrior.

"We've come in peace," Tanner said. "We've brought no harm to you and your people. Now we will return to the fort and see that these murderers are brought to trial."

"We will not wait for white man's justice," Black Beaver snapped. "It is time we avenge the wrongs committed against the Nez Percé." Other warriors raised their voices in support of Black Beaver's words. Spotted Frog had joined them and stood now beside Joseph.

"And bring war down on your heads?" Tanner asked.

"It is not the Indians who make this war. It is the white men who come into our valleys and murder our people," Little Wolf challenged.

"Tanner is right," Joseph said. "It would be unwise of us to seek revenge for one death if it brings about the death of many. We must try to live by the white man's law."

"And no longer be Indian?" Black Beaver jeered.

"If we are dead, we are no longer Indian," Joseph said sadly. "You are warriors, young and strong, and you think only of revenge, but I think of the women and children who will suffer if we go to war. We must be patient and give the white man time to find justice for us."

"I say we fight now and avenge our fallen brothers," Black Beaver shouted. "What do you say, Spotted Frog? You are our war chief." All eyes turned to the tall Indian standing beside Joseph.

"I say we listen to Joseph," he answered somberly. "He cares for the welfare of all our people. I say we wait for the white man's justice."

Tanner nodded. "I'll report back to the fort immediately," he said and helped Sarah into her saddle.

Chief Joseph took a step forward. "Tanner," he called. "You will travel through the Wallowa Valley without harm." Sarah knew the words had been a warning to his angry warriors who might seek revenge on them.

Tanner gave a small salute. "We are grateful for your care," he said. "I will tell the white chief of your friendship." Reining his horse, he headed out of the village. Sarah followed behind, looking over her shoulder to wave at Yellow Bird. There were no cheerful waves of farewell now. The village was somber, grieving that one of them had fallen. Sarah thought of Swan Necklace's grave high on a hill in a secluded place. Now the father of Little Wolf would be buried somewhere there too. Sarah felt sad for the young warrior.

Tanner felt uneasy. He set a swift pace, knowing that Sarah was tiring rapidly yet wanting to put as much distance between them and Joseph's angry braves as he could. When they made a camp for the night, Tanner led them high up the mountainside away from the river. There was no fire. They ate dried fish and the little *ah-pah* cakes Yellow Bird had given them. Before the sun had tinged the rim of the mountain with color, they were up and moving. They had taken three days to reach the Wallowa Valley. By riding hard they returned to the fort in two days.

"Will there be trouble?" Sarah asked when he left her on the porch at the agency. He could see the worry in her eyes.

"I hope not. I'm going to do everything I can to see Wells McNall is brought to trial for this. We can't expect the Indians to quietly accept this kind of persecution from the whites. It isn't fair. No wonder they mistrust our laws."

"Thank you for caring about my people," Sarah said softly and wound her soft arms around his neck. Tanner caught her to him, burying his face in her glossy dark hair.

"I love you, Sarah," he whispered huskily and

was gone. His horses galloped away toward the fort. Sighing, Sarah entered the log cabin.

"I heard you return," Frances Monteith said, "but I didn't want to interrupt you and Major Tanner." Sarah smiled at the other woman's thoughtfulness. In many ways Frances Monteith and Yellow Bird were alike, but she couldn't tell Frances that. She would be mortally offended.

The men came to greet her. "Did you talk to Chief Joseph?" John asked.

"Give her a chance to get her breath and eat a little," Frances admonished and bustled around the kitchen pouring coffee and setting out a plate of little cakes. Gratefully Sarah sank into a chair.

"Was your trip all you'd hoped it would be?" Charles asked. "Did Chief Joseph agree to more schools?"

Wearily Sarah shook her head. "I had no time to talk to him about it," she admitted, "and now our cause is hurt even more. Two white men killed an Indian while we were there. The young warriors want to go to war over it, but Joseph and Spotted Frog wouldn't agree. I'm very worried about what would happen to them if they went to war. There are so few of them."

"There are so few of them." Tanner was repeating Sarah's words to Captain Perry less than an hour later. "The Nez Percé wouldn't stand a chance if they went to war. I think Chief Joseph realizes this."

"Can he control his young hot bloods?" Captain Perry asked. He had been charged with making a report to General Oliver Howard, his commanding officer.

"If McNall and his man are brought to trial," Tanner answered, "Joseph can hold the warriors in check for a while. He carries considerable influence with his people. He seems a peaceful man by nature, unlike his brother, Spotted Frog. Still, Spotted Frog will do as Joseph wishes. He's intensely loyal to Joseph."

"What kind of weaponry did the Nez Percé have?" Captain Perry asked. Tanner took some time reporting on the strength of Joseph's camp, the number of braves, number of herds, and the kinds of weapons. "He had less than a hundred braves, as far as I could tell," Tanner finished.

"Well done, Major," Perry said, getting to his feet. "I'll let you get some rest. General Howard is due here next week. I'd like you to go with me to Lewiston to meet him. I'm sure he'll have questions to ask you."

Tanner nodded. "All right, Captain," he said, getting to his feet. His rangy body sagged with weariness. He sketched a short salute and turned toward the door.

"Oh, Major Tanner," Perry said almost as an afterthought. In reality he'd saved this news for the end because he hated to tell it. "I'm afraid I've had some bad news about your previous unit."

"What's that, sir?" Tanner asked puzzled. His mind was still on Black Beaver and Little Wolf.

"Colonel Custer and the Seventh Cavalry were wiped out at some place called the Little Big Horn. There were no survivors."

Tanner felt the blood leave his face as an awful desolation settled over him. "What about Crazy Horse?" he asked dully. "Did they get him?"

Captain Perry shook his head slowly. "He got away and took his people into Canada. We can't touch him now. That's why General Howard is coming out from Portland. Sheridan is worried about the same thing happening here."

Tanner pulled himself from his melancholy contemplations and shook his head. "Chief Joseph isn't like Crazy Horse," he said slowly.

"Isn't he?" Captain Perry asked sharply. "If he thought he had a chance to drive the whites out of his valley and not suffer any retaliation, don't you think he would try?" Perry's gaze held Tanner's and, having no answer for him, Tanner turned and made his way to the officer's quarters. All he could think of was Gayle Nevins's young face at the battle against the Cheyenne on the Powder River. The soldier had been so young and untried, and now he was dead along with all the rest of the 7th Cavalry.

Tanner threw himself across his bunk and buried his head against his blanket to shut out the awful image of the carnage that must have been at the battle site. He could hear the death cries and smell the gun powder and the sickening odor of blood. His friends, men who had served under him, had fallen, and he could see them lying dead on the prairie, their sightless eyes staring at him in accusation. I should have been there, he thought in despair. Maybe I could have helped. Maybe Gayle and the others would be alive now. He didn't study the irrationality of his thoughts. He was alive, his men dead, and he couldn't erase the guilt of it. He didn't sleep that night, and when he accompanied Captain Perry to Lewiston to meet General Howard, there were bitter new lines about his mouth and a new hardness of purpose in his gray eyes.

Sarah hadn't heard from Tanner for days now and she was worried. John Monteith had gone to the fort to meet with General Howard, and Sarah took solace in the fact that Tanner was involved with his duties. John brought an invitation from Faye Perry for a dinner in honor of General Howard and to introduce her sister who'd come for a visit. Happily Sarah planned to go. It was an opportunity to see Tanner again, if only briefly.

The night of the dinner, she dressed with special care. Her gown was of a black-figured magenta taffeta that rustled pleasantly when she walked. The heavy cross-ribbed material of the skirt had been pulled back into a bustle. Sarah dressed her hair high on top of her head and pinned a wild clemantis flower in it.

"My, you look pretty," Charles teased. "It almost looks like you're going to see your beau."

Winking broadly at Sarah, Frances reprimanded him. "Now Charles, just because a woman fixes herself up a little doesn't mean she's doing it for some man."

Sarah blushed and draped a shawl over her shoulders. The night air would be cool coming home. Her eyes were bright with anticipation.

Faye had once again managed to transform the rough log quarters of the commanding officer into an elegant dining room and parlor. The smelly oil lamps had been banished; the odor of melting candle wax mingled with the delicate fragrance of bouquets of wildflowers. The soft lighting was romantic and intimate and immensely flattering to the ladies. The men hurumphed and teased about the dark shadows, but soon resigned themselves to Faye's spell.

Faye's sister hadn't made her appearance yet, and the talk centered around the general. General Oliver Otis Howard was a vigorous one-armed man who had fought in the Civil War and engaged in many campaigns against the Indians in the years since. He'd let neither age nor his handicap slow him down.

Two years before, he'd been placed by General Sheridan in command of the Department of the Columbia territory and had striven to deal fairly with the Indians. His tales of past Indian wars dominated the conversation in spite of Faye's attempt to direct the talk elsewhere.

Tanner was withdrawn, his expression tight. There was no answering smile when he greeted Sarah. Striving to maintain a lighthearted air, she stood chatting to him, but his thoughts seemed elsewhere. She was hurt and puzzled.

Suddenly all talk and laughter ceased. Faces turned toward the stairway leading down from the second floor. Even Tanner glanced up, his attention caught by something. Perplexed, Sarah swung around and felt concern swell.

Elise Channing, Faye's sister, stood poised on the bottom step, her eyes flashing with laughter as she surveyed the room. Her low-cut gown was exquisite, the delicate pink cloth better suited for an elegant sitting room back East than a rough western post. Above the pale, lace-trimmed bodice her shoulders and the rounded tops of her breasts gleamed like warm ivory. Chestnut hair was piled high on her head, with curls tumbling along the nape and over one shoulder. It was an outrageous hairstyle, not even fashionable, and yet she looked wanton and desirable. Every man in the room was panting, but it was Tanner she sought out.

Faye introduced her sister to one and all, and when they came to Sarah and Tanner, Elise held out her hand prettily and left it in his overly long. Her smoldering amber eyes issued a challenge.

"I already know Major Tanner," she replied, her soft voice implying an intimacy that Sarah was sure didn't exist.

"You have the advantage, madam," Tanner said gallantly. "I don't recall our first meeting."

With a tinkling laugh Elise moved closer so the hand that she still held brushed against the bodice of her gown. Tanner started at the contact and despite himself glanced at Sarah in alarm. "I saw you on the parade ground and asked Faye who you were." Her glance was bold, deliberately provocative. "I feel so safe here, Major, knowing there are men like you protecting us."

"There's little to protect you from, Miss Channing," Tanner said diffidently. Sarah noticed he squared his shoulders a little.

"Welcome to Lapwai," Sarah said, holding out her hand so obviously that Elise had little choice but to release her hold on Tanner. Still she didn't move away from him, so now she stood with her shoulder brushing against his chest. To an onlooker the two of them must have seemed an intimate loving couple.

"Oh, yes, you're the little missionary out at the agency," Elise said, and before Sarah could respond the woman turned back to Tanner. "How long have you been out here in the wicked West, Major?" she cooed. Sarah gritted her teeth, determined not to be outmaneuvered by this woman. And so they stood until supper was announced. Even at the table Elise was seated at Tanner's right while Sarah sat across from him.

Guiltily he avoided her gaze, keeping his eyes downcast. His lips were pressed together in a forbidding line, and Sarah wasn't sure if he were angry with her or the silly situation in which he found himself. He barely glanced at her. Was he having second thoughts about her? she wondered. Was he interested in Elise Channing and her all-too-obvious charms? A sense of forboding settled over her and she fell silent, her sparkle dimmed by Tanner's silence.

If Tanner seemed oblivious to her beauty, General Howard's adjutant, Major Wood, was not. He set himself to charming Sarah. She responded only halfheartedly, not wanting to be rude to him. Tanner seemed not to notice that another man found her attractive. Often his attention was focused on Elise Channing. After dessert the guests retired to the parlor, where the women served tea and the men sipped their whiskey and smoked their cigars. Major Wood hurried to sit beside Sarah on the settee. Tanner contrived to stand across the room from them. Elise was once again at his side, her lovely, animated face raised to his, her tinkling laughter sounding often.

Frances Monteith glanced at Sarah in puzzlement. "Lovers' quarrel," she muttered to Emily Fitzgerald, and the two women smiled sympathetically, remembering the painful misunderstandings of their own courting days.

"Sarah has no hold over Major Tanner," Faye snapped. "Elise can't help it if the major prefers her."

"Ummm, if he does," Frances said. "Either way, he'd best be careful if he doesn't want Henry Wood making headway with Sarah."

Sarah drew little comfort from Henry Wood's admiration. Her heart ached as she observed Tanner bending his head low to catch something Elise said. When he straightened, his eyes swung to Sarah and Major Wood and his lips tightened. Elise's laughter, jubilant and mocking, rang out. Sarah blinked rapidly, her eyes hot and dry with the effort not to shed a tear. She forced herself to concentrate on the conversation, which had turned to the Nez Percé and the threat of war.

"What will be done about McNall and Findley and

their murder of that Indian?" Captain Perry asked. "Rumors have come down that Joseph intends to destroy the farms of some of the settlers if the murderers are not arrested."

"That's not true," Sarah exclaimed. "Major Tanner and I were in Joseph's village when he received the news of the murder. His warriors wanted to retaliate, but Joseph advised them not to. Spotted Frog agreed with Joseph. Major Tanner knows the truth of this. Haven't you told them?" she demanded, rounding on Tanner.

His face was bleak as he returned her gaze. "I told them what we heard and saw," he said gruffly.

"But you say it as if you don't believe Joseph," Sarah challenged. She remembered how sincerely Tanner had pledged justice that day.

"How do I know he spoke the truth?" Tanner asked angrily.

"Joseph wouldn't lie."

"You're besotted by the man," Tanner said so harshly that Sarah blinked and fell silent staring at him in confusion. How could he speak to her like this in front of the others? Elise's smile was little more than a smirk. A flush of humiliation stained Sarah's cheeks.

"I understand they found the missing horses a few days later near Findley's cabin," Emily Fitzgerald broke in quickly, and Sarah was grateful for her attempts to shift the attention.

Sighing, the general leaned back in his chair and rubbed his stump through his empty coat sleeve. "So I've heard," he said, "and those scoundrels McNall and Findley will be detained and tried. They've caused a damn fool lot of trouble."

"Trouble?" Sarah repeated, outraged at his careless attitude toward the murder. "They took a man's life."

"They took an Indian's life, Miss MacKenzie," Howard said, "and they may have started a war in the bargain. I've sent Lieutenant Force and E Company from Fort Walla Walla to maintain order in Wallowa Valley. I want you, Captain Perry, to be ready to move your men out at short notice."

"Oh dear," Faye cried, her blue eyes round and tragic-looking. "Then, you think Joseph will attack." Elise drew closer to Tanner, her golden eyes looking up at him helplessly.

"Of course, he won't attack," Sarah snapped, jumping to her feet. "He wants peace as much as the rest of you. I'm so sure of this that I plan to go back to his village at the first opportunity."

"No, you won't go," Tanner commanded. He stepped forward and glared at her, eyes blazing. Sarah was stunned by his harsh tone. Tanner glanced around at the startled faces of the other guests, and without another word picked up his hat. Giving a quick salute to the general, he stalked out of the room.

"My word," Major Wood said.

Embarrassed at Tanner's treatment, Sarah stood flushed and angry and afraid. "If you'll excuse me a moment," she said to Faye and, catching up her long skirt, ran out of the room and along the porch. She could see Tanner's tall figure halfway across the parade ground.

"Tanner," she called, and to her relief he paused and looked around. Slowly he walked back to meet her. The moon lit the square nearly as brightly as day, but with his wide-brimmed hat, his eyes remained in shadows. Sarah was trembling, wanting to throw herself into his arms and sob out her hurt at his rejection, but she was too intimidated by his stiff, unyielding stance.

"Go back inside, Sarah," he said. There was no softness in his voice.

"Another command, Major Tanner?" she asked, striving to keep her voice light.

"You're new out here. You may not be aware of the dangers."

"Is there danger standing in the moonlight with the man you love?" she asked. She wanted him to reach for her, to kiss her and tell her everything was all right between them. He stood stiff and straight, his long arms hanging at his side.

"Forget what happened between us, Sarah," he said roughly. "It was a mistake."

"I don't understand," she whispered brokenly. "I love you." She reached toward him, but he moved away.

"Go home where you belong, Sarah. Go back east. There's going to be trouble. You don't belong here."

"Does Elise Channing?" she blazed and could have bitten her tongue.

"Elise Channing is not my concern," Tanner answered and, turning on his heels, stalked away.

"Tanner," Sarah called, but he kept walking. "I am where I belong," she cried in frustration. Stalking back into Captain Perry's parlor, she spent the rest of the evening captivating Major Wood.

12

In the weeks that followed that disastrous dinner party, Sarah tried to bury her pain in work. At first she looked for Tanner to come riding into the agency to tell her it had been a mistake, that he hadn't meant the things he'd said, but he never did. Her days became bleak, meaningless measures of time to be gotten through somehow. Owen Thatcher had lost once and for all in his attempt to steal land from the reservation. Carl Pepin and his men waited in the Lewiston jail for the judge to try him for his attack on Sarah. All the buildings had been returned to the agency. Dean Osgood was once again in charge of the mill. Irrigation streams had been reopened and the Indians' crops were being watered. But the hot sun and dry mountain winds had already done their damage. There was some talk of digging camas roots to supplement their diminished harvest.

Sarah opened school in the log cabin and tried to concentrate on her students, but ominous warnings of trouble interrupted their newly won peace. Despite Monteith's militant efforts, bootleggers and unscrupulous sutlers continued to sell whiskey to the Indians.

"The camas digging is the primary target for these troublemakers," he raged one night at the supper table. "Even our reservation Indians give in to the temptation of whiskey and free women and gambling they find at Camas Meadows. There's always trouble."

"What will you do, John?" Charles asked.

The Indian agent slammed his palm against the table. "I'll go with them again this year. I've done it before and I'll do it again. I'll get some soldiers from the fort."

Tension mounted steadily and was felt even in Lewiston. A new rash of complaints were lodged against the non-treaty Indians. Hostility seemed to be directed against John Monteith and the agency people. When Sarah and Frances rode into town for a day of shopping, they were greeted by unfriendly faces and muttered threats.

One day as Frances bought staples and other supplies, Sarah browsed around the general store, enjoying the coolness of the shadowy interior after the hot glare of the sun. Coming to the end of a counter piled high with coal oil lamps and dishes, she was startled to see Annie Red Moccasin waiting for her. The Indian girl stood perfectly still, as if not wanting to call attention to herself. Only her eyes moved, darting a glance from one side to the other.

"Annie, I'm glad to see you again," Sarah whispered and wondered what had prompted her to adopt the same furtive air as the girl.

"Go," Annie hissed in a low, fierce voice. At Sarah's dumbfounded expression she repeated the warning. "Go back to the agency at once. Owen has sent his men."

"To the agency?"

"He makes an ambush for you."

"Where, Annie?" Sarah pressed, but the Indian girl shook her head.

"I must go," she gasped and whirled toward the front of the store.

"Wait, don't go," Sarah called, then fell silent as the door swung open. Scalding yellow light invaded the cool shadows and Owen Thatcher stepped over the threshold.

"Annie," he called in a voice that was deceptive in its mildness. But Annie was already there, slipping past him and out into the street. Thatcher looked after her departing back and his hard gaze swung back to the interior, searching among the shadows as though for any secret Annie might have left behind. His gaze paused on Sarah.

"Minding your own business, Miss Schoolmarm?" he bellowed. Other patrons in the store turned to stare at her.

Sarah raised her chin high, refusing to be intimidated by this evil man. "The Indians, any Indians are my business," she retorted.

Deliberately Owen Thatcher let his lewd gaze drop to her bosom and linger there until her cheeks blazed with outrage. "Seems to me a woman like you ought to have your mind on something else than a bunch of dirty Indians," he said and laughed derisively. Clamping his cigar between his fleshy lips, he tipped his hat and went out, banging the door behind him.

"Sarah, are you all right?" Frances asked, hurrying over to her.

"I'm fine," Sarah declared, brushing her skirt as if brushing away the dirty way Owen Thatcher's glance had made her feel. "Annie said Thatcher's set an ambush for us." She couldn't quite take the warning seriously, but Frances' face blanched with fear.

"We'd better find Charles and John," she said and hurried out of the store, her pile of supplies forgotten. They found the two brothers at the newspaper office. Lucas Tanner was there as well. He gave her a curt nod, then turned away. Hurt, Sarah fell silent.

Quickly Frances told her husband of Annie Red Moccasin's warning.

Tanner turned back to Sarah, his brows drawn down in a frown of concern. "Did Annie tell you where the ambush would occur?"

Sarah shook her head. "There was no time. Thatcher came into the store."

"I have only one man in town with me," Tanner said, looking up and down the street. "If they attack, it won't be here."

"Let's get the sheriff to help us," Sarah cried. All four pairs of eyes turned to her in disbelief.

"Like as not the sheriff's one of the men waiting out there on the trail to ambush us," Charles said glumly.

"Walk down to the general store," Tanner instructed the women. "Act as if you feel no concern. Thatcher is probably having you watched here in town. Charles, take your wagon around in back and load your supplies just as you always do, then drive out of town by the back roads. John, you walk down Main Street. Make sure you're visible. Stop and talk. You're not in a hurry to leave. It's your day in town to do errands. I'll have a horse tied to a tree just outside of town. Make your way there and meet us at the bridge."

Everyone nodded their acquiescence. Adjusting their bonnets, Sarah and Frances sauntered off down the street, stopping now and then to look into windows. Sarah's hands were sweating by the time they got back to the general store, and she couldn't resist a glance over her shoulder. Owen Thatcher was nowhere in sight, but two men were lounging against the posts of the saloon across the street. Although their hat brims were pulled low and their eyes were in shadow, Sarah knew they were watching Frances and her.

Frances paid for her supplies and made arrangements for the clerk to take them out the back door to load. Quickly the women climbed onto the wagon.

"If there's any trouble, lay down flat on the wagon bed," Charles instructed.

"And leave you alone to face everything? I will not," Frances said firmly and sat with her chin high, her hands clenched in her lap.

Charles didn't whip the horses into a gallop as Sarah had expected. He'd been cautioned by Tanner to ride out at a sedate pace, although they did take the back streets. By the time they reached the bridge, John was there along with Tanner and a young, white-faced soldier who kept looking over his shoulder and nervously checking his pistol.

"Let's ride," Tanner said, and Charles whipped up the horses. The road from Lewiston to the fort was well traveled, but the three miles beyond to the agency was a desolate stretch. Its valleys and rocky ravines afforded ample hiding places. Tanner reckoned that was where the attack would occur.

They rode quickly, pushing the horses without mercy for several miles, then slowed the pace to let them rest. They might be needed to outrun the ambushers. When they were a couple of miles from the fort, Tanner sent the young soldier ahead to alert reinforcements. Pale-faced, the boy spurred his horse into a dead gallop that said it would probably not be fit for much after this. Within an hour Lieutenant Dillon and a detachment of soldiers rode out to escort them the rest of the way to the agency.

There was no attack, no gunshots from hidden shadows, no mounted horsemen rushing out of ravines. They reached the agency yard without incident. Sheepishly Sarah looked at the men. "I'm sorry to have bothered you for nothing."

"I'm glad it turned out to be nothing," Tanner said. "Stay on guard. Annie may not have been wrong."

"You don't think Thatcher and his men would try to attack us here, do you?" John asked.

"I don't know," Tanner said, "but I'll leave two of my men to stand guard, just in case."

"You aren't staying yourself?" Sarah asked. Her face reflected her disappointment. He'd been cool and impersonal through it all.

Tanner wanted to walk away from her and not feel the tug at his heart and mind that told him to gather her into his arms and give her the comfort she needed. They'd all been shaken by the threat. Taking out his pistol, he handed it to Sarah. "Keep this with you, just in case," he said.

"Do you think I'll need it?" Her dark eyes were wide and startled-looking.

"Let's hope you don't," he said grimly and studied her face, seeing the fear and the resolution. She might be afraid, but she wouldn't panic as some might.

"I'll report to Captain Perry, then be back to help stand guard," he told the Monteiths. Sarah stood on the porch and watched him ride away, only the cold metallic gun left to give her comfort.

She helped Frances prepare a light supper and carried platters out to the two soldiers Tanner had left on guard. Shadows were gathering in the hollows and among the pine trees. There was no sign of Tanner. Shivering in spite of the warm evening, Sarah hurried back inside. The sense of disquiet stayed with her far past bedtime, making sleep nearly impossible.

The attack came at midnight. Hooves thundered into the agency yard, wild, whooping cries drew the sleeping from their beds. Throwing open the shutters, Sarah peered out. Half-naked bodies smeared with paint gleamed in the light of the torches they held. Shots were fired and more shouting filled the air. Sarah raced to reclaim the gun she'd placed under her pillow. Clutching it in her sweating hands, she pulled back the hammer and took aim out the window, waiting a heartbeat to see what the attackers would do. One of the guards ran forward into the light, his pants hastily donned, his suspenders flapping at his waist. A single gunshot sounded and he fell backward, a bright red stain growing on the white undershirt. He was dead before he hit the ground.

Sarah gasped and pulled the trigger of her gun. One of the riders slumped in his saddle. Another man sounded a bloodcurdling cry and the riders spurred their horses. Flaming brands arched through the air, falling on the roofs of the agency buildings. With tearing eyes Sarah saw the schoolhouse burst into flames. Whooping and yelling, the Indians galloped away. Now a barrage of gunfire stopped them. The attackers were caught between the guns of the agency people and reinforcements.

"Tanner," Sarah shouted in glee and, flinging open her door, rushed into the parlor where Frances and Charles were gathered. John was at the door.

"You can't go out there," Frances pleaded with him. "They'll kill you."

"We've got to put out the fires," John yelled. "I'm not going to let them burn us out."

"Tanner's here with reinforcements," Sarah said. "I'll help you." In the end all four of them did the best they could to save the buildings. Dean Osgood, whose cabin had set away from the other building and so had missed the attack, came running to help as did the reservation Indians from nearby. Buckets of water were passed and flung on the flaming buildings. They managed to save the agency office and cabin, although their roofs would have to be replaced, but the small schoolhouse had burned to the ground.

Dejectedly Sarah rubbed her soot-covered face and looked at the smoldering remains. She was too discouraged even to weep. The gunshots had faded in the distance, and Sarah knew Tanner and his soldiers were giving chase to their attackers. It gave her small comfort.

A shout went up. Charles had found the body of the soldier who'd been on lookout. He'd been shot in the back and clumsily scalped. Sickened, Sarah turned away. She'd seen this once before on a train. Her head came up as she sat thinking about it. There had been several similarities in some of the things that had happened. The men placed the bodies of the two soldiers together.

Tanner and his soldiers rode up. Their horses were lathered and breathing hard, giving testimony of how hard they'd chased the attackers. He slid off his horse and ran to the group huddled on the porch. Sarah was certain the concern in his eyes was meant for her. Again and again his gaze came back to her, as if to assure himself of her safety.

"Did you get the men who did this?" John demanded, wiping his blackened face.

Tanner shook his head. "We killed a couple of them, but they took the bodies with them."

"Both of your men are over there dead," John said. "One of them's been scalped. Looks like Indians to me."

"Unless it was white men trying to start trouble."

"They was Indians," the miller said bitterly. "We

seen 'em as they rode by, laughing and yelling like they was going to a party. Like as not it was some of Joseph's braves. They're getting restless."

"They weren't Joseph's men," Sarah protested. "I don't believe they were Indians at all."

"Why not, Sarah?" Tanner asked.

"I don't know, the way they set their horses, something. I couldn't quite put my finger on it."

"Major," one of his men called. "It had to have been Indians. Look here, unshod hoofprints. Indians are the only ones I know not to shod their horses."

"Then it was Indians," Osgood declared.

"Joseph wouldn't allow his braves to do this. Why would he?"

"He can't control all of them," Reuben, one of the reservation Indians, spoke up. "Black Beaver and Little Wolf are bad medicine."

"I know it wasn't Black Beaver. I would have recognized him," Sarah cried. Tanner studied her face, wondering at her quick defense of the young Nez Percé.

"It seems a little too coincidental that the Indians attacked the agency just after you get a warning from Annie that Thatcher's men were after you." Sarah smiled at him gratefully.

"Annie's Nez Percé," John said. "Maybe she lied. Maybe she knew Joseph's warriors were coming and her conscience wouldn't let her remain silent, so she made up this story that Thatcher's men were after us."

"I don't believe that," Sarah said so steadfastly that John sighed and nodded.

"Perhaps you're right."

"Let's get those men back to the fort," Tanner said. "We'll stand guard tonight." He ordered a detail of men to transport the dead soldiers and deployed his men. Sarah lingered on the porch, hoping he would come back and talk to her, but her wait was in vain. Finally she went inside to bed, staring up at the charred timbers of the ceiling.

Soldiers were left to guard the agency for several nights after the fire, but nothing more happened. With the help of the reservation Indians, new roofs were put on the buildings and things were nearly back to normal. A new schoolhouse would be built later in the summer.

One night as Sarah stood on the porch staring morosely at the moon and thinking of Tanner's continued aloofness, she heard a sound in the bushes. Instinctively she drew back, her gaze darting wildly from one side to the other. Where were the guards? she wondered frantically. The sound came again, mewing and desperate, as if an animal were in pain.

Curiosity carried her to the edge of the porch, where she peered into the shadows.

"Sarah MacKenzie," a voice called weakly, and now she could make out a slight figure slumped on the ground.

"Annie Red Moccasin," she cried, running down the steps. She hurried to the Indian girl and carefully turned her over. Even by the pale moonlight Sarah could see the girl was injured. "Annie. It's me, Sarah," she said urgently.

One eyelash fluttered upward and Sarah perceived that the other eye was swollen shut. "Sarah," the girl whispered. "Owen hurt me, he—" Her words died away.

"He won't hurt you again," Sarah cried. "You're safe here." Annie smiled, a twisted, pathetic grimace in her battered face, and closed her eyes. For a moment Sarah feared she was dead. "Frances," she screamed and her cry brought the Monteiths running.

"Oh, my lord," Frances cried. Charles gathered Annie's slight form up in his arms and carried her to Sarah's bed. Sarah brought water and carefully bathed her face, and Frances smeared salve onto the cuts and bruises.

"It's a wonder he didn't kill the poor little thing," Frances said.

"She can't go back to him after this," Sarah said.

She repeated those words to Annie the next afternoon. After sleeping all night and well past noon, the girl had awakened and tearfully told her story. Owen had been furious that so many of his men had been killed and their attempts to burn out the agency botched. Annie had fallen under suspicion and finally been forced to admit she'd warned Sarah. Sarah's lips tightened in anger. She could well imagine the way Owen had forced the admission. Annie's face and slim body were a horrifying testimony to the man's capability for brutality. Still Annie planned to return to him.

"You can't," Sarah cried, shocked she would even consider it.

Annie shook her head resignedly. "It is better he vents his anger on me than on my grandmother," she said sadly.

"We'll help your grandmother," Sarah said. "She won't want to live on her land if she knows the price you're being forced to pay in exchange."

"She is old. She deserves to live her life in peace," Annie said implacably.

Looking at the pretty face distorted by swelling, Sarah felt like weeping. What could she do to help Annie? she wondered in despair.

Half-Moon provided the solution herself. That eve-

ning as they were about to sit down to supper, two
women rode into the agency leading several packhorses piled high with belongings.

Annie's face lit with pleasure when she saw the
old woman. "Kautsas," she cried and ran to help
her alight.

Half-Moon turned to look at her granddaughter
and nodded her head. "So it is true," she said. "This
evil white man has hurt you. Today he has ordered
me off my land, telling me if you've run away, I
cannot stay in my home."

"I'll go back to him, Kautsas," Annie Red Moccasin said, bowing her head to her grandmother's shoulder. "I am sorry for this pain I've caused you."

The old woman's knobby hand raised the girl's
chin, and she studied her face. "You will not go
back," she said peremptorily. "You are Nez Percé.
You will not be treated like this by a white man."

"But, Kautsas, you will lose your land," Annie
wept piteously.

"There is other land," Half-Moon said. "We will
stay here on the reservation until something can be
done. You will stay with me."

"Are you sure, Kautsas?" Annie asked softly, her
eyes filled with hope.

"I am Nez Percé," Half-Moon said, "and I have
spoken."

Tears were streaming down Sarah's cheeks as she
watched the old grandmother embrace Annie. She
remembered Swan Necklace and the love and comfort she'd known with her.

Frances moved forward and put an arm around
Sarah. "We'll find a place for them," she said kindly.
Sarah went to bed that night with a lighter heart
than she'd felt in some time, but the morning was to
end all that.

Sarah and Annie had gone down to the creek to sit on the bank and talk. Their visit was cut short by the sound of horses riding into the agency. A premonition washed over Sarah and she motioned Annie down out of sight.

The Indian girl pressed herself against the creek bank. "It's Owen," she said, peering over the edge. There was a catch of fear in her voice that tore at Sarah.

"Annie, follow the creek downstream," Sarah whispered, "then head toward the fort. Ask for Major Tanner. Tell him I sent you and he's to take you to Emily Fitzgerald. You'll be safe."

For a moment Annie stared at her in terror. "I'll come get you when Thatcher's gone," Sarah promised and saw some of the fear leave the girl. "Go on, before his men start searching around here for you. Stay low until you get to the trees." Annie nodded and ran along the creek as Sarah had instructed her. Sarah made her way back toward the agency, taking care the men didn't see her until she'd gained the back door. Frances was standing wide-eyed in the kitchen, twisting her apron.

"Monteith," Thatcher called from the front of the house.

"Oh dear, what are we to do?" Frances asked. "The men have gone off to the fort to see Captain Perry."

"Come on out, Monteith. I've got the sheriff with me. He wants to talk to you."

"I'll go talk to him," Sarah offered and walked to the door.

"Do be careful, Sarah," Frances said. "We know what this man is capable of."

"He won't do anything in broad daylight," Sarah said with false courage and stepped out onto the porch.

"John isn't here, Thatcher. What do you want?" she called to the waiting men.

Thatcher sat on his horse, his men flanking him on either side.

He seemed to have an endless supply of saddle bums and killers for hire, she thought in dismay. Sheriff Wilmot was with him. Thatcher let his leering gaze slide over her figure. "So Monteith left a woman to do a man's job," he sneered.

"Maybe he figured that was all that was needed to handle you, Thatcher," Sarah said coolly. "What do you want?"

Thatcher's grin faded. "We're looking for an Indian girl," he snapped. "A thief! She's stolen money and other valuables from me. Is she here?"

"I can't say," Sarah stalled.

"Look here, girlie," Sheriff Wilmot spoke up. "I don't care if this is the Indian agency, you people can't obstruct justice."

"Is that what we're doing?" Sarah asked contrarily.

"You are if you're harboring a thief," Thatcher snapped impatiently. The July sun was growing hot. Irritably he took off his hat and wiped the sweat on his brow. Sarah watched him pointedly and grinned, enjoying his discomfort. Thatcher clamped his hat back on his head.

"We are harboring no criminals here, Sheriff," she spoke to the hard-eyed man with the badge.

"She's lying," Thatcher snapped.

"Now, miss," Wilmot said reasonably. "You're telling me you haven't seen Annie Red Moccasin."

"I saw her in town the other day," Sarah answered evasively.

Thatcher caught onto her game. "Have you seen her since?" he snapped. "Has she come out to the agency?"

Sarah hesitated.

"It wouldn't be smart to lie to the law," Wilmot warned. "We could close down this agency if that happened."

"She came to the agency two nights ago," Sarah admitted and hated Thatcher's sneer of triumph.

"Is she here now?" Wilmot asked, as if speaking to a simpleton.

"No, she's gone," Sarah said and her lips curled in her own smile of triumph.

Thatcher cursed. "Where is she?"

"I don't know," Sarah said and reasoned she really wasn't lying. She didn't know exactly how far along the creek Annie was or even if she'd cut across the fields.

"She's lying as surely as she's standing there," Thatcher said belligerently.

"If you don't believe me, Sheriff, you're welcome to look around. I will have to ask you not to molest any of our people or to damage government property. We've just finished repairs from a fire we had a few nights back."

Wilmot sat considering her words, then shook his head. "Annie ain't here," he said, "otherwise she wouldn't be so all fired fast to let us look."

"That's what she's figuring," Thatcher said. "I'll look myself."

"You'd be trespassing on government property, and I'd have to take steps against that," Sarah replied calmly and nodded. For the first time Thatcher and his men noticed the two soldiers perched on the roof of the storage shed, their rifles in plain view.

Thatcher's face turned a dull red and he glared at Sarah menacingly. "Be very sure you stay out of my way, Miss MacKenzie," he said ominously. "You've crossed my path once too often." With a jerk on the reins he turned his horse and galloped away. Wilmot and the rest of the men followed willy-nilly like the tail of a kite, with no will of their own.

"That horrid man," Frances cried. "He wants to have Annie arrested, after what he did to her."

"We can't let that happen," Sarah said.

"She can't stay here," Frances sighed. "Thatcher will find out and come back for her. John would have to give her up."

"We'll take her to Joseph," Sarah cried in sudden inspiration. "Yellow Bird will make her welcome. I know she will."

"Annie won't leave Half-Moon," Frances said, and Sarah sagged against the porch railing.

"Half-Moon would have to go too," she said finally.

"John would never agree to that," Frances reminded her. "She's a treaty Indian. John wouldn't allow one of his Indians to join Joseph's tribe."

"I know." Sarah nodded. "But he needn't know about it. Oh Frances, I know what I'm asking of you is abominable. I don't want you to lie to John, but Annie needs our help. You know how she feels about Half-Moon. She'll never leave without her and if Annie stays she'll go to jail or worse. It just isn't fair. There've been so many tragic injustices for the Nez Percé. Please help me, so Annie isn't one of them."

Frances listened to Sarah's impassioned plea and nodded her head. "What do you want me to do?" she asked reluctantly.

"Thank you," Sarah cried, throwing her arms around the other woman. Excitedly she drew away, her face lively, her eyes shining, and Frances thought she'd never known a dearer person than Sarah Mac-Kenzie. "The reservation Indians are going to Camas Meadows to dig bulbs in a few days. Annie and her grandmother can go along. We'll hide Annie in a gathering basket or something until we're out on the trail. Once we get to the meadows, Joseph and Yellow Bird will hide her and take her back to Wallowa Valley with them."

"How will you let Joseph know?" Frances asked, trying to keep up with Sarah's rapid plans.

Sarah paused and smiled at her friend. "That's where I'll need your help," she said engagingly. "We'll have to convince John it's imperative that I go along."

Major Tanner and a detachment of fifteen soldiers had been assigned to accompany Monteith and his Indians and to insure peace at the digging grounds. When he rode into the yard at the head of his men, Sarah was waiting, her bags already loaded onto a packhorse, her bonnet tied in place against the hot July sun. The treaty Indians were mounted and waiting patiently in a straggly line. Half-Moon, her daughter, and her packhorses were somewhere in that line, and Annie Red Moccasin was riding in one of the large gathering baskets.

Tanner brought his horse to a halt and doffed his hat briefly at Sarah. His lean, brown face was grim, his expression unyielding, the way it had been the first day she'd seen him on the train. He looked dangerous and not at all like the gentle, passionate man who'd made love to her on the mountain trail.

"Morning, ma'am," he said politely, as if she were a stranger to him.

"Major Tanner," Sarah returned evenly and with equal coolness.

"Fine day, isn't it?" he asked with just a glitter of irony in his eyes. Sarah wanted to rail at him.

"A beautiful day for a journey," she agreed. Her dark eyes flashed with barely suppressed anger.

"Yes, ma'am, it is," Tanner said casting a measuring look at the sky. "It's supposed to rain later on."

"Oh, I hope not," Sarah said, drawing on a pair of riding gloves. "I do hate traveling in the rain."

Tanner sat up as if jolted. "You can't mean you're going on this trip," he demanded in disbelief.

Sarah smiled sweetly. "As a matter of fact, I am," she said firmly and with great pleasure at his expression. Let's see if he can talk about weather for the next two weeks, she thought indignantly.

"It could get dangerous up there," Tanner declared darkly. "It's no place for a woman."

"There are Indian women there," Sarah pointed out.

John Monteith stepped out onto the porch. "Good morning, Major Tanner," he said. "I'm happy you could accompany me this year."

"I must protest Miss MacKenzie going," Tanner said, but the Indian agent had quickly and wisely turned away. Secretly he thought she should stay behind, too, but he'd found she was an adamant and stubborn young woman who generally got her way. He guessed she'd wanted to go in the hopes of finding Annie, who'd run away a few days before. But the final factor in his agreeing to let Sarah come was his formidable sister-in-law. As even-tempered and obliging as Frances usually was, when she set her mind, there was no peace. John had given in to have a surcease of the constant nagging from Frances on the subject. Now he hurried along the line of treaty Indians, pretending to check final travel arrangements with them.

"If there's trouble I don't want to have to worry about a woman," Tanner called after him in frustration.

"Does that mean you won't be protecting the Nez Percé women, Major Tanner?" Sarah asked sweetly.

"You won't find any other white women there," Tanner snapped. His face was tight and angry, and she was pleased by his concern.

"Will there be half-breeds or quarter-breeds?" she asked and saw the sheer fury in his eyes.

Impatiently he pulled the reins of his horse. "Suit yourself about going along," he said flatly. "We'll be traveling fast. You'll have to keep up."

"I always have," Sarah answered, but he'd already turned away, his arm raised to signal his men forward. Sarah climbed into her saddle, straddling the horse as the Indian women did and arranging her long, full skirts the best she could to cover her legs. Two weeks, she thought gleefully. Two weeks and she planned to make the most of them, both in Annie's behalf and her own. Somehow she'd break through Tanner's indifference to her.

"Move 'em out," Tanner called, and the long line moved forward. Two weeks, he thought glumly. Two weeks! How the hell would he be able to stay away from Sarah for two weeks?

If the distance from the Lapwai Agency to the Wallowa Valley had been two days' hard travel, the trip to Camas Meadows must be more than twice that distance, Sarah thought. Tanner set the pace and without complaint the Indians kept up. Sarah floundered along behind, trying hard not to show her fatigue. After her trip to Chief Joseph's village, she'd thought herself trail-hardened. She realized now how easy Tanner had made the journey for her. He made no such concessions now. Each night Sarah fell into her bedroll, grateful for a few hours' rest before having to mount and ride out again. The Nez Percé women arranged impromptu dances and games for the children to play. They were on a holiday and meant to make the most of each day.

Their second night on the trail, Sarah leaned wearily against a boulder and watched the festivities. Tanner paused as he walked past, glancing at her untouched plate. "Trail too hard for you, Miss Mac-Kenzie?" he asked, propping one boot on a rock and leaning forward.

"Not too hard, Major Tanner," she replied. "I'm still here."

"You'd better try to eat or you won't be able to go on for long," he said, nodding at her plate. For a moment she saw the old flicker of concern in his eyes, and it emboldened her to call his name when he would have turned away.

"Why are we like strangers again?" she asked, leaning forward urgently.

"We settled this back at the fort," he answered, looking away from her eager young face.

"Perhaps you did, but I didn't," Sarah said. "I don't understand how you can love me one day and stop loving me the next, unless you never loved me at all. Perhaps the things you said to me on the way to Wallowa Valley were a lie."

"Sarah," Tanner said helplessly.

"Were you lying to me?" she persisted. "Tell me. I want to know what kind of man you are."

His gaze met hers for a brief moment, then flickered away. "I'm a soldier. We're used to telling a woman anything for a few nights' pleasure."

"Is that what you did to me?" she insisted. She wanted to hear it.

"Sarah, what's the point of all this?" he asked.

"The point is I want to know where I stand. Did you lie to me there on the trail that night?" Her voice had gone soft in spite of herself.

He swung around to face her, anger making his face sullen. "Yes." The single word was clipped and cold.

The blood left Sarah's face. "I don't believe you," she whispered and fought the tears that filled her eyes. She would not cry in front of him.

Tanner looked at her in surprise. Any other woman would have dissolved in tears and injured pride, he thought in wonder. But Sarah was still fighting for what was between them. He wanted to take her into his arms and bury his head in the warm, fragrant mounds of her breasts. The pain on her face made him want to weep. He'd put it there, and he couldn't walk away and leave her.

"I meant the words when I said them," he said in a low, quick voice, "but things change, men change, and there's no room for love or all the other pretty feelings. Forget about me, Sarah. Find someone else."

"There is no one else," she cried after his departing back. There was no pause in his angry strides. Sarah sat down on her boulder and thought back over their words. Tears rolled unchecked down her cheeks. She'd seen the sorrow in his eyes. Callous as his words had been, he hadn't meant to cause her pain. He still cared for her, she was sure of it. Somehow she'd make him see he couldn't deny the pretty feelings that bound them.

13

One night Sarah overheard a group of soldiers talking as they sat around their campfire.

"The major's mighty touchy about them Indians," one man said as he stirred a pan of beans over the coals.

"Yeah, reckon I'd be touchy, too, if I'd fought the Sioux like he has."

"I hear tell he used to be with Custer's Seventh," observed one soldier as he cut off a plug of tobacco and popped it in his mouth. Laying back against his bedroll, he chewed with relish.

"That's what I mean," said his partner. "Major Tanner left before the Little Big Horn. If I'd a come that close to having my scalp lifted by Crazy Horse, I'd be a little touchy about Indians myself."

"Reckon he's afraid of Indians?" another soldier asked. He paused in his whittling to look at his friends.

"Naw, the major, he ain't afraid of nothing," said the soldier with the beans. He picked up a spoon and, sitting on a log, began to eat.

"Wonder why he left the Seventh?" The man shook his head. "Whooee, he sure is lucky he hightailed it out of there."

"I don't think he feels lucky," the bean eater said.

The other men looked at him. "How come you know so much about the major?"

"I figured it out. Like you said. He's changed and he didn't do that until he heard about Custer's defeat."

Sarah hurried on to her own campfire, but the things the soldiers had said stayed with her, and they made her waver between despair and hope.

The digging grounds at Camas Meadows were covered with blue flowers so that standing on a high ledge overlooking it, Sarah thought it looked like a mountain lake. Camped along the edges of the camas fields were tribes from the Umatilla reserves, Coeur d'Alene and Columbia River as well as the Nez Percé. Sarah estimated more than a thousand Indians had gathered. Reuben and the Lapwai Indians set up their tipis among the other tribes. Tanner ordered his soldiers to make camp some distance away on a small knoll overlooking the whole prairie.

Sarah helped Martha, Reuben's wife, to set up the tipi and gather firewood, then walked along the Indian camps looking for Chief Joseph and Yellow Bird. A mood of festivity had settled over the camps, and the sounds of laughter and music could be heard. Everywhere Indians, wearing their best finery, called to one another or indulged in games of physical prowess. The rattle of bone die being tossed was lost in the bawdy laughter and shouted bets of men as they gambled. Off in the meadows, horse hooves pounded across the hard-packed racing grounds.

"Swan Necklace," a voice called, and Yellow Bird ran to throw her arms around Sarah. "My sister, it is good to see you again," Joseph's wife declared.

"Yellow Bird, are you well? How are Joseph and

Spotted Frog and the little ones? How is old Running Brook?" Sarah asked all at once.

Yellow Bird laughed. "The old ones are back in the village, but everyone else is here. You will see them before we go. Joseph, come and greet Swan Necklace."

The tall Indian chief came forward and grasped Sarah's arm. "It is good to see our sister at this time of celebration."

"I'm happy to be here among my family," Sarah answered. "Joseph, I've come to ask a favor of you."

"Ask, my little sister," he answered immediately, and Sarah told him the story of Annie Red Moccasin and Half-Moon. "Tell them to come. Their home shall be with us now," Joseph said without hesitation, as Sarah had known he would.

"I'm sorry for the soldiers General Howard has sent to your valley," she said, wishing she could offer him something to repay his generosity toward Annie and her grandmother.

"The one-armed chief has done the right thing. He does not want war, either. Besides, they have captured the two men who killed Eagle Robe."

"I know. I'll speak on your behalf at the trial if it will help."

"White man's justice is for the white man. If you were not there to see what happened, you cannot tell. They will say you are biased for the Nez Percé."

"They'd be right. I am," Sarah replied so steadfastly that Joseph and Yellow Bird smiled.

"You are a good friend as well," Joseph said. "Come, for now we will forget our troubles and enjoy the harvest of the camas bulb. For another year life will be sustained."

Sarah spent the evening in Joseph's camp, taking supper with them and later joining in the games and dancing. For the moment she did as Joseph had suggested; she put aside her worries over Tanner and enjoyed the fellowship with her new friends and family. Black Beaver had finished with the races and other games in which the men participated and now he came to dance. Often he brushed against Sarah, his bold dark eyes admiring as he watched her. Although she felt only friendship for the handsome warrior, she was flattered by his attention. It was very late before she started back to her tent at the Lapwai camp.

"The moon is gone. I'll walk with you," Black Beaver said and fell into step beside her.

Grateful for his presence, Sarah made no protest. Many of the Indian warriors had become drunk. She'd even caught a whiff of whiskey on Black Beaver's breath when he brushed against her, but so firm had their friendship become that she felt no concern. They walked in companionable silence until they neared Reuben's tent.

"I have many horses," Black Beaver said abruptly. "I am a strong warrior. I kill many men in battle."

"Yes, I've heard you're very brave," Sarah said, nonplussed at his sudden need to brag. He was a proud man and wanted her to think highly of him.

"I hunt buffalo for warm robes and meat. My pots are never empty." He paused, waiting for her response, then rushed on. "I have a new rifle which shoots many times very fast." He stepped in front of her, his dark eyes studying her. "Black Beaver is a friend to Chief Joseph and his family. Black Beaver is a tall man among the Nez Percé." He puffed his chest out proudly and Sarah understood he was speaking of his status among the tribe.

She was quite overwhelmed by his revelations, uncertain of their purpose. "That's . . . wonderful,

Black Beaver," she stammered. "Chief Joseph is fortunate to have you for a friend. I am honored you are my friend."

He smiled and seemed to relax. "I will speak to Joseph tonight," he said and stalked away toward Joseph's camp.

Sarah stared after him perplexed and uneasy. A sound nearby made her whirl around in fear. Lucas Tanner stepped out of the shadows.

"Congratulations, Swan Necklace," he said, and she realized that for the first time he'd used her Indian name.

"What do you mean?" she asked warily. She could barely see him in the black night, but she smelled the smoke of his cigar.

"Black Beaver just proposed to you," he paused, "and you've accepted."

"What?" Sarah yelped. "How do you know that's what he was doing? You aren't a Nez Percé. You don't know their customs."

"I'm a man and I know their ways," he said quietly and turned away.

"Tanner, wait," Sarah called in dismay. "What should I do?"

"Prepare for your wedding," he answered contrarily. "Good night, Swan Necklace." His voice floated back in the darkness and she heard no laughter. What had happened to them, she wondered, that they couldn't even laugh at something as preposterous as this? The words she'd overheard between the soldiers came back to her, and thoughtfully she prepared for bed. She couldn't believe Tanner was feeling such prejudice now. He'd known from the beginning of her Indian background. She must talk to him, she decided, first thing tomorrow morning. And she must talk to Black Beaver and clear up this misunderstanding.

But the next morning Tanner and his men were at the far end of the prairie, checking on white traders who'd arrived, bringing more whiskey. Yellow Bird stopped by for Sarah, an extra digging stick in her hand.

"Will you join us in gathering the camas?" she asked.

"I'd like that," Sarah answered, taking the crutchlike stick. One end of the three-foot-long staff was fitted with an elk horn. The other end had been sharpened, its point black and hardened by the fire.

"I had a digging stick when I was a girl," she said. "My grandmother made it for me. I even know how to use it." Delightedly she demonstrated her familiarity with the tool.

"You are very wise about such things," Yellow Bird said solemnly, but her brown eyes danced with laughter. "Perhaps the old one forgot to tell you about the camas. One brings us food and life, one brings us death." She bent to show Sarah the difference. "The white flower tops signify death, the blue brings life. That is why the Nez Percé use blue in their beaded work. You must be careful not to gather the death camas."

"I didn't know," Sarah faltered.

"It is not for us to know all things, Swan Necklace," Yellow Bird admonished gently, and Sarah bent her back to the digging, greatly humbled.

A pit had been dug for steaming the camas bulbs. Flat rocks lined the bottom of the hole and a fire was built to heat the rocks. The cleaned camas bulbs were put to steam overnight, and the women were free once again to play games and visit.

Joseph, as was his custom at this time of year, had

taken some of the men off to butcher cattle. Now he returned with the liver and tongue of the butchered animals. Jubilantly the women roasted the organs over their fires. The spirits had been generous. They would celebrate the first fruits of the mother earth. While the women prepared food, Sarah took the children aside and taught their lessons until she noticed their nodding heads. It had been a long, exciting day for them, she thought and, relenting, closed the book and went away, leaving them to nap in the soft, sun-scented prairie grass.

She was exhausted herself, but once she'd bathed in a nearby stream and donned clean clothes, she felt eager for the evening's festivities. Only the thought that she must speak to Black Beaver cast a pall over her enjoyment. But first, she was determined to talk to Tanner before the day was out. One of the soldiers directed her to his tent. Slowly Sarah walked to the low canvas structure.

Tanner sat on the edge of his bedroll, his long legs stretched out before him, his shoulders hunched over something in his lap. With a stub of a pencil he was making notations in a small black book.

"Tanner?" she asked breathlessly. She'd had to work up her courage to come. He looked up and his lips tightened at the sight of her. His hair was tousled over his tanned brow, and she wanted to smooth it away, just as she wanted to smooth away so much of the misunderstanding between them.

"What do you want, Sarah?" he asked impatiently, closing the pencil stub inside the book and slipping it under the edge of his bedroll. His expression was impersonal.

"I want to talk to you," she said hesitantly.

Tanner sighed and got to his feet. "Let's talk outside," he said and brushed past her. He was observing every formality, Sarah thought, and followed him out of the small tent. In the open he turned to face her. "What can I assist you with?" he asked in that cool, pleasant voice Sarah had come to hate.

"Tell me about the Little Big Horn," she said and saw the start of surprise. Angry color stained his cheeks.

"I thought everyone knew about the battle that was fought there," he said roughly.

"How does it affect you?" she insisted.

"That's really none of your business, Sarah. Don't mettle in what doesn't concern you."

"This does concern me. What happened at the Little Big Horn affects us. I have the right to know why."

"You're wrong," Tanner said stiffly. "What happened between us was a mistake."

"What happened between us was right and good. You said you loved me. I love you. How can that be a mistake?"

"I have no room in my life for a woman. I'm a soldier. The army is my career. It's all I've got. It's all I want." Tears were streaming down Sarah's face and he wished her away. "Why don't you go back down with your Indian family and dance and celebrate?"

"Do you hate me because I'm part Indian?" Sarah asked brokenly. She couldn't bear it if he said yes. Tanner's startled gaze swung to hers.

"I don't hate you," he said. His voice was softer.

"Do you resent me because of my Indian blood, because the Sioux killed all those soldiers? Are you unable to look at me without thinking of them? Tell me the truth about the way you feel."

"I don't hate you," Tanner repeated softly. "I love you." He swung away from her as if he couldn't bear his admission. His shoulders sagged and she heard him swallow in an effort to compose himself. She longed to wrap her arms around him, but she felt the resistance in him.

"If you love me—" she began tentatively.

"Can't you see?" He rounded on her. "You shouldn't love me. I left my men, my unit. I walked away from them when I knew they needed every man to fight the Sioux. I should have been there." He bowed his head as if unable to bear his shame.

"You couldn't have stopped what happened," Sarah cried in amazement.

He glared down at her. "Then I should have died trying," he said. "Stay away from me, Sarah. I'm not the man you want." He stalked away from her, leaving her bereft and torn with pain. Blinded by tears, she walked back to the Indian camp, then veered away to find a quiet spot to cry and think. He blamed himself, she realized, for not being there when Custer and his men fought Crazy Horse. Moreover, he was riddled with guilt for being alive when they were dead, for loving an Indian woman while his friends were being cut down by Indian arrows. He feared he had betrayed them and now he was punishing himself. She wouldn't let him do this to them. Somehow she'd find a way to help him deal with his irrational guilt. Now that she knew what the problem was, she would find a solution. Tanner hadn't reckoned on a woman's stubbornness when it came to the man she loved.

She made her way down to the meadow again and sought out Black Beaver, determined to make at least one thing right. His dark eyes brightened when he saw her.

"I must talk to you," Sarah said. The urgency of

her expression drew him away from the other braves with whom he'd been drinking.

"What is it, Swan Necklace?" he asked. His voice was husky and possessive. Sarah shivered with regret. If she hadn't met Lucas Tanner first, she might have come to love this young warrior, but now there could never be anyone for her but Tanner. Taking a deep breath she began.

"I have considered the words you said to me last night," she began. "I hold Black Beaver in the highest esteem. I see how he stands tall among the other warriors. I would be proud to be his wife, but I have given myself to another man."

A sound deep in Black Beaver's chest made her pause and look at him. His eyes had grown black, his face hard. "Who is this man?" he demanded.

"I have loved Major Tanner for many moons now," Sarah said, "long before I met Black Beaver. I am his woman."

"He does not treat you as his woman," Black Beaver snapped.

"I know," Sarah said. "Still, I have given myself to him and I cannot go with another when I feel as I do. I thank you for the honor you have shown me."

Black Beaver stared at her, anger twisting his handsome features, and without a word, turned on his heels and stalked away.

"Black Beaver, I'm sorry," Sarah called after him, but he didn't look back. Morosely she made her way back to Joseph's camp. Annie and Half-Moon were there with the other women, laughing as they played a game with bones. At least that was one thing she'd done right, Sarah thought, and found little solace. She tried to join in the gaiety, but worry over Black Beaver and depression over Tanner's rejection lay like a black cloud over her. Black Beaver never came to the camp. He was out there somewhere, Sarah thought, looking beyond the campsites to the gaudily lit traders' wagons. Helplessly she turned toward the Lapwai camp. On the knoll where Tanner had pitched his tent, she saw shadows against the canvas. How she longed to run up the hill and try yet again, but she was too discouraged. Settling herself into her bedroll, she cried herself to sleep.

14

The days passed quickly. The Nez Percé women were busy harvesting the camas, cooking and storing it against the lean winter months ahead. The men continued to hunt. In the evenings they gambled and drank too much of the whiskey the white traders provided. Some of the young warriors grew increasingly reckless in their behavior, becoming drunk early in the day and reveling late into the night. Fights broke out. Black Beaver seemed always to be in the middle of it.

"Why doesn't Joseph stop them?" Sarah asked one day as she and Yellow Bird bent to dig under the hot sky. "The soldiers will step in themselves if things get any worse."

"Although Joseph is chief," Yellow Bird explained, "it is not the way of the Nez Percé to tell another what he must do."

"Even if it hurts the whole tribe?" Sarah asked in disbelief.

Yellow Bird nodded. "Each man must follow what his spirit tells him."

"Then how are they made to follow the customs of the tribe? For order there must be law."

"That is so," Yellow Bird agreed. "Our people are taught from childhood to accept the teachings of the old ones, just as your grandmother taught you. They learn to place their beliefs in the earth mother. If they violate those teachings they will bring badness on themselves and the tribe. No one wants to be exiled from their people."

"Yet these young braves buy the white man's whiskey and get drunk and fight even though it is bad for the rest of the Indians."

"Yes," Yellow Bird said sadly. "But the white men sell the whiskey, even though it is against the white man's law. Yet they are not punished. Why should the Indians be punished?" Sarah had no answers for her and turned away.

John Monteith had spent his time at the meadow working to keep the reservation Indians away from the influence of the young braves in other bands, but to little avail. Many of the youths were angry and restless under the strict new way of life and longed for the nomadic freedom of the old. Sarah sensed the Indian agent disapproved of her association with Joseph's people, often referring to them as heathens, but she couldn't let his opinion stop her from being with her new family. She refrained from wearing the beautiful elk-hide dress Yellow Bird had given her, and soon her friend stopped asking about it.

Diligently Sarah worked with the children of the treaty Indians, conducting classes in reading and numbers at the end of the day after their chores with the camas digging and before the revelry began. She longed to have the children from Joseph's and other bands join her in her little prairie school, but knew it wouldn't happen that easily. Joseph had made his feelings clear, and she must respect them or she might be exiled from the tribe. Black Beaver never spoke to Sarah now, treating her as if she did not exist. She missed his friendship and was sorry for the pain she'd caused him.

She often saw Tanner's soldiers patrolling the perimeter of the camps in groups of four. They had been circumspect in their behavior toward the Indians, taking care not to cause unintended offense yet remaining visible enough to act as a deterrent to those young warriors who might be tempted to carry their drunken behavior too far. Sarah knew Spotted Frog and Joseph had counseled their own warriors.

Despite the chief's efforts and Tanner's precautions, it seemed almost inevitable that trouble would break out. One night, having eaten their fill of the wild game, roasted camas bulbs, and berry cakes, Joseph's band began games and races. An air of contentment settled over the camp. Their bellies were filled and so were their cache pots and storage baskets. They had enough food to feed their band for many months ahead. Soon they would return to the rivers for the second and more profitable salmon run. The spirits had been generous with them. Their quiet laughter was carefree.

Sarah joined some of the children in a game of ball. Later she watched as Yellow Bird and the other women vied with each other in a livelier version of the game for cooking pots or prized pieces of hides. Joseph and some of the older men sat nearby shouting encouragement to them.

Their festivities were interrupted by the sound of gunshots. Hoots of triumph came from the end of the prairie where the whiskey men had set up camp. Loud shouts were followed by more gunshots. Sarah heard the quick staccato of hoofbeats as Tanner's men hurried to the site. Many of the Indians had left their games and were streaming toward the whiskey camp. Sarah and Yellow Bird gathered the frightened children, their eyes solemn and wide with concern. More gunshots were followed by bloodcurdling cries of defiance.

"Don't be afraid. Nothing is wrong," Yellow Bird reassured the children, but Sarah saw the worry in her friend's eyes. Joseph and Spotted Frog had hurried to the whiskey camp at the first sound of trouble. Was Tanner there? Sarah wondered. Of course he would be right in the thick of things. That was his job, the reason he'd accompanied Monteith and his reservation Indians here. Sounds of fighting came to her and Sarah leaped to her feet. Tanner might be hurt and she couldn't bear to wait here quietly.

"Go see what has happened," Yellow Bird said understandingly. With a quick apologetic glance Sarah hurried across the meadow. Indians were crowded around watching something. Jubilantly they called out encouragement while others fell to betting. Sarah pushed her way through and stopped, her throat tightening with fear when she saw Tanner and a tall Indian brave warily circling each other. The men shifted positions and Sarah recognized Black Beaver. He held a knife, but Tanner's large hands were empty, held in readiness to ward off a sudden attack.

"Get the red varmint," one of the traders yelled belligerently. "The major ain't even armed." He reached for his gun.

"Sergeant, shoot the first man to draw his weapon," Tanner shouted without taking his eye off the advancing Indian.

"Yes, sir," the soldier answered and, taking out his pistol, held it ready.

The trader eased his hand away from his gun and stood eyeing Tanner. "I place a ten-dollar gold piece on Black Beaver," he called contemptuously and spat in the dust.

Weaving drunkenly, Black Beaver sneered and with a wild cry leaped forward. Tanner jumped aside. The blade of the Indian's knife sliced neatly through the sleeve of his shirt. Sarah screamed. Tanner clamped his hand over his arm, and Sarah could see blood seep around his fingers. She took a step forward, but strong arms wrapped around her middle and held her still.

"You must not interfere, little sister," Spotted Frog said from behind her. Sarah was too caught up in her concern for Tanner to notice his words.

Still circling, his gaze never breaking with Black Beaver's, Tanner quickly took the kerchief from around his neck and wrapped his arm. Once again the Indian warrior lunged. This time Tanner neatly sidestepped, one boot slipping between the staggering brave's feet, his fist coming down in a quick, hard blow that felled the overly confident warrior.

"That's it. Get him back to his camp and sober him up," Tanner ordered. The winners of the betting shouted jubilantly while the losers grudgingly paid up. Both sides were disappointed the fight hadn't lasted longer.

Spotted Frog released Sarah and she ran forward, her soft hands gripping Tanner's arm. "Are you all right?" she asked, looking at his bloodsoaked sleeve.

"It's only a scratch," he said, pulling away from her. Glancing around, he waved to the wagons with every kind of goods displayed. Though not in evidence, Sarah and everyone there knew kegs of whiskey were hidden nearby. "Close them down," Tanner ordered his men.

"You can't do that," one of the traders roared in dismay.

"It's against the law to sell whiskey to Indians," Tanner replied flatly.

"Now, Major, let's be reasonable about this," a man named Joe Craig said. "There's no whiskey here. We traders have brought our goods so the Indians can have a chance to look them over and trade for warm blankets and cooking pots. You can't prevent a man from making a living."

Deliberately Tanner walked to one of the nearby wagons and picked up a coffeepot. "I know all about you, Craig, and the rest of you bootleggers." The accused men exchanged uneasy glances. Tanner glanced around the circle of faces and poured from the coffeepot into a cup. Smiling grimly, he turned the cup and spilled the clear liquid onto the ground. Whiskey! "You didn't come out to sell the Indians anything but whiskey," Tanner stated flatly. "It's all over. Pack up and move out of here."

"Now, Major, be reasonable. A man likes to have a little something to wash the dust out of his throat. You can't prove we've sold them Indians any of that whiskey. Far as you know, they could have brought their own. You can't order us to leave. We've got a right to trade with the Indians."

"Be out of here within an hour, Craig," Tanner ordered stiffly.

"And if we ain't?"

"Sergeant, deploy your men and if these wagons aren't out of here in one hour, go through them and destroy every bottle of whiskey you find."

"Yes, sir," the soldier said. With a wave of his arm he motioned his men into a line, their rifles held loosely but conspicuously in the crook of their elbows.

Without a backward glance Tanner stalked away. Sarah followed. "You need to have that arm looked after," she said.

"It's nothing to worry about," he answered dismissively.

"It could become infected," Sarah insisted.

"Don't worry about it," he snapped.

Sarah stopped in her tracks, staring after his retreating back, then anger took over. Running to catch up, she took hold of his good arm and tugged him around. "Stop trying to be a martyr," she cried.

Startled by her strength and anger, Tanner stared at her. "What are you talking about?"

"You and your willingness to risk infection rather than have an Indian woman tend your arm," Sarah snapped.

"That's not true." He glared at her.

"No? Then let me see to your arm," she challenged, her chin thrust out determinedly. For the first time in weeks, Tanner felt an insane urge to smile.

"All right," he relented and let her lead him to her tent, where she sat him on a patch of grass. Lighting a lantern, she knelt beside him and carefully cut away the bloodsoaked cloth. When she'd bathed his wound, she drew in her breath and glanced at him. It was deep, worse than he'd thought. Her hands were gentle and soft on his flesh, and he had to look away from her sweet mouth. In concentrating on her task, she'd caught her tongue between her even white teeth.

"Drink this," she said and shoved a bottle of whiskey at him.

Tanner held up the bottle. "Don't tell me you bargained with Craig and his cohorts as well?" he asked.

"That's John Monteith's supply," she said primly. "He keeps it for medicinal purposes only. Drink some. You're going to need it. This has to be sewn up." Tanner did as she'd ordered.

Now that the cut was cleaned, Sarah took out a

needle and thread and bent over his arm, her tongue once again between her teeth. Tanner took another swallow of whiskey and looked away.

"What were you trying to prove back there?" she asked, making neat stitches along the cut, pulling the gaping edges together as she worked. Now Tanner watched her nimble, capable hands, marveling at her ability to handle most anything. "Why didn't you have your men help you?"

"Why did you scream when Black Beaver charged me?" he jeered instead of answering her questions. "Worried about your bridegroom?"

Sarah glanced up to meet his gaze and something flared to life between them. "I thought he might kill you," she answered simply. "I couldn't bear the thought of it." Light from the lantern reflected in her dark eyes, quicksilver emotions that she didn't try to hide. Tanner glanced away and she forced herself to a friendly tone. "You didn't answer my question."

"I wasn't trying to prove anything," he answered in his old impersonal way. "If Black Beaver had been killed, the other Indians were drunk enough to retaliate. I didn't have enough men to control them. More people would have been hurt, and my reason for being here would have been undone."

"I see," Sarah answered and put a final knot in the thread. Picking up a piece of clean white cloth, she tore bandages and began to wrap his arm. Her movements were quick and concise. "Still, you could have gotten help," she continued. "It wouldn't have helped matters if you'd been killed."

"But I wasn't," Tanner said lazily. There was something calming about sitting here in the grass beside Sarah and yet something immensely disquieting just being near her. To steady his arm while she worked, she'd clamped his hand with her elbow at her waist.

He could feel the warm, firm flesh of her beneath the cotton gown and remembered their night together on the Salmon River when he first made love to her. Her long hair fell over her face, shining glossy and fine in the flickering light.

"That should hold you until you get back to the fort and the doctor can look at it," she said and let go of his hand. "Try to be careful with it."

"Thank you, I will," he answered, sorry she was finished. "You did a good job."

"It wasn't so much." She shrugged diffidently.

"Not every woman could do it. Where did you learn how—your grandmother."

"My grandmother," Sarah said with a laugh and got to her feet. Tanner stood up, staggering slightly.

"Careful," Sarah cried, steadying him with her strong, young body. "You've lost some blood. You may be a little dizzy for a while."

He could feel her the length of him. So much for all those things he'd told her a few nights back, he thought, and stood straight on his own. "I'm fine," he said gruffly. "I'm much obliged for your help."

"Anytime," Sarah answered quietly, hurt by his shift of mood. "I would have done it for anyone."

"Well, thank you for doing it for me." With a stiff bow he walked away from her. Some part of him cried out to go back and take her in his arms. He longed to taste the berry sweetness of her lips and feel her lustrous black hair against his face. Grimly he walked back to his own campsite and prepared for bed.

Feeling restless, Sarah decided against returning to Joseph's camp. Taking up an Indian blanket, she headed downstream. She would bathe and go to bed early, she decided, but the prospect held little appeal. Her senses felt alive and she knew it was from being so close to Tanner.

Stripping off her gown and undergarments, she plunged into the clear, shallow pool. The water was icy, as she'd known it would be. Melting snow and ice flowing from the high mountain peaks had little chance to warm here at the high altitudes. She remembered another night when she'd bathed in an icy pond and been warmed by Tanner's arms. She could see his lighted tent from where she bathed, his lean silhouette outlined as he bent over his bedroll. A feeling strong and sure welled inside Sarah. They were man and woman, Tanner and she, and he must understand that nothing else mattered in the face of their love for each other. Stepping from the icy stream, she wrapped the Indian blanket around her and, leaving her clothes behind, walked to his tent.

Tanner glanced up when she entered. "What are you doing here, Sarah?" he asked. His voice sounded as soft and defenseless as she felt.

"I've just finished bathing in the stream," she answered, "and I'm cold." Slowly, her dark gaze holding his, she opened the blanket. Water glistened on her bare skin. Tanner drew in his breath as he looked at the firm, high breasts, the tiny waist flaring into the soft curve of her hips, the flat planes of her stomach, and the long legs that could hold a stride like a man or wrap around him in paroxysms of passion. Using one corner of the blanket, Sarah began to dry herself, trailing the soft wool across her shoulders and over the ivory curve of her breasts. Her nipples were dark and taut, and she saw Tanner take a slow, shaky breath.

Slowly she walked toward him and held out the corner of the blanket. "Dry my back?" she asked.

His hands shook, but he took the blanket. Sarah shrugged it away from her and turned her back to him. With slow, circular motions Tanner half dried, half caressed her. One large hand clamped over her slender shoulder, while the other brushed the wool down the graceful arch of her back. Then the wool was gone and it was only Tanner's hands on her, stroking and touching. Sarah's eyes closed as sweet desire washed over her. He pulled her against him, grasping the fullness of her breasts. She could feel the cold metal of his belt buckle and the searing brush of his hands against her flesh. Gasping, she lay her head back against his shoulder, exposing her soft throat. Tanner kissed the satiny, fragrant skin.

"I love you," she whispered. "Don't leave me, don't turn your back on the way we feel about each other."

"I love you too," he said between fierce, passionate kisses. Impatiently he turned her, pressing her against him. Now she felt his buckle against her stomach, the metal warmed by the heat of their bodies.

"Say it doesn't matter that I'm part Indian."

Startled, he drew back, his arms still holding her tightly, his eyes somber. "It doesn't matter, Sarah," he said, and she believed him with all her heart.

"I was afraid you were ashamed of me," she whispered her fears.

"My God," he cried, pressing his lips to her temple. "What am I doing to you? Don't you know how wonderful you are, how much I admire you? You're like no woman I've ever met. I've loved you almost from the first moment I saw you." He rained kisses on her cheeks and lips until she was breathless. His strong arms hooked beneath her knees, and she was lifted and placed on his bedroll. Tanner stood above her, his gray eyes sweeping over the natural beauty of her slender body. His gaze was filled with all the love he felt, and she raised her arms to him. Tanner doused the lantern. Flinging off his clothes impatiently, he lowered himself to her, marveling at the joy of feeling her sleek limbs wrap around his. Her hands were eager as they explored his body. Her chuckle was intimate and satisfied when she felt his arousal.

Tanner lost himself in the warm sensuality of her, and for a while his guilt and shame were blotted away. If Sarah could never overcome the anguished images of his nightmares, at least for a little while she gave him peace and love. Through the night, Tanner clung to the blessed reality of her passion, resting briefly against the sweet comfort of her soft body curled in sleep beside him.

15

Two days later, Monteith ordered his treaty Indians to pack up and return to the reservation. They had been at the meadow for ten days and all the camas bulbs needed against winter hunger had been gathered. After Tanner's interference the bootleggers had taken their whiskey supplies over the ridge a mile away and set up shop again. The young braves raced to and from the circled wagons. Still, no more fights broke out and Sarah was satisfied to see Tanner's wound showed no sign of infection. She bid farewell to Yellow Bird and to Annie and Half-Moon, wishing them well in their new home. Then she joined Monteith and the treaty Indians for the ride back to the reservation. Tanner and his men rode at the front and back of the long line.

"My, it's good to have you home again," Frances Monteith said. "It was just too quiet around here."

"I missed you too," Sarah said, giving the woman a hug.

"Did you get Annie and Half-Moon settled into a new home?" Frances asked anxiously.

"Joseph has promised they may live with his tribe. They seemed very happy with his people."

Frances beamed at her words. "Owen Thatcher is still looking for her. He came out to the agency a couple of times, and Charles finally let him look all around. He questioned our people, but no one gave Annie away."

In the days that followed, John kept Charles busy penning letters and reports to the Indian Commission and General Howard. John had met with Joseph several times at the camas digging, and now he informed General Howard that the chief seemed to care very little for the man killed and seemed satisfied with the state of affairs. But Howard, not willing to take any chances, telegraphed Captain Perry to try to pacify Joseph. When John heard of this, he was irritated and left the dinner party at Faye Perry's quarters early. All the way home he was brooding and silent. Sarah was disappointed as well. She'd looked forward to seeing Tanner again, and Elise Channing had made her intentions toward him very clear.

But Tanner rode over to the agency often after their return from the camas gathering. Sometimes Sarah and he would walk through the pine forests, or sit on the agency porch talking. The development of their whirlwind relationship had been intense, blossoming in spite of the danger and adventure they'd faced together. Now both seemed content to slow down and find out more about each other. Sarah's fears about Elise faded. Likewise they spoke of Black Beaver, and Tanner was elated to hear Sarah felt nothing more than friendship for the Indian warrior and that even that had diminished somewhat since his behavior at Camas Meadows. Lightly he dismissed Black Beaver, but Sarah couldn't. She had seen the flash of hatred in the Indian's dark eyes when he lunged for Tanner.

Tanner courted Sarah gallantly, bringing bunches of field flowers or a box of candy from Lewiston. It had been shipped all the way from back East. Sometimes they sought the privacy of the shady river-banks, where Tanner held her and made love to her. Sarah thought she'd never been so happy in her life.

Toward the end of July new recruits were sent to Fort Lapwai, accompanied by a familiar face. Tanner watched Gayle Nevins direct the men and horses down the gangplank and barely restrained a whoop of joy. The young Irishman hadn't been massacred at the Little Big Horn after all. His glee was short-lived as Nevins caught sight of Tanner and sneered with his old arrogance.

"Hello, Tanner," he said derisively. "So this is where you hightailed it to." He glanced down the street of the rough frontier town. "What they got you doing here, errand boy?"

"Lieutenant Nevins," Tanner snapped coldly, his pleasure diminished by the young man's attitude. "You weren't with Custer at the Little Big Horn?"

"Nah," Nevins grinned. "I was transferred to Major Reno's company. We were patrolling elsewhere when Custer and his men got it. It was a good thing you turned tail and ran when you did." Nevins glanced at his young recruits. Some of them guffawed, then fell silent under Tanner's cold stare.

"Assemble your men," Tanner ordered.

"Yes, sir, Major." Nevins snapped a sloppy, mocking salute. In short order he had his men mounted, but in the process he'd managed to pass along the old rumors of cowardliness, and now the untried young recruits sat watching the major with contemptuous expressions. Although Custer was dead, his legacy of false rumors and unfair condemnations had returned to haunt Tanner. Tanner felt too weary to fight them. Hadn't he castigated himself with the same bitter remonstrations during the past weeks? Never mind that Custer had ordered him to leave. He should have been there with his men.

Tanner never told Sarah of Gayle Nevins's arrival or of the spreading rumors at the fort. She sensed something was wrong, but could get nothing from him. Her old fears about Elise Channing resurfaced. In the weeks that followed, Tanner's life was miserable. He couldn't enter a building or cross the parade ground without the jeers and calls of Nevins and his friends. Yet when he turned to face his hecklers, not one man appeared to be looking at him.

One day Major Wood rode out to the agency to see John Monteith. Frances maintained he'd really come to see Sarah, for he sat during the whole visit staring at her with moonstruck eyes. Sarah was embarrassed, Frances amused, and John and Charles irritated. The major had come at General Howard's request to ask the Indian agent to make arrangements for a council meeting with Joseph. John's thin lips tightened in anger and resentment, but he agreed to make the arrangements.

The council would be held at the Lapwai agency. The morning of the appointed day, Joseph arrived with forty of his warriors and several minor chiefs. Spotted Frog rode beside him. Black Beaver and Little Wolf were among the young warriors. All were mounted on fine horses whose tails and manes had been braided and decorated with shells. Their best saddles had been used, and the men wore shirts and leggings of tanned and bleached elk and deer hide, heavily fringed and beaded. Joseph held himself proudly. All the chiefs wore head bonnets of eagle feathers. They looked like fierce, beautiful birds.

Sarah and Frances watched from the agency porch as the mounted Indians formed a half circle around the designated meeting site. Major Wood and Major Tanner were among the officers who dismounted and solemnly greeted the Indian chief. Sarah could see Tanner's tall, broad-shouldered figure towering over the other men except Joseph and Spotted Frog. They stood eye to eye and even from where she watched, Sarah could see a glimmer of friendship and acceptance in Joseph's eyes. It bode well for the outcome of the council. All that she cared about in the world was represented in these two men, and she prayed the council would bring better understanding between them.

Reuben acted as interpreter as the men began their talks. But all too soon they reached an impasse. The meeting came to an abrupt end, and the Indians and soldiers mounted and galloped away.

"Things don't look too good," Frances said worriedly.

"It was only the first meeting," Sarah reminded her. "More will be accomplished tomorrow."

"Maybe," Frances agreed. "In the meantime, I'd better see to supper." She disappeared inside and Sarah stayed where she was, staring out at the empty grounds where Joseph and his warriors had been a short time before. Tomorrow evening seemed a long time away. Major Wood had chosen to have the meeting at the fort, and she wondered idly if she and Frances would accompany John and Charles. She hoped so. She couldn't bear to wait here, wondering what had happened.

But it seemed none of them would go to the fort. John had been asked not to attend the council, and his fierce pride wouldn't allow him to go as an onlooker.

Tanner rode in late the next night to tell them what had happened. His shoulders sagged wearily and the lines of his face seemed deeper. Sarah knew he'd come straight there to report, and she longed to settle him in a comfortable chair and bathe his face.

Instead she poured him a cup of strong black coffee, and sat across the table from him with Frances, John, and Charles.

"Joseph agreed to a commission if honest men are chosen," Tanner said, sprawling in the roughly hewn kitchen chair. His large brown hands nearly hid Frances's delicate china tea cup.

"I can't say as I blame him for that," Frances said.

Tanner nodded in agreement. "It's not going to be easy, though," he said. "Spotted Frog brought a map of the territory the Indians are still claiming as theirs, and it's considerably more than the amount allowed by the president's last order." He glanced at Monteith, who'd sat tight-lipped throughout the conversation. "I saw Major Wood's report to Howard, and he indicated that the Nez Percé have no complaints against you."

Stiff-necked, John glared at him. "Was General Howard concerned about this?" he asked.

Tanner shook his head. "Not to my knowledge."

"So it was the idea of this upstart, Major Wood," the agent snapped.

"His intentions were good, Monteith," Tanner growled. "We all want these hostilities to die down before we're faced with a full-fledged war."

"That well may be, Major Tanner," John said, getting to his feet, "but I will be sending a letter to the Commissioner of Indian Affairs about this matter. The military had no right to step in without my request to do so. Major Wood's action has given Chief Joseph the idea we hold him in a higher esteem than we do. He will be harder than ever to work with. Furthermore, my position has been undermined. Joseph and his men will think they have some other authority to go to than the agency."

"I'm sure that wasn't the major's intent," Tanner said placatingly.

"That does me little good now," John said unyieldingly.

Tanner sighed and set the delicate cup back on the table. Getting to his feet, he picked up his hat and glanced at the agent. "You seem to forget one thing, Monteith," he said. "If things get much worse with the Indians, the military will have to step in anyway. We're doing everything we can to keep that from happening." With a final glance at Sarah he left.

In the weeks that followed, one trouble seemed to follow another as white settlers continued to encroach on Indian land. Indian and white man fought over fence lines, fences were torn down and men killed. The disputes grew as heated as the hot August sun on the high meadows. One Nez Percé was shot dead when he attempted to stop a settler from plowing up his land, vicious dogs were set to attack other Indians as they passed by, and the continual cheating and shortchanging of the Nez Percé in the general stores and whiskey houses caused more resentment. Joseph's tribe seemed to be singled out for much of the trouble. Sarah suspected Owen Thatcher and his desperadoes were behind it, but she had no proof.

The commission became a reality, approved by the division commander. General Howard proposed Monteith's name to the commission, but the agent, his pride obscuring a broader view of how to handle the Indians, criticized the formation of such a group. When the final commission was formed, the Indian agent had been replaced by a man from Saginaw, Michigan. General Howard and his adjutant, Major Wood, were also part of the five-man group.

"This commission is an unnecessary expense for our government," Monteith fumed bitterly, "and it will accomplish nothing." Sarah said little during these days, keeping quietly to herself. She was ever mindful of her position at the agency and how tenuous it was. Her sympathies for Joseph and his tribe were well-known among the agency people, as was her love for Major Tanner. Now when she wished to see Tanner, she asked Reuben to escort her to the fort or Tanner himself came to meet her halfway. They supped often with Emily Fitzgerald and her family, and with the Perrys when it couldn't be avoided. Elise Channing made such evenings painstaking affairs with Tanner and Sarah parting in polite silence.

By the first week of November the men of the commission had arrived at Fort Lapwai for the first council. Sarah and Frances went to the fort and along with Faye Perry and Emily Fitzgerald joined the other observers at the church, where the meetings were held. Elise Channing didn't attend, claiming the whole affair was boring and unnecessary.

As she climbed the steps to the church, Sarah looked around. Yellow Bird and her mother stood among the Indians crowded outside. They were all dressed in their best clothes, and Sarah felt an irrational thrill of pride at their brave showing. Annie and her grandmother were nowhere in sight. But then Sarah had known she wouldn't be. Owen Thatcher would be in the crowd, and he was still looking for Annie.

Inside the church Sarah took her seat with the other white women, and couldn't help notice that none of the Indian wives had been invited inside, not even as a courtesy to the chiefs. Tanner and the other officers filled the pews on one side of the church. Silently he nodded to Sarah. The crowd of onlookers ceased talking as General Howard and the commission entered and took their seats. Then Joseph, dressed simply in a bleached elk-hide shirt and leggings and wearing the eagle-feathered head-dress of his office entered the church. The high bonnet made him look taller and even more impressive, and a buzz of whispered comments ran along the pews of onlookers.

Faye Perry looked as if she were about to faint, and Emily Fitzgerald held a lacy handkerchief to her nose, as if unable to tolerate the smell of campfire smoke and leather that clung to the Indians. Though she'd liked the doctor's wife for her intelligence and no-nonsense attitude about most things, Sarah felt a flush of anger wash through her. How dare these women, pampered and cared for all their lives, secure in their positions of superiority and righteousness, turn up their nose at the Indians? She bit her lips to keep back her anger.

From his seat, Tanner watched Sarah's face, seeing the play of emotions, feeling that moment when anger turned to awareness of the sad inevitability of the Indians' plight. He glanced away. He couldn't think that way. Once he'd walked away from an Indian fight because of his sympathy for them. He couldn't do so again.

"Welcome, Chief Joseph," General Howard said, standing and holding out his left hand to the Indian. His right coat sleeve hung empty. "I bring greetings from my white father in Washington and a wish for a long and prosperous life for you and your people."

Joseph clasped the hand firmly. "The people of the Nez Percé nation bring greetings. May the Great Spirit guide your heart in this council, for we of the Nez Percé tribes wish to live a long and prosperous life alongside our brothers."

"Yes, well, that is what we hope to accomplish with this council," General Howard said. "Shall we begin?"

It became apparent to the whites who listened that Chief Joseph was not prepared to make any concession about the land he claimed for the Nez Percé. His eyes were alert and intelligent as he listened to the commission's proposals, and he countered every suggestion with one of his own, more favorable to the Nez Percé.

As the council progressed, John Monteith leaned forward. "Is your scalp fastened on tightly, ladies?" he whispered. Sarah's usual patience for the narrow-minded, biased agent was ended. She sent him a telling glance, and he leaned back in his seat and fell silent. Faye, however, had been badly shaken by his comment and by the proceedings, and now she rose, her face sickly pale. Quickly Dr. Fitzgerald and Emily escorted her from the church.

The council ended soon after, and Tanner came to walk Sarah back to Captain Perry's quarters. Joseph and his tribe had returned to their camp outside the fort.

"Don't be too discouraged by today's proceedings," he advised. His hand at her elbow provided some comfort. "They may make better progress tomorrow."

"What kind of progress can we hope for?" Sarah asked. "Either Joseph and his tribe must give up more of their land, or the commission must relent and let him keep what is his. I don't think either one will happen."

"It might. Some compromise will have to be made," Tanner said. "Neither side wants war."

"But the Nez Percé have made compromises for years. Look how the reservation land has slowly shrunk because of the greedy settlers who came first for gold and then land and even for the Indian's ponies and beef herds. Where will it all end?"

"I don't know," Tanner said, but he was afraid he knew all too well. The memory of Cheyenne tipis burning in a March blizzard and of a small face whose terror-filled eyes had widened in death came to him. He pushed it away, deliberately picturing the bodies of fallen soldiers at the battle of Little Big Horn. He'd meant to draw Sarah into some shady, secluded spot for a few stolen kisses, but now he quickened their pace and soon left her on the porch.

Elise Channing was seated among the other women there. Quickly she rose and walked to the railing. "Good afternoon, Major Tanner," she said with a playful air.

"Ma'am," Tanner said, touching the brim of his hat respectfully before walking away.

Sarah couldn't hold back a smile as she met Elise's disappointed gaze. "Good afternoon, Elise," she said playfully as she climbed the steps. Several women had gathered on the porch to discuss the day's proceedings. Sarah found a seat.

"Did you ever smell anything so horrid in your life? They're like animals all wrapped up in those blankets and buffalo robes." Faye shrugged fastidiously. "I don't think I ever saw so many babies before. I understand food gets fairly short out there in the winter time. Why do they have all those babies if they can't feed them?"

Sarah pinched her lips together in order to remain silent but failed. "Maybe they have babies for all the same reasons we have babies," she said crisply. "Children are their hope for the future." Faye fell silent under Sarah's disapproving tone. Elise studied Sarah with bright, speculative eyes.

"It isn't that we mean them ill by our remarks," Emily Fitzgerald said placatingly. "We are trying to understand them, but they just won't compromise at all."

"They have compromised with the whites in the past," Sarah said. "And each time it's cost them more of their land. Now we want them to move on to the reservations and give up their way of life altogether."

"And well they should," remarked Sue McBeth, a missionary who'd come from the Kamiah agency. "They will never achieve salvation living the heathenish life they do." Sarah had only recently met the stern woman who had once held her job as a teacher at the Lapwai agency. When Spalding had died she'd gone to Kamiah, where she taught young Nez Percé men to become religious leaders of the tribes. Though crippled and in feeble health, the dour Scotswoman was diligent in her effort to stamp out all customs and traditions of the Nez Percé. Now she expounded on that theme. The Indians, she'd made very clear, must give up the nomadic lives they led and adhere to the white man's ways if they were ever to save their immortal souls. So earnest was she in her beliefs that the other ladies fell silent and listened to her without demur. All save Sarah.

"The Indians have difficulty in accepting our god who has proven to be vindictive and demanding and harsh, not the loving god they envisioned," she said, trying hard to choose words that would not offend unduly, yet unable to remain silent. To do so would be to betray Joseph and Yellow Bird and even old Running Brook, but most of all Swan Necklace. Her words had shocked the ladies around the porch.

"What heresy," cried Sue McBeth, her jowls quivering in indignation. "Be careful Sarah MacKenzie, that the good Lord doesn't strike you dead. Perhaps you would favor the teaching of this Dreamer religion in our white churches."

"Of course, I didn't say that," Sarah remonstrated, feeling angry at having to defend herself.

"You might as well have," Sue cried.

"I'm sure Sarah meant no insult to you and the wonderful work you're doing with the Indian tribes," Emily assured the teacher. "Let's not be angry with one another. We're all feeling the tension of this council."

"That's true enough," Frances said. "We're all afraid this thing will escalate into a war. Why, John and Charles are constantly working with our Indians to make sure they don't go back out in the mountains with Joseph or Looking Glass or one of the other big chiefs."

"I wish someone would kill Joseph before he kills any of us," Emily said.

Sarah leaped to her feet in shocked outrage. "Surely you don't mean that," she exclaimed.

Emily calmly regarded Sarah. "I do, most fervently," she replied. "If Joseph were dead, his Indians might come into the reservation, and all this fear and danger would be over. Wouldn't one death be better than the many we'll have if there's a war?"

"If there's a war, it won't be of Joseph's making," Sarah declared. She was shaking with anger at Emily's remark. She'd always considered the doctor's wife levelheaded and fair, and now she felt hurt and betrayed by her friend's attitude. "Joseph is doing his best to prevent hostilities between his men and the white settlers, but the more they give way, the more the settlers take. You can't blame him for making a stand now."

The women sat staring at Sarah, their mouths open in consternation at her staunch defense of Joseph. Realizing she'd done nothing to change their thinking and feeling sick with worry for Joseph and Yellow Bird, she excused herself and went to the guest room in Emily Fitzgerald's living quarters. She could hear the women's shocked remarks at her outburst. "Indian lover," Sue sniffed. Sarah heard no more, for she closed the door and sprawled across the bed, tears seeping from beneath her tightly closed lids.

The church was packed with onlookers the next day. General Howard and his commission met Joseph with the same elaborate greetings, compliments, and good wishes as before. They were returned in kind by Joseph. Once again the verbal fencing began, and the commission grew frustrated by the mental dexterity of the Nez Percé chief. For several men on the commission, this council meeting was their first contact with Joseph, and they alternately admired and were angered by his skillful negotiations.

"But," said the gentleman from Saginaw, Michigan, "Lawyer did sign the treaty and you must abide by it."

Joseph considered his words and with calm deliberation replied. "The old treaty has never been correctly reported. If we ever owned the land, we own it still, for we never sold it. In the treaty councils the commissioners have claimed that our country has been sold to the government. Suppose a white man should come to me and say, 'Joseph, I like your horses and I want to buy them.' I say to him, 'No, my horses suit me, I will not sell them.' Then he goes to my neighbor and says to him, 'Joseph has some good horses. I want to buy them, but he refuses to sell.' My neighbor answers, 'Pay me the money and I will sell you Joseph's horses.' The white man returns to me and says, 'Joseph, I have bought your horses and you must let me have them.' If we sold our lands to the government, this is the way they were bought."

Joseph stopped speaking and the onlookers and

commissioners were silent, nonplussed by what he said, for they saw the unfairness.

Finally the commission grew impatient. "I would like to remind the honorable Chief Joseph," said the businessman from Saginaw, "of the other Indian tribes who have refused to cooperate with us, the Modoc, Seminole, and the Sioux." He let his words hang, an ominous threat on the stale smoke-filled air.

With bated breath everyone waited to hear Joseph's response. He remained silent for a time and finally, raising his proud head, spoke. "If it is to be, then we Nez Percé are ready for the soldiers," he replied calmly, and a chill of fear ran through the church.

General Howard cleared his throat. "There can only be one decision from this council, Chief Joseph," he began. "If all the non-treaty Nez Percé do not move onto the reservation voluntarily within a reasonable time, they shall be placed there by force." Sarah felt the blood drain from her head. Chief Joseph's face reflected his shock at the unjustness of the decision.

The council broke up soon afterward, and Sarah and the Monteiths made their way back to Captain Perry's quarters, where a light supper was served. Everyone was morose and quiet.

"By God, he's taken a course of action that will lose all sympathy for him," General Howard said loudly and thumped the table with his good arm. Sarah jumped at the sudden noise.

"He's bound to come around, sir," Tanner said. "He knows he has little choice."

"He'd better," the general exclaimed. "If the trouble in the Wallowa comes up again next summer, I'll send out two men to Joseph's one and whip him into submission." Tanner's hand gripping hers helped Sarah control the anger she felt.

"You seem displeased by General Howard's words, Sarah," Elise said. Her tone was probing. Sarah took a deep breath to calm herself and glanced along the table at the shallow young woman. She was seated beside Gayle Nevins, and it was obvious the young lieutenant was quite taken by her.

"I am displeased at the thought of war and killing, Elise, as any God-fearing person should be," she replied in a low tone.

"We all feel the same way, Sarah," Emily said warmly, and Sarah could have forgiven her for her remarks about Joseph the day before. "Most of us have husbands or loved ones who would be involved. We don't want our men to fight and be killed."

"Oh, David," Faye cried, her slender white hands gripping her husband's sleeve, her blue eyes round with fear.

"It's all right, dearest," he replied, patting her hand reassuringly. "Nothing will happen for the next few months. The Indians will be snowed into their river valleys. Besides, they'll never start a war, they're too ill-equipped. Even Joseph must realize that."

"I wouldn't count on that," Tanner spoke up. "That hasn't stopped any tribe so far."

"The Nez Percé are not the Sioux, Major Tanner," Henry Wood spoke up. In spite of his preoccupation with the commission, he was still slightly nettled that Tanner had won over the heart of the best-looking woman around.

Tanner met his glare, unperturbed. "Indeed the Nez Percé are not the Sioux," he replied quietly. "If they were, you would have been at war with them long before this. Joseph is at least reasonable enough to listen to us and to try to keep his young bucks under control."

"How would you know anything of the Sioux?" Nevins challenged from his end of the table. "You weren't at the battle of the Little Big Horn." Sarah's gaze flew to Tanner's face.

A muscle jumped in his jaw. "No, I wasn't," he said and got to his feet. "But then, neither were you, were you, Lieutenant?" Nevins leaped to his feet, his fists clenched, outrage written in every line of his body.

General Howard looked from one soldier to the other, trying to measure the reason for their animosity. "Gentlemen, let's remember our hostess," he rebuked mildly.

"My apologies, ma'am," Tanner said. "If you'll excuse me, I've some business to attend to before bugle call."

"Of course, Major Tanner," Faye said primly.

"Sir." Tanner sketched a quick salute and with a final glance at Sarah left the room. The people at the table sat silently for a time.

"Well, my goodness, what was that all about?" Elise Channing said, fluttering her hands above the silverware.

"Major Tanner was part of Custer's cavalry before he turned yellow bellied and ran off," Nevins sneered.

"I understand he was transferred," General Howard said.

"Yes, sir. They transferred him after he shot at his own men during a raid on an Indian camp."

"Major Tanner's behavior has been exemplary since he's come here," Captain Perry spoke up. "He's a fine officer." Sarah could have hugged him for his defense of Tanner.

"Yes, that was my impression," General Howard said, casting a disparaging glance at the young lieutenant. "You'd be well advised, lieutenant, to remember he is your superior officer."

"Yes, sir," Nevins said, but he was unchastened. "Requesting your permission, sir, I'd rather be transferred to some other unit. I wouldn't want to be serving under Major Tanner if there's an Indian war."

"I'll take your request into consideration, Lieutenant," Howard said. "In the meantime we'll have no more of this conversation. I won't have my officers gossiped about behind their backs."

"Yes, sir," Nevins said, flushing. "If you'll excuse me, sir, ma'am."

"Excused, excused." The general waved him away. "By the way, Lieutenant, why weren't you fighting at the Little Big Horn with Custer?"

"I was assigned to Major Reno's unit, sir. We missed the action."

"Transferred, eh?" the general said. "The same as Major Tanner."

The young lieutenant colored more. "Yes, sir," he said, and quickly opened the door and made his escape.

The dinner party broke up then. Everyone was tired and still preoccupied by the day's events. General Howard and the rest of the commission would be leaving early the next morning to return to Portland.

This was the last night Sarah would be staying at the fort. The agency people would return to Lapwai sometime in the morning. Restlessly she paced the room she shared with Frances and Sue McBeth until those ladies retired. Then she wrapped a shawl around her shoulders and made her way along the parade ground. There was no moonlight. The barracks rose starkly black against a dark sky. Sarah longed to see Tanner if only for a few stolen moments, but she was hesitant to ask for him at the barracks. Sighing in frustration, she returned to her room and prepared for bed.

True to their word, General Howard and the commissioners left early for Portland. Sarah and Frances packed their canvas bags and waited for John and Charles to bring around the wagon. A light, cold rain had begun to fall. Suddenly there was a shout, and Tanner and some of the other officers came running across the parade ground. Summoned by the commotion, Emily and Faye joined Sarah and Frances on the porch.

"Heavenly days, what is it now?" Emily exclaimed.

"The heathens," Sue exclaimed, eyes riveted on the approaching horsemen. Four Indians rode forward, all of them attired in heavily beaded skins and feathered headpieces. Sarah recognized Joseph and Spotted Frog immediately. For this meeting Joseph had donned a softly tanned skin decorated with ermine fringe along his sleeves and around his knees. Even his headpiece was ornamented with the precious fur. His horse wore a cap over his head and face, all of it heavily beaded with holes cut for his eyes. The warriors' faces were painted and each carried a bow and quiver of arrows, each one decorated with feathers and bits of fur. They looked proud and fierce and noble. Sarah stood gripping a post, her face sad as she watched her kinsmen come to a halt before the onlookers. Rain dripped in a sad, monotonous staccato from the eaves.

"We have come to talk to General Howard," Joseph said pleasantly. He smiled at the ladies.

"I'm afraid he's not here," Captain Perry said, stepping forward. "He and the rest of the commission have returned to Portland."

Joseph's smile faded. "I am sorry to have missed saying farewell to my white brother," he said. All were aware of the insult the general had shown the chief in not bidding a proper farewell.

"We will talk with him again in the spring," Joseph said and, holding his palm out in a final farewell, turned his horse away. Slowly the Indians rode away in the cold rain, and unwillingly tears sprang to Sarah's eyes. Tanner was there beside her. Ignoring the other people, he wrapped his arms around her and held her close. Resting her head on his strong shoulder she quietly wept for Joseph and his people.

"Maybe this is the beginning of a settlement," Emily cried, and the others joined in her happy speculations. Sarah remained where she was. Suddenly she knew the fate of Joseph and his warriors. Their proud nobility would never withstand the force of the white man's greed for Nez Percé lands.

16

The cold rains of November gave way to the first snows, which fell like a gentle mantle over the mountains. Sarah was enchanted by the wonderland around her. But if the land lay at rest, peaceful and serene beneath its pristine white blanket, the people upon it were not.

The Commissioner of Indian Affairs instructed Monteith to notify Joseph and his band that he must come to the reservation. When Sarah heard the news she ran into the woods nearby, where the wind soughed mournfully through snow-laden pine trees. Tears rolled down her cheeks in icy runnels. It had all been to no avail, she though despairingly. All the councils, all the commissions had only delayed the inevitable. Joseph and his people must give up their valley and live on the reservation. Their free spirits would die in such a stifling environment as the reservation. They'd been born to roam the land freely as the eagle roamed the sky, unfettered. How could they submit to the white man's narrow world? She stayed in the woods until the cold drove her back to the agency, where Frances scolded her for her wet feet and frozen fingers.

"How could you go out there without proper clothing?" Frances demanded. "Your lips are blue."

"It doesn't matter," Sarah said, shivering in spite

245

of herself. She raised her tearstained face to the kindly woman who'd been her friend all these months. "What will they do, Frances, Joseph and his people? How will they live here on this small piece of land when they're used to roaming through the mountains and valleys?"

"I don't know, child," Frances said, "and that's a fact. Personally I think it's for the best. They can farm the land and they need not go hungry in the winter as some of them do now. Maybe it'll be hard for them to adjust now, but for their children and their grandchildren, it will be a better life."

"I don't know their grandchildren. I only know them as they are now, and I can't help grieving for them."

John came to the door, his expression guarded when he saw Sarah's tearstained face. She sensed his resentment of her ever since the council at the fort.

"Where's Charlie?" he asked Frances.

"He's coming now," Frances said, nodding toward the porch.

"I need you to write out a formal request to be sent to General Howard," the Indian agent instructed when his brother entered.

"What's this all about?" Charles asked.

"I'm asking the general to send two troops of cavalry to occupy the Wallowa Valley."

Sarah drew in her breath sharply. The cup of hot tea she'd been holding fell from her nerveless fingers. So it had come to this. John glanced at Sarah, then motioned his brother into the hall toward the study.

"I thought the commissioner said to use restraint in dealing with the Indians." Charles's voice was still audible from the hall.

"That's what I'm doing," John replied, "using restraint."

"Won't having the soldiers in the valley stir things up worse?"

"It'll let Joseph know we'll take no more stalling. They have to come onto the reservation." Their voices dwindled away. Sarah buried her face in the warmth of the towel Frances had brought her.

"There, there, Sarah. It's not that bad," Frances said comfortingly. "John is trying to bring the Indians in peacefully." Sarah leaned against the homey comfort of the other woman. Nothing was ever simple, she thought. Frances and Charles and even the stiff, straight-laced John had been her friends these many months, and yet they were the enemies of her people. Faced with torn loyalties, Sarah didn't know what to do, and then she thought of the caged bear she'd seen the first day she arrived. The Nez Percé were like that great wild animal, about to be penned in a cage that was too small.

Monteith acted quickly, for the winter snows would soon close off the passes. He chose four men to go to Joseph's village and try to persuade him to come onto the reservation peacefully. They were gone only a few days before they returned. Their faces reflected their failure before they spoke a word. John ran bareheaded into the snow to greet them. Sarah and Frances stood on the porch, peering through the white flakes.

"Well, what happened?" John demanded before they'd even dismounted.

Reuben slumped in his saddle. "This is what Joseph said," he began. "I have been talking to the whites many years about the land in question, and it is strange they cannot understand me. The country they claim belonged to my father and when he died, it was given to me and my people, and I will not leave it until I am compelled to." It seemed to Sarah that as he spoke Joseph's defiant words, Reuben gained stature. Sarah could read the pride in his eyes. He might have come onto the reservation, but some small part of him still longed for the deep green river valleys and the majestic mountains of his youth.

John Monteith uttered a curse, and Sarah saw Frances's mouth fall open. In all their months at the agency, no matter what the frustrations, they'd never heard the agent utter a blasphemous word. The task was not easy for him, either, Sarah thought, and her anger at him eased somewhat.

The next time she was at the fort, Sarah sought out Tanner and poured out her feelings. She expected his support and was startled at his words.

"It's for the best, Sarah," he said grimly. "Once Joseph is brought onto the reservation, all the rest of the bands will come in and there can be peace in the valley."

"Peace?" she cried scathingly. "At what price? You're forcing the Indians to give up their land, their customs, their whole way of life and adopt a foreign religion that has been used to manipulate them and steal from them for years."

"Sarah, that's the way of things. You have to accept it."

"No," Sarah cried, leaping to her feet. "I won't. I can't. Have you forgotten I'm part Nez Percé?"

Tanner started to answer, but a sound at the door made him pause. Quickly he crossed the room and swung open the door. Gayle Nevins stood on the other side.

"What do you want, Lieutenant?" Tanner demanded.

"I was just passing by," the soldier said, and with a sly sideways glance at Sarah he walked away whistling a little tune.

Thoughtfully Tanner stood watching Nevins's retreating back then closed the door. "It's best if we don't discuss this anymore," he said softly. "Try not to fight it, Sarah. It's going to happen. It's not fair to Joseph and his band or to the other Nez Percé being herded onto reservations, but it can't be stopped."

"If Joseph fights, will you go against him?" Sarah asked the question that had troubled her the most.

Tanner shook his head from side to side. "Don't ask me that," he pleaded.

"Will you?"

"I'll have to. I'm a soldier."

"First you're a man, or maybe you're not. If you ran from the Sioux, can't you run from the Nez Percé as well?" She knew the words were hateful and mean, but she was hurt that he would fight against her people.

Tanner crossed the room and gripped her arms. His gray eyes were icy as they stared into hers. "I will kill any Indian who gets in my way," he said, and Sarah felt frightened by his fierceness.

Crimson color stained her cheeks as she backed away from him. Without a word she walked out of the room. She was too angry to stay at the fort and, requesting a horse from the stables, she left a message for Frances and rode back to the agency alone. Frances was furious with her and rightfully so, Sarah conceded, and to calm her friend, agreed to return to the fort the following week for a Christmas party. How could she go among those people who planned to destroy her people? she wondered bleakly. Tanner hadn't come out to the agency, and she sensed he was as torn as she by all that had been said between them. She wished she'd never uttered those awful words, but she couldn't call them back now. The night of the party Sarah took extra care with her appearance, choosing a gown of a deep red color that was both festive for the season and becoming to her. The heavy damask draped in graceful folds. She wanted to look especially beautiful tonight, not just for Tanner, but for Major Wood, who could tell her General Howard's plans for the spring campaign. Tonight she would hang onto his every word and somehow she would warn Joseph.

Pine cones and green boughs had been brought into the Perrys' parlor. The fresh smells mingling with beeswax greeted the guests when they arrived. A bowl of punch had been placed in the middle of the table with small cookies and cakes set around. Lighthearted laughter filled the air. Breathlessly Faye Perry hurried around the room, greeting newcomers and leading them to the refreshment table or to a group of people. No one was allowed to stand alone on the sidelines. Elise Channing was well in evidence, Sarah noted, and she seemed to be glued to Gayle Nevins's side. At least she'd turned her attentions away from Tanner. Or so Sarah thought.

Sarah knew exactly when Lucas Tanner stepped into the room. The door opened in a rush of wind and snow and he was there, filling more space than the other men, his proud head inches above theirs, the streaked brown hair falling across his forehead, the gray eyes searching the room until they found and settled on Sarah. With a pretty pout Elise went to greet him almost as a lover. Sarah drew a shaky breath and turned back to Captain Whipple, who had recently been appointed to patrol Wallowa Valley. She'd found him surprisingly open and he answered her questions without hesitation.

"General Howard is already moving more troops into Fort Walla Walla," Captain Whipple stated. "By spring we'll be at war with the Nez Percé."

"Be careful what you say, Captain," a deep voice said, and Sarah swung around. Tanner's gray eyes regarded her, a half smile curved his lips. "The lady may be a spy."

"Oh, come now, Major," Sarah replied lightly turning so he could see the tight, low-cut bodice. "Where would I hide my secrets?"

Tanner's hungry gaze swept over the ivory skin of her bare shoulders and slim throat, and she saw a flush rise along his cheekbones. Hope flared within her. Could he forgive her cruel taunts? Her velvety brown eyes showed all her uncertainty and all the love she felt for him.

"Ah, if you'll excuse me, I'll get some more punch," Captain Whipple said, and with a final nod at the two people who seemed not to notice his presence or absence, he went in search of more responsive company.

"Lean pickings," a voice said, and Whipple looked at the young officer standing nearby. He had clear blue eyes and red hair and a face that would be youthful way beyond its years. "Gayle Nevins here." He held out a hand.

Whipple took it. "Lieutenant Nevins."

"I've already checked out the ladies," Nevins continued, glancing around. "It's mostly officers' wives or spinsterish missionaries ready to preach the gospel at the drop of a hat. Except for Elise Channing, and she and I have something of an understanding, if you know what I mean." Nevins winked.

"Looks like Major Tanner's got the only other desirable woman in the room," Whipple said as he glanced with regret back at the couple.

"If you like squaws," Nevins said derisively.

Startled, Whipple looked at him. "What do you mean? She's white."

Nevins shook his head, a knowing look on his face. "I heard it from her myself. She's part Nez Percé. Wonder if the rest of this esteemed company knows it."

Whipple looked thoughtful, remembering the playful remark Tanner had made. Perhaps it hadn't been so playful, but a warning. He tried to remember the questions she'd asked him and how much information he'd given freely. Uneasily he excused himself from the facetious young man and made his way toward General Howard.

"Sir, if I might speak with you a moment."

Sarah didn't see the progression of the two men, Whipple pouring out his suspicions to General Howard, Nevins spreading his bit of information among the rest of the guests. She had eyes only for Tanner.

"I'm sorry for the things I said," she whispered. She couldn't go on until she'd said those words. He saw the sincerity of them in her eyes. "Please forgive me. I didn't mean them. I've been so distraught over this thing with Joseph and his people, my people." Defiantly she uttered the last two words.

"We were both angry. There's something I want you to keep in mind in the months ahead. The Nez Percé may be your people, but so are the rest of us here at this fort. More white blood runs in your veins than Indian."

"I'll try to remember that," Sarah said with sincerity.

Tanner escorted her to the table for refreshments, then guided her to a chair with all the refinement of a gentleman born and bred. Only his weather-beaten face and big, capable hands gave him away. Sarah thought she preferred a man like him to any of the dandified, respectable gentlemen she'd met back East.

"I quite agree with you, Miss McBeth." Nevins's voice rang loudly above the others. People stopped talking and turned toward the jovial young lieutenant. Obviously he'd had a bit too much to drink, but except for the lady with whom he'd been conversing, most of the guests were inclined to be tolerant. It was the holidays, after all, a joyous occasion. Seeing he had an audience, Nevins addressed himself to the whole room. "If the Indians are put on the reservation and educated, they can live civilized, God-fearing lives. Why, Miss MacKenzie is an example of that."

Sarah's face blanched at his words, and Tanner leaped to his feet. The other guests looked at one another and back at the lieutenant in puzzlement.

"Maybe some of you folks didn't know it," Nevins continued affably. "We have a real, honest-to-goodness injun right here in this room. She's been passing herself off as white, with the help of Major Tanner."

"Nevins," Tanner shouted. "Watch what you say."

"I'm only saying what's true," Nevins said with mock piousness.

Tanner's muscles bunched as he prepared to launch himself at Nevins. Quickly Sarah stood up and put a hand on his sleeve.

"Wait, Major," she said in a clear, serene voice. Taking a deep breath to steady herself, she stepped forward to meet her heckler. Elise Channing was smiling with a glittering malevolence. Sarah could see the faces of her friends: Emily's thoughtful and sensitive, Frances' surprised and concerned, and Faye Perry's fearful and anxious, as if Sarah might pull out a tomahawk at any moment and set about scalping all her guests. Sarah pushed back an insane urge to laugh at the image of all of them in their elegant gowns and uniforms and bald heads.

Her glance flicked to Nevins. He stood sneering at her and her chin shot up in pride. She would not apologize or be ashamed. She was sorry now that she hadn't told them sooner. They might see her secrecy as shame. Taking a step toward the tipsy young officer, she looked him straight in the eye and then did the same with General Howard, Captains Perry and Whipple, and so on, and then she spoke, keeping her voice light and friendly.

"My grandfather, as some of you may know" —she nodded to Sue McBeth—"was a missionary here with Reverend Spalding when he first came to Wallowa Valley. My grandmother was Swan Necklace, the daughter of Bright Eagle, sister to the man you knew as Old Joseph. I am Nez Percé. Chief Joseph and I are cousins. My Indian name is the same as my grandmother's." She looked around the room at their shocked faces. Tanner was lounging back against the wall, and she thought she saw pride and admiration in his eyes.

"Lieutenant Nevins has made the point that the Nez Percé should be put on the reservation and reeducated, their old customs stripped away, so they may become more civilized and he offers me as an example. I'm afraid I can't agree with you, Lieutenant. Although I grew up in the white man's world and was educated in his schools, I was also taught the customs and traditions of my people. I think this has made me a better person than I might have been otherwise. If we want to help the Indians, we must strive to give them both worlds, helping them to adopt to the white man's ways without taking away their pride in their Indian heritage. I know the old ways of the Indians are behind them. But surely we—you"—she held out a hand, palm up—"can be more humane, more generous in helping them to accept these changes." She paused and looked around. Her hand fell limply to her side. In the face of her simple declarations, Nevins backed away. He'd expected her to cry and be embarrassed.

"You've made some nice points, Miss MacKenzie," General Howard said at last, and the rest of the room seemed to come awake again. Faye murmured something to Emily, and Captain Whipple gulped down a glass of punch. David Perry lit a cheroot and studied Sarah through the haze of his smoke. "Perhaps you'd like to tell us why you chose to keep all this a secret from the rest of us?" the general asked.

"Certainly," Sarah said candidly. "When I arrived in Lewiston, I was struck by the prejudice that exists toward the Nez Percé. I saw an Indian girl being publicly whipped, and no one stepped forward to help her. I feared my effectiveness here would be lessened if people only thought of me as a Nez Percé and not as a woman who is capable and willing to do all I can to help my people." She could see her last words struck a sensitive spot with some of the guests.

"I'm sure in Missouri you never had to give it much thought," Emily said, crossing the room and putting a hand on Sarah's arm. "Why should you here?"

"Actually, from the time I was a little girl, I knew we were different."

Tanner straightened, hearing for the first time the pain she must have felt all those years when she was made an outsider. He wished he'd been there for her, but then she hadn't been alone. She'd had Swan Necklace.

"General, would you like another glass of punch?" Faye said brightly. How had her party gone awry? she wondered. "Captain Whipple, come try some of the little cakes I baked. Miss McBeth, are you ready for a bit of refreshments? Come on, you all, eat and enjoy." Her manner was brittle and uncertain.

People began milling around the room, smiling brightly, talking of everyday, inconsequential things. No one approached Sarah. She glanced at Frances and saw warm understanding in the older woman's eyes.

Emily squeezed her hand. "That took great courage," she whispered. "I'm sorry for the things I said about Joseph. I had no idea."

"Of course, you hadn't," Sarah answered, giving Emily a hug.

"Let's get out of here for a while," Tanner said, taking her elbow, "unless you're afraid of what they'll say." He grinned.

"I'm afraid it's too late for that," she commented ruefully. Faye and Sue McBeth had their heads together. Elise and Nevins were talking animatedly in one corner.

Tanner grinned. "I'm afraid you're right." He got her cape. Outside, the snow had been cleared from board walks, but it lay trampled and black on the parade ground.

"Have I told you how proud I am to know you, Miss MacKenzie?" Tanner said, intertwining his long fingers with hers.

"I'm grateful for your support back there," Sarah said. "I've wanted to tell everyone, but something always seemed to get in the way. I've felt like a fraud and a liar."

"You could never be that. You're one of the most honest women I've ever known. I've wanted to ask you this almost from the first time I met you."

"What is it?" Sarah asked, laughter suddenly bubbling to the surface. The thing she'd dreaded the most was behind her, and although she'd have to live with the repercussions for months to come, she felt freer than she had in a long time.

Tanner took a deep breath and, giving her a quick hard kiss on the lips, sank to one knee in the snow. "I love you, Sarah MacKenzie," he said earnestly. "I want you to be my wife."

The laughter died as Sarah stared at him in consternation. She'd never expected this. "You aren't asking me out of pity, are you?" she asked hesitantly.

"Pity?" Tanner gazed up at her. "No. Why would I?" he asked, then answered his own questions. "I love you even if you are an old-maid schoolteacher." His words caught her by surprise and suddenly she laughed, wrapping her arms around him where he knelt. His head rested against her soft breasts.

"As pleasurable as this is," he teased, "I'd like an answer soon. The snow is seeping through my trouser leg."

"Oh, Tanner, I'm sorry," Sarah cried, tugging him. "Do stand up."

"Not until I have my answer."

"Yes, yes, I'll marry you." She laughed. With a cry that rivaled any she'd heard from Joseph's braves, he swooped her into his arms and twirled around in the snow. "Put me down," she shrieked, giggling as the ground whirled by dizzily. Their commotion brought people to the door of Captain Perry's quarters. Bright lamplight spilled across the snow just as Tanner gave a final spin and they landed in a drift. Breathless, Sarah sat up and tried to straighten her tangled skirts.

"What's going on here, Major?" General Howard called from the porch.

"I'm about to become a married man, sir," he said, grinning.

"Oh, Sarah, that's wonderful," Emily cried. The other women called their congratulations, all except Elise, who turned and walked back inside. Sarah didn't care. No one could mar her happiness now.

"Come in out of the cold so we can celebrate properly," Frances called, and some of the men rushed down the steps to pull them from the snowbank. Amid back thumping and cries of best wishes they were ushered back into the warm parlor. The announcement had helped clear away the awkwardness that had fallen between them all since her revelation. It seemed a good omen. Glasses of sherry were poured for those who drank, and for the missionary and others of a sterner ilk, cups of hot cider with which to toast the betrothed couple.

When several toasts had been given, Lieutenant Nevins stepped forward and raised his glass. "To the squaw man," he slurred. One quick, hard punch from Tanner's big fist caught him on the chin before the glass reached his lips. He went slack and Tanner hauled him over his shoulder. "I'll just take Lieutenant Nevins back to the barracks," he said affably. "He seems to have had too much to drink." So quickly had it happened that there was barely a pause in the conversation.

"When is the wedding?" Emily asked.

"I don't know," Sarah began.

"Will you be married here?" Faye asked. She'd overcome her irritation that her sister had not won Tanner. Elise Channing was conspicuously absent.

"Will you live here at the fort?" Frances chimed in.

Sarah looked at them with wide, round eyes and everyone laughed. "I haven't had a chance to talk to Tanner yet. I don't know what he wants."

"My, my, my, Sarah," Faye chided prettily. "You

don't ask the bridegroom. You tell him. It's the last chance you'll have. The rest of your life, you'll have to listen to what he wants."

"I think I'll like that," Sarah said.

"Oh, listen to the baby," Frances said. "She'll learn soon enough." Everyone laughed again. Everything seemed incredibly funny. Sarah knew Frances was teasing her, for she'd never seen a more devoted couple than Charles Monteith and this homespun, motherly woman.

"A spring wedding. It should be a spring wedding," Faye said dreamily. "Mine was. We can have wildflowers to decorate the church, and you won't have to worry about mud on your gown. The nights are warm and romantic."

"You can go to Portland for your honeymoon," Frances piped in. "I went there with Charles once and it's a right pretty town, nothing at all like Lewiston."

"I'll help you sew a gown," Emily Fitzgerald offered.

"And I'll make the wedding cake," Faye cried. Sarah didn't know what to say. It seemed as if everyone were rallying around her. She was their friend and they valued her. When Tanner returned he found his bride to be all misty-eyed and his wedding already planned.

The weeks that followed were a strange blend of happiness and sad discoveries. The new schoolhouse had been completed, but when she opened school, she found herself with fewer students than before. The miller's three daughters were missing. Concerned that they might be ill, Sarah donned a heavy shawl and boots and walked down to the mill after school one day. Callie Osgood met her at the door, the baby clasped to her breasts. Her stomach was already swelling with a new one on the way.

"Hello, Callie, may I come in?" Sarah asked. Her cheeks were bright pink from the cold, and her breath was an icy vapor.

Callie looked around uncertainly. "Well, I dunno," she mumbled, but Sarah had already stepped inside the steamy warmth of the cabin. Jane smiled at her timidly from the rough wooden table where she was messily feeding the two-year-old.

"Jane and the other girls haven't been to school for several days," Sarah said. "I was worried they might be ill."

"No, ma'am, they ain't," Callie said.

"I'm glad to hear that," Sarah replied pleasantly. "Will they be there tomorrow?"

Callie shifted the baby higher on her hip and stared at the floor. "No, ma'am, I can't rightly say they will be."

"Goodness, why not?" Sarah asked, her bright eyes studying Callie.

"Dean and me, we figure it's all right for you to be teaching the Indians at that school of yours, but we want our girls to have a white teacher." For the first time Callie met Sarah's gaze. Her expression was defiant. Sarah looked from the mother to Jane sitting quietly at the table. Embarrassed, the little girl looked away.

"I see," Sarah said and was surprised at the pain she felt. "If you change your mind, the girls are welcome back."

"We won't be changing our minds," Callie said and pointedly opened the door. The snow swirled in cold and wet. It clung to the folds of her woolen gown. "Good day to you, Sarah," Callie said as grandly as a great lady speaking to her servant.

"Callie?" Sarah turned back to the woman. "Surely it would be better to have your girls in school than sitting here uneducated because of your prejudice."

"My man said that's the way it's to be. How do we know what heathenish things you're teaching them. The girls know how to write their name and say their numbers. Dean says that's good enough for girls."

"But Jane is so bright. She could go on and become a teacher herself. You can't deny her an education."

"Yes, we can," Callie said defiantly. "She's our daughter and she's white, and we don't want her being taught by no half-breed Indian. Now, you just get on out of here and leave us alone."

Defeated, Sarah left the mill and walked through the fields back to the agency. She never felt the cold snow against her face or knew that the melting flakes mingled with her tears.

Word of her Indian origin spread quickly and when she went into Lewiston, she was accosted by some of the town rowdies. Owen Thatcher looked on as the men jeered at her and even dared to grab at her clothes. Only the arrival of Tanner, with his stern demeanor and steel fists, made the men pass on down the street, hooting and calling obscenities back at her. Tanner saw her safely back to the agency. When Sarah told Frances about the incident, the older woman clicked her tongue in anger.

John Monteith was less sympathetic. "No need to cry over it now," the Indian agent said dourly. "Folks around here don't understand a white Indian." His words were cruel and they cut deeply. Charles nodded in agreement and with a quick glance at his wife turned away.

As the winter winds howled around the mountains, reaching its long, icy fingers deep into the river valleys, Sarah stayed more and more at the agency, avoiding any confrontation with the citizens of Lewiston. She was furious when she heard her charges against Carl Pepin for his attack on her had been dropped. He'd faced imprisonment for assaulting a white woman, but now that she was known to be part Indian, the charges had no grounds. For the first time, Sarah fully realized the injustices the Nez Percé had suffered. Then John Monteith set a deadline for April first for the Indians to be on the reservation.

"This can't be allowed to happen," Sarah said to Tanner one afternoon. She'd ridden to the post alone, needing desperately to see him and to be held in the warm security of his arms. Despite their plans to be circumspect and respectable until their wedding, they'd made their way to his quarters, where they'd stripped away their clothes and made love in a passionate haste that left them sweating and gasping for air.

"I'm afraid there's little to stop it now," Tanner said. His breathing had slowed now, and he pulled Sarah closer, marveling at the satiny smoothness of her skin and the softness of her bared breast pressed against his chest. Her nipples were still tight little buds from their lovemaking.

"Can't you talk to General Howard, buy some time for Joseph, maybe have another council."

Tanner shook his head. "The Secretary of War authorized the use of troops to move Joseph out of the valley."

"If they use force, people could be killed," Sarah said, sitting up. Her face was stark at the thought.

"It won't come to that," Tanner remonstrated and prayed he was right. The image of the little Cheyenne boy came to him, and he wrapped his arms around Sarah. "I promise I will never make war on Joseph's women and children. If shots are exchanged, it will be with his warriors. It's the most I can promise you."

"What are we going to do?" she wept piteously.

"It'll work out, Sarah," Tanner said. "We have to believe that." He held her until her sobs had quieted.

"I'd better get dressed and go," she said finally. "Someone will start terrible rumors about me and my squaw man." She felt the deep rumble of laughter beneath her cheek. Sitting up, she looked at the line of tangled clothes. Voluminous petticoats were twisted with dark blue canvas-lined trousers and jacket. Sarah grinned. "Someone was in a terrible hurry," she said in a playful tone.

Tanner knew she was forcing a lightheartedness she didn't feel, but he went along with it. "That's how we squaw men are," he said and nibbled her ear. "The next time we don't have to be in such a hurry."

"No?" she asked, raising her face to his kisses. "How long until next time?"

Tanner laughed, a warm, intimate chuckle that glided over her skin like a caress. "Anytime can be next time," he said huskily, and she lost the line of their inane love talk in the fire of his kisses.

It was much later before she untangled her petticoats, dressed, and sauntered forth again, and indeed more rumors were added to those already circulating about the white Indian and her squaw man.

17

"My land, look at this," Frances cried one day, and Sarah hurried to the window to look out. Faye Perry and Elise Channing, bundled to the chin in furs, were alighting from a sleigh. "What's brought those two ladies out in this kind of weather? They never come visiting before."

Sarah said nothing, only watching Elise's face as she turned to look at the humble single-story log cabin. A premonition told her this visit was more than an innocent afternoon of tea and chitchat. Frances hurried to open the door for her guests, flustered in spite of herself at the prospect of entertaining.

"Hello, Sarah," Elise said, handing over her heavy woolen cloak and giving her skirts a shake and a brush. "We haven't seen you for a while, and I said to Faye, I just want to go talk to our little Sarah for a while."

"Can you imagine coming out in this weather?" Faye laughed, still taken aback at their outing. She would never have come if Elise hadn't insisted so adamantly.

Frances hurried to make hot tea, fussing that she had only some of the rich dark fruitcake that Charles liked so much, rather than the little iced party cakes Faye was so good at serving.

They settled down in the parlor, and even Elise

appeared friendlier than she'd ever been. The tight feeling in Sarah's stomach began to lift.

"What a cozy home you have," Elise said finally, "but these log cabins are so small. Where is your room, Sarah?" Elise looked around.

"Why don't you show her, honey?" Frances urged. "This cabin is larger than it looks at first." Warily Sarah led the young woman to her room.

"How pretty," Elise gushed, looking around the small homey room. Her bright gaze seemed to take in everything.

"I like it," Sarah said, feeling a little nettled and not sure why.

"Of course, you do," Elise replied, sinking down on the bed, perfectly at ease. It was Sarah who suddenly felt awkward. "And the Monteiths have been so kind to you, haven't they?" Elise continued.

"Yes, they're wonderful."

"It's perfectly understandable that they would feel no prejudice toward you. After all, they work with Indians everyday." Sarah stiffened at the deliberate insult.

"Of course, it's a little harder for Major Tanner." Elise's finger traced the stitched pattern of the quilt, but her eyes were on Sarah, watching for her reaction. "I've heard the cruel taunts and they're really dreadful. There's even been talk that this marriage will ruin his career as an officer. You're so courageous and Lucas Tanner, well—" She rolled her eyes. "It's just so romantic to have a man make such a sacrifice for the woman he claims to love."

"He does love me," Sarah declared, "and he's never said anything to me about this trouble."

"Well, my dear, he wouldn't. He'd try to shield you as much as he can. I overheard him telling David that he feels so sorry for you and so do I,

Sarah, you poor thing." Elise's expression set itself into one of sympathy, but her eyes glittered with mischief.

Sarah made no reply and Elise stood up. "These little cabins are so cold, aren't they?" she said, shivering delicately. She returned to the parlor. "I've caught a dreadful chill, Faye, do you suppose we could go back?"

"Now?" Faye asked in surprise. "We've just arrived." Now that she was here she'd planned to settle in for the afternoon.

"I really feel dreadful," Elise replied, "but of course if you insist on staying—"

"No, no, I'll go with you now," Faye said and turned to her hostess. "Thank you for the tea and cake. I'd like the recipe." Frances smiled in pleasure. In short order their leavetaking was done and in a swirl of snow the guests were gone.

"Well, they didn't stay long," Frances said. "We didn't even have a chance to talk. How strange."

But Sarah knew the visit hadn't been strange at all. It had been perfectly in keeping with Elise's character. She'd accomplished what she'd come here to do.

The question was, Sarah thought, what was she to do about the things Elise had said? Even discounting for exaggeration, there was enough cause for alarm. Was Tanner's career being jeopardized by his coming marriage to her? Did he feel pity for her rather than love? She thought of their last time together, when he'd held her gently and dried her tears. How tender he'd been, how understanding, and there had been passion as well, passion born out of love, she reassured herself. But by the following week, her reassurance had faded. The memory of all the other slights she'd received since revealing her Indian blood only made the things Elise said more real. Was Tanner being humiliated because of her?

What should she do? With every snow-laden day that passed and kept them apart, Sarah's certainty that she must release Tanner from their betrothal grew. She loved him desperately, but they had too many obstacles to overcome. He could never change what he was, a proud, dedicated man who was making a name for himself in his chosen profession, and she couldn't help her Indian blood. If she admitted the truth to herself, she sometimes wished she were pure Nez Percé and she wouldn't feel this pull from one world to another. She'd know who she was and where she belonged. She would proudly take Black Beaver's proposal and become his wife. When Tanner was finally free of his duties and came to the agency, Sarah greeted him at the door with a somber face.

"What is it? What's wrong?" he asked, attuned to her moods more than he'd ever thought possible.

"I've given your proposal some thought these past few weeks," she began, and he felt his heart constrict, "and I realize how foolish this is for us to even consider."

"Foolish to love you, Sarah, to want to marry you?" he asked softly.

"Foolish to think we can put aside our differences and have a life together."

"We can."

"No, don't you see, we can't. People won't let us."

"Who can stop us?"

Sarah perceived that he would have an answer for her every argument, and she couldn't bear to go on. "I'm not going to marry you," she said, her gaze meeting his unwaveringly. "I've decided to become

Black Beaver's wife." She bit the inside of her mouth to hold back the tears.

"Sarah, you don't mean this. You've turned him down."

"I've reconsidered."

"What's happened? Who's been talking to you?" he pleaded. "Whatever problem you perceive we'll find a solution."

"We can't find a solution for what we are. I'm part Indian and you're a soldier committed to fighting against the Indians. Whatever people say at the fort against you, however it affects your career is only part of it. We can't change ourselves. I can't stop being an Indian and you can't stop being a soldier." Her hands spread wide between them as if she were holding him away from her.

"Sarah," he said urgently.

"Good-bye, Tanner. Thank you for all you've done to help me and my people." She held out her hand to him in a final farewell. Tanner looked at it, his lips tight with pain and anger. His eyes searched hers and he reached for her hand. Suddenly he jerked her forward into his arms. His lips settled on hers, bruising and demanding. Sarah pushed at his broad shoulders, trying to break the contact, but he held her tightly, his kiss quelling her resistance until she surrendered and leaned against him. She returned his kiss, feeling the hot, quick passion rising between them, her senses gathering in the manly smell and texture of him and the warm strength of his body. But this only made things more difficult. With a mighty effort she wrenched herself free and backed away, breathing heavily.

"Get out," she cried harshly, while inside she longed to throw herself into his arms again.

Tanner studied her face, a derisive smile curling

his lips. "You say the words, but you don't mean them," he said. "You love me. You want me as much as I want you, and you don't care one whit what people at the fort or down in Lewiston say. You won't marry Black Beaver when you can still respond to me this way."

"Get out, I said," Sarah ordered.

"When you've come to your senses, I'll be waiting at the fort," Tanner said and stalked out of the house, slamming the door behind him. The room seemed cold and dark without him. Sarah doubled over, gripping her middle in a paroxysm of grief.

"What on earth has happened, child?" Frances said, coming into the room. Seeing Sarah's tearful face, she put a comforting arm around the young shoulders. "What happened? Did you and Tanner have a lover's quarrel? My dear, it happens all the time. Things will work out. Take my word for it."

But Sarah was inconsolable. In the weeks that followed, she felt trapped in the tiny log cabin. She longed to see Yellow Bird and Annie Red Moccasin and, yes, even Black Beaver. But the snow fell unrelentingly and she knew it would be several months yet before the passes melted. So she resigned herself to her duties as teacher, slogging through the drifts each morning to the schoolhouse, where she built a fire and readied the single room for her students.

One afternoon when the leaden sky threatened still another blizzard, Sarah released her students early so they could make their way home before the snow began. Absently she moved around the room, putting away books and papers, delaying the time when she must return to the house and the lonely, inconsolable hours of night. A sound at the door made her turn, a bright smile on her face. One of her students had forgotten something, no doubt.

The smile faded as she saw Lucas Tanner standing there. The heavy Mackintosh jacket made him look bigger than ever.

"May I come in out of the cold?" he asked and, at her mute nod, entered and closed the door behind him.

"How have you been?" His gray eyes studied her face. Quickly Sarah turned away. She knew how she looked. She hadn't been sleeping or eating well, her figure was gaunt, her cheekbones too prominent in a suddenly too-thin face.

"I'm just fine," she lied. "How are you and all the others at the fort?"

"Pretty much the same as before," Tanner answered. His gaze devoured her. "I'd forgotten how beautiful you are. You make a man forget about the hardships of getting here." He took a step forward. "Sarah," he said raggedly.

"What do you want?" she demanded, pulling herself up stiffly. "Why have you come here?"

Tanner stopped in his tracks. She could see the will it took for him to look away from her. "General Howard asked me to come talk to you," he said finally. His words surprised her.

"Why?" she demanded. "Is it about Joseph?" He nodded and she rushed on fearfully. "What's wrong?"

"Nothing is wrong," he reassured her and she believed him. "Joseph is all right until spring."

"What does the general want with me?" she asked, startled. Her dark eyes searched his face.

"I'll let him tell you. Will you ride back with me?"

"Yes, of course, if you think it's important." Quickly she damped down the fire and closed up the schoolhouse.

"I wasn't sure a wagon could get through the drifts," Tanner said. "We'll go horseback, so wrap up warmly and bring extra blankets." Sarah nodded and headed back to the agency for her cape and to inform Frances where she was going. In little time she was ready. She'd donned another woolen petticoat for warmth and wound a scarf around her neck and face. Tanner helped her mount, then tucked an extra blanket over her shoulders and around her legs. Climbing into his saddle, he led the way out of the agency yard and along the trail to the fort.

They traveled in a strange world of white shapes and muffled sounds. The gurgling streams had surrendered to the bondage of icy caps. The pine boughs' song was silenced by their blanket of snow. Only the dull plop of the horses' hooves against the heavy wet snow and their labored breathing disturbed the quietness.

Dusk was settling by the time they reached the fort. Long gray shadows lay over the snow-covered humps of log buildings. Tanner led her directly to Captain Perry's quarters.

"Gracious, come right in here," Faye ordered. "You must be frozen." She led Sarah to a chair before the fireplace, then bustled away to bring a cup of hot tea. Sarah sat warming her fingers before the fire.

"Miss MacKenzie, it was good of you to come on a day like this," General Howard said genially. He leaned against the rough oak mantel, enjoying the warmth of the fire himself. On days like this his stump ached wearisomely.

"Tanner said it was important," Sarah said. "Is it something to do with Joseph?"

The general shook his head. "We think you can help both Joseph and us, Miss MacKenzie," he said somberly.

Sarah raised her head and looked at him hopefully. "I'll do whatever I can," she stated fervently.

Howard nodded, pleased at her answer. "You indicated at our last meeting that you're related to Joseph."

"That's right."

"Would he be more apt to listen to you?"

His question took her aback. "As opposed to whom, General?" she asked and wondered at her sudden reticence.

"As opposed to Monteith or me or any one of the other men who've told them they must move to the reservation."

Sarah looked away from him, staring into the fire as if mesmerized by the leaping flames. She felt chilled again and barely repressed a shiver. "I don't think he would," she answered and her head snapped up. "And why should he? Why should he docilely give up his land, the land of his ancestors?"

"Miss MacKenzie, that point has already been settled to the satisfaction of the Commissioner of Indian Affairs, the Secretary of Interior, even to the President himself. What you and I think no longer matters. I have my orders to assist Joseph and his men to the reservation come spring, and that is what I intend to do. I just want to give the hostiles a chance to understand that we are prepared to do whatever it takes to move them."

"Hostiles?" Sarah interrupted. "Joseph isn't hostile."

"He's unwilling to do as our President orders, so we have to consider him hostile to our government."

"Wouldn't you be if you were being asked to give up the home that has belonged to you and your ancestors for centuries?" Sarah flared in indignation. "Right is not might, General Howard. Just because you have a superior number of men and guns doesn't make you right."

He sat silent for a moment, head bowed, staring at

the floor. Finally he sighed and glanced at Tanner. "You've just touched on the reason for my asking you here, Miss MacKenzie," he said. "Our government is going to place Joseph and his people on the reservation. Nothing can stop it. As you've pointed out, we have superior guns and numbers of soldiers. If Joseph has some vain hope of fighting us and winning, he's badly misguided in his thinking. I'd like you to go to his village and talk to him, tell him the things we've discussed here today, and point out to him to what lengths we're prepared to go. Urge him to come into the reservation at the appointed time peacefully."

"I can't help you bring down Joseph and his people," Sarah said shakily, casting a bleak glance at Tanner. Surely he didn't expect this of her.

"You wouldn't be bringing down Joseph, Sarah," he said quietly. "You may save his life and the lives of his people."

"Precisely," General Howard agreed. "We only want you to tell him he hasn't got a chance. Make him see resistance would be futile."

Sarah began to weep quietly. "Only tell him the truth, Sarah, and nothing more," Tanner said gently. "Joseph is an intelligent man. He can come to a clearer decision if he knows some of the facts."

Sarah raised her tearstained face to him, then looked at the general. "You want me to take him military information about your troops?"

For a moment the general looked startled, then cleared his throat. "In essence, yes." He glanced at Tanner, wondering if there were any information the girl could have that he wouldn't want passed on to Joseph. Then he decided there wasn't. Major Tanner had his instructions and the general had learned through long years of battle campaigns which men he could depend on. Tanner was one of them.

"I don't understand any of this," Sarah was saying weakly. "Ever since people learned I'm part Nez Percé, they've acted as if I meant to spy on you and your soldiers and, in truth, the thought crossed my mind. My loyalties have been torn." Her voice shook slightly. The general could imagine her dilemma. The girl obviously loved the major, and yet seemed to feel some commitment to Chief Joseph. Howard glanced at Tanner again. The major himself was in a tight spot. He faced the very real possibility of fighting against the girl's people. Even this mission . . . Howard pushed away his thoughts.

"Now you can do something to help Joseph," he urged.

Sarah sat considering. She was a very pretty girl, the general noticed, and not given to hysterics as was Captain Perry's wife. She was intelligent and not easily routed by the likes of Lieutenant Nevins. That young officer had not made a favorable impression upon the general with his denouncement of the girl. Now the general sat waiting for her decision, sensing all had been said that should be.

Finally she raised her head. "I'll go and tell him the things you've said."

"I think that's a wise decision, Miss MacKenzie. Major Tanner will accompany you. He's been there before and Joseph knows him. You can take the boat downriver for some distance before it becomes ice-locked. From there you'll have to continue overland on horse."

"When will we leave?" Sarah asked, getting to her feet.

"Tomorrow morning if you can be ready in time."

"We can be," Tanner said and, taking Sarah's elbow, guided her from the general's temporary office.

"Am I doing the right thing, Tanner?" she asked,

clinging to his arm and peering up at him anxiously. He looked at her, thinking that in her concern for Joseph and the Nez Percé she'd forgotten to maintain her aloofness toward him. He didn't remind her. It felt good to have her near again.

"If you don't want to see him and his people hurt or even killed, it's worth trying," he said.

She sighed. "I suppose you're right."

"Come on. I'll get you back to the agency so you can pack."

The next morning Sarah was ready when Tanner arrived. Frances ushered him in out of the cold, then knocked on Sarah's door.

"I'll be right out," she called and, gathering up her small bag of clean clothes and a few other items she needed, walked out to the kitchen. John and Charles Monteith sat at the table talking quietly to Tanner about the trip. Frances was bustling over pans of bacon and eggs. Fresh biscuits sat on the open oven door, keeping warm.

Frances was the first to notice Sarah. She swung around, a pleasant greeting already on her lips, a bright, friendly smile on her face and stood gaping, struck dumb by what she saw.

"Good morning, Frances," Sarah said quietly, and now the men turned to glance at her. Sarah saw Charles's frown and the disapproving anger building in John Monteith's eyes, but it was Tanner's face she watched most closely. As usual, it was unreadable when he wanted it to be.

"My lands," Frances exclaimed, looking at the elkhide trousers and Indian dress Sarah wore. She'd laced warm moccasins high on her legs, lining them inside with wool as the Indians did with fur. Her dark hair had been plaited in two braids and decorated with ornamentations of shell and fur. With great care she'd painted her face and the part in her hair.

"This is heathenish. I won't have it in my house," John Monteith roared, getting to his feet.

"Actually, this is a very sensible way to dress," Tanner spoke up. "Those leather leggings will keep her a damn sight warmer than the frilly petticoats she usually wears, and the paint will keep her face from chapping and freezing."

"No God-fearing woman would dress like that," the Indian agent fumed.

"John, leave her be," Frances ordered her brother-in-law. "She's going to Joseph's camp. She's got a right to dress the way she wants."

"Thank you for understanding," Sarah said.

"Oh, you will be careful, won't you?" Frances said, unable to hold back tears. "This weather isn't fit for a body to be out in. You will take care of her, won't you, Major Tanner?"

"I will," he said firmly. "We'd better get a start." He helped Sarah with her warm woolen cape. Frances pressed an extra blanket on her and then they were off. A small boat had been arranged for their use and was anchored at a landing on the Snake River south of Lewiston. They made their way there, and Tanner loaded their horses and the supply mules.

"Go on inside the pilot house and get yourself something hot to drink," the captain instructed. "It's a darn sight warmer in there than out here." Sarah did as she was told and was soon joined by Tanner and the pilot. Expertly the man steered the boat into the current. Ice, thick and menacing, clung to the shoreline of the swirling river.

"Downriver there'll be some freezing. At the first sign of it I'll have to pull over and put you ashore," the pilot said conversationally.

"Is it dangerous?" Sarah asked, gripping the arms of her chair.

"Could be," the boatman said. "Drifting ice'll rip the bottom right out of a boat. We'll be okay for a few miles."

"I'll help keep a watch," Tanner said, and with a last encouraging glance at Sarah went back out in the biting cold. She could see his tall figure standing in the prow, impervious to the wind and snow as he peered into the swirling murky water for any signs of ice forming.

It seemed to Sarah, sitting rigidly in her chair, staring anxiously at the snow and ice-choked shore, that they traveled for hours before Tanner put a hand up, motioning the pilot to the shore.

"You've got ice caking your prow and up ahead the river's frozen over," Tanner said. "The falls aren't too far away anyway; you'd better put us ashore here."

The pilot headed the boat into shore. The wood creaked in protest as it was eased up over the ice. The thin ice crackled a protest, then broke apart. The pilot snubbed the boat against the bank, and Tanner threw out a board from boat to land, then maneuvered the horses over it one at a time. Sarah followed behind.

"Good luck," the pilot called.

"I'll meet you back here in four days," Tanner shouted and stepped back as the pilot drew in the plank, and, revving his engine, backed the sturdy boat back into the current.

"How far to Joseph's village?" Sarah shouted above the whine of rising wind.

"I figure we've come more than halfway," Tanner answered, "but it's still too far to make the village today."

"What will we do? We can't sleep out in this storm." The blowing snow stung her face, and she turned her back into the wind.

"You're right." Tanner cast a glance around and then at the leaden sky. "We'd better look for some shelter." He helped her to mount, then led the way southward along the riverbank. The cutting wind seemed to intensify. Sarah knew Tanner was looking for a bluff or cave, something under which they could shelter, but the river valley was white and flat at this level, dotted only by pine trees. She leaned over the pommel of her saddle, pulling the hood of her cape forward to block the wind from her face. She could feel the heat of the horse as it labored.

"Tanner," she called when they'd traveled on for a while. The wind snatched the breath from her mouth, and she feared he hadn't heard, hunched as he was over his horse. Then he glanced back and she signaled to him.

"What is it?" he shouted, breathing heavily, and she realized the exertion required to break a path through the snow as he and his horse were doing. She had only to follow.

"This is turning into a blizzard," she said. "We've got to take cover."

"I know." He nodded his head.

"Maybe we can burrow under the snow for warmth. My grandmother said she and her family had to do that once when they were caught in the mountains."

"That's an idea," Tanner said, then paused. "See that pine over there?" He pointed to a tree with its branches growing clear down its trunk to the ground. She nodded. "Make your way to that. We'll dig in under it." Dismounting, he caught the bridle of the packhorse and plowed through the knee-deep snow. Sarah followed in his wake, tugging her horse behind. Tanner cut away one of the low-hanging boughs, making a cave for her beneath the tree.

"Grab your covers and climb in there," he ordered

and began unsaddling the horses. Sarah crawled into the space and spread open her bedroll. Its oiled canvas ground cloth would keep the melting snow from wetting them through. Tanner piled the saddles and gear around the perimeter of the tree, and turned the still bridled horses loose. They bunched together for warmth and lowered their heads.

"Will they be all right?" Sarah called from her pine shelter.

"I hope so," Tanner said and slid in beside her. He pulled the saddles and gear around, blocking the opening and closing them in. The drooping branches coated with ice and snow made a natural barrier against the wind and snow. Though dark, their shelter was snug, fragrant, and surprisingly quiet. Opening his bedroll, Tanner spread it over them, then pulled Sarah close for warmth. At first she lay stiff and unyielding.

"Relax," he said. "It's the only way to stay warm." She lay with her head on his shoulder, her eyes bright with curiosity as she listened to the storm howling outside. She felt relaxed and happy. The old excitement of an adventure shared was upon her. A half smile curved her lips.

"This isn't bad," she whispered.

"Not bad at all," he answered and grinned down at her. "Maybe we should just stay here until spring thaw."

"It's very peaceful," she said, ignoring the double meaning in his words. She could feel the tension in his body.

He sighed. "We'd better try to sleep while we have the chance," he said. "This should blow over soon and we can travel a few more miles."

"All right." Sarah closed her eyes, but as warmth returned to her chilled limbs she grew restless and wriggled. Glancing at Tanner, she was startled to see him watching her through half-closed eyes. She lay still, meeting his glittering gaze, feeling the passion that could never be ended between them.

"Tanner," she whispered and it was like a plea. He pulled her forward onto his chest, kissing her hungrily.

"I love you," he whispered hoarsely, and she melted against him.

"I love you, too, Tanner," she sighed and gave herself to the need for him. Their lovemaking was slow and sensuous, a study in contrasts. Their breaths mingled, warming their small bower. Above them the world was harsh and dangerous, here it was secure and peaceful; outside was cold that penetrated to the bone, here was hot, pulsating flesh that yielded to desire; there in the blizzard was death, here was love and tender passion. Their cries of pleasure were lost in the piteous wail of the wind, and then they lay still, their limbs wound around each other in an embrace. They slept and the wind drove itself into a fury through the pines and down the ravines and gullies until it touched even the lodges of the Nez Percé tucked along the protective banks of the river. Then spent, it slunk away. Now the snow drifted down slowly and finally stopped altogether. The sun sent its weak lemon light to the tops of the mountains, making them glisten, and the snow birds ventured out of their nests to see a world made brand-new.

18

Tanner had to lie on his back and kick a way out of their snow cave. Sarah crawled out behind him, blinking her eyes at the dazzling light reflecting off the glistening snow. The horses had stayed close by, finding little forage. They neighed a welcome when Tanner and Sarah approached them, grateful to have contact with humans again. Tanner saddled them while Sarah shook the cold, dry snow from their bedrolls and tied them on the back.

"If we push hard, we could make the fork of the river where Joseph's village sets," Tanner said, looking at the sky to calculate the time. "Are you game?"

"You lead and I'll follow," Sarah assured him. They set out, small specks of humanity in a seemingly unending world of snow and mountains. Tanner hugged the riverbank. The snow might have been less deep up on the ridge under the pines, but he was taking no chance of their becoming lost. He could have managed a few nights camping out in the snow; he wasn't sure about Sarah. She was tougher than her delicate appearance suggested, but he worried about her nonetheless. They slid down the steep inclines, struggling past waterfalls and rapids that had been slowed to pitiful trickles by the encroaching ice. They were journeying downward, going into the deep, protected valleys of the mountains, where the wind was less fierce and the snow not as deep. The traveling got easier and they made better time. Still, it was dusk before they reached the fork, and Tanner debated continuing or camping for the night. Sarah looked cold and exhausted.

"We'll camp here," he called, getting down from his horse. "I'll have a fire going in no time and I'll set up a tent."

"How far are we from Joseph's village?" Sarah asked, looking around.

Tanner kicked a snowbank, searching for wood. "It's a good two-hour ride from here in the dark. If we missed our footing, we could end up in the river."

"I'm willing to take the chance if you are," Sarah said. He looked at her pale face and cursed himself. He shouldn't have listened to Howard's suggestion to bring her here. The trip was too hard on her.

"Can you make it?" he asked, coming to lay a hand on her blanketed thigh.

"Easily," she said and smiled tiredly. "I'd like to spend the night in a warm lodge."

Tanner stood considering. "We'll give it a try," he said finally and climbed back in the saddle. He longed to goad his horses forward, but knew he couldn't. They were tired and winded. The heavy snowbanks had taken their toll. If he pushed them, they might collapse.

Stars, their white light hard and bright in the dark sky, had appeared before they reached the first fringe of Joseph's camp. Lookouts alerted the village with quick, high bird calls. Tanner pushed on, taking no time to stop and identify himself. The first long-houses came into view, and a line of warriors stood in front, rifles and bows and arrows at the ready.

"Greetings to my Nez Percé brothers," Sarah called

in their language. "I am Swan Necklace and I've come to see Chief Joseph."

The warriors parted and a heavily robed man stepped forward. "Welcome, Swan Necklace," the tall Indian said.

"Spotted Frog," Sarah said in relief.

"Spotted Frog, it is good to see you again," Tanner said, getting off his horse and grasping arms with the warrior in an Indian greeting. "We've traveled far today."

"Come, warm yourself by our fires," Spotted Frog said, and gratefully Sarah followed him to the long-house of Chief Joseph. She was bundled so heavily in blankets that no one recognized her when she first stepped into the lodge. She unpeeled the stiff layers.

"Swan Necklace," Yellow Bird called, running to throw her arms around Sarah. The two women hugged and Sarah stood back to look at Yellow Bird's figure. It was hidden by the loose blanket she wore like a shawl around her shoulders, but Sarah had felt the thickening waistline.

Yellow Bird laughed. "Yes, I carry Joseph's child," she said and blushed. "I have prayed to the Great Spirit that it will be a son."

"I'm so happy for you," Sarah cried delightedly. "When will you give birth?"

"The best of all times, in the month of Khoy-Tsahl, when the blueback salmon returns to the lakes and streams. A time of plenty for the Nez Percé. It is a good omen." Yellow Bird's face glowed as she placed her hand possessively over her rounded stomach. Sarah hugged her again and, giggling over all sorts of plans, the two women went to sit beside the fire.

Tanner had seen to the horses and soon joined

them. Bowls of warm stew made from dried salmon
and roots were brought to them, and Sarah and
Tanner ate hungrily. Yellow Bird sat nearby with her
legs folded, her hands resting in her lap. Sarah could
have eaten more, but looking around, she was suddenly aware of the thin, pinched faces of the people
in the lodge. This was the time of dwindling food
supplies and careful rationing. It was the nature of
the Nez Percé to be hospitable and share whatever
food they had, but it was clear they had little food to
make it to the spring thaw when the salmon would
run again. Sarah set her empty bowl to one side and
smiled brightly at Yellow Bird. Suddenly she understood the concern Joseph's wife had for her unborn
baby. Born in a time of plenty, it could grow sturdy
and healthy before the lean, hard winter months.
General Howard and John Monteith's words came
back to her. If the Nez Percé were on the reservation, they could farm and raise more beef and never
know hunger again.

"Why do you look so sad?" Yellow Bird asked.
"You are not happy."

"I have many reasons to feel sad," Sarah said with
a smile that didn't quite erase the melancholy from
her eyes. "We have come with a message for Joseph
from General Howard."

Yellow Bird looked away into the fire. "I see," she
said slowly. "Joseph will come soon to this lodge.
He is seeing to his people."

Sarah sensed her reserve. "How are Running Brook
and Annie Red Moccasin?" she asked, and Yellow
Bird told her the news of the tribe. The chief arrived
shortly after, his tall frame bending down to enter
the opening. His face lit with recognition when he
looked at Sarah and Tanner.

"Welcome, my little sister," he said. "Tanner, it is good to have you in my lodge again."

"The honor is mine, Chief Joseph," Tanner replied.

Joseph waved to Yellow Bird, and with a gentle smile she rose and went to the chest made of buffalo hides. Looking inside, she brought out a pipe and brought it to Joseph. "We will smoke a pipe in honor of our friendship," he said to Tanner and packed the carved wooden bowl with tobacco. When the pipe was lit and had been passed, Tanner cleared his throat.

"We have come from General Howard," he began.

"How is the one-armed general?" Joseph asked calmly.

"He is well and he sends his greetings to his friend, Joseph." The chief nodded his head in acceptance. "General Howard has also sent a message to Chief Joseph. He has asked your kinswoman, Swan Necklace, to bring it to you."

Joseph put away the pipe and turned to Sarah. "What is it you wish to tell me, Swan Necklace?" he asked kindly.

In the face of such gentleness, how could she tell him Howard's threats? She would rather be tortured. But her glance fell on Yellow Bird's slender brown hands resting against the thickening mound of her stomach and she found the courage.

"General Howard has sent me to tell you, you must go to the reservation when the snow is gone."

Joseph looked startled. "Do you join the soldiers against us, Swan Necklace?" he asked in dismay.

"No, of course not," Sarah cried. "But Joseph"— tears started to her eyes and rolled down her cheeks— "the soldiers are many and they have guns. They are prepared to fight if you don't go. Women and children will be killed."

"Why is this so?" Joseph asked. "That men come to your valley and say you must leave the home of your ancestors or we will kill your women and children."

"I don't know," Sarah wept. "I know it's not right, but the soldiers will do this if you don't go peaceably."

"I will inform my council of the things you have told me," Joseph said.

"Joseph." Sarah knew what she was about to say would anger Tanner, but she couldn't abandon the Nez Percé. "General Howard has alerted soldiers at Fort Walla Walla in Washington Territory, and a Captain Whipple and his men are already stationed in the valley."

Tanner's head came up. How had she known that?

"I do not think the general wants to make war on you," she hurried on. "He has his orders from Washington and he must obey them."

"We do not make war. They do. If the white man wants to live in peace with the Indian, he can live in peace. There need be no trouble."

"You must be aware of the seriousness of your position here," Tanner said shortly.

"We are," the noble young chief answered calmly. "We will talk, my council and I, and we will try to determine what is best for the people. Perhaps we can talk to General Howard again. At our last council we agreed to another meeting. He must honor that."

"I will tell him," Sarah said. She glanced around. Spotted Frog had entered the lodge, and Tanner got to his feet.

"Where are all your fine herds now that it is winter?" he asked.

Spotted Frog smiled at his question. "They are

scattered in the hills and valleys. In the spring we will gather them and count the new foals. I will save one for you."

"Thank you," Tanner replied. The men settled around the fire and the pipe was relit. They talked of herds and the buffalo hunt in the spring, when some of the warriors would travel across the Bitter-root Mountain range into Montana. They spoke of the salmon and the elk in the high hills, but they never spoke again of the soldiers or the reservation.

Only Yellow Bird as they prepared for bed made one final comment. "I do not wish my son to be born on a reservation. He should be free to roam his land as were his forefathers."

Sarah was at a loss of what to say.

There seemed little reason to remain in the village. Their message had been delivered, but despite the impending danger, Sarah was enjoying her visit with Yellow Bird and the other women. Annie asked about Owen Thatcher, and Sarah had to tell her that the lawyer still had a complaint out against her. Tanner seemed content to stay for a few days as well. The pilot had said he would be back in four days to pick them up. Everyday Tanner rode out with Spotted Frog and his warriors to hunt or see to the herds of cattle.

Black Beaver avoided her. One day when she saw him walking through the village, she called to him, but he didn't pause. She had hurt him deeply when she refused to marry him. Sadly she turned away. Even now she might yet go to him, but she knew she wouldn't. That brief time with Tanner under the pine boughs had shown her clearly she could never give herself to Black Beaver. Once again she was trapped between two worlds, belonging to neither.

One night Sarah awoke to find Tanner gone.

Quietly she made her way to the door of the lodge and looked out. The moon reflecting on the snow lit the night as brightly as day. As she peered out at the village, she glimpsed the tall, broad-shouldered silhouette of a man moving stealthily among the lodges. Pausing now and then to look around, he made his way toward Sarah. Instinctively she drew back, then quickly went back to her bedroll. Lying tense and still in the darkness, she held her breath as the figure entered the lodge and then Tanner stretched out on the bedroll beside her. Feigning sleep, Sarah could feel the coldness of the night air still clinging to his skin and clothes.

For some reason she felt reluctant to ask him about his midnight excursion. Despite the harshness of their lot, the Nez Percé women were cheerful and optimistic. Soon the snow would melt, the grass would grow green, and the cows would fatten. Then they would be butchered and there would be food enough again. The time of plenty was growing close, its promise reflected in the glistening icicles that hung wet and sleek from the branches. The laughing children gathered and ate them, relishing the icy coldness on their tongues. Only Joseph seemed somber.

"He is worried and sad," Yellow Bird said to Sarah on their final evening in the village. Tanner had said they must leave the next morning, or the boat would leave without them and they'd be forced to travel overland, a journey that could take three or four days. "Joseph does not wish to give up this land. It belonged to his father. His father's buried here."

"So is my grandmother," Sarah said softly, remembering the lonely grave high on the mountain ledge.

"Still, I do not think Joseph will let his people be killed by the soldiers."

"What do you want to do, Yellow Bird?" Sarah asked suddenly, aware that although women were not allowed to speak out in the council meetings, their influence was still considerable.

Yellow Bird met her gaze. "I do not wish my son to be born on a reservation," she said quietly. "I want him to inherit the lands of his ancestors and walk upon them freely."

"But if you don't go, you and your baby could be killed," Sarah said.

Yellow Bird's hands went instinctively to her stomach, but her expression was defiant as she met Sarah's gaze. "So be it," she said with finality.

Sarah paled at such calm stoicism. "You can't mean that," she whispered.

"Death is not an enemy," Yellow Bird remonstrated. "The white man who would take our land is the enemy." For the first time Sarah realized how far apart she was from the Nez Percé, and once again she felt alone. Yellow Bird hadn't meant for her to feel this way, she knew. She was silent and thoughtful throughout the evening, and when Tanner pulled her against him, she lay quiet and unresponsive in his arms.

The next morning, Joseph's braves accompanied them back to the site above the falls where the boat waited. Tanner unloaded the gear and led his army horses back to Spotted Frog. "I will leave these with you in return for the hospitality you have shown us."

"That is not necessary, Tanner," Spotted Frog said.

"I know"—Tanner put a hand on his shoulder—"I want to give them to you as a gift."

"Thank you," the war chief said. Sarah watched

the two men make their farewells. Each seemed to know there would be no such time of friendship between them again. The plank was extended, and Sarah and Tanner walked on board.

"I was beginning to wonder if them injuns had scalped you," the pilot said when he had the boat in midstream and headed back upriver. Impatiently Sarah turned away from him. It hurt her to hear such talk after the hospitality and warmth she'd shared with Joseph and his tribe.

Lieutenant Nevins and Major Wood were waiting when they reached the landing below Lewiston. "General Howard's waiting to hear your report," Major Wood said in an aside to Tanner. Sarah heard him and glanced up. Suspicion and concern warred within her. Tanner guided Major Wood away up the bank, where the two men stood talking privately.

"Lieutenant." Sarah turned back to the young soldier who'd once taunted her so cruelly. "What report is Tanner supposed to deliver to General Howard?"

"The one he went down to that Indian village to get," Nevins said. "He was supposed to find out about Joseph's men and weapons. That's why he needed you along. He figured he'd never get into the village alone."

His words fell like stones around her, dragging her down in a quagmire of deceit and betrayal. As if he sensed her pain, Tanner turned and saw her face. Excusing himself, he ran down the bank toward her.

"Sarah, what's wrong?" he demanded, gripping her shoulder.

"You used me," she whispered harshly. "You used me against my own people. How could you do that?"

"Sarah, it's not the way it seems."

"Then how is it? Tell me, so I'll understand. You

and General Howard with all your fine concerns for the welfare of the Indians."

"The things the general wanted you to say were important, and he really felt Joseph might listen to you when he would no longer listen to the men in council."

"That's not why you had me go. You wanted to get to Joseph and Spotted Frog, to spy on them."

"Sarah, the more we know about the Indians and their strengths, the more we can do to avert a disaster. I did it for Joseph as well."

"I don't believe you," she cried, wrenching away from him. "If you've lied to me about this, how many other things were untrue? You said you loved me and yet you've caused me to betray my people. I don't understand your kind of love."

"I do love you. I've never loved any other woman but you." His eyes were dark with concern. He put out a hand to touch her, then let it fall when she backed away from him.

"Why are you doing this?" Sarah demanded.

"I'm a soldier. I've told you that. I have to do what I think is right."

"So must I. I am a Nez Percé," she answered. Whirling, she ran up the bank toward the waiting wagon.

"Sarah, wait," Tanner called, but she didn't look back. Climbing onto the wagon, she brandished a whip over the backs of the mules.

"Hey," the teamster cried and ran after her, but Sarah whipped the mules to a gallop, ignoring the rushing wind that burned her dampened cheeks. She didn't slow the team until she got to the agency, and when she pulled them to a halt, she sat on the hard wagon seat as if turned to ice. A numbness had settled over her, shutting out the pain of Tanner's betrayal.

"Sarah?" Frances said, coming out on the porch. "Gracious child, are you all right? Did you find out anything on your trip?"

Slowly Sarah raised her head and looked at the older woman. "Yes," she said wearily. "I found out a great many things." She climbed out of the wagon and walked up on the porch.

"Where's Major Tanner? Will he be coming out later?" Frances asked.

"No," Sarah said, and her eyes were stark with grief. "If he comes calling, tell him I have no wish to ever see him again. I'll be leaving the valley as soon as the snow melts and the roads are passable." Shoulders squared, she walked into the log building.

"Another quarrel," Frances mumbled under her breath and shook her head. She didn't see the bleak pain in Sarah's eyes.

19

February melted away to March. Tanner came to the agency several times to plead with Sarah, but each time she refused to see him. He even enlisted Frances to intercede for him, but to no avail. Sarah refused to even discuss what had happened. He had used her and her friendship with Joseph to gain access to the Nez Percé village. Spotted Frog had shown him friendship, and he'd repaid him with betrayal. She could never forgive him for that.

One day when Frances had come to tell her of Tanner's arrival and as usual she'd refused to meet him, the door of the schoolroom was flung open. The children, seeing a huge, ferocious-looking man in a blue uniform, screamed and hid under their desks.

"Children, quiet down. It's nothing," Sarah remonstrated. Then she turned on Lucas Tanner, eyes snapping, elbows jutting, hands on hips. One foot tapped impatiently. "You've frightened the children," she said in her sternest voice.

He wasn't intimidated. His eyes were dark and angry as he glowered at her. "We have to talk," he said, and she knew he wouldn't be put off.

"I'm listening. Talk," she said crisply.

"Alone," he said implacably.

Sarah glanced at the students, who sat listening

with wide-eyed interest. "Children, you're dismissed for the rest of the day," she said. With a loud cheer they gathered their things and raced outdoors. In their pell-mell rush they bumped into Tanner, who was forced to leap aside. The expression on his face softened momentarily.

"All right," she snapped, turning to him again. "We're alone."

He strode into the room and slapped his hat onto a desk. His face was somber, his expression angry and disappointed. Sarah was surprised at his attitude. She was the wronged party. "I think you owed me a chance to talk this out," he began, "instead of just running off with half-cocked impressions." Sarah looked away. She had acted hastily. "I don't know what Gayle Nevins told you."

"Enough."

"Enough for you to turn your back on me and not listen to anything I have to say."

"Nothing you could possibly say can change what you did."

"What about what you did?" he asked quietly. "You gave Joseph information about Howard's troops. Am I to assume you've been spying on us, using me to further ingratiate yourself with Howard and the other officers at the fort? You're a woman of strong principles, Sarah, that's one of the things I admire about you. But I'm a man of some pride and principles as well. You must allow me that."

"You twist everything. You've used me and I can't forget that."

"I thought we went to that Indian village with a common purpose, to avert an Indian war if possible."

"One of us went there for that purpose, the other went to spy for General Howard."

"That's not true," Tanner said raggedly, and the

sincerity in his eyes made her waver. "It was my job to see if Joseph's Indians were joining forces with White Bird and his band."

"And to check on the number of warriors they had and the guns and horses they owned."

"Yes, that's true," Tanner said. Sarah walked away from him, pacing to the far side of the tiny schoolroom. "This knowledge will make it easier for Howard to deal with Joseph in persuading him to go to the reservation."

"You mean it makes it easier for Howard to know how much force to use."

"Sometimes a show of force works when nothing else will."

"Don't you see the unfairness of that?" Sarah demanded, rounding on him.

"Yes, it is unfair," he said, "but sometimes that can't be helped. I've fought in enough Indian wars to know how these things go. So has Howard. You have to give him credit to do what's best for everyone."

"Everyone?" she challenged. "Or what's best for the white settlers who want the land."

"We've been over this before," Tanner said impatiently.

"Yes, we have," Sarah admitted, "and we can't seem to resolve the differences between us. I'd like you to go now. I think we've talked enough."

Tanner thought of pleading more, but pride flared within him and, snatching up his hat, he strode out of the room. Mounting his horse, he spurred it into a gallop back to the fort, cursing Sarah's stubbornness all the way. Sarah was a woman of principles and ideas, and he'd admired her for them, but it was time she understood he was a man of some convictions too. He'd been fighting and powwowing with the Indians for more years than he liked to think about. He knew more about them than most white men. He pitied them, but his allegiance was to his own kind. He'd seen too much killing between the whites and Indians. If he knew the ruthlessness of the white man, he'd also witnessed the savagery of the Indian.

Still, his sense of right could not be ignored. The United States Army was the aggressor. The white soldiers weren't fighting an enemy who had attacked their loved ones and threatened their freedoms. He couldn't blame Joseph and Spotted Frog if they chose to fight, but he prayed they wouldn't. They hadn't a chance. Pity for the Indians wrenched at his conscience, then he remembered Little Big Horn. He didn't want to fight Joseph and his warriors, but if he must, then he would fight to win and conscience and Sarah be damned.

In mid-March Spotted Frog came to the agency. Though he said little about his reasons for being there, it was fairly obvious that Joseph and the other chiefs were giving serious consideration to which reservation on which to settle. Spotted Frog's face was set and he didn't look at Sarah. She stood shivering on the agency porch, yet loathe to go indoors and miss anything.

"Has Joseph come to some decision about the reservation, or is he going to fight us on this?" John Monteith asked, and Sarah strained closer to hear.

Spotted Frog's expression grew sullen. "A great many lies have been told to the Nez Percé and their council," he answered. "Troublemakers say I want to fight. This is not true. I have a wife and children, cattle and horses. I have eyes and a heart and can see and understand for myself that if we fight, we would have to leave all and go into the mountains."

"It's wise of you to understand this," John said. Sarah felt angry at the agent for his threat and for the simplistic tone he took with Spotted Frog. "When are you and Joseph and the rest of your people coming in?"

"When General Howard comes, we will tell him and you what we have made up our minds to do."

"All right, I'll write to him and tell him Joseph wants to talk."

"Spotted Frog!" Sarah called as he prepared to leave. "How is Yellow Bird? Is she well?"

He reined in his horse and studied Sarah for a moment. She wasn't sure he meant to answer. "She is well," he said finally and, kicking his horse with his heels, galloped away.

Chortling with anticipated triumph, Charles and John set about writing letters to General Howard for a proposed council. It seemed they would get all the bands of Nez Percé under the major chiefs, Joseph, White Bird, and others to come into the reservation peaceably.

The conference was set for April 20 at Fort Walla Walla, but onlookers heckled the participants of the meeting so badly that little was accomplished. General Howard set another meeting at Fort Lapwai for the first week of May.

Spring had come to the mountains and valleys. The ice had left the creeks and wildflowers bloomed on the banks. Snowdrops flowered before their foliage had unfurled, and the wild celery pushed its feathery leaves from the dark earth. Wagon trails had opened in the Blue Mountains, and General Howard ordered more troops and supplies to the Wallowa Valley. Two Gatling guns were sent as well. It was the month of Key-Khee-Tahl, time to dig the *keh-kheet*, the first root food of the season.

In the Indian villages, feasts celebrating the first fruits would be held, or would they? Sarah wondered how Yellow Bird and Joseph and old Running Brook were accepting the prospect of leaving the Wallowa Valley forever. Her heart ached for them.

May, the month of the *khouse* root, arrived and with it the final council. Tensions had continued to mount. Civilians fussed over every rumor of aggression by the Indians even when they were proven false. A flurry of robberies had occurred in the stores and taverns along Lapwai Creek, supposedly committed by Indians, but one of the men had been recognized as a white man. Speculations abounded over who was dressing up as Nez Percé in order to stir up trouble. Now Sheriff Wilmot was looking for Carl Pepin and his men. In view of the complaints against Pepin, Wilmot could no longer look the other way. Sarah felt vindicated. Elise Channing returned East, having found her year in the mountains too boring to continue.

For the council meeting a large tent had been pitched in the center of the parade ground. It sat there, bright and colorful as if a circus had come to the fort. Well it might have been described as such, some folks thought. Clearly, great importance was placed on this council, although the outcome had already been determined. There would be no parleying with Joseph. The chiefs would be told the terms by which they must go onto the reservation.

Sarah and Frances had come to Emily Fitzgerald's house to watch and wait for the outcome. Faye Perry fluttered nervously from one window to another, peering across the porch at her own door. Howard and his officers had set up a temporary office in the Perry lodgings.

"I can't for the life of me understand the general

having the council right here inside the fort," she sighed. "He should have had it out away from all of us. What if the Indians decide to attack?"

"I don't think they will, Faye," Emily reassured her kindly. "Besides, General Howard doubled the guards this morning, and he ordered the two companies of men left in the barracks to be armed and ready. He's not taking any chances." She glanced at Sarah's face and looked away quickly.

"I haven't noticed any extra guards or weapons," Faye said in disbelief.

"He ordered them kept out of sight. This is a peace council, Faye. We don't want to scare Joseph and his people."

"Yes, we do," Sarah said flatly. "General Howard's been trying to do that for months now. He'll use any means to coerce Joseph onto the reservation."

"Well, you can hardly blame him, Sarah," Emily said gently. "It's better to frighten Joseph than have bloodshed."

"Oh, I wish David were taking a gun," Faye fumed.

General Howard and Captain Perry stepped out of the captain's quarters. Major Tanner and John and Charles Monteith were with them. Faye threw open the door and all the women hurried out onto the porch. In spite of herself, Sarah's eyes automatically sought Tanner's. His expression was closed and aloof, and he briefly met her gaze before looking away. It was as if they were strangers.

"Ladies." The general nodded a terse greeting and walked to the edge of the porch to peer off into the distance. "By God, this time he's come," he said in satisfaction, and Sarah knew he meant Joseph.

She gazed in the same direction and saw Joseph and the other chiefs ride out of the canyon in a single file. They were followed by their warriors and behind those the women and children, all dressed in their best clothes. All were mounted on Indian ponies.

Instead of riding directly into the post gates, the chiefs spurred their horses and circled the post three times. Cupping their hands to their mouths, they repeated a high-pitched Indian cry over and over. The people on the porch looked at each other apprehensively.

"That's just their way of announcing their presence," Tanner said. "Nothing to get nervous about."

"Nevertheless, we won't take chances, Major," General Howard said. "Have the men been instructed to be at the ready, Captain Perry?"

"Yes, sir," Perry said and cast a reassuring glance at his wife.

To the relief of the general and his officers, the Indians stopped circling and halted before the post gate. Ceremoniously they rode forward one by one and stacked their rifles and other weapons before entering.

The afternoon dragged by and then General Howard dismissed the council. Little had been accomplished. That evening everyone met in Faye Perry's parlor to discuss the day's events.

"Are they stalling on purpose?" Emily Fitzgerald asked.

General Howard shook his head. "I don't know to what purpose. The end is inevitable." Sarah sat quietly in a corner. She knew her presence made some of the others uncomfortable. She'd meant to return to the agency, but Frances and Emily had been so offended by her proposal she'd relented and stayed. Now she sat listening, eyes downcast, perfectly aware of Lucas Tanner lounging in a chair nearby, his big frame giving an impression of tightly coiled tension.

She had no way of knowing that tension was caused by her presence.

Tanner tried to concentrate on the talk in the room, but Sarah was near enough to touch and his big hand twitched on his thigh, wanting to do just that. He'd tried to put her out of his mind, but it was easier to move Joseph and his Nez Percé onto the reservation than it was to forget Sarah. He loved her, he thought morosely, and wondered what she would do if he just turned around and spoke the words. He didn't and the spring coiled tighter, until abruptly he got to his feet and walked out to the porch to roll a cigarette.

Sarah watched him go. Frances glanced at her and Sarah could read what was on her face. Go after him, Frances seemed to be saying. Make your peace and be happy while you can. But Sarah stayed where she was, practicing the control Swan Necklace had taught her as a child. Joseph would have been pleased at the calm exterior she presented to the room, but Yellow Bird would have understood the pain she felt inside. She was grateful when at last the Monteiths rose to begin their journey back to the agency.

The next day the council opened with much the same ceremonies as before, but the discussions quickly reached an impasse. Everyone was frustrated beyond belief. General Howard was concentrating his efforts on Joseph at the moment, John said over Sunday supper. He expected to spend the summer bringing the rest of the non-treaty Indians to the reservation. Joseph was to be the first. He was influential enough with the other bands that if he went peaceably it was expected the other bands would follow. Sarah listened and felt heartsick. She wouldn't go to the next session, she vowed. But when Monday arrived, she couldn't bear the thought of staying behind. She dressed and climbed into the agency wagon for the short trip to the fort.

When they reached the post on Monday, Sarah was surprised to find Faye and Emily more concerned with their clothes and what to serve for dinner that evening than in the coming session. General Howard paced along the porch quoting scriptures in a thunderous voice.

White Bird's people had arrived and there was no reason to delay the council further. Once again the ceremonies were observed, the participants went into the tent. The other Indians settled into their customary places around the perimeter of the tent, and the ladies sank into comfortable chairs in the shade of the porch. Frances and Emily took up needlework. Flies droned halfheartedly in the heat, then, discouraged by the languid brush of a hand, settled into a quiet spot of shade themselves. Suddenly the somnolent quiet was shattered by the sound of harsh voices in heated argument.

"Sounds like General Howard's giving them an ultimatum," Faye said uneasily.

"He can afford to push a little now," Emily said. "Captain Whipple's forces arrived last night. They're deployed close to Lapwai this very minute overlooking the Indian camp."

"How did he get them here so quickly?" Sarah demanded.

"Major Tanner rode out Friday with orders for Captain Whipple from General Howard that he bring his troops immediately," Emily explained. "Two more companies have been ordered from Fort Vancouver." She paused, not wanting to hurt her friend, yet fairness demanded she keep Sarah as informed as the rest of them. "Howard said if Joseph doesn't agree in today's session, he'll have six or seven companies of troops after them by tomorrow."

Tears started to Sarah's eyes and she looked away. She didn't know what to say. Suddenly the shouting from the tent flared again. "The earth is my mother," someone cried in Nez Percé, then all shouting ended abruptly. The flap of the tent was flung back, and Tanner and Captain Perry led an Indian chief toward the guardhouse. General Howard followed closely behind and it was obvious he was greatly agitated. Joseph and Spotted Frog left the tent, and Sarah could see the stunned shock on their faces.

"Why is General Howard arresting that old Indian?" Faye asked in a low voice.

"He can't arrest him," Sarah said in dismay. "This is a council. The Indians are protected under diplomatic immunity."

"Sure looks to me like they're arresting him," Frances said. Suddenly Sarah was down the steps and running across the parade ground. She reached Joseph and Spotted Frog just as they were about to mount their horses.

"Joseph, wait," she called. "What has happened? Why have they taken that man away?"

"General Howard has shown us the rifle," Joseph said bitterly. "He has violated the agreements that bring us here to the council."

"It can't be," Sarah said.

"He will not hear what the Indian has to say. He has made up his mind and we are to obey like children." It was the closest she'd ever seen him to being angry. "There is no goodwill between us now."

Joseph leaped onto his horse and galloped out of the post gate toward his camp. Tanner and the other men were returning from the guardhouse, and Sarah stood in their path, her hands on her hips, her head thrown back in defiance. Tanner saw the determined thrust of her chin and knew someone was in for a good piece of her mind. Sarah's dark eyes flashed with fury and contempt as she looked at him.

"General Howard," she said when the men drew near. "I want to talk to you. What you've done is abominable. Those Indians came in for a council. To throw one of them into the guardhouse is despicable on your part."

"Miss MacKenzie, I've tried hard to appreciate your sympathy for the Nez Percé, but I'll not answer to a civilian for my orders."

"You've acted dishonestly with Joseph and the rest of the chiefs. If there is a war out of this, you will have brought it down on your own head by your actions."

The general's face grew red with rage, and his lips worked before words spilled out. "One more outburst from you, Miss MacKenzie," he snapped, "and I'll clear the post of all civilians." He stalked away.

"Threats and a show of force are not the way to handle things, General," Sarah called after his departing back, but a strong hand clamped over her arm and she was pulled away in the opposite direction.

"Let go of me," Sarah cried, twisting in Tanner's grip.

"Not until you calm down," he answered. "This is a very difficult period, Sarah. You can't become so emotional. It accomplishes nothing."

"The general was wrong to do this to the Indians. They were here to talk. They were immune to arrest."

"We'll let the man out in a day or so after the council. The general lost his temper. He'll cool down. It the meantime, maybe Joseph and the others will listen to reason."

"Joseph won't trust you now."

"Sarah, we're beyond the need for trust," Tanner said, and he saw the resignation in her eyes.

"I know," she whispered so brokenly that he pulled her against his chest, cradling her in his arms, meaning only to comfort. His eyes closed as desire swept through him. He buried his face in her sweet-smelling hair and just stood letting his senses awaken to the familiar feel and fragrance that was Sarah.

"God, I've missed you so much," he whispered. She held her cheek to his, forgetting everything for the moment but the strength of him. His cheek was at once smooth and raspy against hers. Tanner's lips brushed across her cheeks and settled on her lips in a light, tentative kiss. Then with a groan he crushed her to him, his kiss hot and insistent on her mouth. Her breath caught in her chest. She should shove him away, one part of her urged, he had betrayed her. But another part argued that it was not that simple, not that black and white. She returned his kiss, feeling the wholeness that being with Tanner brought her. Then she pushed him away gently, her expression filled with regret. He let her go without a struggle.

Slowly she shook her head from side to side. "I'm sorry," she murmured. "I wish I could forget and go on the way we were, but I can't. This will only bring us more heartache. Nothing has really changed between us."

"No, it hasn't," he agreed and turned on his heels and walked away. Wiping at tears that spilled over, Sarah made her way back to Emily Fitzgerald's quarters. She was grateful to see that John Monteith had already brought the agency wagon around. Tomorrow she would not come again, she vowed.

This time it was easy to keep to her decision. In

the days that followed, Joseph and his chiefs went to inspect sites where they might settle on the reservation. John showed them land in the valley of the Lapwai Creek and along the Clearwater River at Kamiah. On May 15 a final council was held and, true to her resolution, Sarah stayed at the agency. When John and Frances returned, they told her of Joseph's agreement to go to the reservation. Everyone was relieved that a war had been averted. Sarah felt the same relief but she was saddened that a way of life had ended for Joseph and his people. She remembered all the tales her grandmother had told her of the Nez Percé legends and customs. Would they be lost now, smothered by the zeal of missionaries like Sue McBeth and others? Fervently she hoped not.

She had vowed to stay only until the questions over Joseph's people had been answered. Now it was time for her to leave. School was ending for another summer. Soon the treaty Nez Percé would go to Camas Meadows to dig for bulbs, and the summer cycle of gathering and harvesting food they'd grown would begin. It was a process that Joseph and his people must learn. Sadly she went to pack away the books and supplies.

As before, Tanner found her in the schoolhouse. This time, he vowed to himself, the outcome would be different. He would be gentle, patient, tender. He would forget his pride, his duties as a soldier, his convictions. He wanted Sarah. His life was too bleak without her, like the dark shadows in the deepest river valleys where the sunshine never reached. Tentatively he knocked on the door and entered. Sarah turned from her task, startled, a smear of dust on one ivory cheekbone. She wore a plain cotton gown, without bustles and petticoats. Her full red lips were slightly parted, and he wanted to kiss them and touch the smooth mounds of breasts beneath the plain bodice.

"Hello," Sarah said. His face looked leaner if possible, she thought, and went back to packing so she wouldn't look at him.

"Hello," Tanner answered and nodded his head toward the packing crates. "Closing up for the summer?"

Sarah nodded. "The children will be accompanying their parents to the Camas Meadow soon."

"Will you be going?" Tanner asked.

Sarah shook her head. "Not this year," she said, and he heard the regret in her voice.

"Sarah, I came about you and me."

"There is no you and me, Tanner," she answered and concentrated on her task.

Tanner studied her slender back, so rigid and straight. So unyielding, he thought fondly, and yet he knew only too well how soft and yielding Sarah could be. "You can't mean that now," he said. "Joseph has agreed to go on the reservation. The danger of conflict is past. I know you've been pulled in two directions, but that's over now, Sarah. Let's get on with our lives. I love you." His words cut through her defenses like nothing else could.

"I know you love me," he went on. "You haven't been able to put away what we have between us anymore than I have." He was close to her now and as he gently turned her around to face him, he found she was crying. "My sweet Sarah," he said tenderly, stroking her cheek, and once again she was amazed at the gentleness of such a big, hard-driven man. Lovingly he folded her in an embrace. As she had at the fort Sarah leaned against his strength, letting his nearness heal the bruising pain of her heart. Her arms went around his broad shoulders; her soft hands slid over the glossy curls at his nape, the baby-delicate skin behind his ears, the rough-weathered cheek, the stubbled chin, the warm hollow of his neck and the muscular chest.

From the first moment she'd seen him, he'd mystified and amazed her. He'd seldom been far from her thoughts. Even now her body remembered his touch and yearned for it again. Her sooty lashes tangled with tears, Sarah raised her lips to his, not seeking to kiss as a lover, but only to remind herself of the feel of his mouth against hers, the heady taste of him. Smiling tremulously, she drew back.

Tanner smiled and wiped the tears from her cheeks. "Don't cry," he whispered. "Everything will be all right."

"I'm leaving on the next steamboat," she said. "I'll be going back East."

"You couldn't be happy back there. You belong here."

"I'm not sure where I belong anymore," Sarah said. "I've made everyone so uncomfortable here, but I can't change what I am and the way I feel about Joseph and the rest of the Nez Percé."

"No one wants you to," Tanner said. "Your friends understand."

"How can they when I don't understand myself? I'm so confused."

Tanner drew her into his arms again. "The confusion will pass, Sarah. Give it time," he advised. "This has been a difficult time for us all. Joseph and his people will adjust to life on the reservation. The Nez Percé are enterprising people."

"I feel so guilty, as if I should have done something to help them."

"You tried, Sarah. You couldn't do anything more,

but you care and you tried. Joseph knows that. Stay
and help Joseph and his people adjust to their new
life. You can be invaluable to them."

Sarah raised her head and looked at him. In her
preoccupation with the injustices of it all, she'd given
no thought to how the Nez Percé would make the
adjustment to reservation life and that she might
help. Now Tanner held out new hope to her. Eagerly she grasped it. "Do you think I could ease
things for them?" she asked.

Tanner simply nodded and watched her face
change. The sadness and resignation slowly faded
and in their place were the fire and determination of
the old Sarah. Suddenly she laughed, wrapping her
arms around him. He buried his face against her
silky hair. He'd been praying for a miracle. Had that
been all it took, a few words reminding her she was
still needed by the Nez Percé? What would she say if
he told her how badly he needed her not just for a
short time, but for the rest of his life? He'd never let
her go, never. Fiercely he held her. He released her,
then fearful she might change her mind again, he
scooped her up in his arms and carried her to his
horse.

"Are you kidnapping me, sir?" she asked prettily
as he mounted behind her.

"I'll never let you get away from me again, Sarah,"
he said fervently against her ear. Sighing, she leaned
against him. They rode along the river until they
found a secluded spot. Tanner dismounted and pulled
her down to him. She slid the whole length of his
body, and a clamoring set up along every nerve
ending. "Promise you'll never leave me again," he
whispered. "Promise."

Sarah raised her mouth to his in a sweet, surrend-
ering kiss. Tanner lowered her to a fragrant bed of

wildflowers and tender grass. For a moment he hovered over her, drinking in the sight of her. Her dark eyes were wide and loving, her black hair spread around her in a glossy fan. Slowly Tanner lowered himself to her. Gently, passionately he loved her until they both lay spent and satiated upon the new spring grass. Only later did he remember that she hadn't promised after all.

20

Tanner's words had comforted Sarah and given her a reason to continue at Lapwai. His love sustained her in the days ahead. Distraught over the handling of the council, she hadn't stopped to hear the details. Now as John and Charles prepared for Joseph's arrival, they talked of little else.

"Will Joseph make the deadline of June 15 General Howard set for him?" Frances asked one evening at supper.

"He'd better," John answered. "General Howard is prepared to send his soldiers to assist them, and I don't expect they'll be too gentle."

"The order says he forfeits all his property that's not on the reservation by that date," Charles said. "I expect that'll be incentive to Joseph to make it on time."

"That's nearly impossible," Sarah protested. "Joseph's herds are scattered in the valleys through the winter. They won't have finished gathering them."

"They manage to do it every year for the camas harvesting," John said implacably, his pale face flushing slightly at her defense of the Indians. "We've set the deadline. If we go back and make concessions, they'll only ask for more and still more. No, they have to learn to obey now."

"Obey?" Sarah said and her voice shook with fury

at the agent. "They aren't children to be chastised and punished for some minor misdeed. They are proud men and women who've been free to do what they want for generations."

"I'll not have a member of this agency talk to me this way," he roared. "You are relieved of your duties."

"That won't stop me from speaking out when I see an injustice," Sarah said stubbornly.

"John, you don't mean this," Frances said. "Sarah's only concerned about the well-being of the Indians. And Sarah"— Frances, always the peacemaker, turned to her defiant young friend—"you must give John some credit for his work here. He cares about the Nez Percé. He's one of the best Indian agents the commissioner has."

Sarah bit her tongue at Frances's gentle admonitions. The things she said were true. The Nez Percé could have had a much worse man to deal with. "I'm sorry, John," she said.

The Indian agent looked mollified somewhat. "I accept your apology, Sarah," he said, shifting his weight from one foot to the other as he was wont to do when upset.

"But I feel compelled to do what I can," Sarah went on. "I'm going to talk to General Howard and try to persuade him to give Joseph more time."

"Then do what you must," John declared and stalked out of the kitchen.

Sarah glanced at Frances. "I'm sorry to cause problems over this," she said, "but I must do something."

"I understand, child," Frances said. "John will get over his anger and realize you don't mean any criticism against him." To add to her fears the *Teller* reported a drowning. A Dr. G. A. Going had been crossing the Grande Ronde River on horseback along with Lieutenant Whipple's company when he was swept from his horse and drowned. His body was not found. Sarah was beside herself with fear for Yellow Bird and Running Brook. Immediately she went to Reuben for a horse and rode to the fort. But General Howard had already returned to Portland.

In the weeks that followed Sarah knew little peace, torn by fear and uncertainty over the future of the Nez Percé. What if they changed their minds and didn't come? What if many of them were swept away by the raging, swollen rivers?

Then one day Tanner galloped into the agency yard, a smile on his face. "Joseph and his people are across the river. They're heading in," he called from his horse. The relief in his voice was evident, and suddenly Sarah understood he'd been as worried about them as she.

"Did everyone get across safely?" she asked, hardly able to believe Joseph had done it.

Tanner nodded. "All his people. They had to leave behind some of their stock, but most of their horses and belongings are all safely on this side. Owen Thatcher's men are already out gathering the herds left behind."

"We should be seeing them pull in here soon," John said, glancing around.

"Joseph told one of our men that they were going on to Camas Meadows for a couple of weeks first. Chief White Bird and some of the other tribes are going to meet him there."

"We've done it, then," John said, "and without anyone getting hurt."

"Let's hope it lasts," Tanner answered grimly. "Some of the white settlers have been claiming sinister councils and war parades."

"Do you think the chiefs are planning something?" Charles Monteith asked nervously.

Tanner shook his head. "I don't think so. If Joseph were going to resist, he would have done so in his own village. Those valleys are pretty narrow and would have been easier to defend than the open prairie. I think he means to settle as he promised. There's bound to be some resentment among his people, but Joseph seems to have them in hand."

Tanner glanced at Sarah. "Things are going to be all right, you'll see," he said and with a final wave galloped off in the direction of the fort. Sarah stood looking after him for a long time. Her immediate fears had ended. Joseph and Yellow Bird and their unborn baby were safe, as were Annie and Running Brook and all the others. Now her job began, that of helping the Nez Percé adjust to life on a reservation. If it wasn't the best situation, she'd come to realize it wasn't the worst either.

A week later, Red Eagle, whose band had lived south of Lewiston on the Snake River, brought his people into the reservation and settled ten miles north of the agency. It seemed all the tribes would resettle peacefully, and the people at the agency and the fort were breathing easier.

The peaceful interlude was threatened when word came to the fort that Carl Pepin was back in the territory and was selling whiskey to the Indians at Camas Meadows. Tanner rode out to the agency with word of it, and John Monteith's face grew purple with fury.

"Joseph and his tribe are my responsibility now," he raged. "I'll not have these men selling liquor to them. Can I have an escort of soldiers to accompany me to the digging?"

"It might be best not to take a detail of uniformed

soldiers in there now, what with the resentment the Indians feel. I'll go myself as a civilian."

Sarah longed to join them, just to see Yellow Bird and be sure everyone really was safe, but she knew neither Tanner nor John would agree this time. Then one night a treaty Indian stopped at the agency with a frantic message from Yellow Bird. Owen Thatcher's men had discovered Annie Red Moccasin was hiding there. It was only a matter of time before the corrupt lawyer came for her.

Like John, Tanner protested her going when she arrived at the fort the next morning.

"I'll either ride out on my own or ride with you," Sarah declared. "Which do you think would be the safest?"

"Sometimes you're the stubbornest, most unreasonable woman I ever met," Tanner snapped, but Sarah was undeterred. He had little choice but to take her with him.

They pressed hard and by nightfall of the second day were in the foothills overlooking the high camas meadows. Off in the distance they could see the fires of the Indian camps. "We'd better camp here tonight," Tanner said. "No sense to ride in on them out of the night and spook them. No fires. Nevins, you and Fisher take the first watch. Wake me at midnight."

"Yes, sir," Nevins said. He still hadn't gotten over his resentment of the major, and for that reason Captain Perry seemed to assign him to every detail with him. Nevins had had to bite his tongue time and again since. Now, his face sullen, he waved to Fisher, and the two men went forward and settled down behind some rocks with a clear view of the meadow below.

Sarah and the rest of the men laid out their bedrolls, chewed on some dried jerky and hardtack, washing it down with brackish water from their canteens, and stretched out on the hard ground to sleep for a few hours.

"Good night, Sarah," Tanner said softly.

"Good night, Tanner," she answered and knew, like her, he was remembering their first night together in the mountains.

Tanner lay thinking of what their life would be together. How many children would they have? He wanted a girl with dark, flowing hair and fine brown eyes like her mother's. A girl with spirit like Sarah's and strong convictions, and he wanted sons he could talk to and teach things. Sarah would teach them things about her people and their ways. Well, that was all right too.

When Gayle Nevins came to waken him at midnight, Tanner rose immediately and, nudging the soldier nearest him, walked down to take up position. "Something's been going on down there, sir," Nevins said, and Tanner got out his field glasses and trained them on the village below. Warriors were moving around a huge campfire and strewn on the ground at odd angles and poses were bodies of Indians. "What is it, sir?" Nevins asked. "Are they dead?"

"More likely drunk," Tanner said and focused his glasses on the whiskey wagons parked down in a hollow. He could make out white men harnessing their teams and casting stealthy glances over their shoulders as they readied themselves to pull out. Tanner lowered his glasses and sat considering. "Go on to bed, Nevins. I'll call you men if I need you."

"Yes, sir." The two soldiers made their way back to the rocks where the others were sleeping. Tanner trained his glasses once again. Some of the young bucks seemed to be arguing. One of them stalked away in anger, and the others sat cross-legged before the fire. Whatever the problem it seemed to be over, Tanner thought and turned his binoculars on the departing whiskey men. Their behavior seemed more ominous to him than anything else. It wasn't like Pepin to leave when he could still turn a profit. The Nez Percé had managed to bring most of their horse herds. Good steeds could be had for a jug of whiskey. Why then had he chosen to leave and in the middle of the night? The feeling of foreboding stayed with him as he settled against the rock to keep vigil in the dark hours before daylight.

The next morning Tanner instructed his men to keep out of sight in the rocks but to stay alert. He glanced at Sarah. "I don't suppose you'd consider staying here?" he said hopefully, but she only shook her head. Sighing, he mounted and led the way down into the meadow.

There was no sign of the whiskey peddlers and their wagons. They'd made their getaway during the night. Tanner headed directly to Joseph's camp. Warriors cast surly glances in their direction, but no one stopped them. Several women recognized Sarah and waved to her. Tanner drew up before Joseph's tent. Yellow Bird, her slight body heavy now with Joseph's child, came out to greet them. Her face lit up when she saw Sarah.

"Where's Annie?" Sarah asked when she was sure Yellow Bird was well.

"We've hidden her. Half-Moon will take you to her."

"Where's Joseph, Yellow Bird?" Tanner asked and she shrugged.

"Joseph is with the men in the hills, butchering cows," she answered. "I do not know when he will return." Sarah studied the Indian woman. Yellow Bird showed the distress of the past few days, and her shoulders slumped wearily.

"Tell me what has happened," Sarah urged. Glancing at John Monteith, Yellow Bird shook her head.

Sarah turned to Tanner. "While you and John are looking things over, I'm going to visit with Yellow Bird."

"All right," he agreed, realizing he had little choice. Yellow Bird wouldn't talk with the Indian agent there. When the men had left, Sarah followed her friend into her tipi.

Once they were settled around the fire, Yellow Bird began her story. "I am afraid," she said.

"Why?" Sarah asked, alarm growing within her.

"Joseph and Spotted Frog are not here now, so the young warriors talk. They drink whiskey from the wagons, they argue and fight among themselves. They are resentful that Joseph has chosen to come to the reservation. They say they want to fight. Little Wolf has been shamed by the rest of the warriors because he has not avenged his father's death. Black Beaver urges him on and incites the other young warriors to hatred against the whites. Spotted Frog has warned him, but Black Beaver is a brave and well-respected warrior."

"Black Beaver is a fool," Sarah exclaimed.

"He particularly hates Tanner," Yellow Bird warned. "He believes Tanner is the reason you won't marry him. He wishes to be allied with Joseph's family." Sarah was startled by Yellow Bird's words. She'd done nothing to encourage Black Beaver's attentions. Now she shivered with foreboding. She had little doubt that Black Beaver would try to kill Tanner. The fierce warrior who had once been her friend frightened her. She said nothing as Yellow Bird continued with her story.

"Last night, Little Wolf and Black Beaver gathered some of their friends and dressed and painted themselves for war, then they paraded around the campground. Many people cheered him."

"Yellow Bird, are you afraid they will make war?"

Joseph's wife shook her head. "I think they are young men with too much whiskey talk, but I wish Joseph were here." Her slender brown fingers fumbled nervously with the fringe at her thickened waist.

Sarah was reluctant to leave her friend in such a distraught condition, but Yellow Bird urged her to go to Annie. Half-Moon led her away from the encampment toward the bluffs overlooking the meadows. The old woman moved with surprising agility for her age. Annie was hidden in one of the many shallow caves that dotted the bluff. She jumped to her feet when Sarah entered.

"You've come at last," she sobbed, clinging to Sarah.

Sarah smoothed the girl's hair back. "Didn't you know I would?" she asked gently. "We're friends, remember?"

Annie smiled halfheartedly, and it occurred to Sarah she'd never seen the Indian girl laugh. Little reason to laugh in her bleak young life.

"Annie, you must stay hidden for a while longer," she urged. "I'll find a way to get you to safety. Major Tanner will help us."

The girl nodded. "I will do as you ask."

Sarah sat beside Annie and Half-Moon gave her the bundle of food and warm clothing she'd brought. Sarah tried to reassure the girl with her presence, but she sensed her fear. Suddenly Annie glanced toward the entrance of her cave and shrank back in terror.

"Annie, don't be afraid," Sarah remonstrated.

A voice, hateful and evil cut through her words. "Well, Annie, you've come to a sorry pass."

Owen Thatcher stood in the entrance.

"How did you find us?" Sarah cried.

"Why, Miss Busybody, you led me right to her. I knew she'd contact you sooner or later and you'd come running."

"You can't have Annie back," Sarah said. "She doesn't want to go with you."

"She has no choice," the big man said belligerently. "She's a thief. She has to go to jail, unless of course she wants to come back to me. I might be persuaded to tell the sheriff I won't press charges against her."

"No, I won't go back," Annie cried. She leaped to her feet and before Sarah could see what she was about, she sprang forward, a blade in one hand. She drove it deep into the man's fleshy shoulder. With a grunt of surprise and pain he stumbled backward, half sitting on a ledge. His hand fumbled with the knife that still protruded from his shoulder. Sweat glistened on his brow as he pulled it out and pressed a clean white handkerchief to the bleeding wound. Annie stared at him, mesmerized, her slight body trembling as if with the ague.

"Annie," Sarah cried, going to put her arms around the shaken girl. At her touch Annie jumped away with an incoherent cry. Her eyes were wild, like a cornered animal's. "It will be all right, Annie," Sarah said soothingly, but Annie's gaze was fixed on Owen Thatcher. Sarah glanced around and her blood ran cold. Eyes glittering with hatred, he slowly drew his gun, enjoying the terror he saw on Annie's face.

"Run, Annie," Sarah screamed, shoving the girl toward the opening. At any moment she expected to hear the report of a pistol. Then they were in the sunlight and running toward the horses. If only they could make it to the Indian camp. A shot sounded from inside the cave.

"Kautsas," Annie cried and reined in her horse.

"Don't go back," Sarah cried. "He won't hurt Half-Moon. It's you he wants." Annie hesitated, torn with love for the old woman who had nurtured her and fear for her life. "Annie!" Sarah screamed, seeing Thatcher appear in the entrance to the cave. As if in slow motion, he took aim and fired. Annie's body jerked and slid off the horse.

"Annie," Sarah sobbed and raced her horse back to the fallen girl. Flinging herself off her mount, she knelt in the crushed blue flowers of the camas lily beside the body of Annie Red Moccasin. There was no sign of life. She had died instantly, a bullet in her heart.

Owen Thatcher walked from the cave, the smoking pistol still in his hand.

"You murderer," Sarah cried, getting to her feet. The sound of gunfire had drawn other riders. Tanner and Monteith came from the Indian camps, but Sheriff Wilmot and his men reached them first.

"What happened?" Tanner demanded, bringing his horse to a stop.

"She pulled a knife on me," Thatcher said, indicating his wounded shoulder. "I had to defend myself."

"She was running away from you. You didn't have to shoot her," Sarah accused.

"She was coming back," Thatcher said easily. "You saw her turn her horse."

"I saw it," Sheriff Wilmot said. "We've been hunting for this Indian ever since she ran away from Lewiston last year. Funny how they turn mean, ain't it?" Sarah's fists clenched and Tanner feared she meant to throw herself at the man in her fury.

"There's another one in there," Thatcher pointed back at the cave.

"Half-Moon!" Sarah's face crumbled in grief. Tanner gathered her against his chest and she wept bitterly, thinking how the girl and the old grandmother had died trying to help each other. Such would have been the way with Swan Necklace and her, she thought.

Tanner took her back to Yellow Bird's tipi. Joseph's wife listened with horror to what had happened to Annie.

"He is an evil man," she exclaimed. "Many times in the past summers he and his men came to steal our cattle and dig into our land in their search for gold."

"Gold?" Tanner exclaimed. "The gold veins played out years ago."

"Not in Wallowa Valley, not while Joseph was there," Yellow Bird said sadly. "Now Thatcher has Wallowa Valley. His men steal our horses and cattle and still he is not happy. He comes to murder our people."

"He'll be brought to justice," Tanner said, but Yellow Bird only looked at him with unbelieving eyes.

Tanner stepped closer. "The whiskey wagons have left. I'll follow them for a while to make sure they don't come back."

"I'm staying here," Sarah replied. "I'll travel back to the reservation with Joseph's people."

"I don't think you'd better do that," Tanner said. "The mood is pretty hostile right now."

"No one will bother me," Sarah replied. "They know I'm Nez Percé too. I want to be here for Annie's burial."

"Not this time, Sarah," Tanner said firmly.

When she opened her mouth to protest further, Yellow Bird spoke up. "Tanner is right. The white faces only cause resentment among our people now. It is best for all concerned if you return with Tanner."

Sarah looked at her in surprise. "I am no longer welcome to stay here with you?"

"Not now, my little sister." Yellow Bird's expression was regretful but adamant.

There was nothing for Sarah to do but accept things gracefully. She forced a smile. "I'll see you when you reach the agency, then," she said. "I want to be with you when you give birth to your baby."

"I want that too, Swan Necklace," Yellow Bird said warmly.

Sarah felt better. "May the Great Spirit protect you. I don't know what I'd do if anything happened to you now."

"Nothing will. Don't worry. Joseph will come soon and everything will be as it should. We will come to the agency in a few days." She followed them out of the tipi and stood watching as they mounted.

"Give Joseph my regards," Tanner called and led the way out of the camp. Once again sullen, hostile faces were shown to them by Indians who had been friendly and hospitable before.

Tanner collected his men and they set out after the whiskey wagons, always staying just out of sight.

"Doesn't Pepin know we're here?" Sarah asked when they'd stop to watch the progress of the wagons from the cover of a ridge.

"He knows, all right," Tanner said, "but he's not sure who we are or what we want. We'll tail him on to Slater Creek, just to make sure he doesn't turn back."

They rode at an almost leisurely pace for the rest of the afternoon, and that night made camp in a small canyon, well hidden by rocks. Once again Tanner ordered no fires and as a precaution set out extra guards. The other men were ordered to sleep with their guns at the ready. Tanner went up into the rocks himself and settled down to watch. Was he afraid some of the warriors had tracked them and would attack while they slept? Sarah wondered and wasn't able to sleep herself.

A shrill Indian war cry, bloodcurdling and horrible, startled her from a doze. Sarah sat up and looked around. Gunshots sounded in the distance, but she couldn't make out from which directions. Another scream and more shots and she guessed that their position had been surrounded. Joseph's braves had attacked, she thought, and was more heartsick than frightened for her own well-being. This could only mean that Howard's troops would have to use force to subdue the Indians.

Rocks rattled over her head and Sarah crouched under an overhang of stone. A body slid down the steep wall and fell in a heap at her feet. A bullet kicked up the rock dust nearby and she drew back. Someone was there waiting for her to show herself. Crouching beneath the ledge, she waited. Where was Tanner? she wondered. A flurry of gunshots told her he was out there somewhere trying to fight off the Indians. She was on her own. A stealthy, slithering sound came from the right. Relentlessly the stalker moved toward the ledge. As he came closer, Sarah could see that he wore no shirt and his face was painted in a frighteningly gruesome pattern. He wore a feathered headband. The man bent down to peer under the ledge, and his eyes glittered strangely in the moonlight. Carl Pepin!

"You," she cried, backing away.

"Hello, little lady," Pepin sneered. "We've got us some unfinished business to take care of."

Sarah backed away from him. "It was you who wrecked the Union Pacific last year down by Salmon Falls," she accused. She wanted to hear him admit it just once, so her doubts would forever be put to rest.

Pepin smirked and nodded. "I was afraid you and the major would figure it out. I laughed when I heard he was looking for a Mexican. Peppi!" He guffawed and slapped his thigh. Then his grin faded.

"You won't get away with this. You can't pretend you're Indian to cover your crimes for long. People are beginning to suspect."

"Not if you don't run around arousing their suspicions with your crazy accusations," Pepin growled. "But first I'm going to take you with me. My men and me'll have a little fun with you. How long you stay alive depends on how much you please me."

"Tanner will kill you if you touch me," Sarah cried and wished she had a gun.

Pepin laughed again. "Like as not, Tanner is dead now. He thought I didn't know who was trailing me, but I knew when you arrived last night. I hoped the Indians would get you. They was stirred up enough, but I forgot you're Joseph's relative. Well, Joseph ain't here now, so you just start climbing up in them rocks now. Go on, git."

"I won't go," Sarah said, standing her ground.

Pepin's face swelled with rage. "You heard me, girl. I ain't one to mollycoddle a woman. You git on up there and maybe when my men and me's done with you, we'll give you a quick and easy death.

Otherwise, I'm going to stretch you out with rawhide and carve designs all over you the way I seen the Sioux do one time. It's a painful and ugly way to die."

"You don't scare me," Sarah said scathingly, although she was trembling with fear. She raised her chin defiantly and glared at him. Menacingly Pepin advanced toward her and Sarah took a step backward.

"Start climbing them rocks," he ordered, and when Sarah hesitated, he flashed out with his hand, catching her chin and knocking her flat on the ground. Sarah lay stunned. "That's just to let you know I ain't a man to ignore," he sneered. "Now git up and git moving." Slowly Sarah got to her feet, carrying hands full of sand with her. She stood weaving unsteadily and Pepin advanced again.

"I said git moving," he ordered, casting an anxious look over his shoulder. The gunfire had halted. As he turned back to her, Sarah flung the sand toward his face. He ducked and backed away, his hand shielding his eyes, but the distraction was enough for her to slither through a narrow crevice. She could hear him cursing behind her and the ricocheting echo of shots. He was firing blindly under the ledge in case she'd hidden there again.

Frantically Sarah climbed over and around rocks, trying to put as much distance as possible between herself and the whiskey man before he discovered she wasn't under the ledge. Within moments she could hear him coming after her through the rocks. Panic robbed her of breath as she wriggled around boulders and through openings so narrow her arms and shoulders were soon scraped and bleeding. Pepin was gaining on her.

Suddenly she came to a dead end. A wall of granite cut off her escape. Desperately she looked for an opening, but there was none. The moon lit the rocky mountainside, reflecting off the smooth, exposed stones and casting deep shadows. Hurriedly Sarah felt along the wall, seeking an escape, ignoring the sharp edges that tore her soft palms. There was nothing. She heard Pepin behind her and quickly sank into the nebulous cover of shadows.

"You can't hide from me," he growled out of the darkness. He climbed up on a boulder and glared down at her hiding place. His face was sinister in the moonlight. "I see you cowering there against them rocks." Peering into the dark shadows, he laughed and the ugly sound echoed around the rocky canyon. Sarah clamped her hands to her ears so she wouldn't hear it. "You might as well come out," he snarled, raising his gun. "There's no one to protect you now."

Sarah could see the barrel of the gun aimed right at her, and she steeled herself against the bullet soon to tear through her body. But the shot never came. Suddenly Pepin stiffened. His evil expression changed to one of surprise, and the gun fell from his hand and slithered down over the rocks. Stunned, Sarah watched as his knees buckled and he slowly folded and fell off the boulder. He lay still, an arrow protruding from the middle of his back. Now another predator blocked the skyline. Tell and fierce, dressed in rawhide and feathers, Sarah knew instinctively this was not one of Pepin's men dressed as an Indian. The warrior moved forward and the moonlight shone on his painted face. Calmly he fitted an arrow to his bow and aimed it at Sarah.

"Black Beaver," she cried. "It's me, Swan Necklace." He halted, the muscles of his bronze arms flexing as he held the bowstring taut, ready to release the arrow in an instant.

"Why are you here?" he demanded. "Yellow Bird said you and the soldier, Tanner, had returned to the fort."

"No, we followed Pepin to keep him from returning to your campgrounds. Thank God you're here. You saved my life."

"That is not why we are here, Swan Necklace," Black Beaver said. "Where is your soldier now?"

"He's fighting off Pepin's men back up there in the rocks."

"Pepin's men are dead. We've killed them," Black Beaver said.

"Then who are they shooting at?" she paused, her gaze sweeping back to Black Beaver. "No, you can't be serious. Stop your men now, Black Beaver, before it's too late. You won't be punished for Pepin and his men. Tanner will say you did it to help us, but he can't help you if you kill his soldiers."

"We've killed the whiskey men because they have treated us badly. They cheat us at every turn. We will not be silent. We will avenge ourselves. The blood of the Nez Percé flows in your veins. You will live this time. But you cannot live half in the Nimpau world and half in the white world. You must choose, Swan Necklace."

"We can live in peace side by side, Black Beaver. That's what Joseph wishes. That's why he's agreed to go to the reservation. If you harm any more whites, you'll cause all your people to suffer."

She spoke to the wind. Black Beaver had slipped away. Sarah heard gunfire in the distance, and fear for Tanner spurred her back over the treacherous rocks toward the soldiers. The gunfire had faded to nothing long before she reached their campsite. With dread Sarah approached the rocky perch where Tanner and his men had kept watch. Not knowing what to expect, she crept up the rocky incline, pausing often to listen. Who waited at the top, Tanner and his men or Black Beaver and his drunken band? Suddenly a hand clamped over her mouth, and she was pulled backward against the hard wall of a chest.

"Where the hell have you been?" a voice growled low in her ear.

"Tanner," Sarah whispered shakily. She sagged against him in relief.

"Are you all right?" he asked hoarsely.

"I'm fine," she said, half crying, half laughing. Nothing had ever felt so wonderful as his arms.

"We were pinned down. I couldn't get back to you. I've been crawling all over these rocks looking for you. I was afraid they'd gotten to you. You're safe now," Tanner said, running his hands over her face and limbs, reassuring himself that she was indeed safe.

"Black Beaver said he was going to kill you," she whispered, thankful he was alive.

"Black Beaver! So it was Joseph's braves." Tanner swore.

"No, at first it was Pepin and his men dressed up like the Indians. He was going to kill me, but Black Beaver got him first."

"We got most of his men. One or two ran off in the rocks. I don't think we'll see them around here again. They'll probably head south and join up with some of the gangs hiding out along the Snake River canyons."

"Pepin and his men attacked the Union Pacific last year. He bragged about it."

"We'll be able to prove that now," Tanner said. His arms tightened around her spasmodically, and she guessed the anxiety he must have felt when he discovered she wasn't safe in camp.

"Where's Black Beaver now?" he demanded, gripping her arms and shaking her slightly.

"I don't know," Sarah answered wearily. "He just melted away into the shadows. Oh, Tanner, he said they were going to avenge themselves against the whites. What are we going to do to stop them?"

"We'd better get back to the fort and alert the others," he said.

"But can't we do something to stop Little Wolf and Black Beaver?"

Tanner shook his head. "Let's pray Joseph gets back before they cause more mischief."

They made their way back to the fort by midafternoon. People stared as they rode past the barracks and onto the parade ground leading the horses with the dead bodies draped across them. Tanner headed directly to Perry's office. Already alerted that something unusual was occurring, the young captain came out on the vine-covered porch to greet the newcomers. Faye and Emily were right behind.

"What've you got there, Major?" he asked, spotting the feathers and paint. "What's happened?"

"Nothing much yet, sir, but it's going to. This is Pepin and his men. They dressed up like Indians and attacked us down near Slater Creek. Apparently they meant to cause trouble and have it blamed on Joseph's tribe."

General Howard came out of the office and walked down the steps to investigate the dead men more closely. "The dang fools, don't they know we're sitting on a powder keg here?"

"The situation is serious," Tanner said. Howard shook his head and chewed on his lower lip. Sarah had remained quiet. Now she stepped forward. "Perhaps if you send someone to talk to Joseph and his warriors," she suggested.

"That might be worth a try," Howard conceded. Whatever else he'd been about to say was interrupted. Jonah, an Indian guide, galloped into the square. Two Indians followed. Perry and Howard stepped out to meet them, and Sarah hurried to the rail to hear what was going on.

One of the men, a half-breed, stepped forward. "I am called West," he said. "I have a message for the white chief." He handed over the dispatch.

Opening it, Howard began to read, muttering under his breath now and then. "What is it, sir?" Perry asked.

"It's from a hotel keeper, L. P. Brown. He says the Indians have attacked several settlers down along the Cottonwood. They need arms and ammunition. They've got most of the families holed up on a ranch down there, but they need help." There were cries of outrage from those gathered around. Howard looked at the other Indian.

"After West leave, more wounded come in. Brown send me with another message." He held it out.

Hesitantly Howard took it. This time he read it aloud. "The Indians have possession of the prairie and threaten Mount Idaho. All the people are here, and we will do the best we can. Lose no time in getting up with a force. Stop the stage and all through traveling. Give us relief and arms and ammunition. Chapman has got this Indian to go, hoping he may get through. I fear the people on the Salmon have all been killed, as a party was seen going that way last night. We had a report that seven whites had been killed on the Salmon. Notify the people of Lewiston. Hurry up, hurry." Slowly the general lowered the dispatch. His face was grim.

"Those poor people," Emily cried, pressing her

hands to her mouth. Her eyes were wide with sympathy.

General Howard turned to Captain Perry. "Well, Captain, I'm afraid this is serious. Are your men ready?"

"Yes, sir," Perry said.

"I'm afraid we're at war with the Nez Percé."

The words cut through Sarah like a knife, and she pressed her trembling fingers against her lips to hold back the sobs. Her world had just been torn apart and she didn't know which side to choose.

"Sarah," Tanner said urgently. She turned tearful eyes to him. "I'm sorry," he murmured helplessly and then he was gone, running across the compound to gather his men and prepare to attack the camp of her people. Blackness swept over Sarah and gratefully she sank into its comforting oblivion.

21

When Sarah regained consciousness, she was in Emily Fitzgerald's bed and Emily was applying cold cloths to her forehead.

Faye Perry stood nearby, wringing her hands. "This is just dreadful," she said. "It makes me feel quite ill to think of those poor settlers with their mutilated bodies."

"Oh, do be quiet, Faye," Emily snapped. She turned her attention back to Sarah. "She's coming around."

Sarah blinked rapidly to focus, then sat up, embarrassed that she'd given way to such foolish weakness.

"How are you feeling?" Emily asked gently.

"I'm fine," Sarah lied and swung her legs over the bed.

"Oh, don't try to get up yet," Emily remonstrated, hurrying around to settle her back against the pillows, but Sarah refused to be bullied even by so gentle a soul as Emily.

A commotion sounded outside the windows, and all three women turned their gaze toward it. With a rustle of long skirts Faye hurried to the window and peered out. "Major Tanner is organizing the troops," she said excitedly. She drew back and turned to face the other women. "What if the friendly Indians join

Joseph and his tribe? Why, we could be scalped in our sleep," she said, as if the thought had just struck her.

"The soldiers won't allow the Indians to get anywhere near the post," Emily said reassuringly, but Sarah could see the same doubt and fear reflected on her face.

"Joseph won't allow his warriors to come near the post," Sarah said wearily.

"He's already allowed his warriors to attack and kill white settlers along Slater Creek," Emily exclaimed in dismay. "Surely you can't champion him now?"

"Joseph wasn't there. He'd gone across the river to butcher cattle. Some of the young warriors were drinking whiskey sold to them by white men. They got out of hand. When Joseph hears of this, those warriors will be punished."

"In the meantime we have the soldiers to protect us against those heathen savages. I hope they kill every one of them," Faye declared.

Emily saw Sarah's face blanch and pity stirred for her friend. "Sarah needs to rest now, Faye," she suggested gently. "Perhaps you could come back another time."

"Oh! Yes, of course," Faye said and with a final measuring glance at Sarah flounced out of the room.

"Thank you," Sarah said gratefully. "I have to get up. I have to go talk to General Howard and explain how it was at Joseph's camp." She got to her feet. The room spun crazily, then righted itself.

"You've been through some frightful hours, with the Indian attack and all. You came close to losing your life. You're not nearly as strong as you think you are, Sarah MacKenzie," Emily fussed. "I insist you go back to bed."

"I can't, Emily. I have to find General Howard. Maybe I can stop this before it gets out of hand."

"But you've already told him that, and I'm sure Major Tanner informed him as well of what you've found."

"But he must not understand, otherwise he wouldn't be sending so many soldiers against the Indians," Sarah insisted. Her head hurt abominably.

"Sarah, General Howard has been preparing his officers for this for more than a year. We've known for months that war with the Nez Percé was inevitable. Our soldiers are nearly ready to leave. General Howard has sent for four more companies and for hard tack and supplies. Lieutenant Bomus has gone to Lewiston to secure a pack train. They'll ride to Joseph's camp at once."

"Then I must warn them," Sarah whispered fearfully.

"Warn them?" Emily echoed, her face growing pale and disbelieving. "You would warn the Indians against your own people?"

"The Nez Percé are my people as well," Sarah said and wondered at the number of times she'd said that in the year she'd been here. It seemed no one could hear her or understand her ties to the Nez Percé. "I must go to them."

"What manner of woman are you that you would turn against your own kind like this?" Emily asked disbelievingly.

"What manner of woman would you be if you were in my place?" Sarah asked quietly.

"I certainly wouldn't warn the bloodthirsty savages who are killing my people. I wouldn't betray the man I love for them."

Sarah's expression was filled with anguish as she listened to Emily's words. "Poor Sarah," Emily said, patting her back. "This must all be very difficult for you, but you must forget your Nez Percé blood. Look at Reuben and the treaty Indians. They aren't rushing off to support Joseph in his war. They're staying on the reservation and accepting their new lives with the white men. Once and for all you must choose the white world. It's where you belong."

"I don't know where I belong," Sarah moaned, hiding her face in her hands.

"Come back to bed, Sarah. You need to rest," Emily said gently and led her patient back to the big four poster she shared with Dr. Fitzgerald. She tucked the covers high under Sarah's chin and smoothed back the glossy black hair. "It will be all right. Sleep for a little while. When you wake up, you can make a decision. Things will look better to you." Emily glided from the room and quietly closed the door behind her.

Sarah lay back against the white pillowcase, breathing in the delicate scent of lavender and lemon oil. The room smelled like Emily, dainty and fragrant and clean as a rain-washed summer day. No wonder Emily found the 'Indian smells,' as she called them, so offensive. Although they bathed everyday, the Nez Percé smelled of tanned hides and wood smoke, earthy smells that spoke too well of the kind of life they led.

Suddenly the smell of lavender and lemon oil gagged Sarah and she sat up, leaning forward to wretch into the pristine china bowl placed next to the bed. Yellow Bird's face swam before her. She thought of the terror the Nez Percé would feel when the soldiers rode into their camp. Flinging aside the covers, she stood up and shook out the wrinkles of her dark gown. Sounds of horses and men outside drew her once again to the window.

"Sergeant, are your men ready?" Captain Perry called.

"Yes, sir," the man called.

General Howard joined the post commander on the vine-shaded porch. Tanner and Major Wood were there as well. "Well, Captain, this is it. Your regiments are just about ready to ride out."

"Yes, sir," Perry answered. "We're leaving behind a small detail to defend the post."

"More soldiers will arrive in a few hours. I've also ordered up some howitzers."

"Do you think you'll need such big guns against the Nez Percé?" Tanner asked, and Sarah could hear the alarm in his voice.

"I think they will help to end this war sooner, Major Tanner," the general answered.

"If you fire one of those guns into a village, you'll cut down women and children," Tanner said tightly.

General Howard glanced at him sharply. "The Indians are already killing our women and children, Major. They need to be taught a lesson."

"Yes, sir," Tanner answered. His words echoed in Sarah's head and, stifling back a sob, she glanced around the room. Her choice was very clear. She must go to Joseph and warn him. She crossed the room and opened the door. Emily and Faye must be on the porch with the officers. Quietly she let herself out the back door and hurried to the stables.

"Yes, ma'am, what can I do for you?" the private in charge of the horses asked.

"I'm returning to the agency. Saddle my horse, please."

"You ought'n to be riding out alone now, Miss MacKenzie," the man said. "Ain't you heard about the Indians?"

"Uh, yes, I have. I'm to ride with the man sent to

Lewiston to help Lieutenant Bomus with the pack train," she answered. "They're in something of a hurry to leave."

"Oh, yes, ma'am. I'll get your horse." Sarah struggled to maintain her composure and not hurry the man further. He might become suspicious of her story. Soon he brought her horse and held it for her to mount.

"Thank you, soldier. My prayers will be with you brave men in the days ahead," she said and knew it wasn't a lie. She would pray earnestly that something would happen to stay them from fighting the Nez Percé.

Before she could spur her horse away, a shout went up. Tanner ran across the parade ground.

"Soldier, halt that rider," he called, but Sarah brought her whip down over the soldier's face. He flinched and let go of the bit. Her horse reared, then sidestepped nervously. Sarah tugged the reins, turning her mount toward the trail leading out of town, but Tanner's shout had alerted other soldiers. Some of them quickly mounted their horses, and her path was blocked. Desperately she turned toward the parade ground. The assembled men were at the other end. Save for Tanner, the way was clear. Kicking the horse's belly, Sarah rode headlong toward Tanner, but there was no time to gather momentum. Tanner leaped at the bit. The horse neighed and came to a stop, confused by the mixed orders he'd received. He stood quietly, his leg muscles twitching nervously.

Tanner glared up at her. "Where are you going?" he demanded.

"Back to the agency," Sarah lied. "I'm not needed here and I can't bear to watch you ride out against Joseph."

"We have to stop the killings. We'll look for Black

Beaver and Little Wolf first, and we'll try to talk to Joseph. Trust me, Sarah, I'll do what I can to help them."

She wanted to trust him, wanted to believe that the tender, loving lights in his eyes were real and that he wouldn't kill her people. She sat shivering in her saddle, her mind and body exhausted by the turmoil of the past few days, and she wanted desperately to have the world right again, to feel Tanner's strong arms around her. She swayed forward and his arms were there, closing around her, pulling her off the horse. Sarah leaned against him, feeling his strength, needing it. Face buried in the warm hollow of a tanned neck and uniform-clad shoulder, the tears came weakly, but she made no sound. Tanner could feel the tenseness and terror in her slim body, and he longed to ease her pain.

"Let's go back to Emily's and put you to bed," he said. With Sarah's arm still wrapped around his neck and her head resting on his shoulder, Tanner supported her weight as they walked back toward the doctor's quarters. Slowly they climbed the stairs to the porch, where Emily and Captain Perry and General Howard stood waiting.

"Sergeant," the general said when they had reached the top step.

"Yes, sir," the man stepped forward.

"I want you to place a guard at the door of this woman's room. She is under arrest."

Sarah's head came up. Dark, accusing eyes stared at Tanner as she withdrew her arm from his neck and stepped away from him.

"Sarah, I swear this isn't what I had in mind."

"You tricked me," she whispered.

"I had no idea he intended this."

"Mrs. Fitzgerald told me of the conversation she

had with you earlier, Miss MacKenzie," the general said. "I don't intend to have you out there further inciting the Indians or giving away vital information."

"Why don't you just shoot me, General?" Sarah asked scathingly, her gaze never breaking from Tanner's. "Isn't that what they do with spies?"

"Yes, it is," Howard replied easily, "and that is not beyond the realm of possibilities, Miss MacKenzie. You might keep that in mind the next time you intend to go to your Indians. Sergeant, take her away."

"Sarah, I'm sorry," Emily said as they brushed past. "When I found you gone, I had to talk to General Howard."

"I understand, Emily," Sarah said bitterly. "Your loyalty for your people is noble, mine is treacherous." Without another glance at Tanner she walked away.

"Don't you think you're being unnecessarily harsh on her?" Sarah heard Tanner say before the door closed behind her. It no longer mattered. She must never think of Tanner again. Her energy must be focused on Joseph and the Nez Percé, the real people. No one else must exist for her.

She was placed in one of the back bedrooms, where only a high, small window let in light. It was, as were all areas of Emily's home, spotlessly clean, with that same flowery fragrance that Sarah found cloying. A small rope bed with stiff white sheets sat at one side. A carved chest of drawers stood in one corner and a brightly woven rag rug lay on the gleaming plank floor. It was not an unpleasant prison, but a prison nonetheless. The lock was on the inside of the door and she guessed it couldn't be locked from without, but a scrape of a chair told her that someone sat outside the door. There would be no escape.

Sarah thought of the longhouses of the Nez Percé, where several families lived together in harmony, for no one tried to impose his will upon another. There was no need for locks or jails. A man was allowed to do what his conscience dictated. In Joseph's village Sarah would have been allowed to go free. Here in the white man's world she was imprisoned because her beliefs were not the same. She sat on the floor Indian-fashion, bowed her head, and wept heartbrokenly in a fashion that was all her own.

For the rest of the afternoon and evening she heard companies of soldiers ride out; then the fort was quiet again. Once she opened the door and looked out. A young soldier got to his feet, his hand already going for his pistol. She withdrew back into her prison room. The light from the small window grew gray with dusk and finally turned dark. Emily brought a tray and a lamp and tried to talk to her, but Sarah turned away, her face displaying the same stoicism of the Indian that had always baffled the white man. Defeated, Emily went away. Sarah let the food grow cold on the plate while a plan began to form in her head. She would make her escape.

She ate the food Emily had brought after all, forcing it down her tight throat, for she wasn't sure when she would eat again. Bunching the pillow and bright quilt into a pile in the middle of the mattress, she turned the lit lamp onto its side and set the bed ablaze.

"Fire, fire," she shouted, pounding on the door. Hearing excited voices on the other side, she opened the door and rushed out. "Fire," she gasped, pointing with a trembling finger. The soldier grabbed the rag rug and began to beat at the flames. Sarah backed toward the parlor.

Emily ran out of her bedroom, her long hair trailing loosely over her high-necked nightgown. "What is it? What's happened?" she demanded.

"There's a fire," Sarah sobbed. "The l—lamp fell off the table onto the b—bed. I couldn't put it out."

"Dear God, are you hurt?" Emily asked, while casting a quick glance back at the bedroom where her two children were sleeping.

"No, I'm fine," Sarah sobbed. "What about Jeremy and Tommy? Get them outside where they'll be safe." Emily turned from Sarah and ran back to the bedroom, calling frantically to her sons. Sarah watched her go and for a moment was tempted to run to help, but the fire had been contained to the bed and even now she could see the young soldier was bringing the flames under control. There would be little damage. If she tarried any longer, her chance to escape would be gone. Quickly she opened the door and closed it behind her. Footsteps already beat along the porch as men ran to help put out the fire. They knew if it wasn't quickly contained, the whole post could go. In the confusion she made her way along the edge of the buildings, stopping now and then to search the parade grounds for a horse. A supply train of about thirty mules and a handful of packers entered the compound. More soldiers followed behind on horseback. Sarah waited until they had dismounted and moved away before hurrying forward. Unobserved, she reached the mount nearest her and, taking advantage of the noise and confusion caused by the wagon train, led the horse away. In the dark shadows she mounted and, digging her heels into the horse's flanks, galloped away.

She rode hard, traveling by instinct over the trails

that had become so familiar to her, praying her mount wouldn't miss his footing in the darkness and send them both sprawling over a precipice into a canyon. When she was far enough away from the fort and there seemed no outcry or attempt to follow her, Sarah slowed her horse and made her way cautiously. It was imperative that she cover as much distance as possible under the cover of dark, but she couldn't risk detection. The hills and mountains would be well scouted now by troops. Briefly she wondered where Tanner was, pushing his company of soldiers toward Joseph's camp, no doubt. She'd never reach them in time to warn them, she thought and despite her fatigue pressed on.

All night she rode and on into the day, fearful of being spied by lookouts and afraid that she might not reach Joseph's camp in time if she stopped. The trails were muddy and the going hard for the horse. She could feel it struggling beneath her and finally halted for a short while, but soon she was on her feet again, walking to rest her horse. Through the day she pushed on, her only nourishment that drawn from the creek water she drank. The sun slid behind the black wall of a mountain, and finally she was forced to stop and rest. Taking out a soldier's bedroll, she made a pallet on the rocky ground and tried to sleep. Her horse lay down on the ground nearby, too exhausted to forage among the scrawny plants that grew on the hillside. At the first rays of sunlight Sarah was up and pushing forward again. She felt suspended in time, a lost soul, meant to wander the mountains and trails until the Nimpau gods took pity and delivered her to her destination.

It was late afternoon when she reached Camas Meadows. She rode over the last ridge and sat looking down into the empty prairie. There was so sign of any of the Indian camps. Likewise there was no sign of battle, and for that reason Sarah slumped in her saddle and said a prayer of thanksgiving. Finally the nagging worry of where Joseph and his people were cut through her relief and she rode down into the meadow. Tracks were everywhere, some leading off northward toward Cottonwood Creek and others criss-crossing and leading off southward toward White Bird Creek. Which way should she go? she wondered in despair. If she chose wrong, she could lose all chance of catching up with Joseph.

The murders had occurred at Slate Creek, which was south, so Joseph and his people would have fled the trouble, she reasoned, and followed the tracks north. Halfway to Cottonwood Creek she came across a small band of Indians. Boldly she rode forward, refusing to think of what they might do to her. She still wore the clothes of the white man. Holding her hand up in an Indian greeting, she hailed them in the Nez Percé tongue. With troubled, hostile faces the men readied their guns and bows and arrows while the women stood by with extra ammunition. Yet Sarah took heart, for it was obvious by their clothes and equipment that they were treaty Indians from the reservation.

"I mean you no harm," she called. "I am looking for my kinsman, Joseph. Do you know where his tribe has gone?"

Without answering they simply stared at Sarah. "I am from the Lapwai Agency," she said. "I am Swan Necklace, kinswoman of Chief Joseph and Spotted Frog."

"I am Little Elk," one of them said, stepping forward. "We are of the tribe of Chief Looking Glass. We are not part of what has happened here. We want only to return to our village."

"Can you tell me where everyone has gone?" Sarah waved a hand at the empty prairie.

The Indian shrugged. "Joseph has led them to safety at Salmon River."

"Has Yellow Bird delivered her child, then?" Sarah asked eagerly.

Little Elk shook his head. "This I do not know."

"Are Joseph and his people alone there or has White Bird joined him?"

"I do not know," Little Elk said and prepared to depart. Sarah turned her horse south. Weary as she was, she was determined to find Joseph. Her exhausted mind repudiated all she'd heard. She was certain everything that had occurred was a mistake that could be explained away. She had to find Joseph. She had to.

Tanner looked at his men sprawled over the ground like so many broken dolls thrown aside by a careless child. In some cases their horses lay beside them, felled by weariness. They had traveled from Fort Lapwai for forty-eight hours without pausing to rest or eat, slowing their pace only so the supply train could catch up with them. They had gone first to Grangeville, where they'd set up camp. Then word had come that Joseph and his band were camped in White Bird Canyon. Obviously he was planning to flee across the Salmon River and once he did, he could hide in the breaks and steep canyons of the river country. The soldiers had marched most of the night, and now they waited at the head of the canyon. Dismounting, the men had fallen on the ground to sleep for a few precious hours before daylight.

Tanner glanced at the horizon. Dawn was here, the time of reckoning for Joseph and his warriors. What were Black Beaver and Little Wolf thinking? he wondered. Were they giving any thought to the harm they had brought their people with their exploits? Like as not, they lay in a drunken stupor, for Perry had been informed by one of the settlers that the Indians had attacked a pack train of whiskey drums. Black Beaver's following had swelled from a handful of Indians to more than sixty warriors. Tanner's mouth tightened. He was glad Sarah was safely back at the fort, even if she were a prisoner. He didn't want her to witness what was about to happen with Joseph and his warriors.

"Sergeant, pass the word to the men to mount up quietly and move forward." He paused as a match flared and a soldier lit his pipe. In the distance a coyote howled and Tanner felt a shiver of alarm pass along his spine. "Tell that man to put out that light," he snapped. He studied the shadow-shrouded walls of the canyon, trying to peer through the cover of darkness and discern what lurked there in the rocks.

The canyon was a drainage basin for White Bird Creek as it flowed downhill for ten miles before emptying into the Salmon River. The descent to the creek bed was steep, and the valley was slashed with a succession of ridges and breaks, the slopes steep and uneven. Scouts had brought word that the Indian camp was about four miles away in a grassy meadow protected on the north and south by rocky outcrops and sheer drops.

Captain Perry rode up. "Are your men mounted and ready?" he asked.

"Yes, sir," Tanner answered, glancing around.

"I've sent Theller and his troops on ahead. I'll take my men down next in columns of twos. You follow with your company in single-file columns."

Tanner nodded in agreement. "We'll be at a disadvantage, you know. We'll be unprotected riding down into that canyon, and our men and horses are tired. The Indians have been camped here for a couple of nights. They're rested and they know the terrain."

"I know, Major," Perry said wearily. "But if we wait and the Indians cross the Salmon River, we'll be open to censure. I'm counting on them being drunk and unprepared for us."

"I hope to hell you're right, Captain," Tanner said and waved his men forward. A coyote howled again.

She'd been forced to stop for the night. The horse was on its last legs and she was afraid to push it any farther. She'd be afoot if she did. At the first ray of light she rose and started out again. Before leaving Camas Meadows she'd dug a few camas bulbs, and now she peeled one and ate it raw. She'd been without food for nearly two days and at first she thought her stomach would refuse this bit of nourishment. Her shoulders heaved and she willed her body to relax. Finally she swallowed down some creek water and when the weakness and nausea passed, she saddled her horse and rode out again.

White Bird Creek wasn't that far away and she reached it before the sun was very high. Pausing on a high ridge, she looked down into the canyon. She could see Joseph's camp set up a couple of miles from the mouth of the creek. Her relief was short-lived, for her eye caught a movement on the ridge above. A column of troops were spread out in a semicircle, their blue uniforms looking menacing and horribly out of place in the natural beauty of the canyon. As Sarah watched, six Nez Percé carrying a white truce flag rode forward to meet the head of the column. In spite of herself Sarah strained to see Tanner. He sat slouched in his saddle, but she could see by the set of his shoulders and head that the easy posture belied his tense alertness.

A movement at one side drew her attention. A group of civilian volunteers crouched behind a knoll. One of them wore a fancy vest and held a cigar clamped between his teeth. Sarah recognized Owen Thatcher. He pulled his gun and took aim. At first Sarah was too stunned to react, then she opened her mouth to scream a warning to the six Indians. Her cry was lost in the distant roar of the gun. From her position on the high ridge Sarah could see and hear everything. Startled silence followed, then other men began to shoot. "Hold your fire," Tanner shouted, but his commands were ignored by the civilian volunteers.

The Indians who had not fallen under the fusillade of bullets fled back toward the creek. Suddenly the hillsides and ridges came alive with sound and motion as Spotted Frog and his warriors swept down the slopes toward the exposed troops. The soldiers took refuge behind the rocky knolls, but their position was tenuous. Tanner led a group of mounted cavalry into a line and advanced, but Indians bounded out of their hiding places in the brush along the creek and Tanner turned his men aside. The screaming, yelling Indians were bait to draw his men into an ambush. To continue the advance would be certain death under the sniper fire of the Nez Percé crack shots. When it was evident their ploy hadn't worked, the Indians scurried back to their positions in the brush.

"Dismount," Tanner shouted hoarsely. "String out along that ridge. Send your mounts back in the valley behind you." Horses screamed in fear and all was confusion, but in short order Tanner's men had done just as he commanded. Sarah watched as the soldiers and Indians exchanged fire. The Nez Percé had chosen their position well, for the troops were unable to maneuver over the steep bluffs and the Indians held the shallow ravines that led to retreat. The soldiers were pinned down by sniper fire, while their backs were threatened by mounted warriors who dashed right through the lines. In no time at all the soldiers were routed.

Tears rolled down Sarah's cheeks at the carnage, and she struggled to see Tanner through the smoke of battle. He was striding up and down the lines, exhorting his men to greater effort. Panic had set in among the other squads of soldiers. Captain Perry looked on helplessly while his men turned tail and ran. Vainly he tried to turn them back to fight, but ill-trained and inexperienced, they would have none of it. The panic spread to other troops, who followed their example and ran. Perry concentrated only on holding a squad of men to fight until their fellow soldiers had made a retreat.

On the western slope Sarah could see Major Trimble, whom she'd met once at the Perrys', and his detachment of soldiers. Tanner and his men still remained in place. If they stayed much longer they would be cut off from the main body of soldiers.

"Tanner," she screamed, but he couldn't hear her in the clash of battle. She longed to hurl herself down the steep slope and warn him, but common sense and confusion reigned side by side, and she stayed where she was, watching in horror as all chance for a peaceful solution faded with each shot that was fired.

Spotted Frog was everywhere, directing his warriors in darting, clever moves that only confused and frightened Perry's troops more. Even for Sarah, ignorant of battle tactics, it was obvious that Spotted

Frog was a brilliant war leader. She found little solace in that. She'd come to warn Joseph and his
people, fearful they would be cut down by the soldiers' bullets and found them well able to care for
themselves, but the sight of wounded men crawling
uphill toward the safety of the ridge was heartrend-
ing. She watched until she could bear no more, then
she bowed her head over her saddle horn and wept
bitter tears.

At last the sounds of fighting diminished, and
Sarah looked up to see that Perry had reached the
rim of the hill and Trimble's men were staggering up
the trail to meet them. Of the gallant young men
who'd gone into battle a scant few minutes before,
she could count only twenty or so struggling back
up the slope. The valley was littered with bodies.
Anxiously she looked for Tanner and his company
of men. Their numbers greatly decimated, they were
making an orderly retreat up the hillside behind
Trimble's panicky men. Spotted Frog and his warriors continued to harass the retreating men, so that
Sarah longed to cry out her anger at him. Tanner
urged his men on, then glanced around the rim of
the canyon. She knew exactly when he spotted her,
for his body went rigid and even from where she
sat, she could see the anguish on his face.

"Sarah," he called to her and the sound echoed
around the canyon mockingly. "Sarah!"

For a moment she sat as if graven of stone, a final
farewell in her heart, and then she turned away
from him and guided her horse down the ravine
toward the Indian village.

"Sarah!" Tanner cried, but she didn't look back.
Black Beaver heard the cry and his face grew ugly
with hatred for his enemy. Now was the time. Tanner was on foot and vulnerable. Wheeling his pony,

he rode toward the white soldier, his gun at the ready. Spotted Frog galloped up, placing himself between Black Beaver and the major, and the warrior was forced to veer off.

Somberly Spotted Frog gazed up at Tanner. Instinctively Tanner raised his gun and took aim. Over the gleaming, smoking barrel his eyes met Spotted Frog's and slowly he lowered his gun. The two men stared at each other, and the thought occurred to each of them that given other circumstances they might have been friends or brothers, but fate had decreed they be enemies.

Spotted Frog placed his hand to his mouth and made a high-pitched call, then turned his pony and galloped away. His men followed. Without the danger of being shot in the back, Tanner and his men made their retreat.

22

"Swan Necklace! What are you doing here?" Yellow Bird ran out to greet Sarah as she rode into camp.

"Thank God, you're safe." Sarah leaped off her horse and ran to embrace the slight figure. "You've delivered your baby."

A faint smile touched Yellow Bird's face and gratefully she squeezed Sarah's arm. "It's not safe here in the open," she said, looking around. "The soldiers may come back." She pulled Sarah toward a break in the rocky slope.

"How did it begin?" Sarah asked as they crouched in a ravine beside the other women.

Yellow Bird sighed. "When Black Beaver and the rest returned to the village and bragged of what they had done, the people began to weep. Joseph returned and he railed at them. He reassured our people he would speak to the white one-armed general and explain that we do not wish this war. We came here until the council could decide what to do. The soldiers gave us no chance to explain. They fired on our flag of truce."

"It wasn't the soldiers who fired first," Sarah said. "It was Owen Thatcher."

"It makes little difference now," Yellow Bird said morosely, and Sarah's shoulders slumped. The sounds of battle had faded as the soldiers retreated up the hill and moved back toward Mount Idaho. Around her women and children wept quietly, although some of the younger women, wives of the brave warriors who had fought that day, conversed quietly, their faces elated and proud. The Indians had dealt the white soldiers an unexpected and resounding defeat.

Yellow Bird took a small bundle from one of the other women and held it out to Sarah. "Her name is Little Bear," she said fondly.

Little Bear waved a fist and yawned, then opened her black eyes and looked around. Sarah's heart melted. She'd dreamed of someday having a fat little baby like this, one fathered by Tanner. Those dreams were forever gone.

"Joseph is coming," someone called, and the women and children climbed up the ridge. Slowly the chief rode his white Appaloosa toward them, his eyes melancholy, his shoulders slumped even in victory. Behind him rode the older chiefs. Spotted Frog and the young warriors were still pursuing the remnants of Captain Perry's troops.

"Joseph, we have won," the young women cried joyously, but there was no answering smile.

"What will we do now?" Yellow Bird asked, gazing up at her husband, their newborn daughter in her arms.

"The soldiers will come again," Joseph said, and the old women began to weep. Even the proud young wives fell solemn, their defiance gone as they exchanged glances.

Sarah put an arm around Running Brook, who staggered with age and fatigue. "They won't come back soon," she said soothingly. "You'll have time to rest."

Joseph noticed Sarah for the first time and nudged

his horse toward her. "Why have you come, Swan Necklace?"

"I've come to be with my people," she answered simply.

"This is not a good time to be Nez Percé," Joseph said wearily.

"I cannot change the blood of my grandmother," Sarah answered.

"So be it," Joseph said finally and raised his hand to signal the attention of his people. "We will cross the river," he called. "Strike the tipis." The women hastened to obey. Even old Running Brook hobbled to a leather tipi and began to dismantle it.

"I will help you, Kautsas," Sarah said. As she worked beside the frail old woman, it almost seemed to her that she was back in that happier time of her childhood. Then she remembered Tanner and knew she would never again be that carefree, thoughtless girl, never again be free of the memory of him. She would never stop longing for his touch or the feel of his big, rawboned body next to hers. Biting her lower lip, Sarah blinked back the tears. She was Nez Percé. She mustn't cry.

Running Brook looked at Sarah's distraught face and knew she grieved, probably for the tall man called Tanner. The old woman shook her head. Many women would grieve in the months ahead. Many!

Without waiting for the return of Spotted Frog and his warriors, Joseph led his people up the Salmon River to Horseshoe Bend, where most of them crossed on horseback, ferrying their belongings over on clumsy, hastily constructed rafts. Old people rode calmly into the treacherous water; children clung to their saddles, their bright eyes alert and fearless. Up ahead Yellow Bird rode with Little Bear's cradle board on her back. Sarah felt a fierce pride and love for these people.

On the other side, Joseph led them away from the river and into the rugged, wild canyons between the Snake and the Salmon rivers. For now, it was the safest place for them to wait while they tried to end this war no one wanted.

Thirty-three men were dead. Thirty-three raw young recruits who'd given their lives for naught. They'd failed to bring in Joseph and his band. The despair over such losses was heightened when the speculations came that only four Indians had been killed. Perry had lost a third of his command.

At first the battle was called a massacre. The Indians had outnumbered the soldiers and had lured them into a trap under the guise of a flag of truce, rumors maintained. But as the facts came out that only sixty Indians armed with old guns and in some instances bows and arrows had routed more than one hundred soldiers, criticism of Perry grew keen.

The citizens were at once outraged and fearful. What would the savages do next? People flocked to the fort. John Monteith ordered Redfield, the sub-agent at the Kamiah agency to bring his people to Fort Lapwai. Rumors abounded that Joseph planned to burn the Lapwai agency, so Frances and Charles and the miller, Dan Osgood, and his wife and five daughters moved to the post. Sue McBeth arrived with an escort of treaty Indians.

At the fort, panic had set in as they awaited additional troops. A blockhouse was arranged along the line of officers' houses. Stocked with food and casks of water, its exterior reinforced with cords of wood, the house sat as a grim reminder of what could happen. Women and children had been drilled in what to do in case of an Indian attack.

One day, trying to escape the gunfire of some local bullies, two friendly treaty Indians galloped into the fort and the cry went up that the hostiles were attacking. Men hurried to their positions while the women and children ran willy-nilly and finally settled themselves in the blockhouse.

Even the town of Lewiston, perched on its riverbanks, didn't escape the panic. Eighty men patrolled its streets and boundaries every night.

Emily, perhaps because of her calm efficiency, had her hands full with the widows of the men who had fallen at White Bird Canyon and the settlers coming to the fort for protection. Every night her supper table fed more than twenty and sometimes thirty people. She had little time to give thought to Sarah and her whereabouts. When she did, she simply shook her head in puzzlement. How could Sarah have turned her back on her own people and the man she loved?

Lucas Tanner and the surviving officers made their report to General Howard of the battle at White Bird Canyon, and some related seeing Sarah ride down into the Indian camp afterwards. Tanner's eyes reflected pain, quickly covered as Howard questioned the officers.

"You say she rode down by herself voluntarily?" Howard asked. "No one was forcing her?"

"Not as far as I could see," Major Trimble said.

"Is this so, Major Tanner?" Howard asked.

"Yes, sir," Tanner said, and his face was pale, his eyes bleak.

Howard studied his junior officer, then leaned back in his chair and pulled on his cigar, blowing smoke toward the ceiling before hitting his fist against the table. "Then by God, from this moment on, we'll treat Miss MacKenzie as an Indian."

"What does that mean, sir?" Tanner asked, his fists clenched, his eyes sick-looking.

"It means no attempt will be made to rescue her, and we will make no concessions for her safety when we attack."

"You can't do that, sir," Tanner said. "She's confused, caught between two sides, without knowing which side to choose."

"It seems to me, Major, that she's chosen. We will treat her as a hostile, which means that if she makes any attempt to resist us, we'll shoot to kill."

Tanner's face blanched further. "Then I must resign my commission and ask to be relieved of my duties," he said, tight-lipped.

"I can't accept your resignation, Major Tanner," Howard replied coldly. "I need every soldier I can lay my hands on." With a final salute the one-armed general dismissed his officers and left the room.

News of Tanner's request to be relieved of his command spread like wildfire around the post, adding credence to the rumors of cowardice that Gayle Nevins had perpetrated. Men forgot how bravely he'd led them at White Bird Canyon and spit contemptuously in his path when he passed by.

Howard ordered up new troops from as far away as Alaska and Alabama, and ten days after Black Beaver and Little Wolf's first attack on the whites, the general marched out of Fort Lapwai with almost three hundred infantry and cavalry and twenty-one civilians. He was going to punish the hostiles. Major Trimble and Tanner were among the officers. Stony-faced Tanner rode at the head of his column. He'd long since given up trying to sort it all out. The numbness that had closed in on him was welcomed, for it dulled his awareness of the ugly condemnations heaped on his shoulders and dulled, too, the pain of Sarah's abandonment of all that existed between them. She was gone from him, and somehow inside he'd always known it would come to this.

The first day of their march was easy, with the men laughing and exchanging stories. The cavalrymen led on their horses, the infantry followed, and the supply train lumbered along behind. Up Craig Mountain they marched and that night made camp at Cottonwood near the Norton homestead. The sight of the abandoned farm and the destruction of its contents was a sobering reality for the young soldiers.

"Ain't that a scary sight?" Gayle Nevins asked as the men sat around the campfire. "There's something spooky about that empty house." He shivered and glanced around. Tanner was opening his bedroll nearby. "You still here, Major?" he drawled. "I'd of thought you'd hightailed it out of here by now. Didn't you know Indians have been here? They might come back any time."

Tanner straightened and looked at the sneering faces lit by the leaping flames. He'd been bedeviled by Nevins and his cohorts for a week. It was time to end this hate campaign. These men would need to trust him and depend on his leadership in the days ahead if they engaged the Indians. They couldn't follow him if they continued to believe the worst of him. With a look of cold steel in his eyes Tanner walked toward the fire. Nevins leaped to his feet.

"Nevins, you've got a big mouth," Tanner said evenly, "and I'm sorry I saved your life back there in Montana."

The other men looked at each other. This was something Nevins had failed to mention.

"What are you doing now, Major," Nevins sneered, "hiding behind your bars?"

"I'm not hiding behind anything, Nevins," Tanner said. "I whipped you and two of your friends once. I'd hate to do it again."

Nevins glanced around uneasily. "Like I said, Major, it's easy to talk like that when you outrank me."

Tanner began to unbutton his tunic. "That can be easily remedied."

Uneasily Nevins backed up. "Well, now, I know you can beat me up, Major, but that don't change nothing else."

"Doesn't it?" Tanner asked quietly. "You've been calling me a coward ever since you got here. I say you're a liar, and you'd better be prepared to prove what you're saying or fight me over it."

"Well, now Major, I—I," Nevins backed up. "I can't prove anything."

"Then you're going to have to fight me," Tanner said, "because I'm going to prove you're a liar." His long arm lashed out, a raw-boned fist landed on Nevins's mouth, breaking the skin. Blood ran down the young lieutenant's chin. "You're going to tell the truth of what happened back there in Montana or I'm going to beat you until you do."

Nevins looked around for support and saw only avid faces and a few men already betting on the outcome of the fight. Seeing he had no way out, he doubled a fist and swung at the big man. Tanner might have him on size, but Nevins figured he stood an even chance. He had the major on years. His blow landed with a satisfying thud against Tanner's jaw. It was one of the few blows he managed to land. Tanner's mighty arms swung rhythmically, his fists were everywhere, at Nevins's middle, on his chin, punching his shoulder. The man was big, but his size didn't slow him down. He seemed tireless, unbeatable.

To the onlookers it seemed Tanner went at the fight in a methodical, emotionless fashion that had nothing to do with either man. It was something that had to be done and so he was doing it.

General Howard, sitting in his tent studying his field reports, heard the commotion and looked up. "What's going on out there, Major?" he asked his adjutant.

"I, ah, believe Tanner is disciplining one of his junior officers," Major Woods hedged.

"Which one?" Howard asked conversationally.

"Lieutenant Nevins, I believe, sir," Woods answered.

Howard nodded his head. "Long overdue," he said approvingly and continued his perusal of the field report.

Tanner landed another blow to Nevins's bloodied face. "Are you ready to do some explaining, Lieutenant?" he asked.

Nevins shook his head, trying to clear his vision. "There's nothing to explain," he said, and Tanner hit him again. His right fist came around, aimed for Nevins's middle when the young man folded.

"No more," he gasped. "I'll tell 'em the truth."

"We're listening," Tanner said, standing over the defeated soldier. Nevins took a deep breath and began the story of the Cheyenne camp and Tanner's clash with Custer, words that no longer needed to be said, for the men understood that Nevins hadn't told them all the truth and their commanding officer had been unjustly accused. Tanner had walked away long before Nevins had finished telling of how Tanner had saved him in the Cheyenne camp. That his men might come to see him as something of a maverick and a hero didn't occur to Tanner.

Time had labeled Custer a reckless glory hunter who had led his men to death, but whatever the reasons for the disaster the men were still dead and vindication of Tanner wouldn't bring them back. As far as he was concerned, the matter was behind him and now he must find some way to deal with the Nez Percé so as few of them as possible would be killed, especially one who called herself Swan Necklace.

Howard and his men traveled back to White Bird Canyon, where he sent out a reconnaisance westward along the rim of the canyon. In the meantime Perry set a detail to search for and bury the bodies of the soldiers who'd been left behind ten days before. By the time the gruesome business was done, Page and Chapman were back with a report of finding the Indians. Tanner's heart squeezed tightly and the blood left his face.

Now Howard set about the difficult task of fording the river with his heavy artillery and wagons of supplies. As they blundered across, Tanner wondered if the general was giving any thought to the Indians who'd made the crossing with all their old people and their children.

Word came that Looking Glass, who it was believed had remained neutral, was supplying warriors to Joseph. Howard sent Captain Whipple and his cavalry to investigate and bring in the renegade warriors. "I'm also assigning you, Major Tanner, to Captain Whipple's expedition," the general said, chomping on the end of an unlit cigar.

"Begging your indulgence, sir," Tanner said. "I'd rather stay with the main command."

"I'm sorry, Major Tanner, that can't be done," the

general said and buried his head in a map of the terrain.

"Sir, you're going after Joseph and his band. I know Joseph and Spotted Frog. I could be of more help to you here."

"How, Major Tanner?" The general fixed him with a stern eye. "Your knowledge of Joseph and Spotted Frog didn't help Captain Perry's command."

"No, sir," Tanner said.

"We both know why you want to stay, Major," the general said. "Your presence here won't help Miss MacKenzie, and I need you to help Captain Whipple with Looking Glass."

"Yes, sir," Tanner said with a smart salute, but his face was morose as he ordered his men into columns.

"Cheer up, Tanner," Whipple said. "We'll be back before Howard can get his wagons and guns across that river and over those mountains." Tanner looked at the heavy supply wagons and took heart at Whipple's words. It was true. Howard's company moved with ponderous speed.

The trek to Looking Glass's base was longer than reported. The soldiers and about twenty volunteers marched for twenty-four hours, and arrived soon after sunrise at Clear Creek, where Looking Glass and his band were camped. The troops paused on the side of the creek opposite the camp and waited as a warrior rode out to meet them.

"We have come to see your chief, Looking Glass—" Tanner began.

"Looking Glass say, 'Leave us alone. We are living here peacefully and want no trouble,' " the Indian warrior interrupted.

"Tell Looking Glass we have heard he is sending warriors to Joseph. This is not the act of a peaceful man," Tanner replied.

"Look at that red devil," someone jeered behind them. Some of the volunteers had ridden forward. They'd been drinking and had grown belligerent. "Go tell that coward Looking Glass we want to talk to him," one of the men shouted and jabbed the Indian messenger in the side.

Remembering it was a volunteer's shot that started the disaster at White Bird Canyon, Tanner reined his horse around and with a quick clean chop of his hand felled the volunteer. "Get him back up the hill with the rest of the command," Tanner ordered. The volunteers shot him looks of defiance and hatred, but they obeyed. Tanner could feel some of the tension easing out of him as he turned back to the messenger. "Tell Looking Glass he must come and talk with us himself," Tanner ordered. The warrior nodded and started back to the camp.

They waited in the hot sun. Across the creek they could see Looking Glass's lodge and the white flag he'd raised between it and the creek. Several Indians stood talking and gesturing wildly.

Finally one of the warriors rode across. "Looking Glass say you come to his lodge and talk."

Tanner turned back to Whipple. "If anything goes wrong," he said, "come in hard and fast." Whipple nodded.

Tanner followed the messenger across the creek to Looking Glass' lodge. The tall, thin chief came out to greet him.

"I have come on behalf of my chief, General Howard," Tanner began.

"I know him," Looking Glass said.

"General Howard requests that you give yourself up, so we might know that you are not sending warriors and supplies to help Joseph."

"The general has my word."

"He needs more proof than that," Tanner said.

Looking Glass smiled slyly. "Joseph whipped you pretty good at White Bird Canyon." Suddenly a shot rang out. The Indians leaped to their feet. With a wild cry they gathered up their weapons.

"Let's get the hell out of here," Tanner shouted to his two men and, spurring their horses into a flat-out gallop, they dashed across the creek and made it back to the main body.

"Charge," Whipple shouted and signaled his men forward.

"Wait," Tanner called, but his shout was lost in the banshee cry of men and the thunder of hooves as the troops rushed the camp. The Indians scattered into the brush on the hillside, while others mounted their horses and made a dash for freedom. The troops made no attempt to capture any of the Indians, concentrating instead on shooting at the fleeing figures. Helplessly Tanner watched while visions of another attack on a Cheyenne Indian camp flashed before him. That attack had driven the Cheyenne to the Sioux, and now he wondered if they'd just committed a similar blunder.

Several Indians had been wounded. They lay on the ground moaning. The soldiers rushed into the lodges and began looting, then set the longhouses afire. Other soldiers rode their horses through the Indian gardens, trampling the vegetables underfoot.

Ashamed of the men's behavior, he glanced away and caught sight of an Indian woman, a baby clutched to her breast. She leaped on a horse and drove her moccasined heels into its side. The horse spurted ahead, turning toward the Clearwater River. Tanner watched the woman's dark pigtails fly behind her and thought of Sarah. The woman had made the river and unhesitatingly drove her horse into the swirling water. They bobbed there, then the horse went down, the Indian woman and her baby sank beneath the surface of the water, and Tanner never saw them again. Startled, he watched the spot where she'd disappeared, but no dark head bobbed to the top.

Grief washed over him, fresh and raw as if it had been Sarah struggling to escape. Was this the fate that awaited her? His chest felt tight, so he gasped in air. Raising a tearful face to the sky, he bellowed loud and long, releasing some of the tension and pain and fear, but it was little help. He huddled in his saddle, his big shoulders slouching, his head bowed while he prayed fervently that Sarah was safe.

23

If Tanner asked himself why he continued with Howard's company, the answer was always the tenuous hope that his presence might somehow save Sarah when the general finally met Joseph on the field of battle. Somehow he must find a way to rescue her, whether she wanted to leave the Nez Percé or not. He didn't stop to consider the logic or illogic of this reasoning. The thought of deserting so he might travel at his own speed in search of Joseph's band entered his head only briefly. With so many troops in the field he was bound to be caught, and from a stockade he'd be of little use to anyone. No, with General Howard he stood a better chance.

Besides, he was a soldier, had been one all of his adult life. A sense of honor and duty had been bred into him. Something else swayed him. He'd walked away from a fight once, a fight that took the lives of his men. And although Custer had transferred him and he'd had no say in the matter, the unreasonable guilt of that stayed with him.

So Tanner slogged through the rain and mud, over the mountain trails, carrying his burden of guilt and duty and his love for Sarah with him. Leading his company of men, he followed Whipple back to Mount Idaho, where frightened settlers reported that the main body of Indians had eluded Howard, had recrossed the Salmon River, and were now bearing down on Whipple and his two companies. Captain Whipple sent Lieutenant Rains and ten men to reconnoiter. They never returned, wiped out by the Nez Percé. Other attacks on groups of scouts and civilian volunteers further demoralized and frightened the settlers in the Grangeville area. But the Indians bypassed Whipple's force, and Tanner cursed and drove his fist into his palm, not knowing whether to be elated that the Indians had avoided a confrontation that would surely have brought death to some of their band or angered that a chance to rescue Sarah had slipped past him.

"Let me take her for a while," Sarah said to Yellow Bird. The Indian woman's face was pale with fatigue. She'd had no time to recover from her childbearing before being forced to travel. In the days since she'd joined Joseph's band, Sarah had done everything she could to ease the burden for Yellow Bird. Now at her nod, Sarah took the cradleboard that held Little Bear and strapped it to her own back. They'd been moving over the rough terrain for days, pursued relentlessly by General Howard and his large army. Rain had made the steep mountain trails even more treacherous. Now and then a horse slipped in the mud, injuring itself so it had to be left behind.

Joseph led his people through the wilderness and recrossed to the north side of the Salmon. The crossing was even more difficult than the first, and Sarah clung to her saddle with eyes tightly closed. Still, she understood Joseph's strategy when word came that Howard had not been able to cross the river there and had to make his way back over the tortuous mountain trail to his original crossing. Joseph had gained a little time and distance for them. Scouts warned that a large body of soldiers were ahead at Grangeville, so Joseph skirted around and led his band to the south fork of the Clearwater River. They were safe here for a while. The old people set up their tipis, and rested in the sun.

One day the wary peace was disturbed when Looking Glass and his people rode into camp. He was followed by his warriors and their families. The women and children looked tired and scared. Looking Glass's face was a thundercloud, and he spoke to Joseph too rapidly for Sarah to understand everything. Joseph bid the newcomers welcome, and the infuriated warriors dismounted and gathered around the campfires to talk to Joseph's warriors. The women began to set up their own shelters, setting pots of food to cooking over campfires. At last the chiefs emerged from the tipi and Joseph raised his hand for attention.

"Looking Glass has joined us in our resistance to the white man's laws. His warriors will fight at our side. We are brothers."

Everyone cheered. Looking Glass had brought at least forty warriors, but Joseph's shoulders seemed to sag under the added burden of the women and children. Now there were well over four hundred old people, women, and children who were dependent on the warriors to protect and guide them over the steep trails.

Black Beaver came to Joseph's tipi and knelt beside the campfire, his dark eyes studying Sarah. "Have you heard the good news, Swan Necklace?" he asked in Nez Percé, and she shook her head.

"Was there good news?" she asked. "All I have heard is that Looking Glass and his people have been attacked by the white soldiers and will now join us in our struggle. To know that many people have already been killed and more will be in the future is not good news to me."

"Bah, you are like the old women who sit and weep," Black Beaver spat. "You are afraid of war."

"I object to people being killed needlessly and this is needless. The Nez Percé can't change anything with this resistance."

"It is better to resist and die than to quietly accept dishonor," Black Beaver said and leaped to his feet, his dark eyes snapping with anger and hatred.

"That was your decision," Sarah said implacably, "but your need for vengeance will bring death to the old people, who deserve to sit peacefully in the sun."

"They sit in the sun because they can no longer fight. If their bodies would let them, they would mount and ride against the whites as we do." With a final sneer Black Beaver whirled and stalked away, and Sarah was left to contemplate the things he'd said. He had spoken the truth, she thought sadly. No matter what the hardships, most of the people were proud of their resistance. Sarah thought of what this defiance was costing the Nez Percé and what it had already cost her. Where was Tanner now? she wondered, then forced the thought of him from her mind.

Joseph and the council had decided that they might move out of the Salmon River country and make for the foothills of the Bitterroot Mountains. To do this, they must cross the Camas Meadows, which offered no trees or ravines for hiding places. Finally it was determined safe to cross the meadow, and the herds were driven out with the women and children following along behind. Cautiously the warriors rode on the perimeter, keeping a sharp lookout.

It seemed they might make it when suddenly the

lookouts spotted a small group of riders approaching. The women and children drove the herd to the right, circling around the riders. Looking back, Sarah could see a line of Nez Percé warriors stretching nearly a half mile long waiting for the pitifully few riders. They hadn't a chance, she thought and felt like weeping. There was no joy for her in any defeat or victory. She should shout a warning, fire a gun or something she thought hazily, but part of her knew it wouldn't make any difference. If the Indians had been aware of such a small party approaching, surely the white men had been cautious enough to look ahead and see the larger body of Indians. Still they'd continued to approach. They'd wanted this confrontation. What manner of men did these things? she wondered. There was no pride and honor in riding to a foolish death. She turned back to the horse herds. Behind her the first gunfire sounded, but she didn't look back.

Back at the camp, Captain Perry turned away from the sight of the men fighting upon the prairie. His face was pale.

"Requesting permission to ride out and try to give assistance," Tanner said stiffly.

"Request denied, Major," Perry said. "Our job is to protect the supply train when it gets here." Tanner's face blanched. For twenty-five minutes the battle raged. Finally Tanner took matters into his own hands.

"Mount up," he called to his men. Cheering, they vaulted into their saddles.

"I thought I gave you a command, Major," Perry shouted.

"You did, sir, but I'm going against it."

"You know that's reason for a court-martial, don't you?" Perry demanded.

"Yes, sir," Tanner said swinging into his saddle.
"I reckon it is."

"The Indians are withdrawing," someone shouted.

Perry glanced around. "Lieutenant Shelton," he
called. "Take a detail of men and the Gatling gun."
The camp became a beehive of activity. Perry glanced
back at Tanner. The two men stared at each other a
long moment, and Perry broke the contact first, glancing down as if ashamed to meet Tanner's gaze any
longer.

"Let's go," Tanner yelled at his men, and they
galloped out onto the prairie. It was true, the Indians were already withdrawing. Dead and wounded
men littered the flat knoll where they'd fought. Tanner led his men directly at the small bands of Indians who had stayed to harass the wounded. If any
doubts had remained about Tanner's bravery or his
sympathies, this incident dispelled them. He'd been
willing to risk the threat of a court-martial to give aid
against the Indians, and his men were proud that of
all the officers, he had been the first to order them
onto the field.

"Rest, Kautsas," Sarah said to Running Brook,
smoothing back her hair much as she once had Swan
Necklace's. The weeks of flight through the steep,
rough terrain had taken its toll on many of the old
people. Now at last they were safe for a while in this
narrow, steep valley of the Clearwater River. On
either side bluffs rose nearly a thousand feet in height,
the pine trees growing there offering further cover
for the camp. "I'll bring you some soup," Sarah
said. She rose and walked to the campfire, where a
kettle simmered. Bringing back a wooden bowl, she
carefully spooned some of the brew into the old
woman's mouth.

"You are very good to me, Swan Necklace," the old woman said between bites.

"You are my grandmother, my kautsas," Sarah replied gently.

The old woman pushed aside the spoon. "I am weary now. I wish to sleep," she said. Sighing, Sarah set aside the bowl. Running Brook had taken little nourishment. She tucked a soft robe around the old woman and walked back to the campfire.

Suddenly the peace was shattered by the mighty roar of artillery. The shots fell far short of the camp, but the sound frightened the women and children, who ran screaming from their leather tipis. Warriors ran to their horses, and, howling and yelling, began to round up their stock. A few more shots sounded, again far short of the camp, and the warriors turned over the herds to the old men, who guided them into the hills at the rear of the camp.

"Running Brook, come, we must go," Sarah cried, shaking the old woman.

"I cannot move," Running Brook whispered. "Leave me here."

"I cannot, Kautsas," Sarah said. "You must come with me to safety. The white soldiers have found our camp."

"Go without me," Running Brook said.

"Swan Necklace, come, we must hurry," Yellow Bird cried, running to the tipi. Little Bear was clutched in her arms.

"I can't leave Running Brook," Sarah said helplessly, "and she feels too ill to run."

"You must not stay here. The soldiers will find you."

"I can't leave her," Sarah replied. "Go on without me. Perhaps when she's rested awhile, she can ride. Leave a horse for us."

"Swan Necklace," Yellow Bird cried. "I would not leave but—" She looked down at her baby.

"We'll be safe here. Think of Little Bear and go now. I'll follow. I promise."

For a moment the two women looked at each other, then embraced and then Yellow Bird was gone, bending to slip out of the low opening. Flinging herself onto a horse, she rode toward the hills. Sarah sat beside Running Brook and waited. The frantic sounds of flight faded and the camp was quiet, save for the whistle of artillery, which still fell too short to endanger the camp. Occasionally she walked to the opening of the tipi and peered out. Spotted Frog and the other warriors had raced their horses to the top of the bluff, where timber gave them cover. From the crest of the slopes they fired down on Howard's men. Other warriors hurried to join them at this advantageous spot.

From her position in the valley Sarah could see little of the battle, but she could hear the booming of the cannons that brought such death and devastation and the smaller rat-tat of the Gatling guns. Although Howard's men, including volunteers and packers, numbered nearly five hundred and the Nez Percé were outnumbered four to one, Spotted Frog's quick action in taking the timbered ridge gave them an immense advantage. Nez Percé marksmen rained certain death down on the unprotected soldiers, who were pinned without cover in the narrow clearing.

The fighting went on all day long. Now and then Black Beaver and some of the more foolhardy warriors made brave, desperate charges at the soldiers, attempting to capture some of the artillery pieces.

Night brought little surcease. The warriors kept watch, harassing the soldiers when they tried to tend to their wounded. The other women crept back into the camp and prepared food. Some stayed to sleep uneasily in their own bedrolls; others packed up their belongings under the cover of dark and hurried back into the ravines and gullies to hide. Sarah stayed in her tipi with Running Brook, who had not stirred.

Morning brought a resumption of the battle. This time Sarah managed to get Running Brook on a horse and lead her to the safety of the wooded ravines. But now the howitzers seemed to find them no matter where they fled. The women ran to a new hiding place, herding their children and horses before them. Each time Sarah helped Running Brook to her feet and bullied her onto a horse. How long could the old woman go on? she wondered. A high-pitched whistling made her look around. Yellow Bird was just behind her, riding one of Joseph's Appaloosas. Little Bear was strapped to her cradleboard mounted to the saddle just at her mother's knee. The sky lit up orange and black, and dirt rose high in the air and rained down on them. Another whistling sound and this time the shell hit closer. Sarah glanced over her shoulder again. Yellow Bird's saddle was empty. The Appaloosa trotted on without its rider, its eyes rolling in fear. As if aware her mother was no longer near, Little Bear began to wail.

"Yellow Bird," Sarah called and dropped the reins of Running Brook's horse, which she'd been leading. "Wait here," she ordered and turned her horse back to intercept the Appaloosa. Ignoring Little Bear's frantic cries, she turned the Appaloosa back to look for Yellow Bird. She found her slumped beside a tree, her shoulder and arm a bloody mass, her face grimacing in pain.

"Yellow Bird," Sarah whispered fearfully, and the Indian woman opened her eyes. All around them people were fleeing. "Get Joseph," Sarah directed one of them, and with a nod they turned back toward the fighting.

"My little sister," Yellow Bird implored weakly. "Find Little Bear."

"She's safe. Your horse is here. Can you ride?"

White-faced, Yellow Bird nodded. "Help me up." Sarah lent her shoulder to Yellow Bird. Struggle as they might, Yellow Bird could not remount. Her shoulder and arm were so badly damaged, she cried out with each jarring movement. Sarah feared for the blood she'd lost. Joseph raced up as Sarah tried yet another attempt to get her wounded friend into the saddle.

"Yellow Bird," he cried, flinging himself off his horse and hurrying to catch his wife up in his arms. He knelt on the ground, cradling her against his chest. His face was ravaged with grief. A peace-loving man, he'd engaged in this war only because he couldn't abandon his people. Now if it had cost him the woman he loved, he couldn't bear it. Shells exploded nearby. The sound of soldiers howling as they broke through the flank of warriors warned them there was little time.

"Can you ride?" Joseph asked, his mouth pressed against Yellow Bird's temple, his eyes frantic as he looked around for some way out of this. "You must."

"Yes, I will," she answered faintly. "Only get me on the horse."

Joseph rose to his full height, his wife still tucked gently against his chest. Effortlessly he settled her on his big Appaloosa. Another shell whined nearby, then exploded at the base of a tree, sending splinters of wood flying. Yellow Bird's riderless horse bolted, Little Bear's cradleboard still strapped to its side.

"Joseph," Sarah called a warning, and the big

Indian leaped on Sarah's horse. "Get Yellow Bird to safety," he called as he headed after the spooked pony.

Taking the Appaloosa's reins and walking, Sarah led the horse back to where she'd left Running Brook. She gasped when she saw the old Indian woman was gone. She must have followed the others, Sarah thought, and set out at a quick pace, all the while keeping a sharp eye out for the old woman. She wouldn't be able to keep up with the others and was bound to lag behind. Panic-stricken, the routed Indians streamed out of the narrow valley to the riverbank.

Joseph was already there, Little Bear clutched in his arms. Looking Glass and Spotted Frog admonished the warriors to stay and fight. In spite of the rout they'd inflicted much damage on the soldiers. Surprisingly, it was the women who protested. They'd had enough of the fighting and the hiding.

"Enough have been killed," they cried and finally the warriors, tired themselves of the fighting, agreed. They prepared to cross the river to safety.

Sarah looked around for Running Brook, asking all if they'd seen her, but the old woman could not be found. Finally she came back to Yellow Bird, who clung numbly to the saddle. Sarah had managed to pack the wound with moss and stop the bleeding, but now Yellow Bird's lips were white-lined. Her eyes were dark with pain and Sarah knew she was suffering greatly. Grasping her friend's hand, she sought to reassure her.

"Running Brook has been left behind. I must go back for her," she said. "I won't be long. I've asked Red Feather to stay with you until I return."

"Swan Necklace," Yellow Bird said, clasping her

hand tightly. "You must not go back. This is Running Brook's decision."

"No!" Sarah cried.

"She is too old," Yellow Bird said gently. "The trail is too hard for her. She has chosen to stay. When the soldiers find such an old woman, they will take her back to the reservation, where she can rest and die in peace. It is best for Running Brook."

"I wanted to be with her," Sarah replied sadly, but she could see the wisdom of what Yellow Bird said. She was quiet as they crossed the river. Even the cold, tumbling water held no fear for her now. Wearily the Indians fled the river valley. Behind they'd left many of their belongings, their warm robes, their leather tipis, even their cooking pots, some of them still simmering over the abandoned campfires. Left behind, too, were the underground caches holding much of their reserve food supplies, bread root and camas bulbs and dried beef, even the flour they'd stolen in their raids on the stores at Slater Creek and Cottonwood. The worst loss was the ammunition needed for their breechloading rifles. Several hundred rounds of metal bullets had been left. They were desperately short.

Joseph led them to an old meeting ground near Camas Meadows. There a council of the chiefs met to decide what to do next. They had lost seven warriors and many others were wounded. It appeared they had few choices.

"The Crows to the east are our brothers," Looking Glass said. "Many times we have hunted buffalo with them. If we go there and join the Crow, we can live in peace on the prairie. The war would be over."

The other chiefs contemplated his words. They'd fought to remain on their homeland, but now it was obvious they could not stay in peace and although they had proven their bravery time and again, they had no wish to continue at war with the soldiers. One by one the chiefs nodded in agreement. They would go to Montana across the arduous Lolo Trail through the wild and treacherous heights of the Bitterroot Mountains.

"By God, you're right, Major. They're crossing on the Lolo Trail," Howard said, studying his map. They'd been puzzled the last few days as to just what Joseph had in mind. His band had traveled westward for a time and Howard had been certain they were going back to the breaks of the Salmon and Snake rivers in the Wallowa Valley.

"They know they can't do that," Tanner had warned. "They'll have to go east over the mountains. My guess is they'll use the Lolo Trail." Now his predictions had been proven correct. He found little comfort in it. Since the routing of the Indians at the Clearwater, Tanner had grown introspective and quiet. His men sensed his mood and stayed out of his way, not out of anger but respect. So completely had he won their affection and confidence that even the thought that he still loved the quarter-breed Indian woman didn't bother them the way it once would have.

After the Clearwater battle Tanner had looked for signs of Sarah, but found nothing. There was no way to tell how many Nez Percé had been killed. In spite of their hasty retreat, they had gathered their dead. Only a drop of blood on the rocky trail, a broken leaf smeared with a trace of red, testified that anyone had even been wounded. One of Howard's scouts had found an Indian woman near the camp. When Tanner heard her name, he had hurried to the interrogation. Impatiently he'd waited while Howard questioned her.

Tearfully Running Brook had spoken of the dead and wounded. "Even Yellow Bird," she'd mumbled beneath her breath and wiped the tears that rolled over her wrinkled brown cheeks.

Fear started in Tanner and he'd clenched his fists in desperation. At last he had his chance. "Swan Necklace," he asked. "Is she alive and well?" The old woman stared at him with black, unblinking eyes and finally, with a nearly imperceptible movement, nodded her head. Joy flooded through Tanner and he bowed his head until he brought his emotions under control. She was still alive!

Now word had come to them that Joseph and his band were making their way over the Lolo Pass, and a white woman had been spotted with them. Tanner was certain it was Sarah.

Howard folded his map and put it away. "Well, men, there's no sense in delaying longer. Let's go after them."

Gathering their scanty provisions and driving two thousand head of horses before them, the Nez Percé started across the Lolo Trail. From behind they were worried by detachments of soldiers, and from the front they were intercepted by volunteers from the Montana frontier towns. Over the mountain they came, picking their way over fallen timbers and around boulders. It seemed to Sarah that all the mountainous trails they'd traveled thus far had been but a precursor for this rugged and nearly impassable trail. Riding along, she heard the wind soughing through the pines and felt the sun on her neck. How wonderful it would be to simply fall into a patch of grass beside the trail and sleep in the warm sun.

For nine days they traveled through the mountains and, riding though the night, bypassed a makeshift fort volunteers had erected across the trail. By daylight they were well down the trail and the citizens of Missoula, grateful the Indian threat was past, dubbed the log barricade Fort Fizzle. Joseph and his people had no way of knowing this, but they were smiling nonetheless. They were in Montana. Safe at last.

24

Safety was an illusion. There was no safety for them anywhere, not in Wallowa Valley, not in Montana, and not here in Big Hole Valley, where soldiers charged down the hill in a surprise dawn attack. Startled from their sleep, Sarah and the Nez Percé leaped out of bed and struggled into their clothes. Fleeing their tipis, they ran straight into the assault of the troops. Soldiers ran through the camp shooting and clubbing men, women, and children alike. Those who managed to escape fled from the death and violence to the river. Carrying Little Bear, Sarah ran beside Yellow Bird, helping her wounded friend when she might have fallen and pitched forward. They gained the riverbanks and lay down in the mud and water.

Some of the warriors had managed to grab their weapons and ammunition belts before hiding in the willows lining the river. Now the chiefs rallied them and led them back to the camp, where they drove the soldiers back up the hill.

Under Joseph's direction the old men, women, and children hurried into the camp, where they struck their few tipis, gathered their scanty belongings, and, taking up their dead and wounded, fled south. Sarah helped the other women, then seeing Yellow Bird mounted securely on her horse, tied Little Bear's

381

cradleboard to her own saddle and followed the
retreating Nez Percé. By nightfall they were well
away from the Big Hole Valley, their hopes for a
peaceful life dashed. They'd thought they were safe
from Howard, and indeed they were, for he was still
struggling over the formidable Lolo Trail, but they
hadn't reckoned on other companies of troops joining against them. The Crow had refused them sanc-
tion. They would be hounded from every quarter,
Sarah could see, and her heart wept for the plight of
Joseph and Looking Glass and Yellow Bird and all
the others. There was no place for them, no safety.

Howard's troops arrived in the Big Hole Valley the
day after the battle. Colonel Gibbon and his soldiers
and volunteers, totaling in all more than two hundred strong, were still recovering from the defeat.
Gibbon himself was wounded. He had lost thirty-
three soldiers and thirty-eight more were wounded.
Fourteen of his officers were among the dead and
wounded. Howard swore when he learned that once
again Joseph and the wily Nez Percé had slipped
through his fingers.

Walking around the abandoned Indian camp, Tanner searched among the dead and wounded soldiers
for any sign of Sarah, and cursed his luck that no
Nez Percé had been taken alive for questioning. Gibbon reported that his soldiers had inflicted heavy
losses on the Nez Percé before they turned the fight,
and Tanner could well believe him. Once more the
Indians had been forced to leave behind some of
their meager supplies. Their situation must be growing desperate.

Five Wounds was dead, so were Rainbow, Red
Eagle, and other brave warriors. More than seventy

Nez Percé had lost their lives, many of them women and children unable to escape the bludgeoning of the soldiers. In spite of their wounded, Joseph and the other chiefs pressed forward, pausing only for brief respites. There was little hope for them now. The chiefs decided unanimously that they must flee to Canada and join the Sioux. Their way north was cut off, so they would head southeast toward the Targhee Pass that would carry them across the Continental Divide and into the high meadows that made up Yellowstone Park.

Because of the wounded and the exhausted older people, their progress was slow. In the battle at Big Hole, the warriors had managed to destroy one of Gibbon's howitzers by rolling it over a steep cliff and to steal a pack load of two thousand rounds of ammunition, but now they must do something to slow down Howard's progress. Spotted Frog took Black Beaver, Little Wolf, and twenty more young braves and made a daring attack on Howard's camp, driving away their entire remuda of horses. It would take Howard days to round up enough horses and mules to resume his pursuit. Joseph pressed forward with his people.

Only five years before, the area through which they traveled had been declared a national park. Parties of sightseers and campers had come to the vast wilderness ever since to marvel at the deep canyons and timbered peaks. For most it was the great adventure.

The scouts saw the campers first and sent word back to the main body. The warriors, angry, frustrated, and bored, rushed forward, hooting and brandishing their weapons. At first the three men and five women looked startled, then indulgent and attentive, as if this Indian display was a show especially staged for them. It wasn't until Black Beaver rode through their camp, the hooves of his Appaloosa sending their campfire and tripod with its pot of coffee flying that they became afraid. No resistance was made. Stoically the men faced off against their captors, their faces pale, their fear partly masked, while the women responded in different ways, some by tears and hysteria, two with wary caution.

By the time Joseph and the rest of the band arrived, the campsite had been looted, the men were tied and fatalistically awaiting their outcome, while the women struggled in the embrace of the young warriors. When the chiefs rode forward, the warriors released the women and grinned proudly.

"We can take them with us for hostages," Looking Glass said, eyeing the pitiful huddle of frightened people who'd set out so jauntily to find adventure.

"They must not be harmed," Joseph said. "They will be treated with consideration at all times." He raised his voice. "Is that understood, Black Beaver and Little Wolf?" His dark eyes pinned down the two troublemakers. Reluctantly they nodded and moved back to their horses. "Mount up," Joseph said to the captives, and with a final, uncertain glance around the circle of Indians they hurried to comply. Hand-tooled saddles were slapped across the backs of spirited highbred horses. Expensive rifles and pearl-handled guns were confiscated. Food was quickly stored, to be parceled out in meager portions later. Any clothing or utensils that might in some way be useful along the trail were taken, and the camp left in shambles.

One woman caught Sarah's attention by her self-possessed air and calm acceptance. The woman had also managed to bring a pen and paper, and now as they made camp for the night, she found a seat away from the bustle and sat writing hurriedly. Sarah watched her and a memory came flooding back of a female reporter on a train heading west the year before, Audrey Keane. Sarah didn't go to greet her. What could she say? So much had occurred to change her life now. Quickly she returned to her chores and concentrated on tending to Yellow Bird and Little Bear and preparing food for Joseph.

But it was inevitable that the woman reporter, observant and inquisitive as she was by nature, should eventually recognize Sarah. Although Sarah had months before discarded her cotton gown and was now dressed in buckskin like the other Nez Percé women and like them wore her long dark hair bound in two braids, her skin was paler in spite of the hours in the sun and her beautiful features, finely drawn from her ordeals on the trail and the lack of food, still spoke of her white blood. Surreptitiously Audrey studied the beautiful young woman called Swan Necklace, who lived in Joseph's tent. Was she a second wife? How carefully she tended the wounded Indian woman and the small baby.

And then one day she remembered the ride on the Union Pacific with the young missionary teacher. But this couldn't be the same person. That woman had been pale and haggard, her skin sallow, her manner self-effacing and retiring. This young woman was incredibly beautiful, her dark eyes direct and unwavering, her manner sure with no false modesty. She carried herself with dignity and pride not with the shy inhibitions of the missionary. Still it was the same girl, Audrey was sure of it and fell to mulling over her name.

"Sarah?" Audrey stood before her. Sarah hadn't heard her name in so long that at first she didn't respond. Audrey repeated it and, startled, Sarah glanced up. "It is you," Audrey said. "What are you doing here? Were you captured too? Have they hurt you?" The reporter's questions ran together, and finally she ceased speaking and just stared at Sarah.

With a thin smile Sarah answered. "I am well, Audrey. I am here because these are my people. They are gentle and good and wouldn't hurt me just as they will not hurt you."

"This is incredible," Audrey exclaimed. "How can these be your people. Have you adopted them?"

"My grandmother was Nez Percé," Sarah answered.

Audrey waited for more, but Sarah had already acquired the habit of the Nez Percé of not speaking overly much with strangers. Audrey looked around the camp, trying to fathom Sarah's reasons for being here. "Still, you're nearly all white. No one would have known if you'd pretended you were."

"I am proud of my Nez Percé heritage," Sarah said firmly, and Audrey realized she'd offended Sarah when she hadn't meant to.

Brash and bold as she was, Audrey wasn't an unkind person. She had a consuming curiosity about people and events. That was what made her a good reporter. Now she put out a hand to touch Sarah's arm. "Tell me about the Nez Percé," she urged. "Tell me so I might understand your feelings and why you made this choice."

Sarah studied the reporter's face and saw the sincerity there and finally nodded. "All right," she agreed. "I will tell you everything I can if you'll promise to print it as I've told you without editing and without changing."

"I promise," Audrey said. So Sarah began her story, going back to her grandmother and the legends of the Nimpau people. Audrey followed Sarah while she did her chores and rode beside her on the trail; always she wrote in her notebook. Sarah told her of the treaty and of how Wellamotkin had charged his son, Joseph, never to sell the land that held the bones of his mother and father. She told Audrey of the Nez Percé's struggle to stay in the Wallowa Valley and of the unfortunate events that led to the war. Audrey, often insensitive to such matters, discerned a sadness in Sarah and instinctively knew her sorrow was for the doubtful future of the Nez Percé.

As she watched Sarah, or Swan Necklace, as even Audrey had begun to call her, admiration grew for the young woman's quiet dignity. If Joseph was an impressive leader, Swan Necklace was an apt and fitting mate for him. Never mind that he had another wife, Yellow Bird, who was a kind and gentle woman. No, Swan Necklace was the proper wife for Joseph.

Fear of even the most nervous captive toward the Nez Percé had diminished a good deal by now. They were being treated well and with consideration as Joseph had decreed. Obviously the Indians meant them no harm. Their capture took on aspects of an outing. Now the captives could be found playing with the children or talking to the Nez Percé men about their fine horses. The women captives studied the bead and quill handiwork of the Nez Percé women, and closely watched them as they went about their chores of preparing food or tanning hides. Some found the whole experience terribly exciting and romantic; others could hardly wait to be rescued and returned to civilization.

Audrey wrote in her notepad quick impressions of the Nez Percé and Joseph, their noble, impressive leader. She told of his valor and the loyalty and love of his people, and she wrote of his gentleness to his children and his wives, one of whom was a white missionary. No one knew of her misconception concerning Sarah, so no one could tell her differently.

The Indians traveled through the park, past bubbling mud pots and over thinly crusted ground that sometimes erupted into steaming geysers. They moved down the rivers until they came to a lake that stretched away from them for miles. There on the pine tree-lined shores they paused to rest for a day or so.

When Spotted Frog and his warriors ran off General Howard's pack string, Tanner cursed his luck and railed at the delay. With a few of his men he located horses and, going to the general, offered to lead a reconnoitering party. Reluctantly Howard agreed and Tanner set out. He was consumed with an urgency to find Joseph and see for himself that Sarah was still alive. It was mid-August. They'd been fighting the Indians for two months. How much longer could the Nez Percé go on? Their bravery was unexcelled. Their terrible plight had captured the imagination and sympathy of the whole nation, and now General Howard was greeted with daily dispatches of censorship and criticism. None of it mattered to Tanner. He only wanted to find Sarah.

They tracked the Indians over the Continental Divide and down into the Yellowstone Park until at last they found Joseph's band camped on the banks of a river. Tanner trained his field glasses on the group strung out along the banks. Clusters of women knelt at the stream, washing their meager belongings. Old people rested in the sun while the children romped and played.

One group caught Tanner's attention. A white woman dressed in a dark riding skirt and jacket sat on a stump, her head bent over something in her lap. Hope swelled in Tanner, then died as he noticed her blonde hair. She sat talking to two Indian women, then returned to her writing. Was this the white woman seen crossing over the Lolo Trail weeks before? Had he been chasing an elusive dream all this time? Was Sarah already dead? The glasses dipped at such a thought, and for a moment he sat trying to assess what he'd glimpsed. Quickly he trained his glasses back on the two Indian women.

One sat on the bank, cradling a baby in one arm. Her other arm hung limp and useless, caught at her side in a sling. Carefully Tanner studied her face. Yellow Bird! With rising hope he turned his glass to the other woman and had to blink to clear his vision. Sarah knelt beside the stream and even as he watched rose in that graceful, long-legged movement of hers. Taking the baby, Sarah cradled it against her neck for a moment, then bent to give Yellow Bird a hand in rising. Hungrily Tanner watched her every movement, noting the tall, strong body, the way she walked and stood, the swirling long hair and even the way she threw back her head and laughed at the baby before strapping it into its cradleboard.

Sarah was alive. She'd gone back to the river now and knelt to retrieve something. The sunlight spangled the water and shown on her sleek head. Tanner could contain himself no longer. Leaping to his feet, he put a hand to his mouth and shouted Sarah's name, hearing it echo down the mountain and fill the valley.

"Jesus, Major, what are you doing? You want them to hear us?" one of his men cried.

"She's alive," Tanner said. "We have to go get her." His men looked at one another. Gale Nevins straightened and studied his commanding officer. He'd never quite gotten over the humiliation Tanner had dealt him, but a grudging respect for the man had returned.

"We can't go down there, sir," another soldier argued. "There's not enough of us to fight the whole tribe over a woman."

"Stay here if you want, I'm going down," Tanner snapped and turned toward his horse. Gayle Nevins moved without thinking, his gun butt rising in a wide arc and descending on the back of Tanner's head. The big man fell like an ox and lay still.

"Like you're always saying, sir, watch your back," Nevins said.

"Now what're we going to do?" a soldier asked the lieutenant, and as next in command Nevins motioned to the man on the ground.

"Seems the major fell getting on his horse and hit his head. You men want to lay him across his saddle and we'll head back to report to Howard."

The sound startled the birds from the trees. They flew up with a whirring noise and with great sweeping strokes of their wings disappeared.

"What was that?" Audrey asked, looking around. She glanced back at Swan Necklace and Yellow Bird, and was further disturbed by the taut way they held their bodies, their faces turned to the mountain as if they were trying to sniff out any danger.

"Let's go back with the others," Sarah said quietly, and with no sign of panic they quickly gathered up their belongings and hurried to join the other women. Joseph had heard the sound as well, and warriors had already been dispatched along the steep slopes to find what had caused it. In the meantime, their respite was over. The Nez Percé packed up their things and resumed their march. As Sarah rode along she kept hearing the sound over and over. It echoed in her head, and she was as certain as if Yellow Bird or Audrey had spoken to her that the sound had been her name. Tanner was back there somewhere and he still wanted her. For the rest of the day she rode apart and made no answer to anyone around her.

The realization that they were free to come and go pretty much as they pleased came slowly to the captives. One by one they stole away from the Indian camp, and when there was no outcry they understood that the Indians were allowing them to escape. Only Audrey remained. One morning as she mounted her horse to begin the day's march, Sarah reined her horse around, blocking Audrey's way.

"Your time among the Nez Percé has come to an end," she said. "If you ride back the way we have come you will be safe and General Howard will find you."

"I—Sarah, come with me," Audrey urged feeling concern for the young woman.

"I am no longer Sarah. I am Swan Necklace. I have chosen my way with my people. Remember the things I have told you and print them fairly."

Audrey nodded her head. "I will," she said. Sarah turned her horse and followed the departing Nez Percé. Audrey watched them go, hoping Sarah would look back so she could wave good-bye, but she rode straight and sure in her saddle and didn't look back.

On the eastern side of the park, new detachments of troops from the Montana posts rode to intercept them. Joseph led them on a merry chase, pushing through nearly impossible mountainous wilderness to circumvent the army's traps and emerge at their rear. Furiously the commander pursued them.

One day they came upon a stagecoach, which they captured. The passengers managed to escape into the willows along the riverbank near the stage station. Black Beaver and the other warriors gave the children rides in the preposterous, ponderous coach, and for a while man and child alike forgot the stress and hardship of their flight. Their lightheartedness didn't last long. At Canyon Creek the troops they'd managed to outmaneuver had caught up with them. Sarah and the other women drove their herds into a narrow canyon while the braves went out to do battle.

Even Sarah could see they were outnumbered and she feared this would be the end of them, but the commanding officer ordered his men to dismount, allowing the Indians to escape. The soldiers remounted and followed in a running fight, but Joseph ordered boulders and brush to be placed at the mouth of the canyon to block it. The soldiers couldn't penetrate it.

Tired and dispirited, the Nez Percé pushed on. They'd lost many horses through lameness or in their hurry to escape. They'd been marching for more than three months. Their food was scarce and warm robes nonexistent.

If their plight wasn't bad enough, the Crow had joined forces with the army, and now they began to attack as Joseph led his tribe down out of the mountains and across the prairie toward the Missouri River. At Cow Island depot they ransacked the army stores for needed supplies and hurried on. The nights were cold now and there were no robes to warm them. The children cried often with hunger and cold, their pinched faces a driving reminder that time was running out. They must reach Canada soon and seek aid from the Sioux, or they would be caught on the plains in the winter storms and all would perish.

Across the badlands they traveled, where animal

and man alike found no livelihood. Ahead were open plains, which offered no protection, no hiding places from the soldiers who hounded them. But the barren plains must be crossed if they were to reach the Bear Paw Mountains and, beyond the mountains, Canada. Despite their condition, the Nez Percé took heart. Even Yellow Bird, who'd been weakened by childbearing and the grueling trip and her wound, seemed to grow stronger, more optimistic. Sarah looked at the mountains in the distance. She hardly dared to believe they might make it. Howard still pursued them, but he was a few days march behind. She could feel no elation at the thought of their journey's end. They were traveling into exile. None of them would ever return to their homeland again. She would never see Tanner again. Nudging her horse, Sarah rode forward, toward her destiny and, as before, she never looked back.

25

The campaign was over.

Once Howard received word that Joseph had crossed the Missouri at Cow Island, he knew it was no longer necessary to follow the Nez Percé trail. Word was sent to Colonel Miles to intercept Joseph before he reached the Canadian border. Winter was fast approaching and Howard had to make arrangements to send his troops home. Through cold northwest winds that chilled them to the bone, the troops marched to Carroll, where they boarded the steamer *Benton*. It would carry them down the Missouri to Omaha and home. To all intents and purposes, the Indian campaign for the summer of 1877 was over.

Howard kept only a handful of troops and among them, despite his better judgment, was Major Lucas Tanner. In the end Howard had relented, his conscience smitten by the quiet desperation in his officer's eyes. By boat Howard and his men and one howitzer traveled up the Missouri to Cow Island. From there they would march to the Bear Paw Mountains. There was no longer need for urgency.

Tanner disagreed. Miles and Major Ilges from Fort Benton were even now converging on the unsuspecting Joseph. Tanner wanted to be there. Impatiently he champed at the bit, as he had from the beginning. Dispatches and newspapers came up the river on the steamboat, and one day before they left General Howard summoned Tanner to his office.

"I believe you ought to read this, son," he said. "Remember those campers we rescued back in the Yellowstone? It seems one of them was a reporter and she's written an account of her experience." He held out a paper.

"I have no need to read some foolish woman's romanticized account of her ordeal with the Indians," Tanner said.

"Read it, son," Howard said, "the last paragraph of the first column." Tanner picked up the paper. As he read, his face grew pale. He threw the newspaper from him and leaped to his feet.

"I don't believe it," he said, pacing the room.

"It says there that she's the wife of Chief Joseph. I thought you should hear about it before you get out there. It might save you some disappointment."

"It's not true," Tanner said, leaning across the table that served as a desk.

"Keep in mind, son, that it might be. She's embraced the Nez Percé ways as her own. She may have become his second wife. Some of these Indian chiefs take more than one wife."

"Not Sarah," Tanner said, but his voice broke.

Howard studied his young officer and was sorry he hadn't sent him back to Fort Lapwai after all. "When we engage Joseph, I don't want any personal vendettas."

"There won't be," Tanner said stiffly. "Will that be all, sir?"

"That's all, Major," Howard sighed. "Dismissed." He watched until Tanner left the room and sat shaking his head. This had been a long, tough ordeal for them all.

Tanner flung himself on his horse and galloped

away from the depot, oblivious to the cold wind that stung his skin and sucked away his breath. He rode until horse and man were exhausted, and then he dismounted and stood looking around at the barren plains. Joseph had passed this way with his people and Sarah had been among them. Sarah! Her name was like a fire within him, and slowly he sank to his knees on the sparse plain, his head bowed, his shoulders shaking. For the men who had followed him through battle after battle, the sight of their tough, hard-bitten commanding officer crying would have been incomprehensible.

The last day of September was unbearably cold. The wind blustered down from the northwest in unrelenting fury. Joseph had led them to the northern side of the Bear Paw Mountains only thirty miles, a day's march, to the border. Free at last of Howard's dogged pursuit, they'd paused in a deep hollow close to Snake Creek to rest a bit before making the final leg of their journey. They were finally safe. The people relaxed their guard a bit. Although there was little food and the cold wind whistled through their thin, worn skins, an air of elation filled the camp. They'd marched thirteen hundred miles to reach freedom and they'd succeeded. Never mind that their numbers were sadly decimated, that loved ones had been struck down in battle and left behind, buried in shallow graves all along the tortuous trail, never mind that the richness of their horse herds had been reduced to less than half their value and number, Canada was within sight!

The attack caught them unaware, the people spread out over the gully. Some were on the far side of the camp and immediately mounted their horses and rode north away from the fighting. Joseph, Yellow

Bird, and Sarah, carrying Little Bear, found themselves cut off from the rest of the tribe, trapped with the horses. Joseph railed at himself for being caught thus. They burrowed into a shallow wash and looked around. In the distance Sarah could see the women and children caught in the tipis running for cover behind low ridges nearby. The warriors had already scrambled up the steep slopes and taken up positions to return fire on their attackers. Once again their superior marksmanship was inflicting heavy casualties. The soldiers who had charged head on over the open ground toward the camp retreated under this barrage.

"Joseph, the horses," Sarah cried as other soldiers charged through the herd, shooting and yelling so that the frightened horses stampeded. Now the Indians were separated from each other and were forced to fight hand to hand with the soldiers.

"I must get back to the camp," Joseph said.

"No, there's no cover. You'll be killed," Yellow Bird sobbed.

"I am needed," Joseph said. "I cannot hide here like an old woman."

"At least wait for darkness," Yellow Bird pleaded.

Joseph shook his head. "You are safe here. Stay with Little Bear and Swan Necklace until dark, then try to make your way back to the main camp. I must go now." Without giving her time to protest, he crawled out of the wash and made his way on his belly along the creek bed.

All day the battle raged. Sarah and Yellow Bird lay hidden in their hollow, listening to the cries of death around them. Horses thundered by and they crouched low. When the soldiers had passed, Sarah raised her head and gasped. Owen Thatcher sat staring down at them, his gun aimed and ready. He laughed when he recognized Sarah.

"You made a bad choice, teacher," he sneered.

"What are you going to do with us?" Sarah asked fearfully. In answer he thumbed back the hammer of his pistol.

"For God's sake, have some mercy. We're two women and a baby," Sarah cried. Her plea had no impact on Thatcher. Grinning evilly, he aimed his gun. With a last hopeless cry Sarah flung herself across Little Bear. She could hear Yellow Bird's whimpers. A shot rang out. Sarah felt no pain. Warily she looked up at Thatcher.

He was still sitting astride his horse, but his large body had gone slack, the reins dangling, the gun up. Another bullet slammed into him, making him jerk and topple off his horse. One boot caught in the stirrup. Sarah saw Black Bear standing on a ridge, his rifle still aimed at the lawyer. With a high whine a shell landed nearby. Thatcher's mount reared and galloped off across the rocky slope with Owen Thatcher's lifeless body bouncing along behind.

"A fitting death," Yellow Bird spat.

Sarah couldn't have agreed more. "We can't stay here. Can you make it back to camp?" she whispered to her friend, lightly touching her shoulder and arm.

Yellow Bird nodded. "I'll be right behind you. Take care with my Little Bear."

"As if she were my own, my friend," Sarah said, and suddenly the two women hugged, remembering all they'd shared and drawing comfort from each other now in this moment of danger. Sarah crawled out first, scraping along on her belly and following the same path she'd seen Joseph use. She breathed a sigh of relief when the reached the creek bed. At least here there was some protection. The water was freezing cold, a light rim of ice forming along its edges. Ignoring the coldness, Sarah moved forward, taking care not to splash the water unduly and thus draw attention to them. She wasn't sure where to turn away from the creek to the camp, guessing when the time came, and by some miracle they made it back to the main body.

The women were huddled inside the shelter of their tipis, but the men were still on the bluffs. Now and then a shot sounded, reminding them and the soldiers that the Nez Percé warriors would not relax their vigilance again. At some time during the night, fierce fighting broke out as Miles tried to cut the Indians off from the creek, but he was driven back. The temperature had dropped, the night was bitter, and snow fell softly, insidiously, adding to their distress. When morning came neither soldier nor Nez Percé could see their dead for the layer of snow.

Black Beaver brought the news to Joseph that Spotted Frog was dead. A song of keening began and Joseph walked away from his people, no longer a great chief, but simply a man who had lost a beloved brother. Sarah wept, too, remembering the handsome war chief's kindness to her. Spotted Frog was not their only loss. Most of their war chiefs had been killed in the first battle, and a third of their horses had been driven off. The outlook was grim.

With knives and pans, anything they could man, the Nez Percé tried to dig shelters into the steep bluffs. At least more warmth and protection was afforded them there than in their tipis. Or so they thought, until Miles ordered the howitzer fired into the camp. One of the dugouts was hit and a woman and her child buried alive. No one could help her.

Not wanting to expose his soldiers to the rifle fire of the Nez Percé on the bluffs, Miles decided to lay siege to the camp. Snow flurries and the unremitting cold added to the Nez Percé's suffering. Hungry and cold, they proudly, stubbornly hung on. Then Miles hoisted a white flag and Joseph went to parley with his enemy.

But Miles captured Joseph and refused to release him until the Nez Percé captured one of Miles's officers and effected a trade. Joseph returned to his camp and the Nez Percé cheered. Yellow Bird's pinched face brightened with relief and she ran to greet her husband. Sarah watched as the tall chief embraced his tiny wife, and she longed for Tanner and the comfort he'd always given her. She turned away, but not before she noted the look of defeat in Joseph's eyes. He knew it was over, she thought dismally. They would never go to Canada. Their struggle would end here in these mountains.

Sharpshooters from both sides continued to fire on each other. They were at a stalemate. Five interminable days of siege dragged by, and it seemed Joseph and his chiefs meant never to give up. Rumors came that a band of Sioux were marching down from Canada to give aid to Joseph. Then General Howard arrived with reinforcements, and the heart went out of the Nez Percé. Two treaty Indians under a white flag came to the Nez Percé camp to talk to Chief Joseph. If Joseph and his other chiefs surrendered, they would be treated honorably, the treaty Indians said. They would be sent back to the reservation at Lapwai.

A council was held between the chiefs. Sarah and Yellow Bird stood with the other women waiting to hear what the chiefs had decided. They could hear angry voices raised and knew the chiefs were not in agreement on surrender.

Old White Bird and Looking Glass wanted to fight

on, but Joseph pointed to the shivering, emaciated women and children. "For myself I do not care," he declared. "It is for them I am going to surrender."

"If you must surrender," Looking Glass said at last, "give those of us who wish it time to make our escape. Perhaps we can get to Canada and join the Sioux."

"So be it," Joseph agreed, and the two chiefs stood and clasped hands. Looking Glass turned away. A shot rang out and he fell to the ground dead, a neat, round hole in his forehead from a stray bullet. The shocked tribe looked on the fallen chief, hysteria building.

"White Bird," Joseph called to the old chief. "Gather your people if you wish to leave. Now is the time." His words galvanized the Nez Percé to action. Those who still wished to flee to Canada scurried to gather their belongings. With long, quick strides Joseph crossed to Yellow Bird, and took her hand gazing lovingly into her eyes. Sarah felt the blood leave her face, for she knew what the chief was about to say before he'd uttered a word.

"Are we going as well, my husband?" Yellow Bird asked eagerly and Joseph shook his head.

"I cannot go," he said. "There are many here who are too old and weak to make the journey. They would perish on the plains, but you must go, my wife, and take Little Bear with you."

"No," Yellow Bird cried out, her face twisted in anguish, her eyes bright with pain. "Do not ask this of me. I cannot leave you." She threw herself into his arms and clung to him.

"For Little Bear's sake, you must," he answered and smoothed the dark, shiny hair. He had loved this tiny woman well. She'd been the delight of his existence, and now he must send her away for her own safety. "Black Beaver is going and he's agreed to give you his protection. He is a brave warrior. You will be safer with him than anyone else."

"I cannot go," Yellow Bird sobbed, pressing herself against him. With his large hands smoothing her hair and his gentle voice crooning softly, Joseph soothed his wife's grief with such tenderness that Sarah turned away, no longer able to witness the pain between them. At length Joseph convinced his wife, as Sarah had known he would. Now she had only to decide whether to go or stay herself.

Troubled, she walked out along the hills that protected the camp from the soldiers. Climbing to the top, she peered over its rim. In the valley below, soldiers had come to collect their dead. An officer sat on his horse overseeing the task. Sarah studied the big man slouched in his saddle. It was Tanner. Hands pressed to her trembling lips to hold back the sobs, she lay watching him for some time, remembering the feel of his hands and the slow, easy way he smiled.

A flicker of movement made her glance around and she gasped. Black Beaver had spied Tanner as well and even now was sighting along the barrel of his rifle. He was an expert marksman, Sarah knew, and seldom missed. Without thinking she sprang to her feet and screamed, waving her arms wildly. Tanner's head jerked up and he saw Black Beaver. Dropping low in his saddle, he drew his rifle and fired.

Horrified, Sarah watched as Black Beaver crumpled to the ground. Guilt coursed through her. Giving no thought to her own safety, she left the protection of the ridge and ran toward Black Beaver. He lay on the ground, trying to stanch the flow of blood in his side.

"Let me help you," she cried, but he only brushed her hands aside.

"I want no white woman to touch me," he sneered, and with an effort got to his feet and walked toward Joseph's tipi.

The Nez Percé waited for the cover of darkness, quietly preparing for their journey so they would arouse no suspicions with the soldiers. Black Beaver was bridling the ponies, a soft deerskin tied to his wound.

"I'm sorry, Black Beaver," Sarah said contritely, but he made no reply. She no longer existed for him. Sadly, she went away.

"Will you come with me?" Yellow Bird asked later, and Sarah shook her head. "I cannot go into a strange land with you," she said firmly. She didn't tell Yellow Bird of the incident with Black Beaver.

Yellow Bird placed a hand on Sarah's arm. "You are very brave, my little sister," she said gently. "Perhaps the fates will take you and Tanner along the same path again some day. I will pray for this."

"I will miss your wisdom and kindness," Sarah sighed, and the two women hugged each other.

"And I will miss your strength and loyalty. Farewell, my little sister."

"Farewell, Yellow Bird." The two women clasped each other in anguish, knowing they'd never meet again.

Black Beaver had brought around a horse, and now he helped Yellow Bird and Little Bear on it. With a final, unreadable glance at Sarah he sprang into his saddle and, taking up the reins, signaled farewell to Joseph.

"Take good care with them, my friend," Joseph said and pressed one final kiss on Little Bear's tiny face. Carefully he tucked the soft blanket around the cradleboard, so the wind couldn't reach her.

"I will guard them with my life," Black Beaver vowed.

Yellow Bird leaned from her saddle to grasp Joseph's hand. Tears wet her cheeks. "May the Great Spirit be with you," she whispered.

"Go, go quickly," Joseph commanded harshly, and Black Beaver led the horse out of camp and slipped away with the others into the darkness. Joseph stood looking after them long after they'd gone, then he turned back to his tipi. The camp seemed strangely quiet and empty after Yellow Bird and the others had left. Sarah missed having Little Bear to hold and play with. Slowly she went into a tipi and wrapped herself in a tatty fur and forced herself to sleep. Sleep was oblivion. She wouldn't have to feel or think. But her dreams were peopled with all she'd loved and lost: Swan Necklace, Yellow Bird, Annie, and most of all, Tanner.

The next morning Joseph negotiated with the treaty Indians, and at last toward evening returned word to Howard that he would surrender. In return Joseph had been promised that he and his people would be returned to Lapwai. The sun was setting, tinging the sky and flat prairie with bright banners of color as Joseph rode out to meet Howard. Dressed in plain black with beadless moccasins, he'd chosen to ride a black pony instead of his customary white Appaloosa. Only a blanket of red, yellow, and blue stripes knotted around his hips relieved the somberness of his dress. Five of his chiefs walked beside him. Slowly they made their way down the hill. Sarah and the other Nez Percé watched from the bluff.

Standing beside Howard, Tanner scanned the ridge

for a glimpse of Sarah, and when at last he picked her out of the other figures, he couldn't tear his gaze away.

Joseph rode straight toward Howard, his hands crossed over his pommel, his head bowed. His warriors and chiefs talked in quick, angry whispers, but he made no reply. As they rode closer the officers could see the wretched condition of their clothes and the pinched, lean look of their faces that spoke of hunger. Silently Joseph approached Howard and paused a few feet away. Raising his rifle with one hand, he thrust it away from him. Colonel Miles rode forward and accepted it.

Joseph raised his head and spoke for the first time. "Tell General Howard I know his heart," he said. "What he told me before, I have in my heart. I am tired of fighting. Our chiefs are killed. Looking Glass is dead. Spotted Frog is dead." He paused as the mention of his dead chiefs brought him pain. Then he continued and his voice was stronger. "The old men are all dead. It is the young men who say yes or no. He who led the young men is dead. It is cold and we have no blankets. The little children are freezing to death. My people, some of them, have run away to the hills, and have no blankets, no food; no one knows where they are—perhaps freezing to death. I want to have time to look for my children and see how many I can find. Maybe I shall find them among the dead. Hear me, my chiefs. I am tired, my heart is sick and sad. From where the sun now stands, I will fight no more forever."

The men around him were silent. From every direction Indians crept into the soldiers' camp. Tanner looked at the old people, many blind and lame, the wounded young warriors, and the children, and he marveled anew that Joseph had been able to take his people so far and so swiftly. Then he spotted Sarah coming down the hill, leading an old Indian woman, and without waiting for his general to dismiss him, he was running up the steep slope, calling her name.

Sarah heard his cry and stopped to wait for him. How she longed to throw herself into his arms, but she couldn't. The things between them were finished and must stay that way. She didn't know that tears of joy washed her cheeks or that her eyes spoke all too eloquently of the love she still bore him.

"Sarah," Tanner said, coming to a halt below her. His chest heaved from his sprint up the hill and his hat had fallen off. His sun-bleached hair fell across his forehead and his eyes were compelling, entreating as he looked at her.

"Sarah." He put out a hand to touch her, as if he couldn't believe she was finally there in front of him. "I've been so worried about you," he said inadequately and wondered if she knew how much he loved her. "Sarah." He whispered her name as if he couldn't say it enough.

"My name is Swan Necklace," she said, and pain washed across her face. "I am Nimpau." Her dark gaze studied him for a moment longer, touching lightly on his face, then with eyes downcast she slowly walked down the hill leading the old Nez Percé Indian.

He'd lost, Tanner thought numbly. They'd won the war with the Nez Percé, but he'd lost Sarah. There had been too much bloodshed between their people, too much betrayal. His love couldn't overcome all that had occurred. Sick at heart, he made his way down the hill and back to his command.

* * *

The aftermath of the dramatic surrender was disappointing to some, but men like Major Lucas Tanner set about gathering horses, confiscating weapons, and preparing for the long march back to Cow Island and the boat that would take them all out of the snowy battleground. Three days after the surrender they began the trek back to the boat landing. Tanner took care to ride near Sarah. Six days later they reached the mouth of Squaw Creek, where the steamboats *Benton* and *Silver City* waited.

Tanner and some of the other officers met with General Howard to determine the details for dismantling his troops. "Begging your indulgence, sir," Tanner said when he learned that most of the troops would be sent back to San Francisco and thence back to their original posts. "What details will you assign to the Nez Percé?"

"Colonel Miles will be handling that, Major," the general replied.

"Requesting permission, sir, to accompany the Nez Percé back to the reservation at Lapwai," Tanner said.

Howard glanced at his young officer and then away. "I'm afraid the Nez Percé won't be going back to Lapwai," he said, carefully knocking the ash from his cigar.

Tanner looked stunned. "That was part of your agreement with Chief Joseph."

General Howard nodded. "The cost of transporting the Nez Percé back to the Pacific Coast is too great at this time. They'll be quartered in Colonel Miles's district until next spring, at which time if the government hasn't decided otherwise they'll be shipped back to me. I'll be traveling to Washington to confer with General Sheridan about what to do with the Nez Percé during the winter months."

Tanner glanced at Miles, reminding himself that these things took time. He tried to believe that these officers would honor their surrender terms, but a terrible doubt was building inside him.

When the meeting was over, he walked back to the boat landing and sought out Sarah among the Nez Percé. Her face was quiet, unreadable when he approached her. He didn't see the flare of joy when she first caught sight of him.

"I'm afraid you won't be sent back to Lapwai right away," he said. "I'm sorry. It will take time to arrange transportation and it will be easier in the spring."

"Thank you for letting us know, Major Tanner."

"Sarah, if there were something I could do, I would."

"I know," she said, and her words gave him hope.

"Sarah, I love you," he said desperately. When she didn't answer, he pressed forward. "Is it Joseph? Audrey Keane reported you were his wife."

Sarah looked at him with astonishment and he saw the truth in her eyes. Relief washed through him.

"The war is over. Can't there be peace between us?" he pressed.

"Peace is not love," Sarah replied quietly, "and that's what you want from me. I can't come with you, Tanner. I can't turn my back on my people. I have chosen." Her quiet words were so final that he knew she would never change her mind. He walked away from her then, his eyes bleak, his chest too tight to breathe properly. Only later did he realize that she hadn't said she didn't love him, only that she couldn't leave her people. He sat for a long time mulling over her words and what they meant to both of them.

*   *   *

"Swan Necklace, you have not made your peace with Major Tanner?" Joseph asked later as she tended the wounded.

Sarah shook her head. "He spoke of the same thing," she said slowly, "but how am I to forgive the things that have happened to my people? There can never be peace or love between us."

"A war, my child," Joseph said kindly, "is a thing where there are two sides. There have been betrayals on both sides and loyalties that have torn us all apart. It is time to put away our hate and learn to love again."

"I cannot," Sarah replied.

"Then you are more badly wounded than these brave warriors," Joseph said gently. "Just as these wounds cannot heal if there is festering, so your heart cannot heal if you do not drive out the hatred you feel. We must begin to mend. Now is a time of healing." Rising, he walked away.

Sarah thought about Joseph's words and Tanner's declaration of love. She still loved him, God help her, she did. She'd known that ever since she called out in warning, when Black Beaver tried to kill him, but there had been too many betrayals, too many deaths. Still, Joseph's words stayed with her and she resolved herself to talk to Tanner again the next day.

But the next day Colonel Miles escorted the Nez Percé away from the camp at Squaw Creek and marched them by easy stages over five hundred miles to the post at Yellowstone. The trip took them a week and Sarah sat numbly in her saddle, certain she would never see Lucas Tanner again. She would never again have the opportunity to tell him she loved him. Admitting her feelings broke through the wall she'd built against the pain. Tears surged down her cheeks. Bending low over her horse's neck, Sarah gave way to the sobs that welled from the deepest part of her numbed heart and when the tears were done, she knew Joseph had been right. The healing had begun for her as well.

"You wished to see me, Major?" Howard said, looking up at his officer. He frowned and glanced back at the papers on his desk. Somehow he felt uneasy about this meeting, and the look on the big man's weatherbeaten face did nothing to alleviate his disquiet.

"I'd like to give up my commission, sir," Tanner said. General Howard glanced at him, somehow not surprised by his request. He'd been expecting it, he realized, ever since Joseph's surrender.

"You realize what you're giving up, son?" he asked.

"Yes, sir," Tanner said, "but my mind's made up."

"You won't reconsider?" Howard asked, although he knew it was futile.

Tanner shook his head. "My career with the army is over."

"Is she worth this much to you?"

"This and more," Tanner answered.

"You do realize once you've taken this step, there's no turning back?"

"Yes, sir."

The general's shoulders sagged. "You're a good officer, Tanner," he said. "Your men respect you. They would follow you just about anywhere. You know the land and the Indians better than most men out here. We need men like you in the army."

"I'm sorry, sir," Tanner said. "My loyalties would no longer lie with the army's best interests."

"What do you plan to do now?" Howard asked.

"Follow Sarah," Tanner answered unhesitatingly.

"You'll be an exile among your own people, a squaw man, an object of ridicule."

"I'll be a man," Tanner said, "living beside the woman I love."

Howard sighed in defeat and nodded. "Would you consider an alternative assignment?" he asked. "I have need of a man to act as head of a new department to help resettle these Indians on the reservations."

"I'm not sure, sir," Tanner said hesitantly.

"It's a promotion, son," Howard urged him, although he doubted that made much difference to Tanner. "The pay's right handsome, enough to support a wife. You'd be able to help the Nez Percé." He saw relief grow on his officer's face.

"Thank you, sir." Tanner rose. "I'd be happy to continue serving under you if it meant I can find Sarah."

"It'll take a few weeks for the paperwork to go through. In the meantime, you can have a leave of absence to look for your Sarah. Good luck to you, Major, and to Sarah."

"Thank you, sir," Tanner said, saluting smartly.

The general sat staring into space long after the major left the room. He was relieved not to lose Tanner. He'd proven himself a man of strong character. There seemed to be one flaw, and that was his feelings for this Nez Percé woman. Few men would give up their careers for the woman they loved. There were, he guessed, unexpected depths to Lucas Tanner, and Sarah MacKenzie had touched those depths as no one else had.

Sarah MacKenzie, also called Swan Necklace, knocked on the door of the fort commander. Captain Bryan Thornton stifled a sigh of annoyance when he caught sight of her and bid her enter. Beautiful as this woman was, he'd quickly learned she had an obstinate, thorny side to her when it came to the well-being of the Indians.

"Captain Thornton," she said without preamble. "I must protest that cattle and food have not been delivered to the Nez Percé as promised."

"I'm sorry for the delay. There was some difficulty. It hasn't arrived yet."

"Difficulty or not, Captain, something must be done. What are the Nez Percé to eat in the meantime?"

"Yes, ah—I'll see that some army beef is sent over until the other arrives."

"Thank you, Captain," Sarah said primly, and he waited tensely, knowing there was more. "We lost a woman last night to the fever. You'll have to move us to higher ground. The Nez Percé can't live on this swampy ground."

"There is no higher ground," the captain said.

"I'm sure you'll think of something for our people," Sarah said and smiled with surprising sweetness. She was a beauty, Thornton thought for the hundredth time, and for the same number of times reminded herself that she was part Indian and not likely to make a suitable wife for an up-and-coming young officer. The idea of a mistress had crossed his mind once and had been quickly dispelled when he looked at her determined face. Sarah Swan Necklace MacKenzie wasn't the sort of woman a man considered for a mistress. Now as she turned to leave the office, he glanced at the pile of mail on his desk and got to his feet.

"Uh, Miss MacKenzie, these came for you and Chief Joseph in today's mail." He picked up a bundle of letters and eastern newspapers. He couldn't help but notice that some of the letterheads bore the prestigious names of senators and government officials.

"Thank you again, Captain. You've been most kind," Sarah said graciously and left his office. There was, she noted, another letter from Emily. Smiling she slipped it into her pocket. Dear Emily. Her letters had made these past months bearable.

Tucking the bundle of letters under her arm, Sarah shielded her eyes against the glare of sun and looked around. They'd been in this hot swampy land for nearly three months now. Unaccustomed to the heat, many of the old people had already died and more grew ill every day. Chief Joseph had traveled to Washington to plead the cause of the Nez Percé but to no avail. Letters to politicians had brought sympathy and little else. Enlisting the help of Audrey Keane, Sarah had submitted several articles to newspapers telling of the plight of the Indians and although their publication had occasioned much public outcry, nothing had changed. Sarah felt despair. The Nez Percé would not be moved back to the Lapwai reservation.

Sighing in the moist heat, Sarah mounted her horse and made her way back to the fort gate, where Joseph and some of the other men waited for her.

She had long ago stopped dreaming of Tanner. At first she'd clung to the fierce hope that he would find them but finally hope had died. They'd been at the fort in Yellowstone for only a few days before the old and wounded had been loaded into mackinaw boats and taken down the Yellowstone River to the Missouri and on to Bismarck. The rest had been carried overland by wagon. From there they'd been marched here to Fort Leavenworth in the Kansas territory. She'd put her sorrow behind her and concentrated on improving the lot of the Nez Percé.

Now as she approached their camp, she noted the

swarm of people gathered at one end. No doubt some newspaper reporter or do-good senator looking for publicity had ridden out to have his picture taken with an Indian. Not bothering to see who had come, she stopped at her tent and went inside to open the letter from Emily.

"Swan Necklace." A small girl stood in the opening of her tent. "Joseph said come get you quick. Someone's here to see you."

"Who is it, Lily?" Sarah asked, rising from her seat on the ground.

"A man," Lily said with a smile and ducked out of the tent quickly so she wouldn't have to answer any more questions and spoil the lovely surprise. Curious, Sarah followed the girl through the village square toward the crowd. The muscles in her stomach knotted with anxiety. What was happening? she wondered. Who had come? The crowd parted and Sarah stopped in the middle of the square, her eyes riveted on the tall man standing among her people. The dry prairie wind blew the sun-streaked hair. His eyes, mere slits squinting against the sun, studied her. Sarah felt as if the world had stood still.

"Tanner?" she whispered uncertainly. She couldn't breathe. He took a step forward and suddenly she was laughing and running toward him.

"Sarah," Tanner called and his long legs quickly closed the distance separating them. His strong arms gathered her to him, cradling her against his chest. His lips settled at her temple, her eyes, her cheeks, and finally on her mouth.

"You're here," she whispered wondrously.

"I couldn't find you. They said you'd been sent to Fort Lincoln. There are two, one in Dakota and one in Arkansas. By the time I tracked them down and discovered you weren't there, I was frantic."

"Miles took us away before I could talk to you, tell you I was wrong. I was afraid I'd never see you again."

"I'm sorry, so sorry for everything that's happened to you and to your people. I'm sorry for the lies and betrayals. I'll spend the rest of my life trying to make it up to you."

"Just love me, that's all I need," she said, drawing back to look at his dear face.

"I've never stopped loving you, Sarah," he said raggedly. "Don't leave me again. Don't ever go, Sarah. I can't live without you."

"I won't, my love," she whispered and knew this time it was true. She'd hold onto Lucas Tanner as tightly as she did her Nimpau heritage. They were both a part of her. Tanner's lips settled on hers and Sarah understood at last where she belonged.